LV 5055874 9

Liverpool Libraries

THE HUNT

BEAR GRYLLS

ORION

First published in Great Britain in 2018 by Orion Books,
an imprint of The Orion Publishing Group Ltd,
Carmelite House, 50 Victoria Embankment,
London EC4Y 0DZ

An Hachette UK company

1 3 5 7 9 10 8 6 4 2

Copyright © Bear Grylls Ventures 2018

The moral right of Bear Grylls to be identified as
the author of this work has been asserted in accordance with
the Copyright, Designs and Patents Act 1988.

All rights reserved. No part of this publication may be
reproduced, stored in a retrieval system, or transmitted,
in any form or by any means, electronic, mechanical, photocopying,
recording or otherwise, without the prior permission
of the copyright owner and the above publisher of this book.

All the characters in this book are fictitious,
and any resemblance to actual persons, living
or dead, is purely coincidental.

A CIP catalogue record for this book
is available from the British Library.

ISBN (Hardback) 978 1 4091 5689 5
ISBN (Export Trade Paperback) 978 1 4091 5690 1
ISBN (eBook) 978 1 4091 5692 5

Typeset by Input Data Services Ltd, Somerset

Printed and bound in Great Britain by Clays Ltd, St Ives plc

www.orionbooks.co.uk

ACKNOWLEDGEMENTS

Special thanks to the following: literary agents at PFD Caroline Michel, Annabel Merullo and Laura Williams, for their hard work and effort to support this book; Jon Wood, Brendan Durkin, Bethan Jones and all at Orion, for their courage and faith to help bring this story to life – & Malcolm Edwards and Leanne Oliver.

Thanks also to the following: Hamish de Bretton-Gordon, Ollie Morton and Iain Thompson of Avon Protection, for their invaluable insight, advice and expertise on all things CBRN, and their input into the chemical, biological and nuclear aspects of this book, including the defence and protection measures.

Chris Daniels and all at Hybrid Air Vehicles, for their unique insight and expertise on all things Airlander, and for pushing the envelope in terms of what is possible with such an airship; to Paul and Anne Sherratt, for such potent insight into Cold War relations immediately following World War Two; to Peter Fawbert, of Shindo Wadokai, for his self-defence and unarmed combat expertise; to Bob Lowndes, of Autism Wessex, for his psychology input.

And a final special thank you to Damien Lewis, trusted friend and author about many UKSF operators. Thank you for helping to build upon what we discovered together in my grandfather's war chest marked 'Top Secret'. Bringing those World War Two documents, memorabilia and artefacts to life, in such a modern context, has been the adventure of a lifetime.

AUTHOR'S NOTE

This book is inspired by the true life exploits of my grandfather, Brigadier William Edward Harvey Grylls, OBE, 15/19th King's Royal Hussars and Commanding Officer of Target Force, the covert unit established at Winston Churchill's behest at the end of World War Two. The unit was one of the most clandestine ever assembled by the War Office, and its mission was to track down and protect secret technologies, weaponry, scientists and high-ranking Nazi officials to serve the West's cause against the world's new superpower, the Soviet Union.

No one in our family had any idea of his covert role as Commanding Officer T Force – 'T' standing for 'Target' – until many years after his death and the release of information under the Official Secrets Act seventy-year rule – a process of discovery that inspired the writing of this book.

My grandfather was a man of few words, but I remember him so fondly from when I was a child. Pipe-smoking, enigmatic, dry-humoured and loved by those he led.

To me, though, he was always just Grandpa Ted.

Daily Express, 21 May 1945

SECRET ARMY FOUGHT NAZI ATOM BOMB
Four men hid three months in white hell

It can be revealed today that for five years British and German scientists fought their own war-within-a-war. They fought to perfect the atom bomb, which, with the most explosive force in the world, would have given either side walkover superiority.

But it was no war of theorists only. British and Norwegian paratroopers fought it out too, with Wehrmacht men and their quisling supporters, in the white hell of the storm-swept Hardanger Plateau in Norway.

The Germans opened the fight in the summer of 1940. A few weeks after moving into Norway, they seized the vast hydroelectrical works at Rjukan. These works, fed by the famous 'smoking-cascade' waterfall, supply electricity plentifully. And plentiful electricity was essential to the German plan and to the arms plant they intended to set up at Rjukan.

Their plan was to split the atom.

At Rjukan the Norwegians produced large quantities of a substance known as 'heavy water'.

Heavy water contains atoms of hydrogen twice as heavy as those contained in ordinary water, from which it can be made electronically . . .

Scientists the world over had experimented with heavy water and they believed that if they treated the metal uranium with it, under great force, they could split the atom of uranium.

And in so doing they would release terrific energy – and produce a catastrophic explosion.

There are many technical difficulties but the Germans may have been near solving them.

....

Mail Online, Allan Hall, 10 June 2014

Did US fake top Nazi's WWII suicide and spirit him away to get hands on Hitler's secret weapons programme?

The blood of thousands on his hands, SS General Hans Kammler killed himself in 1945 in the dying days of Hitler's Germany.

That, at least, was his official fate. The man steeped in the horrors of the death camps had met his just deserts.

However, it is now claimed that Kammler survived the war, spirited away to America and given a new identity by the US authorities.

For the general wasn't just an expert in the technicalities of industrial-scale slavery and slaughter, he was also deeply involved in the Nazis' secret weapons programme. The Americans, according to a TV documentary, were determined to have his know-how and not let him fall into the hands of the Russians.

Both the US and the Soviet Union tried to recruit Hitler's scientists after the war to help with their own space and military programmes. But it is claimed that Kammler's record was so monstrous that his death had to be faked and he had to have a new identity.

'The whole history of suicide is staged,' said Berlin historian Rainer Karlsch. 'There are several documents that clearly demonstrate that Kammler was captured by the Americans.'

Another expert, Matthias Uhl of the German Historical Institute in Moscow, said: 'The reports from America are more credible than those given about the alleged suicide by Kammler's associates.'

Born in 1901, by the end of the Second World War Kammler was almost as powerful as SS Chief Heinrich Himmler and armaments minister Albert Speer. He had access to the Nazis' most advanced technology, including the 'weapons of retaliation' – the V-1 and V-2 rockets that caused death and destruction in Britain but came too late to turn the tide of the conflict.

He was also involved in the construction of death camps, including the design of the crematoria at Auschwitz which incinerated most of the bodies of the estimated 1.2 million people murdered at the camp in occupied Poland.

The history books say that, one day after the Third Reich surrendered on 9 May 1945, he either shot himself or took poison in the former German city of Stettin, now Szczecin in Poland. His body was never found.

'This whole story of suicide was staged by two of his closest aides who were committed to him,' Karlsch told ZDF TV in Germany.

At the war's end America, while taking part in the punishment of many top Nazis at the Nuremberg trials, also launched the covert Operation Paperclip – the secret exit of top Nazi scientists.

ZDF says in the documentary: 'Sources say that Kammler was captured by the Americans and interrogated by the US Counterintelligence CIC. The secret service man responsible was Donald Richardson, a personal confidant of Allied supreme commander General Dwight D. Eisenhower.'

The sons of the secret service man told programme makers that their father was in charge of the German weapons expert after 1945.

One of them, John Richardson, said: 'This engineer brought a special treasure from the Third Reich into the United States. He offered us modern weapons.

'It was put to my father that he should bring this "useful" German into the United States to prevent him from falling into the hands of the Russian intelligence service.'

It is not revealed under what name Kammler lived or when he died, though some archival material speaks of a 'special guest' living under Richardson's wing.

....

Daily Telegraph, Justin Huggler, 22 January 2015

NAZIS 'BUILT UNDERGROUND NUCLEAR WEAPONS FACILITY USING SLAVE LABOUR'

Austrian documentary-maker believes he has uncovered a sealed complex of underground tunnels in the town where notorious Gusen II concentration camp was, larger than previously thought.

New evidence has emerged of a possible underground nuclear weapons facility built by the Nazis that has lain secret since the Second World War.

Andreas Sulzer, an Austrian documentary-maker, has put forward documentary evidence he claims to have uncovered that a sealed complex of underground tunnels built by the Nazis in Austria using slave labour may be far larger than previously thought, and include rocket launch silos.

Mr Sulzer has previously claimed higher than normal levels of radioactivity in the area are a sign the complex was used to develop nuclear weapons – although local authorities have disputed the results of radiation tests.

The possibility that the Nazis were close to developing an atomic bomb towards the end of the Second World War remains one of history's unanswered questions. There have been persistent rumours of a secret nuclear weapons programme in the final years of the war, but no proof.

Mr Sulzer believes he has found it in a complex of underground tunnels near the town of St Georgen an der Gusen in Austria that have lain largely undisturbed since the 1950s.

The town was the site of the notorious Gusen II concentration camp, one of the Mauthausen-Gusen group, where forced labourers were worked to death. Some 320,000 people are believed to have died in the camps.

The inmates of Gusen II were made to dig the huge Bergkristall underground complex where V-2 rockets and the Messerschmitt Me 262, the world's first jet fighter, were built.

Mr Sulzer believes the network of tunnels he has discovered nearby may have been a separate facility of the Bergkristall project.

But while the main Bergkristall complex was extensively investigated by the Allies after the end of the war, the Nazis appear to have gone to far greater lengths to conceal the second complex, sealing the entrance with huge granite slabs, and it has remained largely undisturbed.

Austria, 24 April 1945

They had been partying for hours.

The Allied guns might be pounding the German positions not twenty miles to the west, but these men in their smart Hitler Youth uniforms were drinking as if there was no tomorrow.

Patriotic songs echoed around the damp rock-hewn walls – the 'SS Marschiert in Feindsland' – 'The Devil's Song' – being tonight's favourite. The verses had been belted out time and time again.

> *The SS marches into enemy land,*
> *And sings a devil's song . . .*
> *We fight for Germany,*
> *We fight for Hitler . . .*

The beer steins had long run dry, but the schnapps had kept flowing, glass after glass being slammed down onto the bare wooden tables, the noise echoing like gunshots off the rough walls.

Though feigning high spirits, SS General Hans Kammler – hawk-faced, sunken-eyed, blonde hair swept back from his high forehead – had barely touched a drop.

He ran a gimlet eye around the vast space, lit by a dozen lanterns. The beast of a weapons system that was secreted within the bowels of this mountain had feasted upon electricity, but forty-eight hours ago, the power had been cut and the machine shut down – hence tonight's flickering illumination, casting grotesque shadows upon the curving walls.

Toast after toast had been drunk to the young men gathered here. Fired up with Nazism and a skinful of schnapps, they would hardly baulk at what was coming. There should be no eleventh-hour objections or last-minute nerves. And for sure, Kammler couldn't afford there to be any, for further back in the shadows of this tunnel complex was hidden the Reich's greatest ever secret.

It represented the fruit of the labours of Nazi Germany's foremost scientists – the Uranverein. Together they had produced a *Wunderwaffe* – a wonder weapon – without equal.

Kammler's grand plan – and arguably the SS high command's most Machiavellian operation – relied upon the Uranverein's work remaining hidden from the advancing Allies. Hence the coming sacrifice – an entirely necessary one as far as the general was concerned.

He glanced upwards momentarily. A narrow shaft rose almost vertically to the starlit heavens: a ventilation duct. These sixty young men would awaken to the dawn light filtering through with the mother of all hangovers. But that would be the least of their worries, he reflected grimly.

The tall, lean SS general rose to his feet. He took his ceremonial sword, its heavy hilt decorated with the distinctive skull-like SS death's head, and rapped it on the table. Gradually the din subsided, and a new cry was taken up in its place.

'*Das Werwolf! Das Werwolf! Das Werwolf!*'

Over and over the chant was repeated, growing in frenzied volume.

This army of fanatical young Nazis believed that they were readying themselves to wage a diehard war of resistance against the Allies. They had been given the name the Werewolves, and their supposed leader was SS General Kammler himself –

Das Werwolf – the key orchestrator of tonight's gathering.

'*Kameraden!*' Kammler cried, still trying to silence the din. '*Kameraden!*'

Gradually the chanting subsided.

'*Kameraden*, you have drunk well! Toasts fit for heroes of the Reich! But now the time for celebration is over. The moment for launching the Great Resistance is upon us. Today, this hour, you will strike a glorious and momentous blow. What you safeguard here will win us the ultimate victory. With your heroic efforts, we will rise up in the enemy's rear! With your efforts, we will wield a weapon that renders us invincible! With your efforts, the enemies of the Reich will be vanquished!'

Wild cheers broke out afresh, the noise rebounding off the walls.

The general raised his shot glass: a final toast. 'To seizing victory from the jaws of defeat! To the Thousand Year Reich! To the Führer . . . Heil Hitler!'

'Heil Hitler!'

Kammler slammed down his glass. He'd allowed that one shot of schnapps to burn down his throat: Dutch courage for what was coming, for the one part in tonight's proceedings that he really did not relish.

But that would come later.

'To your stations!' he called. 'To your positions! It is 0500 hours and we blow the charges shortly.' He ran his gaze around the gathered throng. 'I will return. *We* will return. And when we come to free you from this place, we will do so with unassailable strength.' He paused. 'The darkest hour is just before the dawn – and this will prove the dawn of a glorious new Nazi ascendancy!'

More wild cheering.

Kammler thumped his free hand on the table with a fierce finality. 'To action! To victory!'

The last of the drinks were downed, and figures began hurrying hither and thither. Kammler followed their movements with his cold gaze. Everywhere seemed to be a hive of activity, which was just as he wanted it. He couldn't afford for any soldier to have second thoughts or attempt to slip away.

Having made one last check deep in the guts of the cave to ensure that the massive steel blast doors were firmly closed and bolted, Kammler made his way towards the shadowed entranceway, where men were bent over spools of wire and detonation boxes, busy with last-minute preparations.

With a final word of encouragement, the general strode out of the entrance to Tunnel 88, as the vast edifice was known. In truth, Kammler had no idea how many tunnels made up this gargantuan complex. Certainly, hundreds of thousands of concentration camp inmates had died here, excavating the honeycomb of passageways that bored into the bowels of the mountain.

Not that he gave a damn. He was the architect of much of the mass murder. The genius behind it. Those who had perished here – Jews, Slavs, Gypsies, Poles; the *Untermenschen*, sub-humans – had got what they deserved. As far as he was concerned this was their birthright.

No, this was called Tunnel 88 for entirely different reasons. H being the eighth letter of the alphabet, 88 was thus SS code for 'HH' – or Heil Hitler. It had been named at the personal request of Der Oberste Führer der Schutzstaffel – the supreme commander of the SS, Hitler himself. In this place would be preserved the greatest achievement of Nazi Germany, something that might breathe life once more into the Thousand Year Reich.

For a moment Kammler paused to adjust his cap. It seemed to have fallen a little awry during the partying. As he did so, his fingers brushed against the SS *Totenkopft* – the death's head – emblazoned on its front: blank, empty eye sockets staring into the distance, lipless mouth fixed in a maniacal grin.

It was a more than fitting emblem for what was coming.

2

Cap straightened, Kammler turned to speak to the figure at his side, who was dressed in the uniform of a staff sergeant in the SS. This man too had barely touched a drop of alcohol.

'Konrad, my car, if you will. As soon as the charges blow, we will be on our way.'

Scharführer Konrad Weber gave a smart heel-click and hurried away. Old for his rank – not much younger than Kammler himself – Weber had never married and had no children. The Reich, and the SS in particular, was everything to him. His surrogate family.

Kammler turned back to face the mountainside that towered before him. Already the first bluish hints of dawn were streaking across the heavens, reminding him of the need to get this done. At this hour – this witching hour – few should notice the explosions, not that there were likely to be any witnesses. For days now Kammler had had his troops scouring the terrain to all sides, clearing it of hapless civilians.

From behind he heard the crunch of tyres on the single dirt track that led into this remote region. Hooded headlamps, partially blacked out to hide them from any marauding Allied night fighters, pierced the gloom.

Kammler smiled. Excellent: the ever-loyal Konrad at the wheel of his staff car.

The headlamps illuminated the scene before him, casting it into dull light and shadow. Thick pine forest clung to the lower slopes, making the yawning entrance to Tunnel 88 – and the

5

series of similar openings to either side – all but invisible. From each sprouted a tangle of wires, set all along the rock face.

Kammler waited for his driver to park the vehicle, noting that he left the engine running just as he'd been ordered. Scharführer Weber was a good man, and he had proved an utterly loyal servant. An unspoken understanding – an instinctive empathy – had developed between them.

A pity, in view of what was coming.

A hand emerged from the darkness: it was Scharführer Weber's, holding out the handset of the field telephone.

'Sir.'

Kammler took it. 'Thank you. Wait in the vehicle. Just as soon as I have finished, we will be off – the same route as we came in.'

'Yes, Herr General.'

The car door slammed.

Kammler spoke into the handset. 'Herr Obersturmführer, you are ready?'

'Yes, Herr General.'

'Very good. Proceed when you see my staff car stop at the edge of the clearing. But give me time to dismount, so that I can personally witness this glorious spectacle.'

'Yes, Herr General. Understood. Heil Hitler.'

'Heil Hitler.'

Kammler opened the passenger door of the car and slid onto the polished black leather seat, signalling for Scharführer Weber to drive. The smooth Horch V8 engine rumbled throatily as the vehicle pulled away. A minute later, where the sandy track snaked off into the thick cover of the fir trees, Kammler signalled a halt.

'Just here will be fine.'

He swung his polished leather boots out of the vehicle and stood, facing the direction of the escarpment. As the early rays of dawn peeked over the mountains to the east, they burnished the rock face before him a golden bronze.

Kammler leant on the passenger door, bracing himself for what was coming. As he did so, his thick leather coat fell open a little, revealing the compact Walther PPK pistol he had strapped in a holster at his hip.

He brushed his hand against it, just as he had done with his death's-head cap, checking that it was within easy reach.

Soon now.

Kammler forced his mouth wide open, signalling to his driver to do likewise, and the two SS men faced the mountain, gaping like fish. Even this far away, they needed to take precautions, for a blast this powerful could blow their eardrums.

The explosion, when it came, was all Kammler had hoped it would be.

A series of blasts flashed outwards from the trigger point – Tunnel 88 – the detonation cords igniting with such speed that they appeared indistinguishable from each other. All along a four-hundred-yard front the rock face seemed to dissolve as one, transforming itself into a whirling mass of shattered rubble.

The entire escarpment appeared to rise momentarily as it disintegrated into pulverised granite and boulders. The blast vomited hundreds of tonnes of shattered rock, which began to crash back down in a crushing tidal wave.

An instant later, the shock wave hit the two watchers, rocking the car alarmingly on its springs and tearing at Kammler's cap and his thick leather coat before hammering into the forest to their rear. It was followed almost immediately by the sound wave, an impossible roaring and snarling that broke over them and bored into their heads.

Eventually it dissipated and Kammler straightened up. The sheer power of the explosion had sent him into a defensive crouch – not that he or Scharführer Weber had been in any great danger. He brushed down his coat, removing the thin film of white dust that had been carried with the blast.

He kept his eyes glued to the mountainside. When the air finally began to clear, he found himself marvelling at what he saw. Just as he'd intended, it looked as if a massive rock slide had obliterated one entire side of the mountain.

Here and there a dark slash of red indicated where a rich vein of minerals – iron, perhaps – had been torn asunder and slewed down the slope. Uprooted trees lay like heaps of scattered matchwood, crushed under the weight of the rock. But crucially, there was no sign – not the barest hint – of the tunnel complex that now lay hidden behind the wall of debris, not to mention the sixty young soldiers entombed therein.

Kammler gave a satisfied nod. 'Good. We go,' he announced simply.

Scharführer Weber slipped into the driver's seat and blipped the throttle. Kammler clambered in beside him and, with a last look at the dust-enshrouded scene, signalled the staff sergeant to move off.

The dark forest swallowed them. For a few minutes they drove in silence, or at least comparative silence. Even at this hour the hollow crump of artillery could be heard in the distance. The cursed Americans: how they loved to flaunt their military superiority over the Wehrmacht.

It was Weber who broke the quiet. 'Where to, Herr General? Once we make the metalled road?'

'Where indeed, Konrad? Where indeed?' Kammler mused. 'With the Americans and British to one side, and the Russians to the other, where do we of the Schutzstaffel turn?'

For a long moment Weber seemed unsure of how to answer, or even whether an answer was expected. Finally he must have presumed that it was.

'To the Werewolves, Herr General? To seek out their headquarters?'

'Indeed, Konrad, a good thought,' Kammler answered, staring out of the window at the dark trees. 'A fine suggestion. That's if they had one. A headquarters. But I suspect that no such thing can be found.'

Scharführer Weber looked puzzled. 'But Herr General, a

movement such as the Werewolves . . . Surely . . .'

Kammler glanced at his driver. The younger man was doubtless fitter too, so he would need to be careful. 'Surely what, Konrad?'

Weber's hands gripped the wheel more tightly. 'Well, Herr General, how long can our *Kameraden* beneath the mountain hold out? They will need to be relieved. Dug out of there. As we promised they would be.'

'No, Konrad. Correction. As *I* promised. You promised nothing.'

Weber nodded, keeping his eyes on the route ahead. 'Of course, Herr General.'

The track swung down to cross a rock-strewn riverbed. Scharführer Weber would need to be extra careful not to get a puncture here, or damage an axle.

Kammler stared ahead, eyes piercing the gloom of the dawn forest. 'If you could pull over, Konrad.' He feigned a smile. 'Even an SS general has at times the need to pee.' He gestured at the river crossing. 'Perhaps when we make the far side.'

'Of course, Herr General.'

They crawled across the rough ground, the car groaning and bucking with every turn of the wheels. Once over, Weber pulled to a halt and Kammler climbed out of the car, taking several paces into the forest as if to relieve himself in private.

Once he was out of sight, he eased the Walther PPK out of its holster and cocked it. He was ready.

3

K ammler slid back into his seat.

'I continue, Herr General?' Scharführer Weber queried.

Kammler ignored the question. 'Sadly, Konrad, none of those young men in that tunnel are destined to survive. Like so many others, they will have given their lives for the glory of the Reich.'

'But, Herr General, we told them—'

'Wrong again, Konrad,' Kammler cut in. '*I* told them. If they have been misled, it is none of *your* doing.'

'Of course, Herr General. But . . .'

'You wish to know why. Very well. I will explain.' Kammler gestured ahead. 'Drive if you will.'

Weber eased the car into gear, the dappled sunlight sending beams of light lancing through the thick tree cover, throwing the interior of the Horch into sharp light and shadow.

'Sadly, no one who has witnessed the hiding place of the *Uranmaschine* can be permitted to live,' Kammler continued. 'The reason is simple: the enemy will make those they capture talk, just as we would. That we cannot allow to happen.'

Weber changed up a gear, increasing speed as the track levelled out. A deer, startled by their appearance, darted away at their passing.

'There will be an ordered and quiet vanishing of the senior ranks of the Schutzstaffel,' Kammler continued. 'This we have been planning for some time, ever since it became clear that the enemy would win this phase of the war. We will melt away, to rebuild and fight anew. This will take time; decades even. We have been preparing for many months: the funds, the weaponry, the individuals – key scientists, top leaders – all spirited away to carefully selected safe havens. This we have dubbed Aktion Werwolf – a long-term strategy to forge the Reich anew. It is *we* who are the real Werewolves.'

Kammler paused. Beneath his coat, he checked that he had a round chambered, his index finger seeking out the cold metal of the cocked breech.

'As for any resistance, I am afraid it will come to nothing,' he continued. 'There is no one left to fight. We have thrown everything into the defence of the Fatherland: the old, the young, the war-wounded and the lame; women and girls even. But all to no avail. It is Aktion Werwolf that offers the only real chance of ultimate victory.'

The staff sergeant glanced at him from the corner of his eye. 'But those young men? Those to whom you promised—'

'Doomed,' Kammler cut in coldly, matter-of-factly. 'They will neither suffocate nor starve. It will be their water supplies that will run out on them.' He shrugged. 'Just a few dozen lives lost, and all for the sake of the Reich. It is but a small sacrifice, wouldn't you agree, Konrad? We all have to be prepared to make the ultimate sacrifice.'

Scharführer Weber nodded, understanding slowly dawning upon him. 'Yes, Herr General, of course, if it is for the good of the Reich . . .' He glanced across at his commander. 'But tell me, how may I be a part of this Aktion Werwolf? How might I serve?'

Kammler sighed. 'A good question. Of course, any SS caught by the enemy are unlikely to be treated well. We have all heard the stories, especially those of the cursed Reds. We are the Führer's chosen, so the Russians hate us. And the British and Americans hardly like us a great deal more . . . Which is why I am very likely doing you a favour, Konrad.'

With that, the general eased his weapon out of its hiding place and shot his driver in the head. Moving quickly, he shoved the body to one side, grabbing the steering wheel, and the vehicle came to a halt, the dead driver's foot having eased off the accelerator.

Kammler stared at the bloodied corpse. 'No one means no one, I'm afraid. No one who might talk . . . You, my dear Konrad, have made the ultimate sacrifice, but you still have one last duty to fulfil.'

He slipped out of the passenger seat, opened the driver's door and dragged the dead man's body outside. He proceeded to remove Weber's bloodied uniform, before changing out of his own and into that of his staff sergeant.

That done, he dressed his erstwhile driver in his own clothes, stuffing a wallet and papers into the dead man's pockets. The preparations made by the SS high command had been exhaustive: the papers consisted of forged documents combining Kammler's real identity with a photo of his driver.

When he was done, SS General Kammler was attired in the blood-spattered uniform of a man sixteen ranks lower than his own. If he were captured by the enemy – and he did not intend to be captured – he would stand a good chance of evading notice or retribution.

He dragged the corpse around to the passenger side and bundled it inside. Then, sliding behind the wheel on a seat slick with blood, he began to drive.

After thirty minutes, the Horch emerged from the rough track onto a minor tarred road. Kammler pushed onwards before finally spotting a bend that he thought would prove suitable. He pulled over and found a weighty rock. Dragging the corpse into the driver's seat, he stood in front of the vehicle and emptied the Walther's remaining rounds – eight bullets in all – through the Horch's windscreen.

To a casual observer – even to a half-decent military investigator – it would appear as if the staff car had been ambushed from the front, the windscreen peppered with fire, the driver caught in the onslaught.

Next, he used the rock to jam down the throttle before slamming the car into gear and sending it juddering on its way.

Slowly it gathered speed.

A hundred yards down the slope, and going at quite a pace, the Horch hit the sharp right-hand turn. It veered off the road and careered downhill, bucking its way through a rough field, before crashing into an outcrop of boulders, flipping once and coming to rest on its side.

Kammler stared at it in satisfaction. To all intents and purposes, SS General Hans Kammler had just died in a bloody ambush by unknown assailants.

He set off on foot, his story crystallising in his mind. If he ran into any Germans, he was a comparatively elderly man press-ganged into the defence of the Reich at the eleventh hour. He had fought valiantly – witness the blood – but had lost his brother soldiers in the confusion.

If he ran into the enemy, the story was pretty much the same. A little less valour. A little more shell shock and confusion. A suggestion that the SS uniform was all the hard-pressed Wehrmacht had had to offer him. Heaven forbid he was a member of the dreaded Schutzstaffel himself.

Yes, on balance he should do fine.

But if his luck held, none of that would be necessary. He planned to move cross-country towards a cabin set deep in the mountains – one well stocked with supplies. From there he would make contact with those SS brethren who were likewise in the process of slipping away.

Approaches had been made internationally. Deals had been cut. Vast amounts of Nazi wealth had been secreted in discreet foreign bank accounts to ensure that ratlines – escape routes – would open for the chosen. There was little doubt in Kammler's mind that exotic shores and a new future beckoned.

In time, the humiliation of Germany would be avenged.

In time, the SS brethren would rebuild the glorious Reich.

4

Present day

Picking up Erich Isselhorst had been child's play.
Heidelberg – his place of residence – was a quaint German
city steeped in history and dominated by the hilltop fortress
of Heidelberg Castle. The narrow, twisting alleyways and street
cafés of the old town had provided ample scope for Irina Narov
to lurk unseen, to linger and track her prey.

She had planned this like she would any military operation.
She had watched her target for days, logging his movements, his
routine and his peccadilloes. She knew that she was the type of
woman – blonde, blue-eyed, svelte and super-fit – who would
appeal to his tastes, especially if she hinted at a certain sympathy with his neo-Nazi views.

In his mid forties, Isselhorst was single and childless. Perhaps
he had yet to find the perfect Aryan *Frau* to share his extreme
ideology; one willing to turn a blind eye to his darker dealings.
From the way he was acting right now, Narov reckoned that he
figured she might be the one.

She tried not to shudder as he pulled her closer in the taxi.
Thankfully it was only a short ride through the thick woodland
that fringed the River Neckar – Heidelberg's main artery – to
Isselhorst's home, a modernist slab-sided construction of glass
and steel that overlooked the water.

Isselhorst lived in Heidelberg's most exclusive district and the
house must have cost a small fortune. But he could certainly

afford it, and his ability to do so – the source of his funds – lay at the heart of why Narov had chosen to act the seductress tonight.

She could feel the rise and fall of his chest as he held her close. No doubt about it, he kept himself in good shape. Six foot two, with a thick head of blonde hair and a certain arrogance about his demeanour, he would be no pushover, of that she felt certain.

She had watched him from her hide in the woods as he'd pumped iron in his home gym, putting in a good hour each morning at eleven o'clock sharp, followed by a forty-five-minute jog by the riverside. He was quick, sure-footed and powerful in his movements.

She was ten years his junior, but he had to weigh a good third again as much as she did. She would have to keep her distance, strike hard and give him not the slightest chance to get close enough to land a blow.

Narov was acutely aware that this time, she was acting entirely on her own, with zero chance of any backup. Yet she had one major advantage over her adversary: Isselhorst had consumed a significant quantity of alcohol, whereas she was feigning drunkenness.

Her inebriation was all an act.

Of course, she could have shared her suspicions with the other members of the Secret Hunters – Peter Miles, Uncle Joe, Will Jaeger – the informal band of Nazi hunters who traced their origins back to the war years. But she doubted any of them would have believed her.

That Hank Kammler might still be alive and intent on vengeance: on the face of it, all the evidence suggested otherwise. But the son of SS General Hans Kammler – after Hitler, very possibly the most powerful figure in the Third Reich – hadn't died so easily, of that Narov felt certain.

Well, tonight should go a good distance to proving it.

Isselhorst leant closer. She could smell the alcohol upon him.

'Not so far now . . . You will find I have a particular taste in decor . . . a certain nostalgic bent. For the war years. For when Germany was truly great. One nation. One people. I hope you won't find it offputting.'

Narov steeled herself. 'On the contrary.' She gazed deep into his eyes. 'People still fear even to speak his name. But I find the original aspirations of Hitler strangely appealing.' She paused. 'We all know the kind of man he was. His legacy. His lessons for posterity. Even now, we can learn from them.'

'Exactly. My point entirely,' Isselhorst enthused. He was speaking English, which lent a certain stilted tone to his words. Narov had yet to let on that she was fluent in German. He sighed contentedly. 'I am so glad we met,' he whispered, closer to her ear. 'Fate, the gods – they must be smiling upon us.'

'You are just a hopeless romantic,' Narov teased.

'Perhaps, and maybe if the mood takes us . . . I have a few nostalgic uniforms . . . most dashing . . .' He let the words hang in the air suggestively.

'A little dressing up?' Narov smiled. 'Erich, you naughty boy. But why not? Tell me – you do not have Hanna Reitsch's flying jacket, by any chance? That *would* be something.'

With those with whom she felt no special connection, Narov could play a part to perfection. She could be a chameleon beyond compare. But those she was close to, she found it impossible to deceive. It made for challenging relationships. But not here. This was simple. This was a man she utterly despised, and tonight's little charade came easily.

'My dear, you never cease to amaze,' Isselhorst murmured, stroking her hair. 'You know of Hanna Reitsch? My God, what a woman! What a pilot. What a hero of the Reich.'

'You sound as if you are obsessed with her. Or with her memory.' Narov laughed. 'But Erich, you have a problem. Right now, she would be a hundred and four years old. To be in love with Hanna Reitsch would be a great waste for a man of your . . . potency.'

Isselhorst chuckled, but before he could reply, the taxi pulled into the secluded woodland surrounding his home. He had a cleaner-cum-housekeeper – the ancient, hatchet-faced Frau Helliger, who looked as if her features would crack were she ever to smile – but Narov knew that at this hour, the house would be deserted.

She had watched from the woods and logged Frau Helliger's movements; her routines. She knew she would have a clear run of things until 10 a.m., when the housekeeper came to start her daily round of chores.

Isselhorst paid off the driver and they moved towards the house.

Inside, it was all polished chrome, granite and wood, and clean, minimalist lines. But it wasn't that that would strike any visitor; it was the artwork and Nazi memorabilia that hung from the walls. The place felt more like a gallery or museum – or perhaps a shrine – than it did a normal home.

Narov feigned surprise. From her hide she had observed some of the priceless paintings, though not the full-length portrait of Adolf Hitler that hung in the entrance hall. Encased in a heavy gilt frame, it showed the Führer, resplendent in uniform, standing on the field of battle, his posed expression stern and heroic, eyes on the distant horizon.

Below it was a black swastika, inset in a gold circle, with a point at one end and a mount at the other; she presumed this was the topmost piece of some kind of ceremonial Nazi staff. She turned, acting as if awestruck, noting Isselhorst's obvious enjoyment as he watched.

In a cabinet opposite was a silver-bound edition of *Mein Kampf*, Hitler's hate-filled rant written prior to the war years. Above it was an ornately carved wooden eagle, wings flared and talons outstretched as if to seize the Führer's magnum opus and rise aloft victorious.

The whole effect suddenly made Narov want to vomit, but she fought the reflex. She was in. And she was here to wring from Isselhorst his darkest secrets.

He gestured to the flight of steel stairs that led to the living room, set on the upper floor. 'After you.'

As Narov started up the steps, she could feel Isselhorst's eyes feasting upon her figure.

Let him feast, she told herself, calmly. Soon now.

5

Isselhorst led her to the plate-glass window that filled one entire side of the living room. At the press of a button, the dark blinds whisked aside and the expanse of the city appeared before them: the Neckar floodlit and beautiful, the ancient bridges that spanned the river casting a rich orange glow upon the waters.

At any other time Narov would have found the view breath-taking. But not tonight.

Isselhorst stepped away, returning a moment later with two shot glasses. Peach schnapps, she could tell from the aroma.

He glanced at the view, raising his glass. 'To beauty. To the beautiful of this world. To us.'

'To us,' she echoed, throwing the fiery contents down her throat.

Isselhorst smiled appreciatively. 'You drink like Hanna Reitsch, that's for certain!' He reached for the bottle and poured them both a refill, then leant closer. 'So, I let you in on a little secret: I sleep in Hitler's bed. The one that he had in the Berghof. I purchased it recently at a rather unusual auction. Cost me . . . an arm and a leg, as I think you say. Perhaps you may like to see it?'

'I would love to,' Narov demurred, 'but first I would like to say hello to Oscar. I just love animals, as I think you must, with your home set here in the woodland.'

'You would like to meet my dog? But of course. Come.' Isselhorst ushered her towards a doorway. 'But tell me – how do you know about Oscar? Did I say something?'

For the briefest of moments Narov feared she'd messed up, but she recovered just as quickly. She nodded towards the entranceway. 'You have a dog's collar and lead in the hallway, printed with his name.'

Isselhorst smiled. 'Very observant. Smart as well as beautiful. Come. I introduce you to Oscar. Very big, but very lovable, as you will soon discover.'

Narov had watched Isselhorst take the dog – a large and powerful German Shepherd – with him on his runs. While she was an unapologetic lover of animals, that wasn't why she'd asked to meet his dog. She needed to do so in the company of his master so that Oscar would see her as a friend.

They passed a large oil painting that Narov figured had to be a Matisse. No doubt stolen from its original Jewish owners during the war years, and now hanging on the wall of an ultra-wealthy German lawyer. So much of the Nazis' ill-gotten loot had never been returned, largely thanks to men like Isselhorst.

She paused before it. It showed a naked woman draped across a yellow-and-green-striped sofa, legs dangling provocatively over one arm. The woman had a strip of light, chiffon-like material laid across her lap, obscuring her feminine parts.

'Beautiful. Captivating,' she remarked. 'Do I recognise the artist?'

Isselhorst hesitated for just an instant. 'Matisse, actually,' he boasted, an arrogant curl to his lip. '*Woman in an Armchair*, 1923.'

Narov feigned amazement. 'An original Matisse? Wow. Just what kind of lawyer are you?'

Isselhorst flashed a glittering, perfect smile. 'A very talented one. And some of my clients choose to pay me in kind.'

They moved towards the kitchen, where Narov was introduced to a decidedly sleepy-looking Oscar. She had a magical way with animals. Always had done. She and the German Shepherd quickly bonded, but Isselhorst soon pulled her away, steering her towards the bedroom and Hitler's bed; impatient to get the real agenda for tonight started . . . the one he believed they were here for.

Just as they were about to enter, Narov paused, her head tilted towards the lounge. 'The schnapps. Come on! Just one more.'

She could tell that Isselhorst – a man not used to being denied – was growing impatient. But at the same time he appeared to thrill to his guest's apparently wild ways.

He smiled. 'And why not? One for the road, as you say . . .'

Isselhorst believed Narov to be an American. That was what she'd told him, and indeed these days she mostly was. Recently, she'd taken US citizenship, but she'd been born British and had spent her youth in Russia, for her family was originally Russian.

That part she had kept from him. The Russians and the Nazis had never been the best of friends.

He poured two fresh shots. As he handed Narov hers, she feigned drunken clumsiness, the glass slipping through her fingers. It hit the floor with a sharp crack, shattering into tiny pieces, the schnapps spattering across the marble.

For the briefest of instants, Narov saw a look of anger, bordering on rage, flit across Isselhorst's features. He killed it just as quickly, but still, she'd glimpsed the man behind the mask. He was just as she'd imagined him: bereft of morals, a beast bloated with money and power, and above all a control freak.

But he covered well. 'Not to worry.' He shrugged. 'I have a housekeeper. Frau Helliger. She will clear it up in the morning.'

He turned for the bottle and a replacement glass, and as he did so, he had his hands full and was slightly off balance.

Before he had fully turned back again, bringing Narov into his field of vision, she struck like a coiled snake, driving forwards and upwards with her right hand in a smooth but devastating strike, hammering the fleshy part of her palm directly into the underside of Isselhorst's jaw.

She'd practised the move a thousand times, when she'd served with the Russian Spetsnaz – their special forces. The blow was delivered with all her power and pent-up hatred, and she felt the teeth of Isselhorst's lower jaw being driven upwards, ripping into his upper mouth savagely.

He staggered backwards, spitting blood. Moments later, the schnapps bottle and replacement glass had joined the debris scattered across the living room floor. That blow would have felled most men, but somehow he was still on his feet.

Narov didn't hesitate. She unleashed an open-palmed strike with her right hand, delivering the knockout blow into exactly the desired spot on the side of his neck, three inches beneath his left ear, just where the carotid artery pumped blood to the brain.

Time seemed to hang in the air before Isselhorst's eyes rolled into his head, his knees buckled and he collapsed onto the floor.

Narov glanced down at him breathlessly. He was out cold, a trickle of blood issuing from his mouth and mixing with the pool of schnapps.

She took a few seconds to calm herself before embarking upon the next stage of her plan.

6

Will Jaeger couldn't deny that he was enjoying himself.

When his ninety-five-year-old great-uncle had first suggested the trip, Jaeger had been doubtful. But he had to admit that he needed the break, and where better to come than the place where it had all started.

The Hotel Zum Turken in Berchtesgaden was about as close as one could get these days to Hitler's Berghof, the mountain lair from which he had ruled Nazi Germany. The hotel had stood cheek-by-jowl with the Berghof, being commandeered by Nazi officials during the war. In fact the two had been joined by a network of tunnels burrowed beneath the mountain, but while the Berghof had been destroyed by Allied air raids, the hotel had largely survived.

These days, powerful anti-Nazi sentiments pervaded the area. Andrea Munsch, the hotel's owner, epitomised such feelings. When Jaeger had telephoned enquiring whether they might book rooms, she had warned him that the hotel was probably not going to be to their liking. For a moment he'd worried that the Zum Turken had been turned into some kind of a shrine to the twisted ideology of Nazism, but Andrea had quickly disabused him of that misapprehension.

In 1933, Martin Bormann – known then as 'Hitler's banker' – had seized the Hotel Zum Turken, and its long-time owners – Andrea's parents – had been kicked out by his jackbooted thugs. At the end of the war, they had returned to discover a bare and looted shell. They had decided to rebuild the hotel, but to keep it in the state it had been at war's end as a memorial to those who had died at Hitler's hand. Consequently there were few mod cons, certainly no Wi-Fi or internet, and the only sound system in the place was an old gramophone. Hence Andrea's warning.

That morning, she had taken Jaeger and Uncle Joe into the tunnels, via the Zum Turken's basement. From there they'd wound ever deeper into the bowels of the mountain, descending concrete steps and iron ladders bolted to walls, and stepping through puddles of yellowing water that lingered in the airless damp.

So extensive was the subterranean network that the Bavarian government was still excavating it, to create a permanent exhibit to the dark excesses of the Nazi regime.

At one point, Andrea had paused to allow Uncle Joe to catch his breath, and she'd used the time to relate a story. She spoke impeccable English, and was clearly passionate about keeping such wartime memories alive.

She waved a hand around the tunnel. 'When Bormann seized the hotel, none of this existed. Over time it became the headquarters of the SS, and a key means of maintaining control. As a result, unspeakable things happened here. Perhaps you can feel it in the air? Many visitors say they can. A sense of lingering evil.'

Jaeger pondered this for a moment. He realised that he'd felt unsettled as soon as they'd entered the tunnels, a feeling that only grew the deeper they delved.

'My parents witnessed one of the earliest horrors,' Andrea continued. 'Bormann seized the home of a local man for himself. The man was deeply distressed, so he waited for Hitler's convoy to wend its way down from the Berghof, then placed himself in front of Hitler's car where it slowed at a bend and spoke to him personally, begging that his family be allowed to keep their home.

'Hitler lent an apparently sympathetic ear, and told the man it would be dealt with the very next day. The man returned to his family with the good news: the Führer himself would intercede. The next morning, the Gestapo came. They arrested him, took him into these tunnels and tortured him, then sent him to the concentration camps.

'Just one example.' Andrea paused. 'One of thousands.'

The tour of the labyrinthine tunnel complex had occupied most of that morning, especially as they were proceeding at Uncle Joe's pace. In the afternoon, Jaeger had gone for a run on one of the spectacular walking trails that criss-crossed the mountains, leaving Uncle Joe to his afternoon nap.

He had come here expecting to encounter an atmosphere of oppression and darkness, but what he had discovered was quite the opposite. The breathtaking beauty of the dramatic peaks and valleys had actually lifted his spirits.

And he certainly needed that right now.

The past few months had been anything but easy.

Four years ago, his wife, Ruth, and eight-year-old son Luke had been kidnapped. Jaeger had scoured the earth in his effort to find their abductors. The trail had led him to the son of a former Nazi general, one who had risen to serve in the highest echelons of America's post-war intelligence apparatus. He'd been recruited to help combat the rise of Soviet Russia, the Germans being the only people who had any experience of going to war against the 'Reds'.

That Nazi general was long dead, but his son, Hank Kammler, had good reasons to hate Jaeger, ones reaching deep into a shared family past. Kammler had kidnapped Jaeger's wife and son as a way to exact revenge, and found the means to torture Jaeger remotely with their disappearance, emailing him videos of Ruth and Luke in captivity; bound, kneeling and pleading for help. Each taunting message had ended with the chilling words: *Wir sind die Zukunft* – 'We are the future'.

Following a global hunt, Jaeger had rescued his family, but not before Kammler had infected them with a super-virus with which he had intended to wipe out most of humankind in order to forge a brave new world: a Fourth Reich. The chosen few had been inoculated so that they would survive what he'd named the *Gottvirus*.

At the eleventh hour, Jaeger and his team had foiled Kammler, and the world's military and law-enforcement agencies had gone after him big-time. A scorched body – later confirmed as having Kammler's DNA – had been retrieved from his subterranean command bunker. It appeared he had 'done a Hitler' and committed suicide, possibly by setting himself on fire.

But that had done little to relieve Jaeger's suffering. While Luke had made a remarkable recovery, Ruth had not. She'd languished in the darkness that had gripped her mind, seemingly hopelessly mired within it.

Eventually Jaeger had checked her into a London clinic that specialised in dealing with the victims of trauma. But they were months into her treatment now and going nowhere fast. If anything, Ruth's mood swings, her unpredictability and her violence – she was prone to lashing out – were worsening.

No doubt about it, Jaeger had needed this break big time.

7

The trauma that Jaeger's wife had endured had been horrific. She had been subjected to three years of unspeakable psychological and physical torment at Kammler's hands, and had come back a shadow of her former self.

She was still undergoing various tests, but no one doubted that she had PTSD – post-traumatic stress disorder, a debilitating psychological illness caused by an overburden of horror. While she had recovered physically, the mental scars went far deeper.

Jaeger had endeavoured to be patient, sympathetic and upbeat; to put up with the rage and the outbursts of moody violence.

But in truth it had taken its toll.

He was just glad that Luke and their newly adopted son, Simon, were at a state-run boarding school in the countryside, and so shielded from their mother's more extreme outbursts.

Simon Chucks Bello, an orphan from the East African slums, had played a key role in defeating Kammler and neutralising his *Gottvirus*. Luke had always wanted a brother, and as Simon had no parents, the Jaeger family had decided to adopt him.

But right now, Ruth needed space in which to heal and Jaeger had been in desperate need of a break – hence his spur-of-the-moment visit to the Berghof.

As he sat there on the hotel patio, he let the serenity of the place and its breathtaking beauty seep into him. It was the last

thing he had ever expected: to find solace where Hitler had or-
chestrated so much evil.

Another thought struck him as he ran his eye over the dramatic folds of the forested hills. How could anyone have looked
out over all of this – over the stunning Untersberg Mountains
– and planned the mass murder of so many?

It was inconceivable.

Yet it had happened.

His mind was drawn back to the present by a polite cough.
He turned to find Andrea with the dinner menu.

'No sign of your uncle yet?' she queried. 'He will be joining
you? If not, he can take dinner in his room. He must be tired
after the tunnels. Such a wonderful man. How old is he, if you
don't mind me asking?'

'Ninety-five . . . going on twenty-one,' Jaeger quipped. 'Don't
worry, he'll make dinner. I've just ordered us beer with schnapps
chasers. Uncle Joe wouldn't miss it for the world.'

Andrea smiled. 'You have heard about this new discovery? It
is all over the news. An Austrian film-maker has just uncovered
an entirely unknown Nazi tunnel system not so very far away.'

'Really? They tunnelled everywhere, didn't they?'

'So it seems. But what has made the headlines is what may
be *hidden* there. Apparently this was a top-secret Nazi weapons facility. It is where they concealed the most advanced war
machines.'

Andrea reached for a newspaper, handing it to Jaeger. He ran
his gaze over the newsprint. 'Secret Nazi discoveries,' he mused.
'Always make for good headlines.'

Andrea smiled. 'Indeed.'

It was then that a familiar name caught his eye: SS-
Oberstgruppenführer Hans Kammler.

'I'm curious,' he remarked. 'What does it say there, about
General Kammler?'

Andrea read aloud, translating as she went: 'Found: Hitler's
secret plant. Vast underground complex where Nazis worked

on top-secret weapons systems . . . The entire seventy-five-acre complex was the brainchild of SS General Hans Kammler, who recruited scientists to work on a secret end-of-war weapons programme . . . Austrian film-maker Andreas Sulzer said the site is "most likely the biggest secret weapons facility of the Third Reich". Kammler, who drew up the plans for the crematoriums and gas chambers at Auschwitz, was also in charge of Hitler's V-weapons programmes. Experts say the Nazis may have been developing a variant of the V-2, with a weapon of mass destruction as its warhead.'

Jaeger shook his head. 'Crazy stuff. I wonder how much truth there is to it.'

'Well, it's at St Georgen an der Gusen, which is not so far from here. Maybe two hours' drive. Why not go see for yourself?'

Jaeger nodded pensively. He couldn't deny that he was curious. The possibility that General Kammler had cooked up some last-ditch Nazi super-weapon, and that it had remained hidden until today, was intriguing.

'I'll talk it through with Uncle Joe.' He spied a figure over Andrea's shoulder. 'Talk of the devil, here he is!'

Uncle Joe moved across the patio, a shock of white hair above beady eyes, the thin cane of a walking stick his only concession to age. If Jaeger reached ninety-five and had half Joe's vitality and spirit, he'd be happy.

Together they talked over the St Georgen discovery. They were scheduled to leave for the UK the following morning, but Jaeger figured he could stretch it for another forty-eight hours. They could dedicate tomorrow to visiting the secret caves, followed by the long drive home.

It would be punishing, but doable. Uncle Joe might not be up to all the walking involved, but he could always park himself at a local bar or restaurant in St Georgen.

By the time they had finished eating, they had firmed up their plans.

Jaeger felt a certain thrill of excitement at the proposition

– General Kammler's legacy would always hold a dark fascination for him – but he also experienced a twinge of trepidation. He'd promised to collect Ruth from the clinic just as soon as he was back in the UK. Postponing it by forty-eight hours – well, there was no knowing how she would react.

Ruth Jaeger could be explosively unpredictable these days.

8

Narov watched her hostage come to.

After retrieving her rucksack from her hide in the forest, she'd returned to the house, closed all the blinds and manhandled Isselhorst's bulk onto one of his steel-framed designer chairs, before using a roll of green gaffer tape to fasten him securely.

What she loved about the tape was its utter reliability and functionality. It was quick, easy and ultra-secure.

With Isselhorst she'd been unusually thorough. He was fastened all along his arms and wrists to the flat arms of the chair. His ankles and legs were taped along their length to the chair's legs. She'd used up an entire roll taping his chest, shoulders and neck to its near-vertical back.

And for good measure she'd stuffed his mouth with rags and run a loop of tape around his head, just in case he got any ideas about trying to cry for help – not that there was anyone who might hear.

In short, he was incapable of making any movement whatsoever – the kind of effect you could never pull off using rope alone.

It put your captive completely at your mercy.

She reached out, grabbing hold of one end of the tape covering his jaws, and ripped it free, tearing it off his bare skin. He would have yelled with pain were his mouth not stuffed with rags. With a certain revulsion, she took the end of the bloodied cloth and yanked it free, letting it fall to the floor.

Isselhorst shook his head as he tried to clear it, spitting out gobbets of blood and the odd fragment of tooth. As his eyes focused, he became aware of where he was, how he was fastened and who it was that was facing him.

'What in the name of God . . .' he gasped.

'Be quiet. I do the talking.'

Narov's tone was different now. Cold. Ruthless. And she had spoken in fluent German. Isselhorst, by contrast, had lisped and spluttered as he tried to speak through a mouthful of broken teeth.

She let him see her pistol. It was a compact Beretta 92FS – the one that she always took on operations. It was the civilian version of the Beretta M9, until recently the US Marine Corps' handgun of choice.

The combination of Isselhorst's immobility, Narov's firepower and her cold, fluent German seemed to have the desired effect: her captive remained silent, eyes bulging in disbelief at what had happened.

'I have listened to your egotistical bullshit all night. Now it is my turn,' she grated. 'You are Erich Pieter Isselhorst, grandson of the SS general of the same name. Your grandfather, like you a lawyer, ran an *Einsatzkommando* on the Eastern Front. He murdered tens of thousands of Russians, Jews, Poles and other so-called enemies of the Reich. At war's end he was tried by the Allies for war crimes and executed by a French firing squad.'

She stared into Isselhorst's eyes, her ice-blue gaze seemingly blank of expression or emotion.

'Wrong. Your grandfather's execution was never carried out. Instead, he was recruited by the CIA. He had fought against the Russians, and the Americans felt that former Nazis with such experience could prove useful in the Cold War. In short, Herr Isselhorst, you should not really exist.'

Narov turned away from her captive.

'You are an aberration. Your bloodline should have died with your grandfather's execution.' She pivoted on her heel and stared into his fearful gaze. 'So whatever happens tonight, it is happening to a man who should never have been born.'

Isselhorst gawped. No longer the perfect chocolate-box smile, Narov noted with grim satisfaction.

'Who in the name of God are you?' he slurred.

'I am your worst nightmare.' Narov's reply was flat and un-emotional, and all the more fearsome for it. 'I know all there is to know. I know your bloodline, cursed as it is. I know what you have done for a living these past years. Nazis and mass murderers who were hunted for their war crimes – they turned to you for their defence. And if you could not shield them in law, you arranged for alternative means for them to evade their accusers.'

She gestured at the Matisse. 'Desperate men will go to desper-ate measures to buy their survival. Such artworks are priceless, but hard to place on the open market, for the descendants of the rightful owners do still exist. Despite your grandfather's best efforts, some of those destined for the death camps did evade them.'

Isselhorst scowled. 'None would have if—'

Narov whipped the hard, angular barrel of the Beretta across his face, crunching into the delicate bone structure around the right eye socket. He howled in pain, straining with all his might to free himself from his bonds.

'Did I ask you to speak?' she breathed, her voice like ice. 'Did I ask you to squeal? When I want to hear from you, I will say so.'

She knew from long experience to strike an adversary with anything other than your own limbs. Bone crushed bone. Broken bone injured flesh. The blow had been delivered to cause her minimum injury. You could never be too careful in this kind of game. It was care – minute, pedantic care and preparation – that had kept her alive. That and her training.

'So, I have one thing to ask of you. One question.' She glanced at Isselhorst dispassionately. 'Your answer to this question will determine whether you live or die.'

He glared back at her, eyes brimming with hatred.

'You have recently taken on a new case,' she continued. 'Even for you it is an unusual one. A controversial one. It is your involvement in that case that brought you to my attention.

'Otto Marks versus Justiz Stiftung et al.' She paused. 'Marks claims to be a descendant of Adolf Hitler. As such, he claims the royalties earned by the book you have displayed in your hallway. Hitler's royalties for *Mein Kampf*, stretching back seventy-odd years.'

She paused. 'Just this year, *Mein Kampf* topped best-seller lists here in Germany. In India, Turkey and a string of Arab nations – where I presume its message of exterminating Jews plays well – it is a perennial favourite.

'As you know, Justiz Stiftung – the Justice Foundation – has held those royalties pending the expiration of Hitler's seventy-year copyright, in case a legal heir stepped forward. That copyright recently ran out. Justiz Stiftung announced plans to donate the monies to charities that fight Nazism. Then your client, Otto Marks, stepped forward.

'The amount that you are claiming for Herr Marks runs into many millions of dollars.' Narov paused. She let the silence hang heavy for a second. 'That much I know. Now, my question. What is the real identity of the man you claim to represent? I presume that like you, he is a descendant of a prominent member of the SS. Of the Brotherhood of the Death's Head.'

At the mention of the Brotherhood, Isselhorst visibly stiffened. Narov ignored the reaction. There was so much that she knew. This had been her life's work, and for a very particular set of reasons. But that she would keep until the very end of Herr Isselhorst's interrogation.

'So, his name. His real name,' she demanded. 'Not the one you have used on the documents submitted to the court.'

Isselhorst tried to shake his head, but it was taped rigidly to the back of the chair and it barely moved. 'I don't know his name. He protects it jealously. I only know him by his assumed name: Otto Marks. I'm not lying. You've said my life depends on it. So would I risk a lie? Would I?'

Narov held her silence for a long beat. Then she reached into her backpack. 'This will decide it.' She retrieved two syringes and held them up. 'One contains suxamethonium chloride, a paralytic. The other naloxone hydrochloride, an anti-opioid.'

She paused. Isselhorst's expression was a mixture of fear and confusion as he stared at the needles.

'None the wiser? In layman's terms, this,' she held up the first syringe, 'is a respiratory depressant: it stops you breathing. You remain fully conscious, yet you cannot breathe.' She held up the other syringe. 'And this reverses the effect.'

She paused. 'And I control the timings.'

She glanced up from the needles, eyes cold, expression ice calm. 'Too long under the first shot and you might never recover. You might survive, but brain-dead. A vegetable. Or you might never start breathing again. Either way, you remain totally conscious, so that you get to feel what it is like to die. Over and over again.'

'I tell you, I don't know who he is!' Isselhorst blurted. 'I don't! But there are clues. Other means. My phone. I took a photograph, at dinner, the last time we met. That could help. Plus our next meeting. It's scheduled for three days' time. You stake it out, you get to see him in person.'

Narov glanced at Isselhorst's phone. She'd placed it to one side when she'd searched his pockets, intent on checking it later. Now she reached for it, stood behind him, and held the screen before his one good eye as she flicked through the images.

'There! That's him! Otto Marks, or whatever the bastard's name is.'

Narov studied the photo for a good few seconds, using the

thumb and finger of her free hand to zoom in on the face of the man she sought.

Could it be? The features seemed familiar, but somehow not exactly right. But it was the eyes that were most compelling.

They were his, of that she was certain.

9

Narov moved back to face Isselhorst, taking up her grip again on the pair of syringes. 'It is a start. But I need more. Addresses. Phone details. Email. I need everything.'

'I don't have much. He only makes contact with me, never the other way around. And if he calls, his number is always untraceable. I have never known such secrecy, even with my most paranoid clients.'

Narov pulled out a tourniquet and went to fasten it around Isselhorst's arm. She could see him desperately trying to struggle; to break free from his bonds; to stop her getting the tourniquet fastened. But it was no use: he couldn't move.

'Keep still,' she murmured, almost as if speaking to herself. 'Ah, good. A nice prominent vein.' She moved the needle towards Isselhorst's forearm.

'I tell you, I don't know!' Isselhorst yelled. His terror was plain to see: it had darkened his crotch where he had wet himself with fear. 'The meeting. Three days' time. In Dubai. Please. *Please.* That will get you to him.'

Narov proceeded to extract every last detail she could about the coming meeting: location, purpose, date, time. She realised she would need to hurry. She was never happy to approach a target unless she had done a detailed reconnaissance.

Questioning finished, she settled down for her final chat with Herr Isselhorst.

'There is one more thing about your grandfather that you need to know. In 1944, he was transferred from the Eastern

Front to SS headquarters in Strasbourg. From there, he oversaw a concentration camp called Natzweiler. I'm curious: have you ever heard of it?'

'No. Truthfully. Never.'

She looked him squarely in the eye. 'Few have. It was built on French soil on what was once a beautiful ski resort. At the start of the war, my grandmother joined the French Resistance. She was captured and incarcerated in Natzweiler, on your grand-father's personal orders.'

She paused, gazing at Isselhorst with an odd, unsettling dis-passion. 'You see, in a way we are alike, you and I. I also should not exist. I am the union of two things that should never have been joined.'

She brought her mouth close to his ear, as he had done to her in the taxi. 'My grandmother, Sonia Olchanevsky, was a very beautiful Russian Jew. She was raped by an SS officer at Natzweiler. Repeatedly. That officer was my grandfather, and I – I am the grandchild of that rape.'

With that, she picked up her bag, re-secured Isselhorst's gag, pocketed his mobile phone and left the room. Behind her, she could hear the man sobbing exhaustedly.

She made her way to the kitchen, pausing at the stove and turning all the gas rings to the fully open position. Then she took Oscar's lead, clipped it onto his collar and coaxed him out of his basket. Before she left the house, she struck a match and lit three fat beeswax candles in an ornate silver candelabra.

They flared into life. She placed the candelabra on the shelf and closed the door, Oscar following her obediently. The dog had to be wondering what he had done to deserve such a rare treat as this: midnight walkies.

He paused once only as they walked up the gravel driveway. Narov had dropped something. He pulled on his leash and whined, only for her to signal him onwards, leaving behind a battered, moth-eaten wallet containing an ID card belonging to one Leon Kiel.

Kiel was one of Heidelberg's better-known petty criminals. Narov had observed him picking pockets in the city's narrow, twisting streets. While she didn't exactly relish fitting him up for tonight's crime, there were far greater matters at stake. The last thing she could afford was the authorities somehow linking it to her, or with what was coming.

Wallet dropped, Narov strapped her backpack to her shoulders and hurried into the woods, settling into a ground-eating run, Oscar jogging at her side. Some ten minutes later, the night sky behind them was ripped apart by an almighty explosion, a plume of bluish-yellow flame punching into the darkness as shards of glass and steel tumbled through the air.

The cloud of gas had seeped out of the kitchen, finding its way along the hallways and spreading through the rooms. Finally it had made contact with the candles.

At which point Erich Isselhorst's house – and the man himself – was no more.

10

Jaeger leant back with his feet up on the bed. The Zum Turken hotel was equipped with fine turn-of-the-century furniture. On the far side of the room was a polished oak coffin chest: literally where a coffin would lie in the family home prior to burial.

He hoped it wasn't some kind of prophecy for how the next few minutes might go as he called his wife.

He knew it wasn't Ruth's fault. He knew that it was all due to the years of abuse she'd suffered. But Jaeger was no saint. Try as he might, he couldn't keep taking the punishment; turning the other cheek. There would come a time when he would just want out.

Either the past was the past and they could put it all behind them, or he was done. He had longed for his wife to come back to him; the woman he'd married. But maybe they were beyond that now.

He remembered what had first drawn him to her. She was utterly arresting, with her raven hair and emerald-green eyes. She had the fiery temper bequeathed by her Irish ancestry, not to mention the typical wicked Irish sense of humour.

In short, she had been beautiful, sexy, smart and invariably the centre of attention at any social gathering. Indeed, he'd met her at a friend's party where she was holding court – not that he'd always warmed to the company she tended to keep.

A diehard environmentalist, Ruth had surrounded herself with the kind of crusty Greenpeace crowd that didn't always sit well with Jaeger and his friends. Elite soldiers and the tree-hugging brigade – they weren't natural soulmates.

Jaeger was a bit of an exception, of course. He'd always been drawn to the wilderness and nature. In fact, he shared some of Ruth's fiercest passions. And he guessed that was what had pulled them together.

At first, she'd hated him. Railed against his macho ways. Or at least she'd presumed he had to be the macho type, being a member of the SAS. Then fate had thrown them together. Ruth was paying a visit to a rural school in Devon to give them a talk about 'going green'. Jaeger had offered to accompany her. His excuse was that he had to see some mates at the Commando Training Centre in Lympstone, and she was driving most of the way there. In truth, he'd just wanted to spend some time in her company, to see if he could break through her beautiful but frosty exterior.

He'd worked hard over that long bank holiday weekend. Typically, he'd used his cheeky, teasing humour in an effort to breach her defences. And finally it had worked. On the way back to London, they'd stopped at her parents' country home, and they'd ended up sharing the spare bedroom.

Officially, Jaeger had slept on her parents' fold-down sofa bed.

In reality, their night of passion had been all-consuming.

They say opposites attract. That night was the proof of it.

But now – where had all of that gone? Where had the love gone? When exactly had the incredible passion and joy in each other withered and died?

Jaeger just didn't know. All he was sure of was that he was at the end of his tether. She was the mother of his son. He feared that was the only reason they were staying together these days, and it just wasn't enough.

He steeled himself, grabbed his cell phone and dialled. It was late in the evening and typically the call went to voicemail. She seemed to spend so much of her time sleeping. Maybe it was the drugs the clinic prescribed to help with the trauma.

'Ruth, it's me. Uncle Joe and I have decided to extend our stay. There's a few things we'd like to see. I'll be back a day or two later than scheduled – Thursday instead of Tuesday. If it's an issue, maybe you can call Jennie and get her to pick you up. Either way, let me know.'

He paused uncomfortably. 'Cheers for now.'

That pretty much summed things up. He couldn't even bring himself to sign off with their signature 'Love you.' He felt plagued by guilt. And mostly because he knew in his heart that he was falling for another woman.

Ruth suspected. Lord only knew how. Call it feminine in-stinct. Sixth sense.

Jaeger placed the phone by his bed and went to wash. They had an early start and he would be doing all the driving. He needed a good night's rest.

From the bathroom he heard his phone trilling. He went and checked the caller ID. It was Ruth. Well, that was an improve-ment. At least she'd bothered to return his call. A rarity these days.

'Ruthie, how are you?' he answered.

'Alive,' she said. Not even a hello. Her tone distant, unreach-able, as it always seemed to be these days.

'I've been talking with Joe,' Jaeger explained, 'and we've de-cided to go visit some newly unearthed tunnels. Some kind of secret Nazi super-weapon facility.'

There was a long-drawn-out silence that he sensed was fraught with emotion.

'I could do with you here.' Ruth's voice sounded pained, as if she was in a really bad place. 'Here with me now, not off on some crazy search . . .'

Jaeger sighed guiltily. 'It's just two more days.'

'I'm losing it, Will. Really losing it.' A beat. 'Like I said, I could really do with you here . . .'

Jaeger fought against the temptation to give in. She could be like this – soft, distant, tantalising – then just as quickly flip into a violent mood swing and turn on him. No, he needed a few extra days' break, and the call of the tunnels – Kammler's secrets – was just too compelling.

'It's only two days,' he remonstrated. 'There's been this new discovery. We're so close – we might not get another chance like this.'

'Off searching for a bunch of dusty Nazi memorabilia . . .' There was an intake of breath, heavy with sadness and despair. 'I guess that means you've got your priorities sorted.' A pause. 'Tell me, Will, when did everything between us . . . go so wrong?'

Jaeger could hear her voice breaking. It tortured him. He ran a hand across his brow. 'You know something, the first moment I laid eyes on you, I knew we'd fall in love. I've loved you ever since. But . . .' He paused. 'I just don't know any longer.'

'And you're *surprised*? After all I went through. Waiting for the rescue that never came. For you.' A beat. 'When have you ever taken the time to really try to understand? To get to know the new me? What drives me. And what haunts me . . .'

Her words tailed off to nothing and she started crying. Jaeger was used to the fits of chest-racking sobs. And if he were within reach, her mood turning so that her fists pounded on his chest until he was forced to physically restrain her.

'People change.' She spoke through her tears. '*I've* changed. You think I like the new me? I didn't ask for this to happen.' A beat. A surge of emotion. 'But you, you've just stayed the same. The same old you.'

It was true. Jaeger had always been constant, and in his book, constant was good. A strength. But seemingly not in hers. In Ruth's mind, he should have changed in some indefinable way to keep in step with the new her.

Well, where would that leave the boys? All at sea. Totally messed up.

No. Jaeger had no doubts. He had to stay constant for Luke and Simon. He needed to. And if that meant losing Ruth . . . In truth, he feared he'd lost her already.

'Look, we'll talk when I get back,' he told her. 'Try to get some rest. It's just two days.'

'What you really mean is: take your pills,' she sobbed. 'Get some rest. As if that makes a blind bit of difference. I don't need more pills.'

'Look, I'll be there Thursday,' he told her. 'It's the best I can do.'

'Well maybe I won't be here by then. Maybe I'll be gone. I get a sense that's what you'd like me to do – disappear.'

Jaeger was used to her outbursts by now. Her threats. Mostly they didn't amount to anything. Mostly they were just cries for help, not that he felt he could help her much any more. She needed professional help, that much he understood.

'I'll see you Thursday,' he repeated. 'It's a couple of days, that's all.' He ended the call.

He was used to her unpredictability; her mood swings. But this sense of her slipping away from him still hurt. He didn't know how to reach her any more. The woman he had once loved seemed lost to him completely, and the realisation hit him hard.

He knew that this was Kammler's ultimate revenge.

11

'Hello! Anyone here?'

Jaeger's voice echoed around the rocky hillside. No answer. If anything, the landscape here was even more rugged than that around the Berghof. He noted that he had zero mobile signal. To left and right, massive peaks towered into cloudless skies.

He reached a roped-off area. Plastic warning tape fluttered in the breeze. There were the usual signs, in German: '*ACH-TUNG!* Excavation in progress. Do not enter.' He ducked beneath the tape and made his way towards the rock escarpment that loomed before him.

Dense forest shielded what had to be the entrance to the caves. A path had been beaten through, kept clear by the passage of heavy boots: film people and excavators, moving in both directions.

If he ran into a team at work, he figured he'd play the stupid Englishman: he hadn't understood the warning signs. He doubted they'd believe him, but in his experience, Austrians tended to be endlessly polite and correct.

Finding his way here had been easy enough: a sandy track snaked through the woodland. He'd been forced to leave his silver Range Rover Evoque several kilometres back, as a padlocked forest gate had barred the way, but the trek through the shade had proved a tonic to his soul. This was always where he was happiest. Alone, surrounded by the still quiet of spectacular wilderness. It brought back memories of his time in the Welsh mountains during SAS selection.

The good parts, that was . . .

He'd left Uncle Joe back in St Georgen, at the Tinschert Gasthof, a traditional establishment in the heart of town. It had turned out to be such a pleasant setting, they'd booked rooms for the night. They'd return to the Zum Turken tomorrow, and start the drive home the following morning.

Jaeger had booked a table for two in the Tinschert's restaurant. He'd promised to share everything with Uncle Joe over dinner, as well as to take a bunch of photographs on his smartphone.

He pushed through the foliage and an entrance yawned before him. Correction: there were two entrances. One snaked left, the other right, and he could tell that there had been traffic through both of them.

Jaeger paused, studying the alternatives for a good few seconds. He felt his pulse quicken. Which one to choose?

The right-hand entrance had a heap of basic equipment piled up just inside it: shovels, pickaxes, wheelbarrows, wooden planking. The left-hand opening was clear, apart from a set of rails disappearing into the gloom. Jaeger figured the rails had to be for pushing handcarts laden with excavation debris.

It looked as if the left-hand tunnel was the one to take.

He removed a few items from his rucksack. He tore off hunks of Austrian sausage with his teeth, washing them down with glugs from his water bottle, and stuffing in some bread for good measure. Somehow he didn't fancy lunching in the dark confines of the tunnel.

Then he climbed down the crumbling earth-and-rubble bank and stepped into the shadows. He flicked on his head torch, a fine bluish light stabbing out from the Petzl's pair of xenon bulbs, and glanced ahead, the twin beams piercing the gloom.

What stretched before him was mind-blowing, and all the

more so because he could make out a distant shaft of natural light penetrating the darkness. That slender pillar of sunlight was a good two hundred yards away, giving a sense of the awesome perspective.

The tunnel's profile was roughly semicircular, with the base forming the flat side. He figured the roof had to be a good fifteen metres above him, the width of similar dimensions. Gazing along the tunnel's length, he reckoned that SS General Kammler could have driven an entire Panzer division in here with room to spare.

What on earth had it been designed to safeguard and hide?

Andrea had mentioned that there had been a concentration camp nearby; Mauthausen-Gusen. Some 320,000 of its inmates were said to have perished excavating this dark labyrinth, amongst other Nazi forced labour projects.

That number had seemed inconceivable, but now Jaeger could understand why. Blasting out, digging, reinforcing, roofing and flooring this one tunnel alone would have been an utterly daunting undertaking. He could well understand how building a network of such tunnels beneath the mountain had caused so much death and suffering.

He pushed further into the darkness, his footfalls echoing eerily in the silence and kicking up scuffs of dust. This place was oppressive. Airless. And it resonated with a dark evil.

His sixth sense was crying out 'danger', but he put the feeling down to everything that had gone before; the dark legacy of this place. He had experienced this at various times in his life. Evil: hanging thick in the air like a funeral shroud.

Here, it lingered in the dust at his feet.

It cried out from the dank concrete walls to either side.

It was impossible to rationalise, but it was here.

He recognised the sensation. But all of that was in the past, he told himself. There could be no danger now.

He stopped and listened for a moment. He was maybe fifty yards into the tunnel. He was struck by the deafening stillness of the place. Not a whisper of wind or a hint of birdsong disturbed the silence.

From somewhere up ahead he detected the faintest noise of dripping water. Otherwise, utter deathly quiet.

He pushed on. The floor of the tunnel was mostly clear of debris. The excavation team had done their work well. But the form of a tiny bundle drew Jaeger's eye. It was lying at the very point where the curved side wall met the floor, lost in the shade.

He bent to inspect it: a small heap of rags, no larger than a child's shoe. He brushed aside the rock and dust. Something gleamed white amidst the musty grey. He recognised it instantly. A bone. A human bone. One of the metacarpals – those that formed the front of the fist; that would strike an opponent in hand-to-hand combat.

What Jaeger was looking at here was the skeletal remains of a human hand.

He told himself he shouldn't be overly surprised. If 320,000 souls had died here, whoever had opened this place up would be bound to stumble upon human remains. There was something else, though: his twin xenon beams glinted upon a form half hidden, glowing in the light.

He reached for it and brought it fully into his view. Unmistakable: a thick cloth badge displaying the distinctive silver SS runes against a plain background.

Jaeger studied it for a second. What was an SS badge doing here, amongst the skeletal remains of those who had perished? Maybe the hand that lay here had ripped it off in a final act of defiance, before the SS soldier had killed him. Or her.

He would never know. It was one of history's lost moments. He got to his feet, stuffing the badge deep into his pocket.

He pushed on for what seemed like an age. Finally, and for

no discernible reason, the tunnel came to an abrupt stop. Jaeger faced a wall of concrete, which ballooned out in bulbous steps. He could climb it, but there was little point.

As far as this tunnel went, he had reached the end of the road.

12

Narov had had no option but to fall back on her training.

In a city like Dubai – a tightly packed, ultra-high-rise, high-tech 24/7 metropolis – there was pretty much nowhere to hide.

But the Spetsnaz had a saying: *Any mission, any time, any place: whatever it takes.* She'd reminded herself of that as she'd steeled herself for what was coming. She had resolved to hide in plain sight, where everyone could see her.

She'd also reminded herself of one of Will Jaeger's maxims, one of the few sensible things he had had to say when they had operated together; when he hadn't been teasing her or playing the fool: *Fail to prepare; prepare to fail.*

She'd been scrupulous in her preparations – or at least as much as she could, given the time available. Getting hold of the fluorescent workman's jacket and trousers hadn't been so difficult, not for a woman of her means. It had involved a little partying, a smidgen of seduction, a dose of Rohypnol – a heavy sedation drug – and the subsequent theft of one set of workmen's clothing.

Routine.

As a bonus, the high-vis clothing was emblazoned with the name of the service company – Brown, Smith & Hudson – that looked after the target building.

The climbing gear she'd purchased in a local store. She had it slung around her person now, her high-vis suit sprouting harness and coiled ropes, plus some unusual extra pieces of kit that should come in very handy.

To the lay observer it would all look like standard maintenance gear. With her hair bunched up under her fluorescent orange safety helmet, and her figure obscured by the bulky suit, she would appear gender-neutral; unrecognisable as female, at least from a distance.

And she didn't intend for anyone to get a closer look at her.

Brown, Smith & Hudson held the contract for external maintenance for the Al Mohajir Tower. Not Dubai's tallest by a long chalk, but still a seventy-seven-floor space-age monolith of strengthened glass and steel. Internal security was another company's responsibility, but Narov didn't plan to blag her way into the meeting that way.

It was too obvious. Too many security personnel would be in place to stop her.

Hence the pre-dawn start, and the journey she'd made in the tower's external elevator – the one reserved for taking workmen to the higher reaches of the exterior. The code to access the elevator had been easy enough to extract from the drunken workman, especially as he'd believed that Narov was intent on getting down and dirty with him on the seventieth floor.

Seventieth, because that was as far as the elevator went.

Floors seventy-one to seventy-seven were cantilevered outwards, the Al Mohajir Tower seeming to bloom like a flower at its zenith. It was designed so that the upper floors cast cooling shade over those below. Plus the interior of the flower sheltered its own massive roof garden, complete with a forest of tropical ferns.

Those top floors, reaching out over the city, could only be accessed externally by climbing them. At first Narov had considered simply acting as though cleaning or inspecting the glass, hanging outside the window of the room where the meeting was scheduled to take place.

But there was a problem. She needed a voice recording of the man she hunted, to be absolutely certain.

The more she'd studied Isselhorst's photographs – she'd

transferred several from his phone to her laptop, to view them at the highest resolution possible – the more she'd become convinced that they did show the man she sought. Yet he'd changed. Subtly, but enough to ensure he wouldn't easily be recognised.

Narov had a good idea how he'd achieved such a clever transformation, but it made nailing him somewhat more challenging. His eyes – those killer eyes – appeared to be unaltered, but she couldn't be absolutely certain. The secret was his voice: whatever else he might have doctored, his vocal cords would remain unchanged.

And that meant she needed a recording.

There was no way to secure that through several inches of toughened, soundproofed triple glazing. She needed to get inside the meeting room; or at least to insert a microphone.

Typically, the level of security inside the Al Mohajir Tower lessened the higher you climbed. At the ground floor it was a veritable Fort Knox: there were metal detectors, detailed ID checks, scanners, security guards frisking would-be visitors, and CCTV cameras at every turn. Getting into the lifts was equally challenging.

But by the time you hit the seventy-seventh floor, there was very little of that. The philosophy seemed to be that if you'd reached that far, then by default you must have every right to be where you were.

Hence the present plan.

Narov leant out from the elevator's cage, reached up and attached the first double suction device, placing it flat on the glass, her hand gripping the tough aluminium handle that ran between the cups. Suction pads firmly applied, she flipped down the locking handles that secured the apparatus in place.

Designed for construction workers, the suction cups allowed for teams to carry large panes of glass in relative safety – crucial when building a complex skyscraper. But in a typical piece of lateral thinking, the elite of the world's military had realised that such devices could also enable the scaling of otherwise un-assailable structures.

Narov reached higher, attaching another double cup and testing it with her weight. Each device was designed to hold one hundred kilograms; Narov, at five foot nine, weighed just under sixty.

She attached one more at thigh height, the handle positioned horizontally to make a foothold. Then she levered herself upwards until she had three points of contact with the glass – feet on the lower suction pad and her weight supported by the thin climbing slings that she looped through the two middle cups. She took out one last device, reached up as high as she could and fastened it in place.

Then she carefully swung out over the abyss.

The routine was simple: the two central cups held her weight, whilst she stood on the lower one. She then lifted herself up and forward, reached as high as she could and reattached the top cup. Shifting her weight onto that, she began to move the lower cups upwards.

Then she repeated the process.

It took time, and it was all about moving calmly and efficiently, letting her legs and the cups do the work. Otherwise she would tire quickly.

In such a fashion, Narov inched her way up the first few feet of glass, being careful not to snag the bulging pack of gear she had strapped to her front for ease of access. She had a second, smaller pack strapped to her back, but she wouldn't be needing that if all went to plan. The glass flared outwards at thirty degrees. Scaling seven floors – maybe one hundred feet – at such an angle was hugely tiring.

But it was doable if she paced herself, scaling one massive pane at a time, clinging to it like some kind of giant spider.

13

As she passed the seventy-second floor, Narov could detect a faint bluish tinge to the horizon: first light was maybe an hour away. Plenty of time to get to the top. It was never truly dark in this city: the glare thrown off by the jungle of brightly lit skyscrapers ensured that she had more than enough light by which to climb.

She'd opted to scale the building at night chiefly because of temperature. Come dawn, the heat and humidity would rise and the fierce Dubai sunlight would be reflected off the glass, making the present task near-impossible.

At least at this hour it was still relatively cool.

She felt her heart rate rising as she edged further and further away from the safety of the elevator cage. She ensured that she was always secured by at least three cups, yet still it was daunting hanging off the wall of glass.

She'd first learnt this climbing technique in England, courtesy of Will Jaeger. Following their mission to stop Kammler, Jaeger had been invited to the passing-out parade of a group of Royal Marines recruits at the Commando Training Centre in Lympstone, Devon, known simply as CTCRM.

Eighteen young men had just completed the gruelling thirty-two-week selection course, and they were scheduled to be awarded their coveted green berets.

Jaeger, a former commando officer, had asked Narov to join him for the ceremony. He'd intended to take his wife, but at the last minute he'd realised that her behaviour was far too unpredictable these days.

Since her rescue, Ruth Jaeger had grown increasingly introverted, spurning most of their family and friends. Jaeger had confided all this to Narov during one of their quieter moments. He hadn't told her that Ruth was growing increasingly moody and prone to violence, but Narov knew as much from what others had said. It pained her to think of Will Jaeger being on the receiving end of so much psychological – and physical – hurt.

With his chiselled features, longish dark hair, grey eyes and wolfish demeanour, Will Jaeger was blessed with gaunt, rugged good looks. Over time, Narov had fallen for him hook, line and sinker. She'd got skin-close. Heart-close.

She'd longed for him. Dreamed about him. Believed in him.

And then his wife had come back from the dead.

Well, shit happened. Narov wasn't one to hold grudges. She'd accepted Jaeger's invitation to Lympstone because you never knew. For someone like her, who found it difficult to get close to anyone, hope sprang eternal. And with Will Jaeger, she sensed there was reason to hope.

At CTCRM, she'd learnt how the Royal Marines prided themselves on recruiting the 'thinking man's soldier'. Their motto was: *Royal Marines: It's a state of mind.* They stressed that being a commando was as much about mental as physical ability.

'Be the first to understand,' the commanding officer had urged the new recruits, 'the first to adapt and respond; the first to overcome.' He'd finished by reminding them that 'In the midst of every difficulty lies opportunity.'

Narov had been sceptical at first. She'd heard too much bullshit military-speak in her time. But then they'd taken her for a tour of the mountain cadre, where they trained some of the world's most accomplished combat mountaineers.

It was there that she'd watched a demonstration of how to scale a glass-fronted skyscraper using nothing more than what looked like a set of builder's tools. Of course, when they offered her a try, she couldn't resist. She'd been an instant convert.

But what had impressed her most was the character of the Marines. They knew their job, they did it well, yet there was a humility to their words and actions that she hadn't seen before in fighting men. Even with the inevitable banter, the soldiers seemed to have respect at the heart of all they did.

Indeed, Lympstone was where the young Will Jaeger had been shaped as a soldier, and as a man.

The words of the chief instructor ran through her head now as she scaled the highest floors of the Al Mohajir Tower: *Trust the gear, it works.*

From her dizzying vantage point she could hear the distant hum of traffic, the city's heartbeat, punctuated by the blaring of horns. She glanced east. Sunrise soon. A thin blanket of white coated much of the coast, where smog mixed with the mist sweeping in off the sea.

Narov didn't put much store by the climber's mantra: *Never look down.* She *liked* looking down. She liked to see how high she had come. She knew how far she had to fall. It was a fact. So how could seeing it unsettle her?

She didn't understand fear of dying. She always took risks in the full knowledge of what the consequences might be. That was her way.

She turned back to the task, shoulder muscles bunching as she detached a suction pad, reached higher and clamped it on again. Just a few more panes of glass and she'd have made it.

Show time.

14

Having reached the dead end, Jaeger had turned around and decided to investigate the second tunnel. But something didn't feel right. *Absence of the normal; presence of the abnormal*: the phrase had crept unbidden into his mind.

But why? Why now? What had triggered it?

He paused. Old habits died hard, and he'd been counting out his paces as he moved. Two hundred and fifty steps at roughly eighty centimetres per step; he was around two hundred yards in.

But what 'normals' were lacking?

What 'abnormals' were present that shouldn't be?

He flashed his torch around. Nothing jumped out at him.

Then the answer hit him. It was the silence.

If there was a team in this tunnel carrying out excavations, why couldn't he hear anything? And there would be a film crew with them, making all the usual noise. He strained his ears. Nothing. You could hear the proverbial pin drop.

This tunnel seemed even quieter than the first. Plus there was something else, something that creeped Jaeger out, his sixth sense screaming danger at him. No way was this some throwback to the past; to seventy years ago.

This was danger *now*. Present, immediate, life-threatening.

Jaeger considered his options. He had no weapons apart from his bare hands. In the pitch dark he needed his head torch to find his way, which meant that anyone out there was bound to see him coming. He could turn back, but he felt driven to continue.

He made a decision: he'd give it another hundred yards; one hundred and ten paces. That should take him to the dead end, if this tunnel had the same configuration as the first.

One hundred yards: no more.

Jaeger needed out of here. He needed to see the sky and to breathe clean, fresh air. Plus he needed to make his way back to Uncle Joe, who would be wondering what had kept him.

He pushed on for another eighty paces, creeping forward, moving silently on the balls of his feet, trying to stick to the cover of the walls. It was then that he spotted it, almost at the limit of his head torch's reach: a shapeless bundle lying on the floor.

He knew instantly what it was. He'd seen such things too many times before. Plus he caught the faint tang on the air: a sharp iron scent.

Too familiar.

Blood.

There was a body in the tunnel, and this was no World War II-era corpse; no musty, desiccated skeleton. From what Jaeger could make out, this one was but a matter of hours old.

He approached with infinite care. As he moved closer, he could make out a horrifying scene: other bodies, a half-dozen scattered around the floor, and lying amongst them the smashed-up remains of the tools of their trade – video cameras, tripods, sound-recording gear.

He came to a halt. The first corpse was more or less at his feet. He swept his torch around the space. Not thirty yards away, the tunnel ended in a jumbled wall of rock and debris. This was as far as the excavations seemed to have reached.

No immediate sign of whoever had done this.

No movement.

No noise.

He switched off his torch. He waited. Utter darkness. Utter silence. The stench of death in his nostrils. There wasn't the faintest hint of any light, apart from that thrown down by the ventilation shaft a good hundred yards to his rear.

If the killers were here, they were doing a fine job of hiding.

Jaeger flicked his torch back on and inspected the first corpse. A young woman, probably in her late twenties, executed with a single shot to the head. The muzzle had been so close, he could see the scorch mark around the entry wound.

The bullet had made a tiny hole. It hardly seemed enough to kill a human, but Jaeger knew better. Whoever had done this was a true professional. They'd used .22 pistols – far smaller than your average calibre handgun.

The .22 was fairly useless at any kind of range, but up close and personal it was a hugely efficient killer. A heavier round would tear through a human skull, leaving an exit wound. Jaeger didn't need to check: this round hadn't done that. It didn't have the mass to break through.

Instead it had bounced around inside the victim's skull, ripping her grey matter to shreds.

The .22 had other advantages as an assassin's weapon. It was small and lightweight. Being a sportsman's and huntsman's weapon, it was readily available on the open market.

Easy to get hold of; easy to dispose of.

Jaeger checked the other bodies. Each had been killed in the same way. He had an image in his mind's eye now: the victims kneeling on the floor of the tunnel as their executioner stood before them firing shot after shot.

A terrifying way to go.

Whoever had done this had also indulged in a frenzy of destruction, either before or after the executions, smashing the filming kit to smithereens.

But why? To what purpose? To what end?

It just didn't make any sense.

Jaeger had to presume that they'd wanted to destroy all record of whatever the film crew had recorded. But surely nothing of any great significance had been found. Just a long and very ghostly set of tunnels.

He flicked his light back to the mound of earth at the far end. It was then that he spied it. Footprints ran up the near side. It wasn't just one set of boots that had made that climb: scores had.

But why, if it was a dead end?

Jaeger moved closer. He followed the same path up the hillock of dirt. As he neared the top, he felt it. The pile beneath his feet began to shift. All of a sudden the wall of debris before him collapsed in a mini landslide.

The noise in this enclosed space was deafening.

He flicked off his light, and froze.

15

The sound of the landslide echoed along the length of the tunnel that had opened before him.

Unlike the first tunnel, this one certainly led somewhere. But just as the film crew and their team of excavators had made their discovery, somebody – some force of gunmen – had smashed apart their film kit and executed them all.

Jaeger figured he had his answer as to why they had been murdered: they had been snuffed out in an effort to hide whatever they had discovered. But surely someone would come to investigate? They'd find what Jaeger had found. They'd look deeper. And they'd discover whatever the film crew had stumbled across.

Unless . . .

He stepped back a few paces and flicked his light on again, running it back and forth over the path beaten across the pile of rubble and dirt. A lot of people had walked this way, and in both directions.

Which begged the question: had whatever the film crew discovered been *removed*?

It must have been secreted here for seventy-odd years. Presumably those who had hidden it had wanted it to remain utterly secret. So had a force of gunmen been sent in here to retrieve it and silence any who had borne witness to its existence?

It was the only thing that made any sense.

But what was so valuable that it could warrant seventy years' dark secrecy and such a brutal mass slaying? A hoard of Nazi gold? Precious antiquities? Priceless artworks? What exactly was it that had cost these young people their lives?

And then another thought hit Jaeger: what if the killers were still here? What if they were deeper in the tunnel complex, and busy with their task of retrieval?

He ran his eye across the corpses. Eight dead. He figured there had to be several assailants; three at a minimum, and very likely more. Though he hated to admit it, they had been good at their work. Cold-blooded, efficient killers.

And he was alone and unarmed.

One of the basic skills of elite-forces soldiering was deciding when to fight and when to flee. In World War II, the SAS had made its name with 'shoot-and-scoot' tactics: striking an enemy by utter surprise, then melting away before they could respond with any significant force of arms.

Hit and run.

Jaeger might have the element of surprise, but he was heavily outnumbered and hopelessly outgunned. Not for the first time in his life, he decided that discretion was the better part of valour. He flicked off his torch and turned to leave, pausing for a few seconds to let his eyes adjust to the darkness. He'd move through it now, using it as his cloak and his protector.

Jaeger set off, skirting around the corpses, but something made him pause. A memory, tugging at his adrenalin-hyped senses. For the barest of instants he was in the depths of the Brazilian Amazon, on the trail of a lost warplane – a stupendous Luftwaffe Junkers JU 390, the largest aircraft ever to have flown during World War II.

That had been the start of the journey that had led to his ultimate showdown with Hank Kammler. Jaeger had had a film crew accompany the expedition. The cameraman had been in the habit of secretly filming the team when he'd been forbidden from doing so.

His favourite trick was to plonk the camera down as if it wasn't running, but to leave the lens facing the direction of maximum interest and the machine on record. He'd taped over the red filming light, so no one could tell if the camera was live.

Jaeger bent to inspect the remains of the nearest camera. As he did so, his eyes flashed across the features of the corpse lying beside it. Somehow it looked familiar. He risked momentarily flicking on his torch. It was the Austrian film-maker; Jaeger recognised him from his photo in the newspaper.

The dead man's camera had been seriously smashed up, but still he could see that the red record light had been covered over with a length of gaffer tape.

Jaeger hesitated for just an instant before feeling around in the camera's innards for the memory card. He stepped across to the other camera – most crews carried two – but as he bent to retrieve the second card, a spear of light pierced the gloom.

It had come from the far end of the tunnel, and was accompanied by heavy footfalls. The sound of running. The gunmen, whoever they might be, were coming.

Jaeger figured they must have spotted the flash of illumination from his torch as he'd studied the dead cameraman's features. His pulse pounding like a machine gun, he grabbed the second memory card and stuffed it into his pocket, then turned and ran.

As he pounded up the tunnel, he caught sight of a figure from the corner of his eye. Massive, muscle-bound, the man had clambered up the far side of the rock pile, torch dazzling Jaeger's eyes.

Held before him he had his .22 pistol, sweeping the space ahead.

16

Narov made her way through the dense foliage of the Al
Mohajir Tower's roof garden as if she had every right to
be there.

She knew exactly what she was looking for. The garden sat
within a courtyard made up of the four sides of the skyscraper.
Basically, she had scaled the glass exterior, only to abseil back
down to where she was now.

Which was just as she'd intended.

Kammler's meeting was scheduled to take place on Executive Level Platinum, the floor that lay directly below the roof
garden. It had the benefit of natural light, which filtered through
the foliage via a series of skylights.

She found the one that she was looking for.

With barely a pause to check whether she was being observed
– a workman going about his everyday tasks at 6.30 a.m.; why
would anyone pay any heed? – she dropped to her knees, unloading a set of tools from her chest pack.

She took hold of a simple glass-cutting tool and proceeded to
score around the edge of one of the skylight's panes. With a pair
of suction handles attached, she lifted free the glass with a sharp
snatch of the hands. She did a repeat performance with the
second pane – the skylights were double-glazed – and suddenly
she was gazing down into the building's interior.

The skylights themselves were alarmed, but would trigger only
if you opened one. Cutting the glass avoided that. She'd chosen
to enter the seventy-second floor via one of the restrooms, and

she was looking down at a row of sinks, with directly beneath her a line of cubicles. There was CCTV, but it would not cover the cubicles, for obvious reasons of privacy.

Before allowing herself to drop, Narov removed a small video camera from her rucksack. She held it rock-steady, braced against the side of the skylight, and filmed three minutes of the empty restroom. Then she stuffed the camera deep in her pocket, dropped her rucksack through the opening and lowered herself, landing cat-like on the bare floor of one of the cubicles.

It was still only 6.45, so there were unlikely to be many people about. Even so, she needed to hurry.

Bracing her legs against the cubicle's sides, she levered herself upwards until she could reach the ceiling. She pulled out a small, commercially available laser, popped it above the cubicle and fired the beam directly at the CCTV camera.

The laser would instantly white out – blind – the camera, overloading it with light. Quick as a flash, she reached over and slipped a small clip with wire teeth onto the cable leading to the camera; the cable that would carry the images back to the CCTV monitoring room.

A wire led from the clip to her own camera. She set it running on a pre-programmed loop, playing over and over the footage that she'd filmed from the roof, then clamped the clip firmly shut, the metal teeth cutting into the CCTV cable and taking over its circuit.

The images she had filmed of the empty restroom were now being beamed along the cable, and would do so for as long as her camera kept playing. If anyone had noticed the CCTV image whiting out for a few seconds, it was apparently back to normal now.

That done, she fastened her own camera and cabling to the CCTV apparatus with plastic ties. It didn't look pretty, but the CCTV was positioned discreetly in one corner of the ceiling, so who was going to notice?

She dropped down again, then removed the glass-cutter from

her bag and moved to the restroom's one external window. Working quickly, she cut away two of the panes at around waist height, lifting each free. The third she scoured around at the edges but left in place.

She carried each pane down to the furthest cubicle, placing them inside against one wall. Finally she ran some red-and-white-striped workman's tape across the space where she'd removed the glass, as if the window was in the process of being repaired.

That done, she headed for the cubicle where she'd stashed the panes, locking the door behind her. She removed a small hand-operated drill from her pack and selected a spot at the top right corner of the wall. Climbing onto the toilet seat, she began to drill.

Narov sweated as she worked. Fine plaster dust drifted down from the drill bit. Every minute or so she removed it and blew into the hole, trying to gauge how close she was to breaking through. Gradually she slowed the rotations, trying to feel for the moment when the tiny tip cut into open space.

She tensed for the sound of a picture being knocked off the wall and glass smashing on the far side. That would spell the end of this little venture. But hopefully by choosing a high corner she'd avoided any risk of that happening.

She sensed the drill bite through. She removed it, reversing the direction to help ease it free, then took a tiny brush from her pocket and dragged back as much of the drilling waste as she could. That done, she put her eye gingerly to the hole: she could just make out light bleeding through from the far side.

She reached into her pocket and removed a slender optical cord, on the end of which was a minute fish-eye lens. She eased it into the hole, centimetre by centimetre. After some minutes, she paused what she was doing and attached a recording device equipped with a mini viewing screen. She fired it up and was able to monitor the last few millimetres of insertion.

The fish-eye didn't need to be forced all the way: its

280-degree vision enabled it to capture the image of the room while remaining flush with the wall's surface. As long as Narov hadn't dislodged too much plaster dust, it should be largely undetectable.

It was 7.35 a.m. The spy camera was in place. The meeting was scheduled to start at 9 a.m. sharp.

She pulled on a set of headphones and settled down to wait. She stilled her breathing and consoled herself with the thought that at least she didn't have far to go if she needed to pee.

It was the noise that pulled her mind back to the present: the thump of a door being thrown open, and the guttural arrogance in the voice that bled through on the headphones. It sounded so familiar and so utterly, utterly chilling.

'So where is the lawyer? Isselhorst. Damn him! He was supposed to be here by now.'

Narov knew instantly that she was right.

Grey Wolf: he was alive.

17

Narov's eyes were glued to the mini screen. The speaker was a middle-aged man, face hawkish, nose beak-like, gaze radiating a burning fanaticism and an innate cruelty. There was a fierce arrogance to his look, as of a man crazed with power.

It was always about power, Narov reminded herself. And this was her target all right. Grey Wolf: the man who would stop at nothing . . .

The person he was speaking to was younger, swarthy and tough-looking; he had a soldier's demeanour, though right now he was dressed in a slick business suit. He didn't look particularly comfortable.

He shrugged. 'I called Isselhorst's mobile. Earlier this morning. Some woman answered.'

The older man glared. 'A woman? What's he doing with a woman here in Dubai? He isn't married. He doesn't have a secretary. He's a one-man band. Flexible. Discreet. That's why we use him. And more importantly, he's under strict instructions.'

The younger man sighed. 'Sir, I know. I figured it was just some woman he'd picked up. Dubai. You know how it is.'

'What did this *woman* have to say?' the older man demanded, ignoring the remark.

'They were caught in traffic. Figured they might be twenty minutes late.'

The elderly man growled his displeasure. 'Whatever happened to lawyerly punctuality?' He made a visible effort to get his irritation under control. 'So: how long before the legal team for the other side get here?'

'Fifteen minutes. Thereabouts.'

'Do we need Isselhorst? I thought it was a done deal. If he's late, we start without him.'

'The lawyers have advised the foundation to sign. It was the threat of the court action that swung it. That, plus the adverse publicity. And charities always do what their lawyers say, apparently.'

'Ha! Adverse publicity. Seventy years of revenue from the Führer's literary masterpiece, and they want to give it to charities that promote the very things he abhorred: racial harmony, refugee rights, cultural understanding! What a load of horse shit. They deserve all the adverse publicity they get.' He glared. 'So, the question is: do we need Isselhorst? And this woman?'

'Sir, I doubt he's bringing her to the meeting.'

The old man's eyes narrowed. 'He'd better not.' A beat. 'I don't like this new development. Getting a woman involved. Would Isselhorst really be that stupid? Find out who she is. And tighten security. No one else gets close to this room. Understood?'

'Sir.'

The younger man barked a series of instructions into a radio mic that was clipped discreetly to his jacket. From the series of responses, it was clear that he had security teams ringing the Al Mohajir Tower.

He glanced up. 'Done.'

'Right, we have ten minutes to kill. Tell me: the other business. Is all going to plan?'

'Which other business, sir? We're quite . . . busy right now.'

'Moldova! What else?'

'All sorted. They're only awaiting the final payment.'

The older man's face brightened. 'Excellent. And the conduit? Is it "all sorted" too?'

'It is. The Colombians are on standby to take delivery. Bout's airline is ready to ship as planned.'

'Good work, Vladimir. I'm impressed.'

In her cubicle, Narov's eyes narrowed. Vladimir Ustanov: she'd thought it was him.

Ustanov had commanded the force that had pursued Jaeger and his team halfway across the Amazon when they had first been hunting Kammler. He'd proved a diehard, merciless operator, with a sadistic streak to boot. Narov and Jaeger had assaulted Ustanov's base, hitting him and his fellow mercenaries with a lethal gas, but somehow he had survived.

'Tell me,' the older man continued, 'why d'you still refer to it as Bout's airline? The Americans put him behind bars several years ago.'

'Simple: he was a hero to the Russian people. Still is. To us it remains Viktor Bout's airline in his honour.'

The older man gave a bark of a laugh. 'Bout! He became too notorious for his own good. Sailed too close to the wind. Believed the myth of his own invincibility. Arms dealers need to fly beneath the radar. As, indeed, do we.'

The younger man shrugged. 'That's the Americans for you: one moment they're your best buddies, the next they slam you behind bars. No honour. No loyalty. Only money and power.'

'And the big man? The English oaf? What news of him?'

'Austria's more or less sorted. Just a few loose ends to tie up, and then the ore will be on its way.'

'Good. I don't like him, you know that. He's English, which is enough. But he can be . . . useful.'

'He can.'

The older man glanced up, eyes searching his surroundings. 'This room – it was checked? You have scanned it?'

'Yes, sir.'

'When?'

'Last night.'

'But not this morning?'

'No. Not this morning.'

'Well do it. This "woman" development – I don't like it. It's making me doubly mistrustful.'

The younger man got to his feet. He pulled a bag from under the table and removed a small hand-held device: a scanner for checking for bugs or other suspicious electrical signals. He flicked it on and moved over to the nearest wall.

Behind it, Narov tensed. Her tiny camera used such a minuscule amount of power, she doubted the scanner would detect it. It was the hole she had drilled and the dust that worried her.

She watched as the scanner moved back and forth, sweeping across the wall, moving over the section where she'd embedded the camera. Ustanov was about to carry on, but paused. Something had caught his eye.

He glanced at the side table pushed against the wall. It was crammed full of bottles of mineral water and glasses, plus flasks of coffee. All seemed in order, but something had disturbed him.

He reached out a hand and ran it across the polished wooden surface of the table. It came away streaked with white: plaster dust. Fresh, by the looks of things. He picked up a glass and inspected it. Dust free. The plaster had fallen prior to the trays of drinks being delivered.

He ran his eye up the wall, searching.

On the far side, Narov barely dared to breathe. She was glued to his every move. She saw his gaze come to rest directly on the camera lens, seemingly staring at her. His expression changed. An arm reached out towards her.

In a flash, she yanked the optical cord free, stuffing the device deep into her pocket. Then she slammed back the bolt on the cubicle door and dashed into the open. From behind her she heard a guttural yell of alarm, followed by a deafening series of gunshots ripping through the wall where she had just been sitting.

She sprinted down the length of the restroom. Outside, boots thundered along the corridor. She reached the end of the cubicles, turned left and lunged for the window. As she did so, the door behind her was booted open, a stocky figure spraying an arc of fire in her general direction.

She threw herself forward.

Her crossed arms made contact with the window, and the pane gave way, popping free where she had scored it with the glass-cutter. Seconds later, she was tumbling through the screaming blue.

Narov had 1,100 feet to fall, and she was gaining momentum rapidly. She forced herself to calm her nerves and count out the seconds. She'd once made a parachute jump with Jaeger from 250 feet, a fraction of her present altitude. But still, she needed to get this just right.

She hit 800 feet and triggered the parachute that was strapped to her back. An expanse of fine silk shot out into the sky above, pulling her up short. She'd deployed a compact sports chute, one designed for a rapid but manoeuvrable descent: perfect for steering a path between Dubai's high-rises.

Her first priority was to put space – and ideally the solid form of a skyscraper – between her and the gunmen now gathered at the window high above in the Al Mohajir Tower.

Her second priority was to fly.

She needed to cover enough distance to evade the security teams that even now would be racing from the tower to nail her. But she'd planned for this. She knew where she could put down in relative safety. She'd recced a clear spot where her touch-down should go relatively unobserved.

As Jaeger always said: *Fail to prepare, prepare to fail.*

It was now a race between her and Grey Wolf's gunmen.

She steered left, dropping in a series of super-fast tight loops before using her accumulated speed to swoop around the side of the nearest high-rise. As she fell into its shadow, she knew she was out of her pursuers' immediate line of fire.

She felt a tingling in her right calf muscle and glanced down. She was surprised to see that the fluorescent trousers had been torn apart, and her calf was dripping blood. She'd been injured.

Either she'd caught herself on the glass as she'd dived free, or Vladimir had clipped her with a round.

She was so hyped on adrenalin that she hadn't even felt it. Even now, she had little sense of pain. It was an odd fact, but Narov's pain threshold was not normal. In fact little about her was particularly normal. Pain simply didn't seem to bother her. She could never understand how it caused others such suffering.

She made a mental note to do something about the leg; stop the bleeding.

But first she had to fly like the wind and make safe landfall.

18

Jaeger probably should have left the memory cards for the Austrian police to recover. Probably. Plus there was a part of him that felt guilty at not having made himself available to help with the investigation. After all, he had been first at the scene of the crime.

But something told him it was better this way.

In any case, he'd made it out of those tunnels only by the skin of his teeth, and thanks to his alertness and his training. *Expect the unexpected*: it was a rule drilled into SAS operators. That and *Never underestimate the enemy*.

Jaeger had seen the imposing bulk of his adversary. He'd also seen and heard the other gunmen a few vital seconds before they had put in an appearance. And by that time, he was pretty much out of the range of their .22s.

They'd loosed off several shots down the tunnel, but Jaeger had proved a far faster runner. He figured he knew why. Each of the mystery gunmen had been laden down with a massive pack. Those, Jaeger suspected, contained whatever the men were removing from the tunnel.

Once back at St Georgen, he'd made it clear to Uncle Joe that they needed to get the hell out of town. They'd paid for their rooms, made their hurried excuses to the owner – a family emergency back in England – and hit the road.

There would be no returning to the Zum Turken hotel. Jaeger would phone and offer the same kind of explanation. Instead, they'd stop at some anonymous chain – a Holiday Inn maybe

– and try and digest the full import of his discoveries.

He'd made the call to the Austrian cops from a phone booth on the A1. By then, he and Uncle Joe were well on their way, the Range Rover eating up the miles. He'd given a short report about the mass killing, but refused to provide his name. He'd taken basic precautions to disguise his voice, presuming all such calls were recorded.

Jaeger just had a feeling, a hunch, an instinctive sense that he was being pulled back towards a dark past that he'd been trying to put behind him. It was his soldier's sixth sense, and as Uncle Joe had reminded him, he should never ignore it.

They'd pushed on across the German border. On the face of it they were heading home. But it would be just as easy to turn a little further north and east and make for the Falkenhagen Bunker, the makeshift headquarters of the Secret Hunters. But only if whatever they might discover on the memory cards from the tunnel seemed to warrant such a diversion.

As luck would have it, the first opportunity to stop proved to be at the Munich Park Hilton, on the outskirts of the city. Once they had checked into their room, Jaeger made sure that Uncle Joe was comfortable, settling him in an armchair, amply propped up with pillows. 'You good? It may take some time. Each of the cards can hold several hours.'

Uncle Joe forced a smile. He was tired, but he was also incredibly resilient. 'Will, my boy, I'm fine. Let's see what you've got here.'

Jaeger pulled out his MacBook Air and placed it on the desk. With a feeling of foreboding, he slotted the first memory card into the laptop's port. He tried several times, but no joy. It wouldn't open. It must have been too badly damaged.

The second card looked somewhat more promising. Jaeger slid it in. On the third attempt, an icon popped onto his screen: 'SONY XDCAM'. He double-clicked the icon, his MacBook automatically pulling up the video-player screen, then clicked the play button.

A ghostly image appeared. It showed a figure seated in the tunnel entrance, giving an interview. Jaeger had little idea who it was, but he recognised him as one of the bloodied corpses lying deep in the tunnel's interior.

It was like the man had come back from the dead.

From his dress and manner, it was clear he was some kind of expert; a World War II historian no doubt. He was speaking German, but even so Jaeger could tell by his hand gestures that he had been one excited interviewee.

He used the digital menu to flip through the scenes. They were deep inside the mountain now. The tunnel was lit by powerful film lights, set on tripods to either side. Figures worked at the slope using pickaxes and shovels to clear a wider path.

Jaeger pointed at the pile of rubble. 'See. By the time this was filmed, they'd already made the breakthrough.'

Uncle Joe nodded. 'The man giving the interview – was he speaking about whatever they had discovered?'

'Most probably.'

Jaeger spun through the footage at twelve-times speed. There was nothing much of note, until the screen went suddenly very dark. He stopped, and replayed the image at normal speed. All was seemingly normal, until a harsh yelling could be heard echoing down the tunnel.

The words were in German and hard to catch, but the aggression and menace was clear. Moments later, the film lights were extinguished, as if by order. A few seconds after that, the camera was removed from its tripod, the image going wobbly as it was lowered towards the floor.

Jaeger could sense hands flipping various switches, then the screen suddenly turned a weird, smudgy fluorescent green, producing an image that was instantly familiar.

Even as he'd lowered it, the cameraman had flicked his camera on to night-filming mode. Jaeger recognised it instantly: it produced the same kind of grainy green image he'd experienced so often on elite operations when using NVGs – night-vision goggles.

Crucially, as he'd placed it on the ground, the man had left the camera running. Given what he had been facing – the shock and fear of an assault by a gang of armed gunmen – Jaeger was amazed by his poise and bravery.

Figures stepped into view: ghostly, menacing, sinister. They were dressed in black, with balaclavas covering their faces. Jaeger counted six of them. Two stood back, pistols at the ready, herding the camera crew and excavators against one wall, while a third started smashing apart the filming gear.

Jaeger figured there was only a few seconds remaining before the image would die on him, and as yet there was nothing to give the barest hint as to the identity of the gunmen. Moments later, the camera gave a savage jerk as the blade of a shovel smashed into it, and the image went suddenly very dead.

He replayed that section of footage several times, trying to glean something of value from the vital last minutes of film. There was something tugging at the edge of his consciousness. He was missing something. A vital clue. He knew it, and yet he couldn't put his finger on what it was.

Finally, he ejected the memory card and stared disconsolately at the blank screen. 'Anything, Uncle Joe? Anything that strikes you?'

No answer.

He turned to check. His great-uncle had fallen asleep in his chair.

Jaeger smiled to himself. He guessed the question could wait until morning.

He suddenly felt utterly shattered. He lifted his uncle onto the bed, marvelling at how light his elderly frame was. Then he lay down on the floor and pulled a blanket over himself.

Just like the old days, he thought. He'd revisit this enigma with a fresh head come morning.

19

Jaeger awoke sometime later. The stress and shock of the day had exhausted him. But now he sat bolt upright, the image of the nightmare playing through his mind.

He'd been underwater. At sea. Fighting against a hated assailant. He'd already stabbed the man, using Irina Narov's dagger, but his opponent just wouldn't die. This was the man who had kidnapped Jaeger's wife and child. Jaeger hated him as he would never have imagined possible.

His opponent was massive and hugely powerful, and not the type to give in. That much Jaeger knew, for way back they had been on SAS selection together. Jaeger had passed, but the big man had crashed and burnt, and all because he'd tried to cheat by taking performance-enhancing drugs.

It was Jaeger who had discovered that he was doping, and he was immediately binned.

In that moment had been born a lifelong enmity, although Jaeger hadn't realised it at the time. Hence why the big man had been so keen to come after Jaeger's wife and child. Revenge. Sweet revenge. But not so sweet when Jaeger had finally tracked him down, driving the blade in deep.

Steve Jones. Jaeger had left him entangled within a mass of writhing sharks driven wild by the smell of blood. A dead man, or so he had presumed. So why were those dark scenes coming back to haunt him now?

A new set of images came unbidden into his head. He remembered how, as he'd swum towards the surface, he'd dropped

Narov's knife. An iconic commando fighting knife, the razor-sharp tapered blade had slipped from his grasp and sunk from view.

But now he could see its fate somehow playing out before him: the knife drifting downwards . . . coming to rest in Steve Jones's grasp . . . The big man using it to eviscerate the nearest shark, slicing its gut cavity open . . . The wounded animal spinning away voiding gouts of blood . . . the other sharks following.

Blood was blood: the sharks didn't care.

And a final image: Steve Jones, one hand gripping his wounded neck, the other the knife, kicking for the surface.

Jaeger flicked on the light. He sat for several seconds in utter silence. Jones alive? Was it even possible? And what had made him imagine all of this now?

The answer came to him with a jolt. He roused himself and moved to the desk, powering up the laptop. He stared at the screen as he replayed the last few minutes of footage, showing the team of killers going about their murderous work.

There. He punched pause. The image froze and he gazed at it in silent disbelief. There, strapped to the thigh of the largest of the mystery gunmen, was a Fairbairn–Sykes commando fighting knife, to give it its full name. The same knife that Irina Narov had carried, and Jaeger had let slip from his grasp in the sea.

He lived by the mantra: *Expect the unexpected*. It was what had kept him alive all these years. But this – it just seemed so impossible.

He pressed play, eyes glued to the movements of the hulking figure. There was little doubt about it any more: the bulging forearms and shoulders; the sheer power of the man as he smashed apart the film gear with his bare hands.

The way his stance radiated rage and hatred; hatred and rage.

No doubt about it: it was Jones.

Jaeger killed the image, then sat back and tried to get his breathing under control. The realisation alone had set him hyperventilating. One thing was clear: if Steve Jones had survived, Jaeger was going to have to kill him. Again.

He was tempted to fire up the Evoque right now and drive hell for leather for St Georgen, in case Jones was still somewhere in those tunnels. To finish this for good. But gradually he gained control over his blind shock and rage. Jones would be long gone, he reasoned. Even if he wasn't, there were more of them, and Jones alone had proved a fearsome adversary.

But most importantly, Jaeger had Uncle Joe to care for.

Plus there was something else. Something that went far deeper. Jones's reappearance was shock enough: but his reappearance *there*, at St Georgen, in a top-secret tunnel built by the Nazis and overseen by SS General Hans Kammler . . .

Well, the ramifications were hard even for Jaeger to fully comprehend.

If Jones had been placed in command of a team of killers charged with evacuating the tunnel and terminating all who might have discovered its dark secret, what was that secret? Who had sent him? And why?

Whatever the answers, Jaeger sensed they couldn't be good. Not with Jones involved. Not with such a direct link to a dark Nazi past and to SS General Kammler himself.

This was bigger than Jaeger alone. Jaeger knew in his gut what he had to do: he had to make for Falkenhagen, to see if the full resources of the Secret Hunters might fathom this one.

He picked up his smartphone and dialled. It was four o'clock in the morning, but Peter Miles – the group's chief – had assured him that he was always on duty. No matter what time of day, Jaeger should feel free to make contact.

A sleepy voice answered. 'William? What time d'you call this?'

Despite everything, Jaeger smiled. Miles's voice had that effect on him. No matter what might happen, the man seemed imperturbable; he had an unshakeable calm about him. It made him the perfect boss for the movement, and for brainstorming what on earth Jaeger's discoveries might signify.

'Something's cropped up. We need to meet. I'm with Uncle Joe, so summon whoever else you can muster.'

Miles chuckled. 'Funny you should say that. I was about to call you. Though I would have left it to a more sociable hour. Something's cropped up our end too. So yes, we very much do need to meet.'

'Fine. We'll come to you. Normal place?'

'The usual.'

'We'll be there by midday.'

Jaeger signed off the call and logged onto the internet. Even as he'd been speaking to Peter, he'd made the decision that he needed to let Ruth know – at least the very basics.

He didn't know what the St Georgen discovery might signify exactly, but the last thing he wanted was for Ruth to read something in the press, finding out that way that their nemesis might still be alive.

That would send her into a total tailspin.

He typed out a short email. After their last, fractious phone call, he figured he'd keep it businesslike and short.

Hi Ruth,
Listen, don't want to alarm you, but I've stumbled upon
something here. There's a chance that Kammler might
still be alive. I'm looking into it – low-profile, so don't fret
– but it'll delay me a day or so. Didn't want you to see
something on the news that might freak you out.
W

Email sent, he googled the quickest route from Munich to Falkenhagen.

20

The Falkenhagen Bunker: it was a while since Jaeger had been here. It brought back memories both good and bad. It was from here that they'd masterminded the destruction of Kammler and his co-conspirators, or so Jaeger had thought; but after the last thirty-six hours, he was assailed by doubts.

The Secret Hunters had been gifted the use of the bunker by the German government. As Miles had reminded Jaeger, if there was one nation who would never forget the excesses of the Nazi regime, it was the Germans. It was a somewhat ironic venue: a vast subterranean complex where Hitler had manufactured his most fearsome chemical weapons.

At war's end it had been seized by the Russians, who had transformed it into a Cold War headquarters complete with a command bunker that could survive a nuclear meltdown – a massive domed structure set six storeys below ground.

Peter Miles had made this the nerve centre of the Secret Hunters.

There were few creature comforts in the bare and echoing concrete chamber, and Miles liked it that way: it kept meetings short and focused. There was one bare wooden table, bearing Miles's laptop, with some plastic chairs arranged in a semicircle facing it. That was about all.

Apart from Jaeger, Uncle Joe and Miles, there was one other figure present: Takavesi 'Raff' Rafarra, long hair braided Maori-style. Maori by birth, Royal Marines by training, and a fellow veteran of the SAS, Raff was larger than life in every sense.

Jaeger and he had gone through their commando training and SAS selection together, and they were inseparable.

Tough, resourceful, a natural-born warrior, Raff was the kind of guy Jaeger would choose to fight back-to-back with every time. There was no better soldier or more loyal friend. He was also a fearsome drinker, hopeless where women were concerned, and incapable of accepting orders from those he didn't respect, which had pretty much done for his prospects in the military.

Jaeger and Raff had left the SAS at around the same time to found an executive adventure company – though that had taken something of a back seat once they'd been drawn into the world of the Secret Hunters. They'd just started trying to resuscitate the business when the present unforeseen developments had transpired.

Considering what had happened over the past few days, Jaeger was doubly glad of Raff's presence. He was the man to have beside you if the likes of Steve Jones were back on the scene.

It seemed odd not to have a fifth figure present: Irina Narov. Jaeger had asked. Miles hadn't been able to shed much light. A few weeks back, Narov had disappeared: no email, no phone contact, nothing. Miles wasn't overly concerned. She had a habit of doing this. She'd be back in her own good time.

As succinctly as he could, Jaeger proceeded to deliver a briefing on all that had happened in the St Georgen tunnels. Once he was done, they played the footage from the smashed camera.

Neither Raff nor Miles had laid eyes on Steve Jones before. It was only Jaeger who had got close enough to the man, and the more he watched the footage, the more convinced he was that it was Jones giving the orders. Which begged the million-dollar question: what had he and his team been seeking at St Georgen? What had they retrieved?

With Jones back on the prowl, did that mean that his employer was too? Had his mission been ordered by his erstwhile boss, Hank Kammler? It seemed possible, and it was a deeply disturbing proposition.

Kammler's death had been confirmed by none other than Daniel Brooks, the director of the CIA and a good friend and ally to their cause. Likewise, Jones had been left for dead by Jaeger: shark food, or so he'd presumed.

But had both returned to haunt them?

It seemed unthinkable, but footage didn't lie.

Miles powered down his laptop. He turned to Jaeger. 'You say you're certain it's Jones. Is there any way we can get absolute proof?'

'Even if we do, it doesn't prove that Kammler's alive,' Jaeger reasoned. 'One doesn't follow from the other.'

'It doesn't,' Miles agreed. 'But I have a separate – as yet un-corroborated – report suggesting Kammler may still be with us. More of that shortly. If we can be certain this is Jones, we may be able to use him to lead us to Kammler.'

Miles was right. Jones was a fighter and a killer, but he wasn't necessarily the sharpest tool in the box. He might blunder, and that might lead them to the kingpin.

'I reported the murders forty-eight hours ago,' Jaeger an-nounced. 'The police investigation will be well under way. It's got to be high-profile: eight people – a film crew and historians – murdered in a secret Nazi bunker. It'll hit the press, and that will flush out more detail.'

'It should,' Miles confirmed. 'I'll use our sources and dig up as much as I can. Plus I'll find a way to quietly pass them a copy of this film, if you don't mind.'

'Please do. It's been bugging me. Feeling kind of guilty.'

A steely look came into Miles's eyes. 'Well don't. What we're about here – trust me, it's far bigger than whatever happened at St Georgen.'

Silver-haired, blue-eyed and with a neatly trimmed beard, Miles had to be in his late seventies. His air of calm compassion masked an iron will and an unshakeable determination to do the right thing. A young Jewish boy during the war, he'd been saved from the Nazi death camps at the eleventh hour and brought to Britain, though his family had all perished in the camps. The experience of losing a family had been his bond with Jaeger. With his quietly spoken transatlantic accent, Miles was a citizen of the world and Jaeger trusted him absolutely.

'We can hoover up whatever media coverage there is,' the older man continued. 'If Kammler is alive, we have to find him . . .'

He left the rest unsaid. For a moment, a dark quiet settled over the room.

They all knew what such a man was capable of.

21

Unexpectedly, unbidden, a voice shattered the silence of the bunker.

'Trust me – Kammler is alive.'

It had come from the entranceway, and to Jaeger it was immediately and powerfully familiar. It sent a shiver – and not an entirely unpleasant one – up his spine.

He whipped around. There, framed in the doorway, was an unmistakable figure: Irina Narov. How long she'd been standing there, he wasn't certain.

'Narov!' he exclaimed.

By way of answer, she stalked over to where Miles was standing and tossed something onto the table. It looked to Jaeger like a memory card.

'Play it.'

Miles couldn't suppress a smile. 'Hello, Irina, nice to see you again, and welcome back.'

Narov turned away without a word. She was limping slightly, dragging her right leg. As she went to take a seat, her gaze swept across Jaeger and Raff, her eyes blazing. 'Pay attention, you two. This very nearly cost me my life.'

'Jesus,' Raff muttered, 'talk about making an entrance.'

Miles picked up the memory card. 'Perhaps you wouldn't mind giving us a little background. An idea maybe of where you've been and what you've been up to these past few weeks. Context – so we can better appreciate whatever may be on this.'

'Just play it.'

Miles rolled his eyes. Irina clearly was not in a talkative mood.

He slotted the card into the laptop, clicked his mouse a few times, and the images began to play. The four men sat through the surveillance footage that Narov had filmed at the Al Moha-jir Tower. As home movies went, there was none better.

To top it all, when Narov had dragged the optical cord from the cubicle wall and fled, she'd left the camera running. The grand finale showed her diving through the window amidst a hail of bullets, and her subsequent freefall, followed by her pull-ing the chute and floating free over the Dubai skyline.

At which stage she urged Miles to kill the video. 'The rest is boring. Just my escape.'

Miles did as she asked.

Irina Narov, Jaeger reflected. What was there to say, other than: *What in the name of God have you been up to these past few days? And how on earth did you get hold of that footage?* But he'd leave it to Miles to do the cross-examination. He'd learnt the hard way how combative Narov could be.

And as Jaeger was acutely aware, the two of them had a cer-tain . . . history of recent months, which could make matters somewhat delicate. When it came to matters of the heart, Irina Narov could be particularly spiky.

Miles probed gently. Bit by bit he got the basic story out of her. Her stalking Isselhorst. The interrogation. The revelations about Hitler's royalties. Staking out the Dubai meeting. What she had discovered.

A few details were glossed over: the gas-fuelled explosion at Isselhorst's house being one. Occasionally Narov figured it was just better for her boss not to know. If he found out, she could always own up to it then. They were all volunteers. Freelancers. It was a question of seeking forgiveness, not permission.

When she had finished, Jaeger couldn't resist popping the one question. 'What got you thinking about Hitler's royalties? I mean, what kind of mind asks: *I wonder who earns the revenues from* Mein Kampf? Just came to you over your cornflakes?'

Narov glared. Jaeger's teasing was in part how he'd broken down her defences the first time. How he had melted her icy exterior. Well, she wasn't about to fall for it again.

'I was in Turkey. A holiday. I read a newspaper. *Mein Kampf* had topped the best-seller list. Again. A summer blockbuster. So naturally I wondered who was getting the revenues. As anyone would.' She stared at Jaeger hard. 'Anyone with half a brain, that is.'

Jaeger smiled. 'So in between ordering a double-choc Cornetto and lathering on the suncream, you thought you'd go find out?'

Narov turned to Miles. 'Do I really have to listen to this *Schwachkopf?*'

Jaeger smiled. *Schwachkopf.* German for dimwit or knucklehead. Narov's favourite insult, for him especially.

It felt great to have her back.

'I think we're all a little curious,' Miles ventured. 'As Einstein once said: "Imagination is more important than knowledge, for knowledge is limited, while imagination embraces the entire world." And I have to say, Irina, your mind – your imagination – is perhaps a little more all-encompassing than most. We're just trying to understand, so we can better assess our next moves.'

'Very well. I called the publisher.' Narov turned on Jaeger. 'And yes, before you ask, it was from my hotel, poolside. The man was very guarded. It turned out someone else had been making similar enquiries. An investigative journalist. A German. He had ended up very dead.

'A certain figure had recently laid claim to Hitler's entire literary estate,' Narov continued, 'including all the Führer's back-earnings. Any idea how much money we are talking about? Millions of dollars. I found out who the lawyer was: Erich Isselhorst. The rest you know.'

Miles rubbed his chin pensively. 'Well, not exactly. I mean, how does someone claiming Hitler's royalties lead you to suspect it was Hank Kammler? I for one don't get it.'

'Me too,' Raff growled. 'You lost me.'

Narov sighed. 'The journalist who was killed, he had also been tortured. Someone had carved an image into his living flesh. A *Reichsadler* . . .'

Jaeger stiffened. Mention of the *Reichsadler* brought back dark memories of Andy Smith, who along with Raff had been Jaeger's closest buddy in the SAS. Smith had been murdered by Kammler's people. He'd been discovered with that stylised eagle symbol so resonant of the evil of the Reich carved into his back.

Jaeger had vowed to avenge his death. He'd thought he'd done so. But if Kammler was still alive, not to mention Jones, then he hadn't even got close.

'I understand,' Miles said quietly. He was silent for a moment. 'One last question, and then I think perhaps we should try to determine what all of this might mean. Why didn't you share this with us earlier? Weeks back. Why the need to go off radar? Solo?'

Narov raised her chin defiantly. 'I never believed Kammler was dead. You all did. All too easily. So the CIA had a DNA sample. So what? We have been misled before. People like Kammler do not die so easily.' A pause. 'You can't deny it any more: Kammler is alive. Which means we need to go after him.'

Jaeger snorted. 'And you never thought to breathe a word about your suspicions?'

'What would have been the point? You all wanted to believe he was dead. The threat extinguished.' She eyed him dismissively. 'Plus you had other things on your mind.'

In a sense, Narov was right. For three long years Jaeger had been missing his wife and child. When he'd got them back, he'd focused on them to the exclusion of everything else, leaving it to others to hunt Kammler. After all, the entire CIA and the world's militaries had been involved by then.

When Jaeger had been told they'd got him, he'd believed them. It took a mind like Narov's never to give credit to anything, not unless she'd seen it with her own eyes.

'One more question.' It was Raff. 'That was Kammler's voice all right. I'd never forget it. But he looks different. Like the face doesn't fit the voice any more.'

Miles pulled up an image from Narov's surveillance footage and zoomed in on Kammler's features. 'Look closely. His face shows all the signs of having had plastic surgery. It's something that wasn't unknown during the war. Allied agents known to the Gestapo went under the knife, and they did the same on their side.'

Jaeger stared at the image frozen on the screen. 'One thing's for sure: he's learnt well from his Nazi forefathers.'

22

They'd eaten a rushed lunch huddled round a couple of laptops, digging up the basics on the St Georgen murder investigation. One point jumped out from all the press and police reports: the investigating team had penetrated far into the tunnels, but had eventually been forced to turn back.

The deeper they had gone, the higher the level of radiation they'd detected.

'Haigerloch,' Uncle Joe ventured. 'The missing uranium. It has to be.'

'Exactly,' Miles agreed.

'Fancy enlightening us?' Jaeger prompted.

'Haigerloch, a pretty village in southern Germany,' Miles explained. 'Towards the end of the war, the Nazis moved their top nuclear scientists – the Uranverein; the Uranium Club – plus their technology, out of Berlin, and secreted it in caves beneath Haigerloch's pretty baroque church.

'They presumed, rightly, that Allied warplanes would never venture there,' he continued, 'and even if they did, all they'd see was a quaint church. As matters transpired, American forces overran Haigerloch before the reactor could breed enough raw material to build a bomb. Or so everyone thought.'

'US forces dismantled the reactor. They recovered 664 cubes of uranium, forming the core. Each cube weighed roughly half a kilo, so 332 kilos all told. But Nazi records showed that one and a half tonnes of uranium had been trucked out of Berlin, which left over a tonne unaccounted for. The suspicion was that the

Reich had established a second, ultra-secret reactor.'

'So that's why Jones and his gang went to St Georgen?' Jaeger queried. 'That's what's been hidden there all these years? A pile of uranium ore?'

'It would make a certain degree of sense, yes.'

'But what can they do with it?' Jaeger probed. 'Practically speaking?'

'Yeah, like does it spell kaboom?' Raff added.

'Nuclear reactors can breed the raw material for an atomic bomb,' Miles confirmed. 'But it all depends how enriched the uranium is. To give you a sense of the amounts involved, Little Boy was packed with sixty-four kilos of highly enriched uranium when it was detonated over Hiroshima.'

Jaeger's face darkened. 'So you're saying they've got enough to build several bombs? Potentially.'

Miles shrugged. 'Not necessarily. To do that, you'd have to master hugely complex technology.' He flashed a look at Jaeger. 'But there is another possibility . . .'

'Which is?'

'I'm no expert,' Miles continued, 'but constructing an IND is relatively easy. In fact the main challenge is getting your hands on enough highly enriched uranium. Once you've done that, it's fairly straightforward.'

'IND?'

'Improvised nuclear device. Basically, a modern nuclear weapon achieves ninety per cent efficiency in terms of fission – so turning uranium into an unimaginably powerful explosion. It does so by firing a hollow tube of uranium onto an interlocking cylinder, at tremendous speed. When they impact, fission occurs . . . and kaboom, as Raff would say.'

'And an IND?'

'Far cruder. In essence, you clobber two lumps of uranium together, achieving around ten per cent efficiency. But it's still a staggeringly powerful weapon. To give you a sense of it, an IND fitted with twenty kilos of highly enriched uranium would create a blast equal to one thousand tonnes of high explosives.'

'Plus the radiation poisoning and contamination,' Narov added.

'Yes. Plus that.'

'So practically speaking, what would a twenty-kilo IND achieve in terms of destruction?'

Miles eyed Jaeger. 'If you detonated it in the City of London, it would flatten the entire Square Mile.'

'Shit.'

'Indeed. There's one other advantage to an IND. Despite its name, Little Boy was a big device, weighing in at around 4,500 kilos. An IND is a fraction of that size and weight.'

Jaeger's face hardened. 'Which makes it the perfect weapon for a terrorist outfit . . . or a madman like Kammler.' It was stating the obvious, but it needed to be said.

'It does.' Miles paused for a second, massaging the bridge of his nose. 'And that brings me to why *I* wanted to call you all here. How many of you have heard of Moldova?'

'Moldova?' Raff snorted. 'Heard a joke about it once. Why do Moldovan football fans need two seats? One to sit on and one to throw when the fighting starts.'

There was a ripple of laughter. It was one of the things that Jaeger loved about Raff: no matter how dire a situation, he could always find humour in it. It was so often humour that carried them through.

Typically, Narov had failed to crack the barest hint of a smile. Humour was rarely her strong point.

'Moldova's an impoverished, chaotic, lawless mess of a former Soviet state,' Miles continued, 'not to mention the world's foremost black market for uranium. There have been several attempts to flog former Soviet stocks. It culminated in an effort to sell forty kilos to ISIS. Note the amount: more than enough to build an IND.'

'Who stopped it? I presume it *was* stopped?'

'It was.'

'Who by?'

'As it happens, our old friend Daniel Brooks. The CIA infiltrated an agent into the network, and when the money was handed over, the bad guys were busted. But this year the Moldovan mafia moved on to a new deal, this one involving a mystery client. We know his code name only: Grey Wolf.'

The room went silent. All eyes were on Miles.

'Brooks, obviously, found that rather suspicious. Worrying. When he raised it with me, so did I. I don't believe in coincidences.'

'But surely Kammler wouldn't be that stupid,' Jaeger objected. 'Grey Wolf is known. It's blown. So why use it again?'

'But he would be that *arrogant*,' Narov interjected. 'It is deeply symbolic. He will never drop it, bearing in mind who the original Grey Wolf was.'

'You think he believes he's Hitler?' Jaeger queried.

'Hitler's modern incarnation, at the very least.'

Raff nodded. 'Ego. The big killer and the big banana skin.'

'Kammler does see himself as the Hitler of today,' Miles confirmed. 'Plus he feels protected. Shielded. Invulnerable. Assuming the DNA sample that proved he was dead was doctored, then Kammler has friends in high places.'

'Okay, so let's presume Grey Wolf is Kammler,' Jaeger mused. 'What else do we know about this Moldovan deal?'

'Dates, plus destination the goods are being shipped to. All the Moldovan mafia is waiting on is the final payment. And believe me, this stuff is obscenely expensive. Once they get their money, they're flying it out to a particularly nasty narco gang based in Colombia.'

'Kammler mentioned Moldova, in the Dubai meeting,' Narov interjected. 'It's on the tapes. Something about the Columbians being on standby to take delivery.'

'Did he?' Miles gave an appreciative nod at Narov. 'Good work. That pretty much confirms everything we've been hearing.'

'You're saying Kammler's in bed with Colombian drug

traffickers?' Jaeger ventured. 'How does that work?'

'Arms dealers, drugs runners and terrorists – the nexus of evil draws ever closer,' Miles explained. 'You couple that with a hatred of the West – of America in particular – and the Moldovan mafia, Colombian narcos and Kammler can make common cause. Plus, a remote, lawless jungle base: in a sense, it offers the perfect place for a man like Kammler to hide.'

'Then there's Kammler's former role at the CIA,' Narov volunteered. 'He was big into developing narcotics as tools of espionage and warfare. LSD. Heroin. And worse. You name it, he dabbled in it. He has to have contacts in that world. Maybe he called in some favours.'

'Then why not roll it up?' Raff queried. 'Now. Kill the network before the shit has a chance to hit the fan.'

'Because if it is Kammler, this is the means to track him,' Miles answered. 'We trace the cargo, we trace Kammler.'

'Do we know the exact location the uranium's being routed to?' Jaeger asked.

'We do,' Miles confirmed. 'Dirt airstrip hacked out of the Colombian jungle. One of the narco trafficker's drugs-smuggling hubs, for onward shipment to the US.'

Jaeger eyed Miles. 'Okay, so the contention is that Kammler's set up some kind of IND lab alongside the drugs-processing facilities? Am I right?'

Miles nodded. 'That's what we're thinking.'

'Right, let's do a pre-emptive strike. Before the flight leaves Moldova and has a chance to jet in, we hit Kammler's jungle base and blow his labs to shreds, then get in there and kill or capture the man himself – that's if he's there.'

Miles smiled. 'My thoughts exactly.'

Jaeger got to his feet. 'Then what're we waiting for?'

23

'This time, just who is the "we"?' Raff queried. 'Who exactly is going to be backing us? Where's our top cover?'

'Myself. Daniel Brooks,' Miles confirmed. 'Plus a few other highly placed and trusted individuals. The usual suspects.'

Over the decades, the Secret Hunters had cultivated a network of powerful backers, encompassing the elite military and intelligence agencies of the major Allied governments.

'But I'll level with you,' Miles continued. 'Brooks is worried. If Kammler's DNA sample was doctored, then he's got problems in his own agency. Until he proves Kammler's back in business, he can't do much about it. Hence his need to keep this low-profile.' He ran his gaze around the room. 'Hence the desire to use you.'

'I am curious about one thing,' Narov volunteered. 'How much is the final payment the Moldovans are waiting for? To green-light the shipment?'

'Tens of millions of dollars.'

'The kind of money Kammler's trying to grab via Hitler's literary estate.'

'Indeed. Using the revenues from *Mein Kampf* to wreak some kind of nuclear carnage in memory of the Reich. Well, it would appeal to Kammler's ego, not to mention his sense of the dramatic. But we won't know for sure until—'

'He is smarter than that,' Narov cut in. 'If he aims to spread terror, it won't be only revenge he is after. He will do so to light a fire, one that will scorch the world, from the ashes of which he will build anew. Bringing back the Reich, that was always his aim. A Fourth Reich. With him as Führer. I don't believe it will have changed.'

'Quite,' Miles agreed. 'But as I was saying, we won't know for sure until we get eyes on, and that's down to you guys.'

Jaeger, Raff and Narov glanced at each other. Either they agreed to Miles's proposition, or potentially they'd have the blood of millions on their hands. But beyond that, this was deeply personal.

Narov had her own reasons to hate Kammler, reasons rooted deep in her family's dark past. As for Raff, he'd seen good friends die horribly at Kammler's hands. And for Jaeger, this was the man who'd murdered his best friend, and very nearly succeeded in doing the same to his wife and child.

They broke for a brew. Jaeger found a quiet place where he could make a private call via his computer. He needed to let Ruth know that he wasn't about to make it home any time soon. He steeled himself for what was coming: he didn't figure this was going to be easy.

Predictably, her mobile went to voicemail. He decided to call home. Maybe she was there. A woman's voice answered. For the briefest of moments he was hopeful, but it wasn't her.

'Who's th——?' he demanded. What was a stranger doing answering the home phone?

'It's Jennie, Will.'

Jaeger felt a sinking feeling. Jennie was Raff's long-term partner, and one of Ruth's closest friends. She'd proved a constant support. But why was she there now, at their home?

'Is everything okay? Where's Ruth?'

'No easy way to say this, Will: she's disappeared from the clinic. I've been trying to call you for hours. It kept going to voicemail.'

No surprise she couldn't reach him: the Falkenhagen Bunker had zero mobile coverage. Jaeger's mind started to race. Ruth had been acting increasingly erratically. But pulling a disappearing act? What on earth was going on?

'Will? Are you there?'

Jennie's voice dragged Jaeger's mind back to the present. He forced himself to speak. 'I am. Tell me – how long has she been gone?'

'It happened yesterday. The clinic people tried calling. They couldn't raise you, so they got hold of me. I've been trying to reach you ever since.' A pause. 'Plus there's this. They say she left in the company of a suspicious- looking individual.'

'Suspicious like how?' Jaeger queried. 'Any description?'

'Not much. Big shaven-headed guy. Man of few words. "Scary looking" was how they described him. But the clinic's not a prison, so they couldn't exactly stop her.'

Jaeger felt punch-drunk. What the hell was going on? There was more than a hint of Steve Jones in the description of the individual who had taken Ruth away. Maybe she'd been kid-napped by Kammler's people. But Jones couldn't be in two places at once – the tunnels under St Georgen and the London clinic.

Jaeger thrust out a hand to the wall to steady himself. He had a terrible feeling that history was repeating itself.

'Any idea where she went?' he asked desperately. 'Any clues as to where she might be? Anything? It's important, Jen. Vitally so.'

'No. Nothing. Just what the clinic people said. Plus the fact that she's gone.'

Jaeger thanked her and killed the call.

Another thought struck him, one so dreadful in its im-plications that it was almost as if he couldn't breathe. Fighting to keep his hands from shaking, he punched speed dial for his sons' mobile; Luke and Simon shared the same phone.

It rang out and went to voicemail. It was lesson time, so the phone would be off.

With a mounting sense of panic, he called school reception.

'Luke and Simon Jaeger, Year 8,' he blurted out. 'They're

both still at school? No one's come to pick them up in the last twenty-four hours?'

'Just a moment . . . Mr Jaeger, is it?'

'Yes, it is. And it's urgent.'

'Just one moment while I check.'

Music began to play. Jaeger had been placed on hold. The tune was supposed to be comforting. Calming. Well, no parent had ever called as stressed out and messed up as he was right now, of that he was certain. *Come on. Come on.*

If felt like an age before the receptionist was back on the line. 'Their mother came to see them yesterday evening. She took them for a bite to eat by the sea.'

Jaeger felt his blood run cold. The school lay on the Somerset coastline, and Jaeger was in the habit of taking the boys for fish and chips by the harbour. But Ruth's visits had been few and far between, for obvious reasons.

'Apparently she came to say goodbye, before she went off on an overseas trip. The boys were back before lights out. They're both here. If you're worried, I can get them to call you once class is finished.'

Jaeger forced himself to speak. 'Please, I'd really appreciate it. As soon as they're able to.'

'Of course. They'll call around three forty-five.'

'One more thing: did my . . . wife leave any indication as to where she might be going?'

'Not that I'm aware of. But the boys may know more.'

Jaeger thanked the woman and sank back against the cold concrete of the wall. How had life come to this – to a point where he was worried that his own wife might snatch their sons and return them to their tormentor? She'd been acting so un-predictably recently, and if she'd fallen under the influence of Kammler's people anything was possible, that's if it was them who'd taken her.

Jaeger's mind was spinning. He didn't know what to think anymore. But of one thing he was certain: it was Kammler who had done this to them. Directly or indirectly, it was his fault. In his dark, fucked-up, vengeful fashion, Kammler was behind it all.

It was time to end it, once and for all.

24

Hank Kammler bristled as he eyed the figures in the room, his gaunt face cloaked in shadow, his gaze distinctly predatory.

'You don't like it?' he demanded. 'It offends your sense of entitlement? Your precious positions of influence? Let me ask – what is the point of influence, of power, if you never see fit to use it for the sake of the Reich?'

A man of around Kammler's age – Ferdinand Bormann, the son of Martin Bormann, Hitler's banker – knitted his brows. He was a very different character from Kammler, as he himself was well aware. Where Kammler was driven, merciless and utterly single-minded, Ferdy, as his friends called him, was a little more circumspect and conservative. A banker by nature. Something of an accountant. A 'bean counter', as Kammler had once so cuttingly said. Well, Kammler might be Grey Wolf, but they were still a team, and that demanded a certain accountability.

'It is only that the *Mein Kampf* settlement brings with it certain dangers, risks, in the form of scrutiny,' he ventured. 'A mystery figure claiming the Führer's royalties: press interest is inevitable. We must anticipate that it will bring attention our way. Which could prove . . . difficult.'

Kammler stalked across the room, throwing open the curtains. Light flooded in; the fine sunlight of an early spring day. He ran his eye around the perfectly manicured grounds. Yes, Ferdinand Bormann had done well for himself. You didn't run a Zurich bank of such global reach without being amply rewarded – this fine country estate being a case in point.

But that was just the problem. Bormann and the rest of the Kameraden had grown fat and bloated, seduced by the trappings of wealth and power. None of that did anything to bring back the Reich. To reclaim the Führer's legacy. To purge humanity of its present sickness.

And by God, was it sick.

By contrast, he, Hank Kammler, son of SS General Hans Kammler, had sacrificed so much. His position as deputy director of the CIA. His friends. His freedom. His very face, even. He ran a hand across the recent scarring. He had sacrificed his looks – the hawkish, aristocratic Kammler features – and all for the cause.

Yet still greater sacrifice was required, and he was ready. To start a fire. A fire to burn and sear the dead wood. Destroying all to start anew. He for one would enjoy sitting back and watching it burn.

But the men in this room: how would he galvanise them?

He glanced at his watch. 'It is six forty-five p.m. on the fourteenth of March. Tonight, the Moldovan flight will take to the air. If all goes to schedule, I expect delivery in seventy-six hours.'

He paused. 'I should be there, overseeing the building of the last of the devices. Instead, you call me here to quibble about the *Mein Kampf* settlement? To complain that it may attract a little *unwelcome publicity?*'

His eyes flashed a momentary rage, verging on the brink of madness. '*Mein Kampf*, the Führer's masterpiece, banished! His royalties going to fund the very causes we abhor! They try to do this with his message, his glorious inheritance, and I am surprised – and disappointed – that you are not as incensed as I am, *Kameraden.*'

Boorman and his fellows remained silent. Kammler's words had stung them. There was a sense that they had hit home.

'Look at us,' Kammler continued. 'Eight men. Eight, the

sacred number of the *Schutzstaffel*. Eight men in the sunset of our days, yet we are so very, very close. So close to fulfilling our pledges to the Führer. And yet you call me halfway around the world to tell me this? That the *Mein Kampf* settlement is a little *risky*?'

'You cannot act alone,' a figure sitting to Bormann's right objected. 'You did so with the *Mein Kampf* settlement, and out of what motive? Hubris? We do not need the money. The sum is paltry compared to the finance and power in this room. I repeat: you cannot act alone. You are not yet the Führer of the new Reich. We are the Kameraden. The Brotherhood of the Death's Head. We act as one or not at all.'

Kammler couldn't hide his scorn any longer. 'Well there hasn't been much action to date! Seventy years of *inaction*, by my reckoning. What do you suggest? We dither for another seventy? You think we can pass such responsibility to a new generation? You really think they will care? Understand?'

He paused and tapped his chest steadily. 'You think they will feel it? In their hearts? Do you think they will even remember?'

'Heady rhetoric,' the figure retorted. 'You have your father's flare for oratory. But that doesn't alter the fact that we act as eight, united, or not at all. That is the way.'

Josef von Alvensleben – son of Ludolf von Alvensleben, the SS *Gruppenführer* who had run the infamous Valley of Death, an SS extermination camp in Poland – wasn't about to be bullied by anyone. His father hadn't exterminated hundreds of thousands of Polish Jews and communists for his son to scare easily.

'We share your sense of urgency,' he continued. 'The world must be purged of the *Untermenschen*. We Aryans must take our rightful place. And we will, of course. But cautiously. And with proper planning. Don't mistake our caution for reluctance to act.'

Kammler fought to suppress a sneer. He had grown accustomed to their reticence. To the snail's pace at which they tended to act. To their cursed caution. And he abhorred it.

'Eight devices; that we are agreed upon,' von Alvensleben continued. 'But do we have enough raw material? How much was retrieved from the tunnels at St Georgen?'

'Two hundred and forty kilos,' Kammler volunteered. 'That was before the idiot film crew stumbled upon the tunnel complex. From that we hope to isolate a hundred and twenty kilos that is highly enriched and usable.'

'Correct me if I'm wrong, but each device requires twenty kilos of HEU?' The speaker was Walter Barbie, son of SS and Gestapo officer Klaus Barbie, the so-called 'Butcher of Lyon'.

At war's end, Klaus Barbie had been recruited into the CIA to serve as an agent in South America. He'd led a long and happy life, raising a family in the southern Argentinian town of Bariloche. Hence Walter, his eldest son, spoke German with a strong South American accent.

'It does,' Kammler confirmed.

'Eight devices each of twenty kilos: the St Georgen haul leaves us a shortfall, does it not?' Barbie pressed.

Kammler found the inquisitorial tone grating. He did his best to hide his resentment. 'It does. Hence the need to go ahead with the deal offered by our friends in Moldova. Once we take delivery, we should have more than enough for our plans.'

'You are to be congratulated,' von Alvensleben remarked. 'This is certainly progress.' He paused, running his gaze around the others in the room. 'But we also understand your plans have altered somewhat. Is that true?'

Kammler's eyes grew cold. 'Plans evolve, Josef.'

Von Alvensleben's gaze didn't falter. 'Yes, and with each evolution we need to be kept informed. Fully briefed. We are your paymasters, your protectors. You know the protocols.'

'Those who have money will always make money, no matter what catastrophe may befall humankind,' Kammler remarked by way of answer. 'The more dire the catastrophe, the more money there is to be made. This we all understand. And crucially, we have unrivalled finances and we will have ample forewarning.'

'That's as may be,' von Alvensleben countered. 'But still we need to be kept informed. We are hitting purely military and political targets, as agreed? That has not changed?'

'It hasn't,' Kammler confirmed.

'So what *has* changed?' von Alvensleben pressed. 'I have word that you have altered our plans significantly.'

Kammler eyed von Alvensleben. Who had given him word? Could there be a mole in Kammler's set-up; a leak? He would check. Root it out mercilessly.

He brought himself to his full height. 'It is a work in progress, Josef. Eight INDs simultaneously detonated at the targets we have agreed upon. I'm proud to say that we have managed to accurately predict the radiation envelope from each strike. We can now forecast precisely where the devastation will fall.'

Von Alvensleben gave a curt nod. 'This is only as we intended.'

'But it means we can better protect ourselves. Greater safety equals greater predictability for us all. A vital evolution, as I think you'll agree?'

'This is an improvement,' Von Alvensleben conceded. 'This is what we had hoped for.'

'It is.' Kammler smiled. 'As for those who are not forewarned – those who are not the chosen – the results will be exactly as we intend.'

'But this is still nothing *new*,' von Alvensleben pressed.

Kammler feigned a smile. 'I was holding back the best to last. Consider where the blame will fall. I have made certain arrangements so that responsibility will be placed at the feet of the North Koreans. Or at the very least, rogue elements in the North Korean regime.'

He gazed around triumphantly. 'By fingering North Korea, we prove how communism really is a scourge on the earth. Doubly fertile soil for fascism to triumph. A stroke of genius, don't you think?'

'A stroke of genius,' a figure sitting to the right of von Alvensleben confirmed. It was Wolfgang Eichmann, son of Adolf Eichmann, one of the chief architects of the Holocaust. 'But how will you achieve it?'

'North Korean teams are building the devices,' Kammler replied. 'Their expertise has proved critical. Without it, our plans are impossible to achieve. I'll make sure the evidence is in place to reveal their involvement.'

The Kameraden nodded their approval. The North Korean factor was indeed a stroke of genius.

With it, Kammler figured he was winning them over.

25

'We shall light a fire,' Kammler announced, excitement burning in his eyes. 'In the chaos and panic that ensues, we will seize power in all the ways we have planned. Between the eight of us in this room, we control a good slice of the world's media. We will pump out the message even before the dust starts to settle: it is time for a new world order, one that only we can provide.'

Kammler gesticulated wildly. 'Economies will lie in ruins. We will show that iron law and order is needed to build a sustainable future. And that is something that only we – the global Nazi brotherhood; fascism – can deliver.

'The world's public – bloodied, reeling, thrust into a terrible recession – will be ready! At last, right-thinking people will be ready. The message of liberalism and tolerance – of equality – will be exposed for what it is. A sham that has robbed the Aryans of our birthright.'

'And the targets – they remain the same?' von Alvensleben queried pointedly. He was nothing if not persistent. His repeated circling back to this question was starting to grate. Maybe he did know something.

'They do, Josef, as I've already said. Why would they have changed?'

'The countries to be attacked?'

'We've been through all of this before,' Kammler snapped.

'The countries?' von Alvensleben pressed.

'China. Russia. The US. Britain. France. Canada. Then Israel, as the grand finale. You'll be pleased to know the prevailing winds will ensure that much of Israel is enshrouded in fallout.' Kammler flashed a thin smile. 'Gentlemen, what Hitler began, we will finish in one fell swoop.'

'That's seven by my count,' von Alvensleben pointed out. 'Seven nations. Eight is the sacred number.'

'China will be hit by two.'

'Why China?'

'The Americans and British like to perpetuate the myth that they won the war. More lies. The single greatest loss of life was suffered by China. Over twenty million dead. In essence, the Chinese – along with the Russians – bled us dry. For this, we will make them suffer disproportionately.'

'And the targets – they remain exclusively political, military and economic?' von Alvensleben pressed. 'There will be no mass murder for mass murder's sake?'

Kammler eyed the man. He was nothing if not sharp. 'Correct.'

'Please send me an up-to-date target list. Indeed, you might circulate it to all.'

'Gladly.'

'Timings,' von Alvensleben remarked. 'Has there been any impact upon the schedule?'

'None. We go ahead as planned. We strike on the thirtieth of April, the anniversary of the Führer's death. And in doing so we prove that he did not die in vain. Quite the contrary: his legacy lives. The Reich will rise anew and conquer!'

'That's only six weeks from now. You can still meet this deadline?'

'I can.'

'Timing is utterly critical,' Bormann interjected, a hint of excitement in his voice. 'This is our chance to seize control financially even before we do politically. From finance all else flows. Stock markets, currency trading, futures – the financial system will survive. We can profit massively, as long as we know the day and hour of the strike!'

Kammler smiled. 'Exactly. And trust me, we will.'

It was a high-risk strategy, one that could backfire. The world might spiral into a dark chaos from which it would never recover. It could spell the end of humanity. Of civilisation.

But what true civilisation was there left that was even worthy of the name, Kammler mused. Jews, blacks, Muslims, Asians, homosexuals, the disabled: all had been raised up with the fall of the Reich to a perverse equality with their obvious masters.

The natural order of things had been turned on its head, and it enraged him. Tortured him. In short, all of Hitler's warnings had come to pass, as the human race, plague-like, devastated the natural world. On balance, what was at risk? The present unnatural, sick order of things wasn't worth saving.

Now, to seal the support of the Kameraden. Kammler pulled a sheet of paper from his pocket.

'At this juncture it seems opportune to remind us of the final words of the Führer,' he announced portentously, 'written just hours before his death. From his last will and testament, I quote.

'"This war will one day go down in history as the most glorious and heroic manifestation of the struggle . . . Centuries will go by, but from the ruins of our towns and monuments, hatred of those ultimately responsible will always grow anew. They are the people whom we have to thank for all this: international Jewry and its helpers!"'

On hearing those words, a reverential silence had settled upon the room.

'"Do not give up the struggle under any circumstances",' Kammler continued, '"but carry it on wherever you may be against the enemies of the Fatherland . . . The surrender of a district or town is out of the question . . . Above everything else the commanders must set a shining example of faithful devotion to duty until death."'

He paused for effect.

'He wrote those immortal words even as Russian troops advanced to within five hundred metres of his Berlin bunker and his men were all but out of ammunition. Such defiance. Such purity of vision. That, *Kameraden,* is our inheritance. Our legacy. That is what the Führer charged us to fulfil.'

Kammler glanced at each of the figures in turn: Bormann; von Alvensleben; Barbie; Eichmann; Gustav Heim, son of Aribert Heim, who'd earned the nickname Dr Death in the concentration camps; the two Mengele brothers, sons of the infamous Angel of Death. From each he received a solemn nod of approval, his appeal to the Führer's memory a master stroke.

They broke for refreshments, Bormann and Kammler drifting into a private corner. 'What of this Narov woman?' Bormann queried, a hint of worry in his voice. 'Was it her in Dubai? Is she on to us? On to *you*?'

'I'm unsure. Whoever did this was a consummate professional. Not a trace of CCTV footage to identify the culprit.'

'And Isselhorst? The lawyer. Is his death linked somehow? Surely it has to be?'

'Ferdy, you worry too much. It will end up killing you.' Kammler gave a thin smile. 'But yes, we assume the two are linked. Whoever was spying on that meeting, we presume they got to us via our unfortunate – and very dead – lawyer.'

'So those who hunt us, are they on to us again? And if so, how close are they?'

'We have to presume they are. And that means we can afford no delay. No dissent. So I'm doubly glad to see we have reached firm agreement.'

'Indeed, but . . .' Bormann paused. 'If we are forced to take the kind of action we have discussed, it will be hugely expensive, not to mention risky.'

Kammler stiffened. 'Then perhaps it is time to dig deep into your own pockets. After all, just look at what our efforts have cost *me*. We are on the brink of the final solution. By the end, we will have finances and power beyond our wildest dreams. No cost is too great.'

'I have funds that can be made . . . available,' Bormann

conceded. 'But even my resources are not inexhaustible.'

Kammler smiled. 'They won't have to be. Not long now, Ferdy. Not long.'

A third figure joined them. They made space for von Alvensleben. Kammler the mastermind; von Alvensleben the intelligence chief; Bormann the banker – these three formed the inner circle of the Brotherhood.

'We would do well not to underestimate them,' von Alvensleben remarked. 'The Secret Hunters. They frustrated us once before, remember.'

'They did.' Kammler's face grew cruel. 'If we sense they are too close, we must resort to the ultimate sanction. We have people in place. We must hit them where it hurts most. We must cut the head off the snake.'

'We must,' von Alvensleben agreed.

Kammler eyed Bormann. 'It is the only way. Whatever the cost and whatever the risks.'

Somewhat reluctantly, Bormann signalled his agreement. He was a banker; he knew the costs would prove exorbitant. But so too would be the profits he would reap, armed with the foreknowledge of what was coming.

'Warn your contacts to be doubly vigilant,' Kammler continued, speaking to von Alvensleben. 'Even if the agencies of the enemy are officially doing nothing, that means little. They are smart. They'll run any operation off the books. Covertly. Get your people asking the right questions, in the right places. If the Secret Hunters get too close, we hit them without delay and without mercy.'

Von Alvensleben nodded. 'Understood.'

'One thing,' Bormann ventured. 'This person we have on the inside. Is now not the time they should be used? Surely they must know how close the Secret Hunters are.'

'Ordinarily speaking, yes,' Kammler agreed, 'but right now, they've dropped off the radar. I believe it's only temporary. I will let you know. We will determine then how best to act.'

An hour later – he could afford to linger no longer – Kammler strode out of the front entrance of the Chateau de Laufen and slid into the rear seat of a chauffeur-driven black Mercedes. The vehicle pulled away from the grand turreted building, which was enshrouded in thick forest overlooking the waters of the Rhine.

He allowed himself a thin smile. He'd won the Kameraden's blessing.

But unbeknownst to them, he had so much more in mind . . .

26

S ometimes contacts could save your arse.

Contacts and the shared brotherhood of warriors.

In Jaeger's world – the world of black ops – it was often down to who you knew.

The Colombian narco gang – the one scheduled to receive Kammler's Moldovan flight – called themselves Los Niños – 'The Children'. It was a piss-take of a name, of course. There was nothing remotely childlike about their activities – not unless you included kidnapping kids from the jungle villages and recruiting them as foot soldiers.

When a child was forcibly taken from his community – having first been made to commit unspeakable atrocities, often against his own relatives – there tended to be little he wouldn't do for his new family.

The narco chief was the infamous Camilo Abrego, whose gang name was El Padre – 'The Father'. He was rumoured to have a squad of teenage soldiers as his personal bodyguard.

There was one upside, as far as Jaeger was concerned: the gang's main base lay close to the remote border with Brazil, and in Brazil Jaeger had some of the best contacts imaginable.

During his time in the military Jaeger had trained the elite Brazilian Special Operations Brigade (BSOB), their equivalent of the SAS. The BSOB were commanded by Colonel Augustine Evandro. When one of the colonel's patrols had gone missing in the jungle, Jaeger had led the team that went in to rescue them from the narco gang's clutches.

Colonel Evandro had never forgotten what Jaeger had done for his men, and he'd been only too happy to help when he'd got in touch explaining the nature of their present mission. The Colonel's keenness was also driven by his own recent experiences: he, too, had crossed swords with Kammler, some of his people getting burnt in the process.

As a result, he was keen for payback.

Just days after the Falkenhagen meeting, Jaeger, Raff and Narov had flown into Cachimbo airport, situated in the heart of the Brazilian Amazon. Colonel Evandro was waiting for them. Reserved exclusively for military operations, Cachimbo was a perfect jumping-off point for their mission.

From there, they'd deployed to a remote airstrip on Brazil's north-western frontier, just a few kilometres short of the border with Colombia. That place – Station 15, one of many such dirt airstrips that the colonel maintained for anti-narcotics work – would be their forward operating base.

Upon arrival, they'd boarded a chopper for the flight onwards into 'Dodge City', as Jaeger and his crew had nicknamed Los Niños's base. If all went to plan, they would be in and out without anyone in Colombia being any the wiser.

Prior to take-off, Jaeger had given the helicopter pilot a short briefing over his maps. 'We need you to get us into here.' He'd pointed out a clearing in the dense jungle, some seven kilometres east of Dodge City. 'Get us in there, or as close as you can. We've ID'd a second LZ here, in case the first is a no-go.'

Now they were whipping over the jungle canopy at 130 knots airspeed, the Brazilian Air Force CH-34 Super Puma cutting through the dawn sky, rotors seeming to skim the very treetops. Any lower, Jaeger figured, and the pilot would be slicing the tops off the tallest of the rainforest giants.

Mist swirled around the helo as the heat started to build and the jungle sucked moisture from the forest floor. The Puma's side doors were wide open, the wind noise killing any chance of talk. Occasionally there was a break in the forest cover, revealing a stretch of open water or a cluster of huts.

But mostly it was impenetrable jungle.

Narov was seated with her back to the cockpit, silent and utterly composed, as she always was when going into action. Raff was perched on one of the fold-down canvas seats that ran along the helo's side, equally calm and collected. Jaeger was on the rearmost one, next to the pile of bergens – military rucksacks – and weaponry netted down on the Puma's floor.

Sandwiched between Jaeger and Raff was a third figure, a massive African American named Lewis Alonzo. CIA chief Brooks had insisted on there being an American on Jaeger's team – his eyes and ears on the mission. Alonzo, a former SEAL now working in close protection, had been the obvious choice.

Alonzo had formed a part of Jaeger's team on his previous Nazi-hunting operations, and had more than proved himself. With Mike Tyson's physique and Will Smith's humour, he liked to act the fool; the big muscle-bound oaf. In fact, his mind was as sharp as a pin, as Jaeger had soon learnt.

Fearless, generous-hearted and trustworthy, he was a man who liked to fight fire with fire. Oddly, his one bête noire was fish. Alonzo hated fish. Set upon by piranha during their previous Amazon venture, he'd been one unhappy dude. He'd agreed to the present mission as long as rabid shoals of piranha were well off the menu.

Jaeger settled back in his seat and closed his eyes. The last few days had been a crazed whirl. He'd spent much of the time trying to trace Ruth. He'd heard nothing and had failed to locate her at any of the obvious places she might have gone. The police had been informed, but they too had zero leads.

He felt guilty at abandoning her in the clinic while he'd crawled around those Nazi-era catacombs. He hoped her doing a runner was a fleeting moment of madness, that maybe she just needed space and time alone, after which she'd come to

115

her senses. But in truth, he feared the worst – that she had been abducted; in which case he was chiefly to blame.

Hence he was doing the only thing that made any sense: hunting the source of the threat.

27

A day earlier, they'd been flying across the Atlantic on an airliner routed to Rio when Narov had levered open the topic of Ruth's disappearance with all the subtlety of a bulldozer.

'I have been thinking about your wife's condition,' she had announced flatly. 'I know about the diagnosis of PTSD. That might be a part of what she is suffering. But I don't believe that is all that is wrong with her.'

As she'd been speaking, Narov had rearranged the food on her plate. For dinner she'd chosen grilled salmon fillet with bulgur wheat and green mango salad. Typically, she'd separated out the foodstuffs so that none touched, sorting them into their various colours.

As Jaeger knew, Narov was autistic; high-functioning, but autistic nonetheless. It explained so many things about her: her apparent icy reserve; her odd, robotic way of speaking; the fact that she seemed to mimic so many different accents – American, English, Russian – her speech a total mishmash.

And of course, her absolute perfectionism about the thing she did so very well, which was soldiering; or more specifically, man-hunting.

Plus it explained why foods of differing colours should never be in contact with each other, especially green on red. By way of answer, Jaeger had prodded the fish so that it touched the salad – a real no-no as far as Narov was concerned.

She'd glared at him. 'Look, you know why I do this. With my food. I have explained it to you, so why mock?' She paused.

'You may not understand it, but equally I cannot understand why you bury your head in the sand. Nothing about your wife's disappearance makes any sense, yet you stay loyal to her, blindly.'

Jaeger's face hardened. He could sense Raff shrinking in the seat beside him. There were clearly far gentler ways to broach such a topic – not that Jaeger agreed with her in any case. Narov was hardly unbiased. She'd never warmed to Ruth, and he figured the reasons why were anchored in the attraction she'd felt towards him from the get-go – one that Jaeger had found it hard not to reciprocate.

But right now, she was really riling him. 'She was escorted out of the clinic by an unknown male,' Jaeger grated. 'She was abducted the last time. Taken captive. Stands to reason it's the same now.'

'And her visiting your boys? How do you explain that? How does that fit with an abduction?'

They'd lapsed into a moody silence. It had given Jaeger more than a moment to reflect. He was stressed – tight as a razor blade. For a moment he'd wondered whether he should continue with the mission. Wasn't it more important to be at home with the boys, to protect them? Maybe start the search for Ruth from that end?

But if she had gone after Kammler, then this was the only way to find her. On balance, he had no choice.

Or maybe this was all total bullshit. People suffering from PTSD tended to act irrationally. Unpredictably. Maybe she had disappeared as a veiled cry for help, taking herself off for some quality 'alone' time. It wouldn't be the first time. There was just no way of knowing.

Jaeger forced his thoughts back to the present: he could feel the Super Puma starting to lose what little altitude it had.

Moments later, it flared out, the rear end dropping into a jungle clearing some ninety yards across, the turbines screaming at fever pitch. The Puma's loadmaster – the guy who looked after the passengers and cargo – was hanging out of the doorway, checking the rotors weren't about to slam into one of the massive trees that fringed the clearing.

A sudden jolt signified that the rear wheels had made contact with the hot earth. The loadie spun around and gave a thumbs-up – the universal signal for 'go, go, go'. Keeping low, Jaeger and Narov leapt off the helo and Raff and Alonzo started hurling packs down to them.

They grabbed the bergens and got down in a crouch, covering Raff and Alonzo with their weapons. The Super Puma was still turning and burning, the downwash of the rotor blades kicking up a storm of choking dust and vegetation. Jaeger flashed a thumbs-up, and seconds later, the chopper had pulled away from the clearing and was gone.

The key priority now was to get off the LZ, in case any of the narcos were around. But first, Jaeger needed to check they'd been dropped in the right location. He pulled out his map, compass and GPS. Having used these to verify their grid, he took a compass bearing pretty much due west, checked the map for any obvious features, and signalled the off.

Heaving his massive pack onto his shoulders, he led the way silently towards the ragged fringe of trees, pushing beneath the canopy, where all was shade and shadow. A hundred yards in, he halted, signalling the others to do likewise. Here they'd execute a listening watch, crouching in silence, using eyes and ears to scrutinise their surroundings.

If anyone had got wise to their arrival, now was the time they were likely to put in an appearance. Silent and watchful, Jaeger and his team would be ready to mount an ambush, as opposed to blundering into one.

As he crouched there, letting the sounds, sights and smells of the jungle seep into him, Jaeger felt his mind wander. Losing Ruth again, and in such shocking circumstances, had hit him hard. He'd been totally blindsided. And it hurt. Really hurt.

He'd barely slept this past week. He had dark bags beneath his eyes. He hoped that the present mission, and the sheer physical exertion, would help drive the worry from his mind.

Deep in his heart he still loved her. She was the mother of his son, and the woman he had fallen for all those years ago, with those magical green eyes flecked with gold. She could light up a room with her laughter and her razor-sharp sense of humour. But that had been Ruth Jaeger prior to Kammler getting his hands on her.

If she had been kidnapped, the present mission was the best way – perhaps the only way – of finding her.

28

Jaeger made some final adjustments to the straps on his pack and hefted it onto his shoulders.

He was using his trusted seventy-five-litre ALICE pack, a US military-style bergen designed specifically for jungle work. It came with a strong metal frame, which held the pack a good inch or more off the back and shoulders, allowing air to circulate and helping to prevent prickly heat and skin rubbing raw.

Most large backpacks were wider than a man's shoulders, with all sorts of pouches sticking out the sides. As a result, they tended to snag on vegetation. The ALICE pack was no broader than Jaeger's torso, and all the pouches were slung on the rear. He knew that if his body could squeeze through a gap, his pack would too. Lined with a tough rubberised canoe bag, which made it waterproof, it could also double as a buoyancy aid.

All four of them were armed with Colt Diemacos, the assault rifle of choice for special forces operators, and BSOB's standard weapon.

Recently the Colombian government had made great strides in tackling the narco gangs, but not in this remote area. Here, where the borders of Colombia, Peru and Brazil converged, was a vast lawless region. A swathe of jungle the size of France, it was home to drugs smugglers, people traffickers and illegal mining and logging camps.

Few here respected frontiers very much.

For Jaeger and his team it was all about stealth, secrecy and surprise now; about remaining unseen and undetected until the moment they blew their demolitions charges. The plastic explosives, detonators and related kit were an extra burden weighing on their shoulders.

Jaeger picked out a distinctive tree some fifty yards ahead – his first point to aim for – and set forth. He'd taped a tiny plastic counter to his Diemaco, of the kind an air hostess would use when counting passengers onto a plane. Covered in green gaffer tape – DIY camouflage – it had a push button and a tiny mechanical wheel, presently set to 000.

After counting ten left footfalls – Jaeger was left-handed, and favoured his left side – he pressed the button, the numbers flicking around to 001. From long experience he knew that ten left footfalls under such a heavy pack amounted to 8.3 metres of terrain covered. When the counter clicked around to 012, he'd know he'd covered the first hundred metres of terrain. At 120 he'd have completed his first kilometre, and so on and so forth. A simple navigational system called 'pacing and bearing', this was the bread-and-butter of SAS operations in the jungle. Amidst such dense vegetation, and with the sky obscured by a thick canopy, it was a vital tool in their navigational arsenal.

Normally Jaeger tended to use a more old-school system: he'd pass a small pebble from one pocket to another, each pass recording paces covered. But right now he needed a system that took less focus, meaning he could concentrate on what lay ahead.

He was acutely aware of how distracted he was at the moment; how difficult he was finding this. Part of his mind was on Luke and Simon back at home, another part on Ruth, wherever she might be. That left little room for the mission, and he had to get a grip. Right now, Raff, Narov and Alonzo were as reliant upon him as he was on them. He had to shake himself out of it and focus.

He eyed the vegetation. It was what was termed 'dirty jungle' – dense and suffocating. From floor to canopy was a mass of musty, dank, decaying leaf matter, interspersed with half-rotten branches and slabs of fallen bark. Underfoot, a thick layer of mouldy detritus cushioned each footfall, and everywhere thick clouds of bugs misted the hot, moisture-laden air.

They say you either love the jungle or hate it. Generally, Jaeger was of the former disposition: he thrilled to its raw primeval otherness, the sense of a land lost in time; the sense of entering an environment unchanged by human hand for millennia. But this jungle would test even him.

There was no slashing through this with a machete. That would leave a trail like a motorway for any bad guys to follow. Instead, he had to wriggle and thread his way through. At each step detritus rained upon him and began to work its way down his back.

After each hundred paces, Jaeger grabbed his compass where it was slung around his neck and took a new bearing – due west towards another distinctive feature: a vine twisting around a tree trunk, or a broken branch suspended halfway to the forest floor.

Operating like this meant he didn't have to keep checking the compass. Instead, he kept eyes on the feature up ahead as he moved. 'Move like a panther, not a Panzer,' he'd been told on SAS selection. Stealthy, not tank-like. He'd always remembered.

He kept both hands on his weapon in the 'patrol alert' position – slung low across the body, ready to unleash controlled bursts of fire. Here, being fast on the draw was key to survival.

In the jungle you were taught to open fire from the hip, putting a burst of rounds into the enemy's position, forcing them to go to ground. Then you'd take two steps left or right, so when the enemy looked to nail you, you were no longer visible. It was then that you'd bring your weapon into the shoulder to unleash aimed shots, good marksmanship and weapons drills being key.

After years of practice, this had become instinctive. Second nature. Something that Jaeger didn't need to consciously think about. Which was fortunate, because right now he was struggling with some particularly nasty undergrowth, plus a mind plagued by dark worries about his loved ones.

When his counter reached 240, Jaeger called a halt. The others drew in close, down on one knee and heads practically touching. Jaeger pulled out a map as they averaged out the distance they had covered. They were some two kilometres in, with four to go before they reached the ridge overlooking Dodge City, their intended destination.

Jaeger gulped some water. He felt a dark foreboding about the jungle here, a palpable sense of unwelcome.

His nerves were on edge; his eyes seeing enemies in every patch of shadow.

29

'We hit the LZ at 0800,' Jaeger whispered. 'We're three hours in, averaging seven hundred metres per hour. Last light's at – what – 1900 hours?'

'Under this depth of canopy, 1800, at a push,' Raff volunteered.

Jaeger had learnt to trust Raff on most things when it came to the jungle. He scrutinised the map for any signs of serious obstacles, such as ravines or rivers.

'We should make the ridge before dark, but only if we keep up the pace. All good?'

Three sets of eyes stared back at him, white in the darkness, faces streaked with dirt and grime and rotting leaf matter. None of them were wearing camouflage cream. Years of experience had proved it to be more of a liability than a blessing on a mission such as this.

Over days spent on covert ops in the jungle, no washing was possible. Camo cream would dry thick and stiff on face and neck. It became unbearably itchy, and it was movement – always – which drew an aggressor's eye. Raff had long ago taught Jaeger that nature was the best camouflage: 'Go dirty early.'

Jaeger stood, his sodden combat fatigues clinging to his skin. They were all dressed the same, in the unmarked jungle uniforms provided by Colonel Evandro. Jaeger's shirt and trousers were dark with sweat.

'Keep drinking. Keep rehydrating,' he whispered. 'The humidity's off the scale.'

He pulled out a compact Katadyn filter from his bergen. He

dropped the end of the intake tube into a patch of stagnant-looking water and began to pump, refilling each of their water bottles. The Katadyn employed a series of ceramic filters impregnated with silver to remove dirt, bacteria and protozoa – the kind of nasty single-celled parasites that abounded in the Amazon. Unless the water source was contaminated with man-made chemicals – which was highly unlikely here – it could render just about anything drinkable.

Water bottles replenished, they pushed onwards, Raff now taking point, a sense of urgency driving them.

By the time they reached the base of the ridge, Narov was leading. Jaeger joined her as she studied the slope that reared before them. He eyed her for a second. She seemed to be in bad shape, even considering what they'd just been through. She was limping, and Jaeger figured she'd yet to fully recover from her Dubai injuries. Typically, she'd said not a word, despite carrying the same load as the others.

The heat and humidity had been building through the day, and now they faced a stiff climb with little light remaining. In truth, Jaeger felt like death himself. He was light-headed, soaked to the skin with sweat, and had a pounding headache. First signs of a lack of fluids. Exhaustion and a rapid deterioration in his mental capacity would quickly follow if he let the dehydration really set in.

They'd done their best to keep the fluids going down, replenishing their bottles every two hours, then filter, drink, repeat. But even so, Jaeger had just sweated the liquid out again. It was the same for all of them, sweat running off like water in a shower.

He glanced to the west, where beams of sunlight were filtering low through the canopy. Last light was maybe forty minutes off, and with sundown it would grow dark as the grave. Only ten per cent of the light filtered through the jungle canopy, so even with a full moon and stars, visibility would be zero.

Every second was precious now.

Jaeger glanced at Raff. 'You good for the recce ascent?'

Raff nodded. Without a word, they dropped their packs. Jaeger turned to Narov and Alonzo. 'Keep drinking, and get some food down you too.'

Narov glanced at Alonzo. 'Typical Jaeger,' she grated. 'Treats us like children.'

Jaeger grimaced. Typical Irina Narov, more like.

He and Raff started the climb with only the bare necessities – weapons, compass, plus a couple of water bottles – to hand. They fought their way upwards, mouthing silent curses as rotten vegetation and dirt gave way underfoot. The temptation was always to use your assault rifle as some kind of walking stick, which would free up one hand to grab at branches.

But tradecraft forbade it. You needed your weapon always at the ready, and free from dirt and vegetation.

Digging in with his tough Salewa boots, and clambering over the last of the fallen tree trunks, Jaeger approached the high point. They needed to move with extreme caution. Here the vegetation thinned and it was rocky underfoot. Sunlight broke through, bathing the terrain in fine evening light. The last thing they needed was to be silhouetted on the skyline.

Jaeger dropped to his hands and knees, Raff doing likewise. They crawled ahead, waiting for the terrain to fall away on the far side. There should be nothing between them and the narco base but half a kilometre of open air. They found an opening in the low tree cover and inched forward, lifting their heads slowly.

Before them, the ridge plunged away. Smack-bang ahead lay a clearing hacked out of the thick jungle – the base of Los Niños. Two things struck Jaeger: one, it was simply massive; and two, there was a well-used dirt airstrip that ran along the southern edge of the clearing.

Burnt stumps marked where the forest had been stripped away, the underlying soil laid bare to form the landing strip, like an angry red scar. To the north lay the base, resembling some kind of a frontier town – all galvanised-iron roofs and rough dirt streets. Two of the buildings were huge, as though a pair of giant warehouses had been parachuted into the jungle.

Those, Jaeger figured, were the drugs processing and storage facilities, where the raw coca paste was refined into pure cocaine. From there it would be loaded aboard aircraft and flown north at low level en route to the USA.

Some would doubtless be routed east, on an island-hopping journey across the Atlantic, bound for some of the less law-abiding states in Africa. There, the narcos had set up transit points for shipping the deadly white powder north into Europe.

Everyone at all levels was paid off, and no one tended to ask too many questions. Those who did invariably ended up dead.

As Jaeger gazed down upon Dodge, he just hoped their fate wouldn't be the same.

30

Several roads bisected Dodge, each a rust-red highway that terminated in a dark wall of trees. At the far end of one lay a rectangular expanse of flat ground, with a sagging set of football posts at either end. Like kids anywhere, El Padre's child soldiers needed to boot a ball around after a hard day's graft.

Jaeger could see 4x4s buzzing along the dirt roads. Stick-like figures were crammed into the vehicles. He didn't doubt that most of them were armed. All in all, he reckoned the base was a good kilometre square. This was a serious operation; they had to be running industrial-scale quantities out of here.

But Hank Kammler here, in such a remote and lawless outpost? Or Ruth? To Jaeger that just didn't add up. Plus what reason would El Padre possibly have for dabbling in uranium trafficking? That was a whole different level of bad than narcotics.

Smuggling cocaine was one thing. Smuggling the raw material for a nuclear weapon – that was inviting a world of unwanted attention and trouble. If El Padre was messing with highly en-riched uranium, the powers-that-be would have every excuse to flatten this place.

With the amount of cash that was obviously being spun out of the drugs trade, why would anyone take the risk? It was tan-tamount to suicide. Any way Jaeger looked at it, it didn't make sense.

They inched backwards into the tree cover.

'Well, the nav's been spot-on,' Raff rumbled, 'but buggered if the place isn't massive.'

'Yeah. A major facility, with several hundred men needed to run and guard it.'

'Plus the wife and kids.'

Raff was right: Jaeger hadn't missed the smaller figures dashing about the dirt streets. Many of the narco workers had brought their families. And as both men were well aware, that complicated matters: neither of them was keen to get into a fight that risked women and children getting caught in the crossfire.

Jaeger glanced around at their ridgetop location. 'Positions? Defences?'

'Keep two on permanent watch, looking west with eyes on. And the others in the rear, resting. The ridge's northern wall falls away almost vertical, so no one's about to take us from there. East is the slope we just climbed: no one's coming up that without us knowing it. South the ridge rolls on for a good few kilometres. That's the main threat.'

Jaeger nodded. 'Agreed. Let's go.'

As silently and swiftly as they could, they dropped down. The last of the light was fading to deep shadow by the time they reached the foot of the descent. Jaeger gave a quick heads-up before they all heaved up their bergens and began the climb.

It soon became clear that Narov was having real problems. She was moving slowly, and twice she took a fall, once collapsing against a tree and the next time plunging face forward, awkwardly catching her side on a rock.

Finally, wordlessly, Jaeger managed to prise away her assault rifle and pass it to Alonzo, whilst he and Raff each took one of her arms and more or less propelled her up the steep slope.

Narov hated accepting the help and didn't offer the slightest word of thanks, despite the fact that it was almost dark by the time they reached the top. Another few minutes on the slope and she would have been trapped there in pitch darkness.

They crawled across to the point that Jaeger and Raff had

selected as their base of operations – their observation post, or OP. Jaeger gave Narov and Alonzo a quick brief about their position, plus the orientation of the narco gang's base.

'I'm setting an ERV seven hundred metres due east, so at the base of the slope we just climbed,' he explained. 'If we're hit, or split up, that's where we regroup.' ERV stood for emergency rendezvous point, which pretty much did what it said on the tin.

That decided, Jaeger went about making contact with their Falkenhagen headquarters. He pulled out a compact military-spec Thuraya satphone and punched in a short message: *In position. Grid 183746. Nothing further. Out.*

Using an inbuilt cipher programme, he encoded the message, sending it in data burst, which basically meant it was compressed to a tiny fraction of its size, taking barely a split second to bounce to the satellite orbiting high overhead, and from there to where Peter Miles would be listening.

Jaeger lived by the mantra that presumption was the mother of all screw-ups. If they presumed El Padre had no monitoring and direction-finding kit in place, they would likely die by that presumption. The gang's boss was running a multi-billion-dollar narco business, and he could afford to hire the best. Hence the precautions.

Message sent, they set the first watch rota. Jaeger and Raff would take up position at the vantage point, while Narov and Alonzo got their heads down. Much as she tried to hide it, it was clear that Narov was beat. By contrast, the hard-as-nails African American still looked relatively fresh.

That was Alonzo: unbreakable. He would keep a watch over Narov while she rested.

As Jaeger crawled forward, he reflected upon Narov's condition. He'd never known her anything other than indestructible. He was getting a sense now of what the Dubai mission, plus her subsequent escape, must have taken out of her.

There was no doubt she'd suffered to prove her conviction

that Kammler was alive and plotting mayhem and mass murder. And it was her balls and brass that had brought them here to uncover the dark truth and put a stop to him.

Quite a woman, Jaeger thought.

31

With darkness, Dodge truly came alive.

The throbbing beat of generators reached Jaeger and Raff clearly, as DIY street lighting sparked into life. Bare bulbs were strung from wiring looped along the dirt roads on make-shift telegraph poles. And with nightfall the narcos appeared to love nothing more than parading their weaponry.

As the ridge was shrouded in shadow, Jaeger and Raff didn't need to worry too much about being spotted. There was no need to use night-vision goggles either. They could scan the well-lit streets with bog-standard binoculars.

They counted the individuals as they moved about, and ID'd their hardware. The gang was remarkably well armed. Apart from the ubiquitous AK-47 assault rifles, Jaeger noted rocket-propelled grenade launchers, scores of M60 light machine guns, and even the odd .50-calibre heavy machine gun mounted in the rear of a pickup truck.

In short, a ready-made war in a box.

But it wasn't until approaching midnight that things really started to get interesting. Horribly distorted Latino-style music started pulsating out of speakers set around the central cross-roads. More and more figures gathered in that area, nearly all of them male. They were drawn to a couple of neon-lit buildings – Dodge City's main drinking dens. Every so often a pickup would arrive, disgorging more figures. Occasionally a scantily clad woman would emerge from a bar and drag one of the men inside.

It didn't take a genius to work out that these had to be ladies of the night.

Shortly after midnight, the shit truly hit the fan. A group of men came tumbling out of a doorway and a massive brawl ensued. It culminated in several of them drawing their sidearms and loosing off wild shots. The chaos only subsided when a couple of trucks arrived, complete with some seriously tooled-up narcos.

The fight was broken up, some of the worst offenders relieved of their weapons and sent on their way. No one had been shot, and despite the obvious lawlessness of the place, there seemed to be a means of keeping order. Clearly El Padre would tolerate a degree of high spirits, but nothing that would endanger his operations.

At 0100 hours, Jaeger signalled that he was heading for the rear position. His five-hour watch was done. They'd stagger the changeover so that there was always one set of eyes on Dodge. Raff would be relieved in turn by Narov.

'Change of shift,' Jaeger whispered to Alonzo. 'Raff'll brief you *in situ.*'

Feeling exhaustion creeping up on him, he curled up on the waterproof poncho that Alonzo vacated. He dragged his lightweight sleeping bag out of his pack, zipped it open to act like a blanket, and got his head down. He was fully clothed and still wearing his boots, and his weapon was cradled at his side. That way, if they were hit during the night, he was good to move and fight.

He sensed the scores of mosquitoes homing in on his position. They began to dive-bomb him, their incessant whining drilling into his head. He flailed around groggily, found his mozzie head-net and pulled it on, bagging it out around his face like a beekeeper's helmet.

Then he lay back and drifted into a deep sleep.

He awoke sometime later with a start.

He sat bolt upright, his hand on his weapon.

Gunfire cut the night; that was what had woken him. This time, though, it wasn't pistol shots. It was the distinctive crack of 'longs' – assault rifles.

He glanced across at Raff, who was equally wide awake. 'What the hell?'

Raff shrugged and glanced in Alonzo and Narov's direction. 'If it was aimed at us, they'd be here by now to warn us.'

'High spirits in Dodge?'

'Sounds like it's party-bloody-city.' Raff gave Jaeger a hard look. 'Hardly strikes me as the kind of place where Kammler's gonna build his INDs.'

'Don't I know it.'

'Plus there's no visible sign of him or his people.'

'There isn't.' Jaeger paused. 'You know what, mate, there's only one way to prove this. We've got to do a CTR.'

CTR: close-target recce. SAS speak for getting spitting-distance close to the enemy.

'We execute a CTR,' Jaeger continued. 'If we find Kammler or his people, we move in with the demolitions charges and blow the place to shit.'

Raff nodded. 'Agreed. But that's one for you and your Russian lady friend. You'll enjoy it. Plus you two hide better than Alonzo and me.'

'Makes sense. You wouldn't be able to resist getting stuck into the nearest brothel or brawl.'

'My kind of town.' Raff smiled, his teeth showing white in the darkness. 'You clock those ditches? Running from the edge of the clearing right into the heart of the place?'

'Yeah. Why?'

'Figure they're a solid route in.'

'What d'you reckon to them? Defensive?'

'Nah. Drainage more likely.'

Jaeger shuddered. 'Great. Another midnight crawl through a sodden jungle shit pit . . .'

He settled back to rest. Tomorrow promised to be a long day.

32

It was late afternoon on their second day when Jaeger and his team withdrew from the ridge, descended the slope at the rear and set out due north. They'd kept a close watch on Dodge all through the hours of daylight, but there had been zero sign of Kammler or his cohorts, which made the CTR a real priority.

They looped around their former hilltop position until they were barely 250 metres short of Dodge. There they cached their bergens, covering them in thick vegetation, at a point they could easily find their way back to. Each prepared a separate day sack stuffed full of the bare necessities – medical pack, twenty-four hours' rations, batteries, spare ammo – which they could grab and go if compromised.

That done, Jaeger and Narov set about ensuring that any exposed skin was streaked with mud and dirt, to break up the human form. Once they had finished the DIY camo, they stood nose-to-toe, scrutinising each other minutely. She was barely an inch shorter than him, and it was easy enough to check for any exposed skin that might have been missed. As he did so, Jaeger found himself catching her gaze.

Narov's ice-blue eyes betrayed not the slightest hint of emotion: not excitement, not trepidation and certainly not fear. They were about to step into the heart of the narco gang's territory, and capture would lead to a whole world of horror and pain.

In fact, it would be much better not to allow yourself to get captured. Better to save a final bullet for yourself.

But Narov appeared to be not the slightest bit fazed.

If he hadn't known her better, Jaeger would have worried that she was in shock or denial. But he'd seen her like this before: suffused with an empty-seeming calm. It made you wonder if anyone was at home. And then, in an instant, she'd transform into a lightning-fast killer, as if some switch had been flicked inside her head.

It was weird. But that was Narov. And Raff was right: on a CTR, she made for perfect company.

They did a final check of their kit, making certain nothing would clatter or clunk as they moved about. Anything that threatened to make the slightest noise was coated in layers of khaki gaffer tape, deadening it.

When they were done, they could move silently as panthers.

Finally they settled upon some comms-under-duress key words. If either was captured and forced to make contact, they needed some seemingly normal phrase to insert into their messages. Otherwise, with a gun held to their heads, they could be forced to call for a rescue helo, luring it straight into a trap.

Key words sorted, and with the evening shadows lengthening, Jaeger gave the signal to move out. All knew the plan. As far as possible, the CTR would be done silently, without a word being spoken and using hand signals only.

Silent as ghosts, the four flitted through the trees. They reached a point set a hundred metres back from the fringes of Dodge – the drop-off point for Raff, who would be acting as their backstop.

As they crept closer to the clearing, Jaeger rolled out a length of paracord. This was their insurance policy: he and Narov could trace it back to Raff's position, moving in utter silence and darkness.

The sights and sounds of the narco base were beginning to bleed through now: slivers of light, the put-put of generators, plus the odd burst of Latino beat blaring distortedly through the trees.

Alonzo took up position just inside the cover of the ragged

fringe of jungle. He was here for two reasons. First, to provide fire support if it all went noisy. And second, to act as a marker to guide Narov and Jaeger back to their entry/exit point, from where they could trace the paracord back to Raff and their route to safety.

Jaeger moved ahead in a low crouch, Narov following some five feet behind him. They crept a yard or two into the open and went down on one knee, utterly motionless. They needed to allow their eyes to adjust to the change in light: from the dark of the jungle, they were now at the outer limits of Dodge City's makeshift street lighting.

Before them stretched a patch of rough ground, littered with burnt tree stumps and waist-high bushes. Heaps of recently cut vegetation lay drying in the sun, ready for burning. From long experience, Jaeger knew that regular clearance and fire were the only ways to keep the jungle at bay.

Eyes adjusted, he turned left and crept along the fringe of vegetation, counting his left footfalls. After a minute or so, he found what he was looking for. He went down on one knee again, Narov doing likewise at his shoulder.

He nodded at a massive skeletal tree just to his left, glowing silver in the moonlight. It was strung with vines thick as a man's thigh. 'Okay, that's our datum point.'

'Got it. A hundred and forty paces.'

'One forty,' Jaeger confirmed. 'We get here, it's a hundred and forty paces north to Alonzo.'

Fixing the datum point was crucial. Alonzo was a dark figure crouched amidst a fringe of trees. They'd never find him without an instantly recognisable feature that would lead them back to his exact location.

From the skeletal tree, Jaeger set off due south, towards the point where the drainage ditches should intersect with the fringes of the forest, the lights of Dodge throwing an eerie halo into the dark sky.

Sound drifted across to them. A burst of raucous laughter.

Someone singing. The howl of a scooter burning down the nearest dirt track.

Jaeger could feel the tension gripping him as they pushed into more open terrain. The adrenalin was pumping. His senses were incredibly heightened.

A part of him loved it, as he sensed the danger crackling back and forth between the shadows. But he had no illusions as to what he and Narov were heading into.

The two of them were pitting themselves against several hundred of El Padre's gunmen. An anarchic drugs mafia in a land of chaotic lawlessness.

As enemies went, it didn't get much worse.

33

Ending up dead would be far better than being captured, Jaeger reflected. Although getting out alive and returning to Luke and Simon would be infinitely preferable. If Jaeger was taken alive, they'd torture him, body and soul, until he would be begging for his own death.

As for Narov . . .

Jaeger realised he felt strangely protective towards her. He could not let harm come to this extraordinary yet infuriating woman. In spite of everything, there was something bewitching about her; something that brought out in him the desire to break through her ice-cool shell.

A thought struck him, as horrific as it was dark. If Narov was about to get captured, would he shoot her himself? He just didn't know. All he could do was live the mission with one hundred per cent focus.

Finding this shitty drainage ditch was crucial.

By rights, it should lie just a few feet in front of them. Jaeger went down on one knee, turning to Narov. Their eyes met across the darkness. They didn't need to speak. Her expression echoed what he felt. *This is hellish, but it's what we came here for. Just do it.*

They turned to face Dodge Central, settling down to observe. Being watchful was everything. They squatted shoulder to shoulder, rock still and utterly focused.

Jaeger's legs and back were soaked with perspiration, but worse were the mosquitoes. He was being eaten alive. There was nothing he could do about that. Sudden movement would be a dead giveaway. Swatting at a cloud of buzzing, biting insects was likely to invite a hail of bullets.

'Two o'clock,' Narov hissed. 'Car. Hazards on.'

'Seen.'

Hammering down the main drag was a pickup truck, lights blaring. It had to mean something. But what? Was that code to get the narco gunmen on standby when a hostile force had been spotted? Or was the driver signalling that more bales of cocaine were needed at the airstrip?

No way of knowing.

Keep watchful.

Silent.

The preep-preep of cicadas echoed deafeningly in Jaeger's ears. It provided the bass track to the heartbeat of Dodge: the pulse of the Latino dance tracks that were being pumped out with increasing gusto from the nearest of the bars.

'Eleven o'clock,' Narov hissed. 'Airstrip. Movement.'

Jaeger swung his eyes around. Sure enough, a group of males were milling about on one side of the dirt strip. He counted around three dozen, all armed. Question was, what were they there for? To usher in a narco flight, or to mount up the gun trucks and come racing after Jaeger and his team?

He couldn't believe that they'd been detected, but it was crucial to be ready. *Fail to prepare, prepare to fail.*

Jaeger signalled to Narov that they should move. In a low crouch, and hugging the earth, he turned north, creeping towards the dark heart of Dodge. The nearest buildings were no more than fifty feet away. His every sense was projected forward, focused on the potential threat.

As a result, he almost tumbled into the ditch.

He regained his balance at the last moment, then tentatively eased his leading foot forward, advancing with the slow, calculated movements of a predator. Ahead of him yawned a dark pit maybe five feet wide. He flicked his eyes down its length: it stretched dead straight right into the heart of Dodge.

As Raff had suggested, perfect cover for executing a CTR.

Two things struck Jaeger. First, the smell. He twitched his nostrils: something distinctly chemical, mixed with the rank scent of stagnant water and human faeces. Second, the lack of any noticeable reflection. A patch of still water normally mirrored the moon, stars or street lighting. Here, there was nothing. The ditch had to be coated in a thick scum.

Jaeger pulled out a scarf made of a light khaki cotton, brought with him for this very purpose. On an Afghan mission in 2001, his SAS squadron had been tasked to snatch an HVT – high-value target – from a heavily defended compound. A veritable fortress.

They'd needed a way in that would take the defenders by utter surprise. As a captain commanding D Squadron's mountain troop, Jaeger had chosen what he deemed was the best option: a sewer of sorts; an open ditch that ran beneath one of the walls, emptying into a river. The lads hadn't thanked him for that one.

Before entering, they had wrapped their faces in shemags; traditional Arab headscarves. It had helped filter out the stench. He and Narov did the same now. When they were done, only their eyes showed above the swathe of cloth.

Without a word, Jaeger turned, placed his hands on the side of the ditch and lowered himself in.

34

The crawl through the ditch had been grim, even by Jaeger's standards.

For the most part he'd been fighting back the gag reflex, as unidentified *things* bobbed and hissed on the rank surface. There was one upside: this place had to be so toxic that nothing else would surely venture into its putrid depths.

Jaeger dreaded to think what prolonged immersion was doing to him and Narov. They were probably going to grow an extra head. But there had been no other way.

He figured the ditch served a dual purpose: it was Dodge City's main sewer and drain, plus the coca refineries dumped their used chemicals here. Though it was largely stagnant, he figured there had to be a net outflow at the far end, where the toxic crap drained into the jungle.

But right now his senses were focused very much elsewhere.

Inch by inch he raised his head towards the lip of the ditch. The noise here was deafening: to his right, the bars were cranking out the Latino beat. He could feel the sound waves pulsing through the shitty water.

As he slipped above the lip, he sensed Narov right beside him. Two heads emerged into the open, two sets of eyes behind gaping gun barrels. Each chose a 180-degree arc to scan.

No doubt about it: they had penetrated into the very heart of El Padre's narco fortress. All around them were the sounds, sights and smells of the place.

It had taken almost an hour to reach this point; it was approaching midnight, and Dodge was busy. Loud drunken laughter rang across the water. Crowds surged back and forth from bar to bar. Neon signs flashed their gaudy glare. Engines revved and horns blared as a pickup forced its way through.

Jaeger and Narov kept up a whispered commentary to each other.

'Warehouse, nine o'clock, one hundred yards,' Narov noted. To her left lay one of the massive buildings they figured were the cocaine refineries. 'I see a gun truck pulling up. Six guys in the rear.'

'Weapons?'

'Longs. All of them.'

Jaeger swivelled his eyes around his 180-degree arc. Where the hell should he start? Narov had the easy bit: she was checking south, over the warehouse district and airstrip. He was gazing north, into Dodge's chaotic drink- and drug-fuelled heart of darkness.

The nearest bar was maybe thirty yards away. It was made of galvanised iron, and Jaeger could see where a set of speakers were bolted to the roof, belting out the party beat. The neon beer-bottle sign pulsed with the throb of a generator, the strength of the current matching the thud of the engine.

Out front, a crowd swayed to the music. It was almost exclusively male, and all were clutching beer bottles; most also sported a sidearm. From the steps, a woman in a very short skirt yelled taunts at them. Jaeger figured she was trying to drum up custom.

He was about to start relating all of this to Narov when a series of shots rang out. Jaeger forced his head into the dirt, his mind processing the sound: low-velocity rounds, 9mm for sure. Pistol shots. Which more than likely spelled trouble at the bar. Sure enough, a series of hollow thuds and angry yells rang out as the narcos started beating the crap out of each other.

Jaeger raised his head again and eyed the scene. 'Bar brawl. Four o'clock. I figured you got that. Plus I got a pickup incoming, with what look like enforcers. I got—'

More gunshots. Jaeger hit the dirt again and froze, face scrunched into the mud. Those had been high-velocity rounds from an assault rifle. Most likely an AK-47. They'd sounded up close and personal. The only thing he could do now was keep utterly still, and use his sense of hearing to try to work out what the hell was going on.

Yelled orders drifted across from the direction of the bar, punctuated by the crunch of rifle butts on human flesh. From the sound of things, the brawling had come to an abrupt halt.

Jaeger raised his head a little, using the back of his hand to wipe the gunk from his eyes.

Absence of the normal, he reminded himself. There was nothing he could see that wasn't symptomatic of a normal night in Dodge, which was a huge relief. It meant that their presence here was unlikely to have been detected.

He glanced at Narov. 'Warning shots?'

'Got to be.'

Dodge's enforcers had seemingly broken up the brawl. They'd been on it in record time. Jaeger figured El Padre wasn't going to put up with any kind of serious ruckus, which maybe meant that there was important business being done tonight.

Narov resumed her commentary, as the gunmen in the pickup dismounted at the warehouse and others took their place. Two took up position at the building's massive sliding door, which was open just a crack, light bleeding out. The others dispersed inside. It was a change of sentries.

Further to Narov's left, figures were still busy on the airstrip. Dodge seemed to be split into two categories of activity. On one side, off-duty narco workers getting in some serious partying.

On the other, on-duty workers engaged with the core business of refining and trafficking drugs.

There was a businesslike feel to the warehouse side of town; a sense of dark purpose.

As if to confirm this, the airstrip itself suddenly flared into life. Shadowy figures darted up and down its length, lighting a series of beacons, metal baskets stuffed with paraffin-soaked rags. Put a light to the rags, and hey presto, you had crude runway lighting.

Moments after the flares had been lit, an aircraft put in an appearance. The Latino beat that washed over the ditch was so loud that Jaeger and Narov barely heard it, before the shadowy form swept across at low level and bumped down onto the dirt.

The light aircraft – a Twin Otter by the looks of things – taxied to a standstill at the warehouse. Figures gathered at its cargo hatches, unloading sacks of what had to be raw coca paste, and loading up bales of white from the warehouse in turn.

The entire operation took maybe ten minutes. It was smooth and well practised. But when they were almost done, one of the men dropped a bag of refined cocaine, which split open, spilling its contents across the dirt. As the hapless worker went to try to scoop it up, a voice started yelling maniacally and a figure strode out of the shadows, machete clutched in his hand, a small entourage of bodyguards with him. With barely a pause, he brought the cruel blade down hard. The man who'd dropped the cocaine let out a bloodcurdling scream and keeled over, wailing pitifully. The man who had struck him didn't let up. Instead, he started to put the boot in.

Jaeger watched with a growing sense of unease. 'El Padre,' he whispered to Narov. 'Like the briefings said, he's one evil fucker.'

Moments later, the Twin Otter taxied to the end of the runway and took to the skies again, banking hard. Even as the shadowy silhouette disappeared over the jungle, the DIY runway lighting was being doused.

Slick. This was the business side of Dodge.

And here, cocaine was serious business.

35

One thing had surprised Jaeger. No one had seemed to bother to check either that the coca paste being unloaded from the aircraft was genuine coca, or that the cocaine being loaded aboard was genuine cocaine. But then why would they? If whoever supplied El Padre had tricked him, they wouldn't get to live for long.

That was how the system worked. Billionaire narco barons had a long reach. It was a system based not upon mutual trust, but upon mutual fear. If you messed up, you died. And probably most of your loved ones as well. Men like El Padre had been known to wipe out entire families – infants and babies included – to drive their message home.

Dodge City was a Class A narco operation, that was for sure. But as to Kammler and his IND team being here? Jaeger hadn't seen the slightest sign that this was the place where his arch-enemy was going to mastermind his dark machinations.

There was only one way to know for sure, and that was to get closer. Jaeger's eyes met Narov's across the surface of the stinking water.

'We need a close-up look at the warehouse,' he whispered. 'To be certain.'

Narov nodded. 'I will go.'

Jaeger was about to object, but her look silenced him. They'd found themselves in a similar position a while ago in Africa. They'd needed to get inside an elephant poachers' camp. Not easy. Narov had argued that she should go because she could move more stealthily. The same argument held true now.

She handed him her assault rifle. 'Cover me.'

With that, she grabbed some of the stinking gunk from the edge of the ditch, smeared it over her face and hands as an extra layer of camouflage, wormed her way over the lip and was gone. Swallowed into the darkness.

As best he could, Jaeger traced her movements with his weapon. She was far from easy to follow. Repeatedly he lost track of her as she flitted to and fro, silent as a wraith. Finally he glimpsed a darker patch of shadow flattened against the wall of the nearest warehouse, a hundred yards away.

For the briefest of moments Narov's head was silhouetted against the oblong of light that bled out of the building. Jaeger could envisage her eyes making a rapid sweep of the warehouse's interior. Just as quickly, she ducked down again.

He lost sight of her completely now. She was moving almost due west, sticking to the thick scrub that fringed the dirt airstrip. That would take her to the second warehouse, a couple of hundred yards away.

For a moment he wondered what he would do if he saw her surrounded or captured.

Go in solo, all guns blazing?

What other choice was there?

Either way, it would be a suicide mission.

He kept his eyes glued to that distant building, squat and dark against the moonlit sky. He figured he saw movement: a silhouette working its way along the nearside wall. Narov – had to be. He saw the flash of a head at the window. *Good girl: almost done.*

But then his grip on his weapon tightened. Narov had levered open the window, and moments later, she'd slipped inside. As Jaeger waited with bated breath for her to emerge, he spotted a figure heading around to her side of the building. The guy was moving with the bored gait of someone coming to the end of yet another long night's watch.

Jaeger tracked him with his gun sights. If he were forced to open fire, their cover would be blown. He had to hold off doing so until all other options were exhausted. Out of the corner of his eye he saw Narov slip back out through the window. Maybe the guard would fail to spot her.

She melted into the shadows and Jaeger lost track of her.

Suddenly a lithe form rose behind the sentry and an arm whipped around his neck, choking off all possibility of a cry. The other arm came around, driving a blade downwards behind the sentry's clavicle and clean into his heart.

Jaeger knew the move well. The victim would be dead within seconds. He watched as Narov lowered the body to the ground, before dragging it into the undergrowth.

A couple of minutes later she was back, slipping into the ditch like a bloodied eel. The sentry had bled profusely, that much was clear.

'We need to go,' she mouthed.

Jaeger nodded. Time was running out. Plus there was that dead sentry now to factor into the equation. If his body was discovered before Narov and Jaeger made the cover of the jungle, all hell would break loose.

Narov eyed him for an instant, then reached into her backpack. 'There was this,' she volunteered, holding up a brown leather-backed ledger. On the front cover was scribbled in Spanish: *Registro de Vuelo*. It was Los Niños's flight log.

Jaeger shook his head in amazement. 'Bloody brilliant. Right, let's get the hell out of here.'

He turned to go back the way they'd come, lowering his head down to the stinking water and pushing off, Diemaco held at the ready.

Most CTRs went wrong when those executing them rushed the withdrawal.

As he began his slow and steady crawl, Jaeger wondered for an instant if Narov felt anything for the man she'd just killed. There was little sign if she did. It was typical: when she had to kill, she did so seemingly without hesitation or remorse.

Another thought struck him. He'd realised with a shock what all of them had perhaps been missing. The best way to bust Kammler's network was staring them right in the face, here in Dodge.

In a sense, it had been all along, but it had taken this crawl through this hellish shithole for him to realise it. He'd share his thoughts with Narov and the others, but only once they'd got the hell out of Dodge.

And much as he hated it, they still had a good twenty minutes of crawling ahead of them.

Shit happens, he thought to himself wryly. But he would have his moment.

And this mission – it was only just beginning.

36

The trek out to the LZ had taken considerably less time than the journey in. They'd stopped at one of the first rivers they came across, so that Jaeger and Narov could scrub themselves clean of the blood and the stinking gunk from the ditch. But otherwise they'd moved relatively swiftly. They were carrying lighter loads and they were more attuned to the jungle.

They were also buoyed by the success of the CTR. To have penetrated right into the heart of such an operation and got out again undetected and unscathed – that had taken some skill, and balls.

If Narov's handiwork with the knife had been discovered, there had been no sign of it while they were exfiltrating from Dodge.

They'd arrived at the clearing with a good sixty minutes to spare before the chopper arrived to pluck them out. They settled in some cover, Narov pulling out the flight log from her pack. She flicked through the pages, stopping here and there at key entries. Much that Jaeger marvelled at her focus after such an exhausting mission, he was impatient to know what Los Niños's flight log might reveal.

'So, what's it tell us?' he pressed.

Narov glanced up at him. 'I need to go over it in more detail. But two things jump out. One, the Moldovan flight doesn't end in Dodge. It's a refuelling stopover, no more. Where it's headed after that isn't entirely clear.'

'So the hunt for Kammler is far from over.' It was obvious, but Jaeger felt it needed saying.

'Exactly,' Narov confirmed. 'And second, it looks as if three previous flights have been routed via Dodge, all at the orders of Kammler. If they were loaded with uranium, Kammler is even further ahead of the game than we feared.'

'Good work, you gettin' that,' Alonzo cut in. 'Game changer. Freakin' game changer. Worries me shitless, though . . .'

In truth, the flight log had them all worried. The revelation of those three previous flights lent an added sense of urgency to their mission. It was a ticking time bomb. But it had triggered something else – building on the flash of inspiration Jaeger first had as they'd crawled out of Dodge. He had a growing sense as to how they might use all this against Kammler, to nail him. He set about explaining it to the others.

'So, it's a part of SAS folklore. Beirut, 1976. The SAS were on a covert mission. There's a great book about it I read once. Figured we could use something similar now.'

Narov looked askance at him. 'You? Read a book?'

'A book?' Raff echoed.

'Yeah, a book,' Jaeger confirmed. 'Don't sound so surprised.'

Raff shook his head in disgust. 'Bloody Ruperts and their books.'

Alonzo grinned. While he didn't completely get the British sense of humour, he couldn't help but find it funny. As long as it wasn't directed at him.

'So what did this book say?' Narov challenged. 'And what makes it relevant now?'

'The book's called *Cobra Gold*. SAS troop gets sent into Beirut to lift some sensitive documents from a bank vault. Lebanon's one massive war zone – Beirut's been shot to shreds. The SAS blow their way into the vault, but along with the documents, they discover a shedload of gold bullion.'

Jaeger could tell he had their attention now. The SAS and an epic bank robbery – what was not to like?

153

'They figured they'd nab the gold along with the documents. A bit of freelance larceny. We know that the robbery took place. Fact. It's recorded in the *Guinness Book of Records*: British Bank of the Middle East; the world's biggest ever bullion robbery – some $150 million at today's value.'

'So what?' Raff challenged. 'Every chancer and their dog has a story about the Regiment and its supposed dark arts. I just wish they were all true.' He paused. 'In fact, I wish I'd been in on the act.'

Jaeger laughed. 'During the exfil, they were forced to cache the gold. It was ten years until they came back to retrieve it. Trouble was, they knew that as soon as they set foot in Lebanon, the bad guys – the terrorists – would be onto them. They realised they needed a decoy. A Trojan horse.'

'So where did they hide it – the gold?' Raff queried.

'Dumped at sea. Not that that's crucial to the story.' Jaeger couldn't keep the excitement out of his voice now. 'Tungsten. You've all heard of it, right? One of the heaviest metals known to man. Used for tipping bunker-busting bombs and such like. It also happens to be more or less the same molecular weight as gold.'

Raff kicked the bottom of Jaeger's boot. 'Get to it.'

'They built a decoy. A pile of tungsten machined into bars and plated in gold. It looked like bullion. It weighed practically the same. It even smelled right. They allowed the terrorists to seize the decoy and take it right into the heart of their camp. That golden decoy contained a hidden charge of explosives. When it reached the bad guys' base, someone pressed a button and . . . *kaboom*. The tungsten went up a like a massive nail bomb and flattened everything.'

'Nice story,' Narov grated icily. 'But what's its relevance now?'

Jaeger eyed her. 'Highly enriched uranium is the heaviest naturally occurring element. It has a very similar molecular weight to gold. Or tungsten, for that matter . . . So here's the plan: *we switch cargoes*. We swap the uranium for a lookalike tungsten cargo. One with a massive charge set at its centre and primed to blow.'

Narov shook her head despairingly. 'This is your great idea? This is why you told us this bullshit story? *Schwachkopf*.'

'And? What exactly is your problem?'

'First, how do you switch the cargoes when the uranium is being flown here by the Moldovan mafia in an aircraft operated by Eastern European arms dealers?'

'And second?'

'What is the point? We don't believe that Dodge is the final destination for the shipment, especially not after getting this.' Narov brandished the flight log. 'Dodge is a narco operation through and through. The CTR proved that. So how does destroying it help get us to Kammler? Yours' is the plan of an idiot.'

'Second answer first,' Jaeger volunteered. He was used to Narov's outbursts. Mostly they were neither personal nor meant with ill intent. 'The decoy shipment is fitted with a tracking device. You don't blow it upon arrival at Dodge. You follow it, and it leads us to Kammler.'

'But the switch?' Narov challenged. 'How on earth is that possible?'

By way of answer, Jaeger turned to Alonzo. 'You ever served on any DEA missions?'

Alonzo shook his head. 'DEA? Bunch of cowboys. Generally we steered well clear of 'em.'

'I guess we didn't have that luxury.' Jaeger paused. 'A few years back, I was on a DEA sting. Texas. The boondocks. A bunch of narcos were bringing in a drugs flight to a tiny bush airstrip. That part of Texas, every farm seems to have one.'

'You got it,' Alonzo confirmed. 'That, plus a Lone Star flag, and a barn stuffed full of baked beans and assault rifles.'

'Pretty much. Anyhow, the DEA got wise to the shipment. The night of the flight, they jammed the narcos' radio frequency, plus the beacons the aircraft was to home in on. They fired up

155

their own radio on a slightly different frequency, on an airstrip not so far away. The incoming pilot lost contact with the narcos. He began scanning the airwaves. He found the DEA's signal, and the DEA – posing as narcos – began to talk him in.'

Jaeger eyed his audience. He wondered if they could see what was coming. 'The pilot flew in to the DEA's airstrip and landed. They seized him, his crew, the aircraft, plus several hundred million dollars' worth of the purest cocaine. The op was code-named Angeldust. It went down in the annals of DEA history.'

'And so?' Narov challenged. 'We don't want to seize this shipment. You said so yourself – we want it to lead us to Kammler.'

'Okay, so we think laterally,' Jaeger suggested. 'Imagine we do the same with the flight from Moldova. You saw Colonel Evandro's strip at Station 15. At night, under floodlights, there's nothing much to mark it out as military, or to distinguish it from Dodge. The colonel likes to keep it that way: low-profile, low-key.

'We lure the flight in to Station 15,' he continued. 'It's just across the border, so with guidance from a friendly radio operator, we reel the pilot in. Acting like narcos, Colonel Evandro's men unload the cargo. They roll it into one of the hangars. Then they let the pilot know there must be some kind of mistake. They were expecting bales of raw coca paste. Instead, they've got a heap of insanely heavy metal.

'They roll the shipment out to the aircraft again and load up – only they've made the switch. The pilot and his aircrew are a bunch of Russians who just want in and out without getting kidnapped and boiled alive. The Russian pilot believes he's at the wrong strip. If El Padre finds out, he's a dead man. The "narcos" advise him to take to the skies, and make hell-for-leather for Dodge.

'Plane takes off. We've already unjammed El Padre's radio frequency. Mr Very Scared Russian Pilot flies onwards to Dodge. He's not going to breathe a word about what's happened, for obvious reasons. He tells some bullshit story about losing their signal and flying a holding pattern – hence the delay. Switch done. No one any the wiser.'

Jaeger gazed at the others, eyes burning with excitement. 'Our version of Operation Angeldust – done 'n' dusted.'

37

'GPS. What about his GPS?' Narov ventured an objection. 'The pilot would know he was being lured to the wrong strip.'

'Easy,' Alonzo interjected. 'The US military has made sure that pretty much any civilian GPS system can be disabled. Reason being, if a rogue state or terrorist outfit fits a nuclear missile with such a guidance system, we need to be able to stop it. So we disable the aircraft's GPS.'

'Any other objections?' Jaeger queried. 'And quick, 'cause the helo's inbound.'

'What the fuck made you think of it?' Raff queried. 'I mean, Jesus – it's genius.'

'That's a question, not a material objection to the plan.' Jaeger grinned, his teeth shining white from his mud-splattered features.

Raff snorted. 'All right, what about this. You seem to know an awful lot about that Lebanon gold. If we ever get out of this shit storm, I want to hear how we can get our hands on some of it!'

Jaeger laughed. 'You got it.'

'But will Colonel Evandro even agree to the plan?' Alonzo queried. 'I mean, that's one out-there kind of an idea.'

'Agree?' Jaeger countered. 'You don't know the colonel. He'll bite our arms off.' He flashed another of his wolfish smiles. 'He wants Kammler as badly as anyone. Plus his BSOB lads – they're good. They're as capable of pulling this off as anyone.'

'Who builds the decoy? And gets it in country?' It was Alonzo again. 'Plus in the time available? That's a pile of tungsten, machined into blocks and disguised as uranium, with a freakin' great Semtex charge at its core . . .'

'Daniel Brooks,' Jaeger answered. 'He's the director of the world's foremost intelligence agency. He's got the ear of the US president. He sent us in here on the QT. Brooks sorts the decoy and its means of delivery. It's well within his capabilities.'

'I guess.' Alonzo nodded. 'If anyone can, he can.' He paused. 'But what if we've got it wrong? What if Kammler is in Dodge and gets wise to the switch?'

'If Kammler's in Dodge, I'm a bloody monkey,' Raff growled. 'That place is a hellhole. No way is he there building his INDs.'

Everyone was quiet for a moment.

It was Narov who broke the silence. 'I am no expert, but as I understand it, refined tungsten ore and highly enriched uranium are both extremely heavy grey metals. I doubt if you can tell them apart, not unless you do some serious technical testing. Plus, it would need to be shielded with lead to stop radiation from leaking. Kammler's people are hardly going to dismantle a lead shield to check on the shipment, and all in the midst of Dodge.'

Silence. Jaeger could hear the faint beat of rotor blades cutting through the air.

A Super Puma, inbound.

'There's one other reason no one will check the shipment,' he volunteered. 'Because that's not how it works. No one checked the coca paste and cocaine handover. Why? Because if anyone pulls a fast one, they die. There's no trust, but there's bucketloads of fear. With the kind of reach El Padre has, if the uranium's not uranium, the Moldovan mafiosa leader takes a bullet.'

Nods all around.

'Guys, trust me, it's doable,' he continued. 'Imagine it: we get Kammler to embrace the engine of his own destruction—'

'Helo inbound,' Raff interjected.

As one, the four figures shouldered their bergens and headed for their cab ride out of the jungle . . .

And into the coming storm.

38

Professor Pak Won Kangjon picked up the chopsticks that lay next to his computer. A fly had buzzed past the screen. It was warm in the lab, and the professor needed to kill a few minutes before Mr Kammler arrived and the proverbial shit hit the fan.

He snapped the chopsticks in midair as the fly zoomed past, trying to catch it and crush it. An old Chinese proverb said: *Man who catch fly with chopsticks, he can do anything*. Professor Pak Won Kangjon could do with that kind of a lucky break right now. He snapped the sticks again nervously.

He wondered what malignant alignment of the stars had been in play the night he had been born. No one, surely, deserved the kind of luck he was having.

A refugee from the utter horror and madness that was North Korea, he'd spent what felt like a lifetime serving one nuclear madman – North Korea's Glorious Leader – only to end up working for another.

Of course, the money had been the draw. Wasn't it always? If the money was right, you could get people to do just about anything.

Usually.

At first he'd been showered with comparative riches, which had been like a miracle. Too good to turn down. And now, as the saying went, he was in too deep. Over his head and drowning, you might even say.

Building an IND: at first it had been child's play compared

161

to what he had been tasked to achieve in North Korea's nuclear programme. But then his boss had decided to change things; alter the plan in an act of self-proclaimed genius. Hubris, more like.

It had made Professor Pak Won Kangjon's job a whole lot more difficult.

Kammler had added imponderables to the plan. The professor was an expert in nuclear weaponry, not nuclear power. He'd tried to explain the difference, but his boss wasn't listening. No – it had to be his way or the highway, and Professor Kangjon had few illusions about what a dark and bloody end the highway might lead to.

It was all very well in theory, of course: hit a nuclear power station to achieve meltdown. Fine on paper. The ratchet effect. Use the power station's stocks of uranium to multiply the destructive power of the IND's blast, not to mention the radiation poisoning. Ratchet up the fear and the death factor.

Professor Kangjon had few reasons to lament the coming loss of life, incalculable though it would doubtless prove. So far as he knew, the populations being targeted were those that had mocked and emasculated his once great nation. His homeland. For at heart, the professor would always be a proud North Korean.

They'd openly laughed at his country's Glorious Leader, otherwise known as the Great Leader Comrade, the Sun of the Communist Future and the Father of the People. Tauntingly, they'd christened him 'Little Rocket Man', 'Kim Fatty the Third', or even 'Kim Fat Fat Fat'.

Well, it enraged Professor Kangjon. Those who belittled his homeland should be made to pay. They deserved to.

Why should he lift a finger to save them?

Yes, his boss's idea was clever. Very clever. In theory. In practice, it hadn't quite worked out that way, and mainly because he, Professor Kangjon, had screwed up the calculations – or at least he was pretty certain that he had.

To cause meltdown at a first-world nuclear power station, he'd presumed you'd have to overcome the same kind of safeguards – shields – as at a standard North Korean nuclear plant.

Wrong. You actually needed enough highly enriched uranium to punch through *twice* the level of protection, and that basically required twice the destructive power. So, not twenty kilos per device. Oh no. *Forty kilos.* Professor Kangjon now believed a forty-kilo charge was required to achieve meltdown at a nuclear power plant in Britain, France or the USA.

The specific reasons why were immensely complicated. Too complicated to explain to his boss. You needed a lifetime's devotion to nuclear physics just to begin to understand the kind of complex theorems that were involved. But any minute now, his boss, Mr Hank Kammler – he'd tried to use a different name, Mr Helmut Kraft, but Professor Kangjon was too smart; he'd long figured out his real identity – was going to pay a visit to his laboratory, demanding answers.

The professor wasn't looking forward to it, to put it mildly. He snapped in the air again with the chopsticks. Again he missed.

Behind him, a bank of giant 3D printers whirred away. Their steady beat was somehow reassuring. They were working to exacting digital plans inputted by Professor Kangjon, building up layer by layer the components required to smash two ten-kilo lumps of HEU against each other.

With his new calculations requiring a forty-kilo device, he'd need to alter the printer dimensions accordingly. No great drama. A little tweaking here and there, that was all.

It wasn't re-engineering the components that worried the professor. It was explaining it all to Kammler. After all, three of the twenty-kilo devices had already been dispatched, and he figured it would be next to impossible to call them back again.

He'd suffered the full blast of his employer's ire over the phone earlier, when he'd made the call to confess his mistake.

What was it going to be like up close and personal? He dreaded to think.

The door behind him opened. Professor Kangjon put down the chopsticks. He'd not caught his fly.

From the sound of the footsteps, he could tell that it was Kammler.

He spun around in his chair and got to his feet, a little unsteadily.

Kammler grinned.

Odd, that. The professor felt utterly thrown.

'No need to get up.' Kammler beamed his crocodile smile. It was taking a superhuman effort to mask his fury, but he was capable of it. Just. All necessary measures – whatever it took – to further the cause.

'Please don't unsettle yourself, Professor,' he continued, through gritted teeth. 'I need you calm and lucid to continue with your work. But just so we are clear: each device needs twice as much uranium? Am I right?'

'Exactly, Mr . . . Kraft. I am so sorry for this recalculation . . .'

Kammler waved a hand impatiently. 'These things happen at the cutting edge of science. So, if it's forty kilos per device, we will need to utilise more HEU from the stocks we're amassing. We should still have enough for the sacred eight.' He eyed the professor. 'But of course, I will need you to redouble your efforts.'

Professor Kangjon bowed stiffly – a bob of the head and shoulders. 'Naturally, Mr Kraft. I would never give less than one hundred and one per cent. Perhaps if I might move my sleeping things into the laboratory?'

Kammler nodded curtly. 'That would certainly aid the cause. Time is pressing, as always.' He glanced at his watch. 'It is the fifth of April. Twenty-five days and counting. We must not miss the scheduled completion date. Do you understand?'

Professor Kangjon bowed more deeply this time. 'Nothing will delay us, Mr Kraft, of that you have my solemn word. I will work my fingers to the bone, and the machines will run day and night to achieve this great and illustrious . . .'

But Kammler wasn't listening any more. He'd already turned and stepped towards the door. His mind was crunching the numbers. With the amount of HEU they'd amassed already and the incoming flight from Colombia, they should have enough at a stretch. But the North Korean professor would have to pay, of course. This was unforgivable, and the bastard would have to be made to suffer. Probably a job for Steve Jones. Yes, Jones. But first, let Kangjon work his fingers to the bone: fear would make him doubly diligent.

That was one of the major upsides of operating from a location such as this, Kammler reflected: scores of disaffected nuclear scientists on your doorstep. Most of them desperate for a way out and willing to work for peanuts. And most – like Professor Kangjon – nursing a bitter grudge against the world powers.

A grudge that Kammler was more than happy to harness to his own ends.

39

As Kammler stepped out of the lab's front entrance, he caught sight of an arresting scene. To one side of the building a diminutive figure had been lashed to a post. A giant of a man pivoted this way and that, administering a punishment beating.

Even from a distance Kammler could hear the distinctive crunch as a blow from a massive fist shattered bone, though the victim was tightly gagged and thus unable to scream. Kammler smiled his approval. He didn't want any cries of agony to unsettle the professor and his team. To disturb their vital work. But at the same time, he wanted the beatings carried out in public as a warning to any who might consider stepping out of line.

The facility was basically a prison camp. No one got in or out without Kammler's say-so. And for those local workers – Korean or Chinese – who did try to escape, there had to be consequences. A deterrent.

There was none better than Steve Jones.

Kammler watched as the tattooed bulk of the man danced on his feet and hammered home the blows. To Jones, violence was an art form. Brutality a religion. No beating was the same, or so it seemed to Kammler. Jones used each as a chance to experiment with another technique designed to deliver maximum pain and damage.

He was breathing hard and pouring with sweat. But what struck Kammler most was the man's obvious enjoyment of what he was doing. No doubt about it, Jones was an animal, which made him the ideal enforcer. He never seemed happier than when doing as he was now – beating the living daylights out of a woman.

Amongst the Chinese they had enslaved here were several dozen women, kept for menial cooking and cleaning duties. One of them had clearly stepped out of line. A group of local workers was being forced to watch the savage punishment. That way, Kammler was confident that word would quickly spread.

Jones came to a halt and wiped sweat from his forehead. The bound figure slumped from the post, more dead than alive. Kammler nodded his approval.

No doubt about it, Steve Jones's methods were crude but effective.

He strolled past the scene. He didn't feel the slightest sympathy for the victim or the watchers. Non-Aryans, they were subhumans as far as he was concerned. Racially and intellectually his inferiors. Fit only to be workers and slaves. The sheer audacity of any who might object or resist took his breath away.

'Well done,' he remarked, as Jones stepped back from his bloodied handiwork. 'Nothing quite like it *pour décourager les autres.*'

'What?' Jones scowled. 'That French? I don't do French. As a rule. Bunch of cheese-eating surrender monkeys in my book.'

'To discourage the others,' Kammler translated. 'I was commenting on what a fine example you've set.' He nodded in the direction of the workers, dressed in stained and ragged overalls. His lip curled. 'For them. The scum. The expendables.'

Jones shrugged. 'Plenty more where they came from. A billion of the fuckers, or so I'm told.'

Kammler gave a thin smile. Though he heartily approved of the sentiments, Jones's way of expressing himself was hardly refined. Yet what should he expect of an Englishman?

'There will be a few billion less after we're finished,' Kammler remarked. He couldn't resist the quip. 'Something to look forward to other than your next punishment beating. I have a fancy

Kangjon is going to need similar treatment fairly soon . . .'

Jones nodded darkly. 'Can't wait.'

Kammler walked on, making for his quarters. There he would have the benefit of an altogether different kind of companion from Steve Jones. One who was intellectual. Educated. Cultured. As convinced as he was that the world could only be saved if the vast majority of humankind were to be exterminated.

He strode into his study. 'My dear, I have good and bad news. Which would you prefer first?'

'The bad,' a female voice answered from an adjoining room.

'The power-station busters – they need to be forty-kilo devices to achieve our goal.'

'And the good?'

'I think we have enough raw material. In fact, I'm sure we do.'

'So where does that leave us?'

'In a nutshell, in pretty good shape. We'll need a little luck on our side, but when did good fortune ever desert the faithful, the constant, the brave?'

'So we cull the human population to something a little more sustainable?'

'We do. We remove a plague from the earth. And not a moment too soon in my book.'

'And my family? Or at least those I still care for. What about them?'

'You'll have plenty of warning, as will we all. We'll get our loved ones – the chosen – to safety.'

'I have your word on that?'

'You have my word.' Kammler paused. 'Now, Falkenhagen. Tell me again what you learnt about its defences.'

40

Colonel Evandro had been inundated with volunteers. Few had wanted to miss out on the sting. Unsurprisingly, as far as Jaeger was concerned, the colonel had been its single greatest advocate, once Jaeger had shared the proposition with him.

Station 15 had taken a little disguising. They'd run down the Brazilian flag and sloshed some paint over the few obvious military insignia, shoving the Super Pumas into a distant hangar. The colonel had also set up extra floodlights to illuminate the incoming aircraft when it taxied to a standstill on the runway. That way the pilot would be partially blinded, and less likely to notice any anomalies.

Not that Colonel Evandro figured there were any.

He'd even gone as far as getting his BSOB engineers to weld together some crude iron baskets on stakes, which had been planted along either side of the dirt strip. They were burning fiercely now: DIY landing lights – an added touch of authenticity.

Peter Miles had taken a little more persuading, but once he'd checked into the history – the Lebanon sting by the team of former SAS – he'd seemed happy. A few calls to Daniel Brooks, and some due diligence on the science and technology, and Miles had really started to come onside.

Apparently Narov was right. Refined tungsten ingots and highly enriched uranium appeared almost exactly the same: an insanely heavy silver-grey metal. It would take a metallurgist with some fancy equipment to tell the two apart, and then only once he'd dismantled the lead sarcophagus making up the radiation shield.

And no way was all that going to happen in Dodge.

But the clincher had been getting hold of the DEA's files on Operation Angeldust. Angeldust was a little more complicated and technically accomplished than Jaeger had remembered it, but the basics were just as he'd described them. After reading the file, Miles had come fully on board.

Brooks had taken charge of building the fake shipment that Colonel Evandro's men would switch with the incoming cargo of uranium. In the depths of some woodland in a small, unmarked hangar in rural Virginia – one of the CIA's many black facilities – a specialist team had been ordered to drop everything else and concentrate on the task.

Brooks's demolitions expert, Theo Wallis – something of a magician with anything that could be made to go *bang* – realised from the get-go that the device would have to be a trade-off between maximum destructive power and the amount of space the explosive charge would need.

His greatest challenge was the incredibly small volume that the tungsten ingots would occupy. His chosen explosive, RDX, had a density of 1.8 grams per cubic centimetre, as opposed to tungsten's 19.25 grams. Volume for volume, it weighed less than a tenth of the tungsten ingots within which he would need to conceal the charge.

RDX was actually a World War II-era explosive, but it remained one of the most powerful available. It had had an interesting history. The story went that in the process of developing the explosive, Britain's Research Department 11 blew itself to smithereens – hence the name RDX, short for 'Research Department X'.

X – as, in the past. Dead and gone. An irony that Jaeger found amusing.

Wallis needed to cover six faces of the block of RDX with metal ingots, being careful that none of the explosive was visible, for then even a cursory inspection might give the game away. Plus he needed to insert the tiny Retrievor tracking device somewhere it wouldn't be discovered.

The great upside of combining RDX with tungsten was the sheer destructive power that resulted. Tungsten was the material of choice for bunker-busting bombs, forming the tip of any such projectile. Its enormous weight and density, coupled with its stupendously high melting point, made it ideal for slicing through steel, concrete, earth or brickwork.

Its capacity for causing lethal harm was practically unlimited, especially when hurled at its target with the explosive velocity of RDX – some 8,750 metres per second. The biggest downside was what a surprisingly small block the right amount of tungsten made – not a great deal larger than your average computer printer.

Wallis figured he could afford to build the block of explosives-cum-tungsten somewhat larger than the equivalent weight of uranium ingots, for the simple reason that he could compensate in the thickness of the lead shield. Because his tungsten bomb wasn't radioactive, he could thin the lead to allow for a larger charge of RDX.

That was the answer.

With the team working around the clock, the dummy-shipment-cum-bomb had been sealed in its lead sarcophagus, packed into a wooden crate and flown to the nearest military airbase, where Brooks had had it loaded aboard a non-stop flight to Brazil. Jetted direct into Cachimbo airport, it had been ferried out to Station 15 and hidden in the hangar where – all being well – the switch would occur.

Tonight was show time.

Jaeger, Narov, Raff and Alonzo had joined Colonel Evandro in a makeshift operations room, set a good way back from the airstrip.

The man chosen to front up the ruse was a Captain Ernesto Gonzales, a short, stocky, dark-skinned guy in his early thirties, who had the demeanour of a farmer rather than a special forces warrior. Indeed, that was exactly the kind of background he hailed from before being recruited into BSOB.

His face was scarred and pockmarked, his hair longish and greasy, and he looked as if he'd had a hard life, which in truth he had. Dressed as he now was, in scuffed cowboy boots and a mixed bag of ragged unmarked combats, topped off by a wide-brimmed Stetson, he looked every inch a narco.

As a bonus, he spoke decent English, which was the lingua franca of global smuggling operations. Equally as important, he had one of those classic poker-faced demeanours, his features rarely giving anything away. He was a consummate bluffer – which was why the colonel had used him for various under-cover ops in the past.

In short, Gonzales was the obvious choice for tonight's dark and dangerous charade.

41

The inbound aircraft was an Antonov AN-12. Fitted with extra internal fuel tanks, it had a range of over 6,000 kilometres and an unrivalled STOL – short take-off and landing – capability. It could put down on a dirt strip 600 metres in length, and on an airbase at several thousand metres of altitude.

In short, it was perfect for flying into rugged, mountainous territory, and landing on a runway hacked out of the jungle. It was also highly manoeuvrable and well capable of low-level flying, so keeping below any radar.

With four powerful turboprop engines and a massive cargo-carrying capacity, the AN-12 was overkill for such a small load, but it was one of the few aircraft capable of executing such a challenging transcontinental delivery.

For the past forty minutes, the pilot had been guided by a VOR/DME system – a VHF omnidirectional range, combined with a distance measuring equipment device. In layman's terms, a homing beacon. All airports had them. In fact, the AN-12 had been using three VOR/DMEs – those stationed at the nearest commercial airports to Dodge – and triangulating its position from their signals.

The self-appointed air traffic controller at Dodge had been talking the pilot in by radio, using vectors from those VOR/DMEs to cross-reference distance and position. While it sounded complicated, it was pretty much the standard operating procedure for bringing in a ghost flight packed full of illegal cargo to an uncharted bush airstrip.

Normally the narco boss wouldn't provide the end location to the pilot, for that risked the DEA getting wise to their base. Hence the need to use VOR/DME triangulation to keep nudging the aircraft in. Hence why El Padre's air traffic control guy kept talking to the AN-12's pilot via their prearranged frequency, guiding him ever closer.

Normally, the procedure was pretty much foolproof. Normally.

Tonight was a little different. Tonight, things had got a little complicated.

First, the signal emanating from Dodge had got scrambled. El Padre's radio operator had lost contact with the incoming aircraft. No matter what he tried, the AN-12 was unreachable: in the place of the Russian pilot's voice, there was a weird, echoing, hollow, howling scream.

Electrical storm, it sounded like. But the operator was well aware that thunderstorms didn't affect VHF radio signals. Not normally. Hence his discomfort and confusion at having lost contact with the incoming aircraft.

'Try another frequency,' barked a stout, barrel-chested figure at his side.

It was unusual – very – to have El Padre himself standing by for such a delivery. The radio operator blanched and began punching buttons, scrolling through the digital frequencies, but he didn't hold out any great hopes.

In the AN-12's cockpit, the pilot was having little better luck. He could see the three VOR/DMEs transmitting their bearings, but without any guidance from the ground, he was screwed. He too began to prod at his radio. Maybe the narcos had drifted across to a different frequency without telling him. Sure enough, as he scanned the airwaves, a voice came up asking him to check in.

'Bear 12, come in. Bear 12, come in. We lost your signal. Repeat, we lost your signal. Come in, Bear 12, come in.'

The pilot grabbed his radio handset. 'This is Bear 12. Where the hell have you been?' he growled. 'I lost you for fifteen minutes. Why you change frequency?'

Colonel Evandro's radio operator smiled. 'You want me to guide you in, or you want to bitch?'

'I want you to guide.'

'Okay, this is your landing bearing and vectors.' The radio operator passed the pilot a series of bearings from the VOR/DME stations that would bring him directly into Station 15. 'You're twenty minutes out.'

'Twenty,' the pilot confirmed. 'Make sure you have runway lights on. Is a big jungle down there.'

'Affirm. Out.'

The radio operator flashed Colonel Evandro a smile. They'd just taken control of the inbound aircraft. They knew its call sign – Bear 12 – because they'd been tracking the aircraft's radio communications as it approached Brazilian airspace. All seemed to be going perfectly, but twenty minutes was a long time in show business. Any number of things could still go wrong.

The jam on Dodge's radio signal might collapse, enabling the narcos to alert the pilot. If his navigator was any good, he might realise they were being lured down to a strip the wrong side of the border. Or Captain Gonzales might screw it up on the ground.

Jaeger felt horribly restless. He checked his watch, stepped outside and gazed into the heavens. Fifteen minutes to go, and not a sign of any aircraft. Not a glimmer of moonlight on metal. Not the faintest rumble of engines.

So much was hanging on this moment. The hunt for Kammler. The means to derail whatever he was up to. Jaeger's search for his traumatised and now missing wife. Plus the sting had been his idea in the first place.

It couldn't just fall apart now.

He felt others join him. Narov. Alonzo. Raff. All craning their necks skywards. He flicked his wrist, checking his watch for the umpteenth time. Ten minutes. Surely they should be able to see and hear something?

Silence. The thumping of his pulse in his temples. Jaeger could sense the tension, taut on the still air. He shivered as though someone had walked over his grave. The aircraft wasn't coming, he knew it.

They'd been rumbled.

42

'Eight minutes,' someone said.

Silence; all eyes scanning the darkened heavens.

Jaeger shook his head darkly. 'They're not coming.'

'Shut up.' It was Colonel Evandro. It was unlike him to be so brusque. 'I hear something.'

Jaeger strained his ears. Sure enough, a faint, barely audible rumble reverberated over the treetops. An aircraft was coming in low and unseen from the west, the noise masked by the dense vegetation.

Moments later, the eerie form of the AN-12 lumbered out of the blackness, flying at a little above its 70-knot stall speed. It was showing no lights across its 125-foot wingspan, so it appeared like some kind of giant ghost plane. It did one pass low over the airbase before executing a smart turn and touching down smoothly on the dirt strip.

Unbelievable, Jaeger told himself, his adrenalin pumping. This guy sure knows how to fly.

For several seconds the 100-foot-long aircraft slowed on the runway, as if coming to a standstill. Yet when it was maybe a third of the way in, its four Ivchenko turboprop engines began to pour thick black smoke as they went to maximum power. The Antonov gained speed rapidly, and in a thunderous roar it clawed its way back into the darkness.

Jaeger sprinted for the radio room. The pilot must have noticed something was amiss. But what? What had they overlooked when preparing the airstrip for the sting? He burst inside to find

Colonel Evandro's radio operator firmly on the case.

'Bear 12, you've aborted the landing. Why the abort?'

Silence. A long beat of echoing static in which the Antonov's pilot didn't respond. Jaeger feared they'd spooked him. Or maybe Los Niños's radio operator had managed to make contact, alerting him to what was going on.

'Bear 12, Bear 12, why the abort?' the radio operator repeated.

A moment of silence, followed by a throaty chuckle. 'No abort. Old Soviet trick. Testing if your strip is good. I touch wheels, see if strip holds up. Don't worry. Is good. Bear 12 now making final approach.'

By the time Jaeger had got his pulse back to something like normal, the AN-12 had touched down and was coming to a halt on the dirt runway.

All eyes switched to Captain Ernesto Gonzales's point of view now, as it was transmitted to a laptop set on the desk before them. Jaeger felt his heart race as he eyed the screen. It had made sense to rig the BSOB captain with a tiny surveillance device so they could monitor the sting as it went down.

A figure stepped into view dressed in grubby overalls. Using two fluorescent panels, he guided the aircraft towards the target hangar; the hangar that concealed the decoy cargo.

The AN-12 taxied to a standstill. Captain Gonzales strolled over, using one hand to anchor his Stetson against the aircraft's powerful backwash.

The pilot powered down his engines. Once the deafening racket had died away, he slid open the cockpit's side window. His face appeared: mid fifties, jowly; former Soviet military if the greying crew cut was anything to go by.

'You're late,' Gonzales shouted up at him.

The pilot peered down. 'You change frequency. Why the change?'

Gonzales's face remained impassive. 'You never heard of electrical storms? We get a lot of 'em around here.'

'Thunderstorm not affect VHF.'

'Well something did.' A beat of silence. 'You wanna bitch about it, or you wanna unload?'

The Russian shrugged. 'We are here. We get unloading, comrade.'

'You are. Let's get started.'

There was an audible clunk from somewhere, and the AN-12's rear ramp whined down. Captain Gonzales yelled out some orders and a bunch of narco lookalikes roared over in a pickup truck fitted with a hydraulic tailgate.

Moments later it had backed up to the AN-12's ramp and disappeared inside. A minute ticked by. Gonzales wandered around to the AN-12's rear and started yelling orders, gesticulating wildly, just to lend an added sense of chaos to the scene. The colonel had made the perfect choice – Gonzales was a natural.

The pickup drove down the ramp with a wooden crate the size of a small fridge-freezer strapped to its rear. As it headed across to the nearby hangar, Captain Gonzales moved back to the cockpit.

'You wait there while we inspect the cargo,' he told the pilot.

The pilot shrugged. 'Cargo is good. No need to inspect.'

Gonzales moved his hand more firmly onto the AK-47 slung across his shoulder. 'You wait while we check. *Comrade.*'

The pilot didn't respond. He clearly wasn't going anywhere until this narco gunman was satisfied.

There was a yell from the direction of the hangar. In Portuguese. 'El Commandante! You need to see this!'

Gonzales eyed the pilot. 'Something I need to check. You wait here.' He strolled across to the hangar.

'It's a heap of bloody metal in a crate,' one of his men complained, gesturing at the cargo. 'What do we want with a heap of useless freakin' metal? Take a look for yourself,' he announced, feigning anger.

Gonzales and his men were keeping it one hundred per cent real, just in case any of the Russian crew spoke Portuguese and overheard. Gonzales made a show of peering into the crate. He frowned. 'What the fuck? What is this shit?'

He turned around and strode back to the aircraft. There was a certain menace to his step now.

He eyed the pilot. 'You just delivered a crateload of metal. This is not what was agreed. Where's the coca paste, comrade?'

The pilot did a double take. 'What?'

'Coca. Paste. From Ecuador. Like last time.' Gonzales's tone was level and calm, with just the right hint of menace. 'Plus we got the refined product to onload. Just like always.'

The pilot's face darkened. 'What is this bullshit?'

Gonzales placed his hand on his weapon. 'We do this a hundred times, comrade, no problem. A hundred times. Then tonight we get a crateload of useless fucking scrap. No bullshit, comrade; you got some explaining to do.'

For a moment Jaeger wondered if Gonzales was laying it on a little too thick. This was the moment when the bad guys had to fall hook, line and sinker for the ruse.

The pilot glanced around, the spotlights blinding him. His gaze came to rest on Gonzalez again. 'Look, brother, I load up at Moldova. I bring cargo here as instructed. I land.' The pilot paused. 'So, like I say: what bullshit is this?'

Gonzales unslung his weapon. 'Mister, right now it's me asking the questions and you giving the answers.'

The pilot was a tough old bird, but Gonzales's act was getting to him. 'Look, I have never been to this Ecuador. I have never fly the drugs. I fly the weapons. And tonight, I follow instructions to letter.'

Gonzales fixed him with a look. 'Comrade, who exactly is your patron? Who is your customer for this pile of useless scrap?'

The pilot stiffened. He clearly wasn't inclined to answer.

Gonzales ratcheted a round into the breech of his AK-47. 'Mister, let me make this easy on you: you start talking and you start making some motherfucking sense, or things are gonna turn very ugly very fast.'

The pilot blanched. 'El Padre,' he growled. 'Los Niños. I fly in here for El Padre.'

Gonzales scratched his head, his features displaying a certain incredulity. Then he let out a short bark of a laugh before glancing at the pilot again.

'You're on the wrong strip, comrade. I'm expecting a shipment of coca paste from Ecuador. End of.'

The pilot's mouth hung open. Speechless.

Gonzalez shrugged. 'Listen, we don't mess with El Padre. No one does. Not if they want to live. So best you turn this crate around and get airborne again. Pronto.'

The pilot seemed frozen, his face drained of all colour.

'Comrade, you're free to go. But I gotta tell you something. You're not just at the wrong strip; you're in the wrong goddam country. This is Brazil. You want the other side of the border. Colombia.'

'So who are . . .' the pilot stuttered. 'Who are you guys?'

Gonzalez shook his head. 'Not your need-to-know.' There was a steeliness to his gaze now. 'Like I said, we're done. *Adios.* You need to spin this crate around and get airborne.'

The pilot turned and barked a few orders in Russian at his co-pilot and navigator, then reached for his instrument panel. The colour was starting to return to his features. Maybe he was going to get away with this. Maybe he wasn't about to die.

Gonzales yelled for his boys to load up the cargo once more. In the hangar, the dummy shipment was manhandled into the pickup, driven up the ramp of the AN-12 and deposited in the aircraft's hold. With barely a second glance, the loadmaster got it strapped down and headed for the cockpit.

Gonzales's men exited the aircraft, switch done.

'Word of advice, Igor,' Gonzales volunteered to the pilot. 'You get to El Padre's place, you may want to keep quiet about your little fuck-up. He doesn't take kindly to . . . fuck-ups.' A beat. 'Good luck, comrade. Safe flying to wherever it is you're headed. This side of the border, we're the only guys in town.'

The pilot cracked a smile. He reached behind him and pulled out a bottle. 'You like vodka? Khortytsa vodka. The best. All the way from Ukraine.'

Captain Gonzales shook his head. 'I'm a tequila kind of guy. Maybe you'll need that where you're heading. If El Padre finds out what really happened here tonight . . .' He let the words tail off menacingly. '*Adios*, comrade, and say hello to Moldova for me, or wherever the hell it is you come from.'

The pilot punched a button and there was the distinctive whine of the starter motors firing up the first of the aircraft's engines. 'Ukraine. I come from Ukraine. Oleksandr Savchenko, Ukraine's finest pilot. But right now, we have cargo to deliver all the way to fucking China. If you ever come to Ukraine, please, you . . .' The last of his words were drowned out by the howling of the engines.

'Sure, I'll look you up.' Gonzales slapped the fuselage theatrically. 'Safe trip! And next time, get a better navigator, Comrade Savchenko!'

He stepped away from the aircraft, his part of the mission complete: so far, so good.

43

Jaeger and his team were gathered around Colonel Evandro's computer, the military-encrypted internet link providing a secure video feed to their distant Falkenhagen headquarters. Peter Miles was speaking, and they were glued to his every word.

'We agree with your analysis, plus all intelligence from our end suggests that the plane isn't terminating at that jungle strip. It's a stopover. Refuelling. Time for the crew to grab some shut-eye. But mostly it's a ruse. A cut-off. A decoy destination.'

The switch had gone like clockwork. The AN-12 had flown on to Los Niños's base with its Trojan horse tungsten-bomb cargo, apparently with no further dramas. Which must have been as much of a relief to Oleksandr Savchenko, Ukraine's finest pilot, as it was to Jaeger and his team.

Right now, the tracking device revealed that the crate was sitting on that aircraft in Dodge, beaming out its signal as regular as clockwork.

'So what d'you reckon to the China connection?' Jaeger queried. 'What the pilot mentioned. Is it credible?'

'Yes, as it happens.' Miles replied. 'We figure they've flown to Colombia as a blind. It's not unusual with these criminal-narco-mafioso networks. Colombia's where the trail goes cold. Or at least it's supposed to. Meanwhile, the HEU gets spirited to the other side of the world.'

Miles searched out Narov. 'Plus, there's been an unexpected development . . . Irina, I have something of a personal question for you. You and Falk Konig – Kammler's son – you made something of a special connection on your last mission, I understand?'

'You can say that again,' Jaeger cut in. 'Became intimately acquainted. Sparks flew.'

Raff practically choked on his coffee. Alonzo tried to kill an almighty great snigger. Narov gave the daggers. If looks could kill, Jaeger was dead and buried.

'Falk and I shared a mutual interest, yes,' she replied tightly. 'For wildlife. For animals. So yes, by the time we left, I viewed him as a . . . close friend. That was all. Nothing more.' She glared at Jaeger. 'Nothing like what that *Schwachkopf* is implying.'

With that, she stalked out the room.

Her sudden departure was met with an uncomfortable silence. It was Raff who broke it. He eyed Jaeger despairingly. 'That went well. Always had the touch. And still got it, by the looks of things.'

Jaeger winced. 'Well, it's true. They were like a couple of lovebirds.'

During their previous mission, Kammler's son, Falk, had played a somewhat ambivalent role. While Narov had believed he was on the side of the angels, Jaeger hadn't been convinced.

Falk had changed his surname from Kammler to Konig, apparently in an effort to distance himself from the family's Nazi legacy. But after Jaeger and his team had nailed Kammler's dark plot to bring back the Reich, Falk had dropped off the radar. Completely.

Jaeger's last communication with him had been a text message, in which Falk had tried to exonerate himself: *My father has taken refuge in his lair . . . I am innocent. He is a madman.*

After that, silence.

In Jaeger's book, that was suspicious. You didn't do a disappearing act like that unless you had reason. Why run unless you were guilty?

'Falk's been calling Irina,' Miles announced. 'Repeatedly, over an eight-hour period. He's been using a Chinese-made

ETACTO TLX, a kind of poor man's satphone. It's got great connectivity over China and comes equipped with two SIM slots. He chose to use his regular SIM card, in spite of the fact that it's at the top of our global watch list. Seems he set his phone to automatic call repeat. Of course, he got no answer, Irina being in the Brazilian jungle.'

'So Falk's surfaced. Where is he?' Jaeger queried.

'Well, there's the thing. He's in China. A remote border region in the depths of the Himalayas.' Miles eyed Jaeger for a long moment. 'Go fetch Irina. Say sorry, and get her back in here. You all need to hear this.'

Jaeger headed outside. Finding Narov alone, he didn't know quite what to say. He figured he'd keep it simple.

'Look, I'm sorry. I was just messing with you. It didn't mean anything.'

Narov turned on him. 'You know something? I'm sick of you and I am sick of your blind stupidity.' A beat, fraught with emotion. Jaeger knew exactly what she was driving at: the bond – the electrifying attraction – between the two of them.

He knew in his heart that he'd fallen for her. It was the love that wouldn't speak its name. Guilt over Ruth made him try to bury it; deny it.

'You want to know the truth?' Narov continued. 'You want to know why I went off hunting Kammler solo? Because I no longer trusted you. I needed to hide it from you, Kahuhara'ga.'

Kahuhara'ga. The Hunter. Months back, Jaeger had been given that name by a tribe of isolated Amazonian Indians who had sacrificed themselves in order to aid his mission. Narov had started using the name teasingly. Yet now she seemed to have lost all faith in him.

Jaeger ran a hand through his hair. He couldn't find any words.

'You think I would have shared what I was doing, knowing you would repeat it all to your wife?' Narov demanded. 'To her. As if you can still trust her!'

'You think she'd betray us? You think she'd feed it to

Kammler? But you've got no proof.' Jaeger had found his voice at last. 'Not one shred of evidence. There's no way you can be certain . . . Anyway, the fact is, you never liked her.'

Narov shook her head despairingly. 'Tell me: prior to her disappearing act, did you speak to her? Tell her anything about Kammler that could have triggered her to leave? Did you?'

Jaeger cast his mind back to the email he'd sent shortly after the St Georgen tunnel discoveries: *I've stumbled upon something here. There's a chance that Kammler might still be alive.*

Maybe it wasn't an abduction. Maybe that email had caused his wife to run. But to run to Kammler? The more he tried to fathom it, the more he just couldn't be certain. He didn't know what to think any more.

'She's got PTSD,' he objected mulishly. 'She's not thinking straight. She's confused and damaged and acting irrationally. Plus there are any number of ways to explain her disappearance, starting with the obvious: Kammler's people seized her . . .'

His words tailed off to nothing.

He needed to start being more honest with himself. Long ago he'd fallen for Narov's elusive charms. At the time, he was married, with kids he adored and a wife he loved. Not any more. He knew he was losing Ruth; maybe he'd already lost her. At the same time he was still trying to push Narov away.

But try as he might, his connection with this enigma of a woman was growing more powerful by the day. His heart was being torn away from the woman he'd once loved, and he feared that if he stepped closer to Narov's fire and ice, he was going to burn.

With a supreme effort of will, he forced all of that from his mind.

There was only one way to settle this: *find Kammler.*

44

Jaeger and Narov stepped back into the ops room, an uncomfortable silence hanging between them. No one asked how things had gone outside. In a sense, it didn't matter. What mattered was that time was running out, for all of them.

As quickly as he could, Miles narrated to Narov the history of the calls from Falk Konig. 'We traced his cell phone to a remote part of the Chinese Himalayas. There is some sensitivity over China, but we've managed to secure some high-resolution imagery. We think – we strongly suspect – that this may be Kammler's new base of operations.'

'Why there?' Narov demanded. In an instant, she'd switched back to one hundred per cent focus.

'It's got everything. Remote. Inaccessible. Self-contained. But most importantly, it's got perfect cover. You could raise an army in the place – or build a salvo of IND-tipped missiles – and no one would turn a hair. I'll email you the images and you'll see what I mean.'

'One question,' Jaeger cut in. 'Why would Falk Konig make repeated calls on a mobile he's got to know is red hot? If he is with his father, the world's most wanted man, what would make him break his silence?'

'That's the point,' Miles replied. 'We don't think he's trying to hide. We think he wants to be found.'

'You think he is being held against his will?' Narov queried. 'His father's captive?'

'We suspect as much. He blipped up for one night. We figure

187

something happened that enabled him to make those calls, but just for that brief time window.'

'The number's specific to a SIM card that he knows is hot,' Jaeger ventured. 'Traceable. He uses it just that one night, when he has the chance. Come morning, he goes silent again.'

'We figure something like that, yes,' Miles confirmed. 'But we can't be certain. For all we know, he could be reconciled with his father. In league with him. Those calls could easily be some kind of decoy or ambush.'

'Unlikely,' Narov remarked. 'From what I know of Falk. And from what I know of his father.'

Jaeger shot her a look. 'Expect the unexpected. Day one, lesson one.'

'I do. But I also trust my instinct,' Narov countered. 'Trust me, this is a cry for help.'

'We've triple-checked the location,' Miles cut in. 'The only way to be certain this is Kammler's new base of operations is to deploy you guys. We'd like you to get eyes on as soon as possible. That way, when the decoy is delivered we can be certain it's in the right place before we trigger the blast.'

'So when do we deploy?' Jaeger demanded. 'And how? It's a long way from here to Beijing.'

'As soon as humanly possible. We have very little influence on when that flight leaves Dodge and recommences its journey. Brooks has got a C-5 Galaxy inbound. You RV with it at Afonsos Air Force Base, in Rio, deploying directly from there.'

'Got it.' Jaeger glanced briefly at the others. 'Understood.'

'One more thing,' Miles added. 'You're going in trans-border to China, which is about as sensitive as it gets. We need a means to deliver you to your end destination that is utterly covert and untraceable. We're talking China, remember, with their state-of-the-art tracking and surveillance systems. We're in one hell of a hurry, but don't go screwing this up China side of the border.'

'Send us the surveillance photos,' said Jaeger. 'We'll think of something.'

'You'll have them,' Miles confirmed. 'Finally, a warning. We've detected signs that Kammler and his people may know we're onto them. Narov's Dubai mission left a signature.' He paused. 'Take every possible precaution. Do not under-estimate Kammler. His back's to the wall, which makes him doubly dangerous. Make sure the hunters do not become the hunted.'

As they gathered around Colonel Evandro's laptop, Jaeger, Narov, Raff and Alonzo scrutinised the satellite photos that Miles had sent through. The thing that struck Jaeger most forcibly was the endless expanse of mountains, snow and ice. But chiefly, snowfields. Vast, rolling, freezing drifts of glittering white.

To trek cross-border through that – it wasn't possible, not in the time they had available. To parachute or make a helicopter insertion was also a non-starter, for this was the most monitored and watched airspace on earth. Then a thought struck him. It was risky – crazily so – but it might just be doable.

He turned to Raff. 'Mate, remember that insertion we trialled in Antarctica? Years back. There was a spike in tension be-tween us and the Argentinians. HMG figured it might kick off between our Antarctic survey teams and theirs.'

'Yeah. Break a leg. I almost bloody did.'

Jaeger gestured at the surveillance photos. 'Well?'

'We *trialled* it. It was a trial. And we knew the depth of the snow, plus its density.'

'Yeah, but feast your eyes upon those drifts. Brooks is bound to have some boffins who could take a closer look. Give us a steer.'

'We'd need a discreet base somewhere near the border to do a stop-short,' Raff mused. 'We'd have to transfer to a low-key aircraft that can execute that kind of drop with little or no sig-nature.' He paused. 'It's one hell of a challenge, and we don't have the time to screw up.'

'Any better suggestions?'

Raff stared at the images for a second. 'Fuck it. It's no crazier than your Angeldust sting.'

Jaeger gave a thin smile. 'Yeah, and beggars can't be choosers.'

45

The massive US Air Force C-5M Super Galaxy – powered by four giant General Electric turbofan jet engines – was eating up the miles.

Flying at some 35,000 feet, and with such a light load as she was presently carrying – four operators, plus their hastily assembled kit – she had a range of some 10,500 kilometres. It would get them to their refuelling stop at Camp Lemmonier, the US military base in Djibouti, on the east coast of Africa.

Upon take-off, Jaeger had done what he normally did when facing a long flight by military transport: he'd slung his hammock in the massive hold and zoned out. He'd awoken some eleven hours later as they approached Camp Lemmonier, based at Djibouti's Ambouli International Airport, feeling remarkably refreshed.

The stress and tension of the last few days had proved draining. Alonzo had cobbled together a makeshift bed on the Galaxy's floor, and Narov and Raff had each taken a row of the giant aircraft's seats. The three of them appeared to be comatose still.

Before departing Brazil, Jaeger had had to sort some kind of arrangements for his boys. It was the Easter holidays, school was breaking up, and he needed someone to take care of them for as long as might be necessary.

The obvious solution had presented itself when Uncle Joe had offered to have them to stay at his place. He lived in a beautiful wooden cabin set at the foot of Buccleuch Fell, in the Scottish Borders, a natural paradise in the heart of dense woodland, complete with a series of lakes.

Uncle Joe's Cabin, as they called it, was far more sumptuous than the name suggested. It had become something of a home-from-home for the Jaeger family. Luke loved it, and Jaeger felt certain Simon would too. They could go climbing in the woods, fish in the streams and cycle the forest tracks. Plus Great-Auntie Ethel's cooking was an extra draw.

A part of Jaeger had felt homesick, especially when he'd spoken to the boys. He'd told them as much as he could. They knew their dad would be doing everything possible to get back to them safely. He would have moved mountains to be there with them right now, running wild. But what would he tell them about Ruth? How would he explain her absence?

Any way he looked at it, he was in the right place – hunting down Kammler. And very possibly his wife too, perish the thought.

His parents had offered to have the boys, but Jaeger had been wary. His father had long since gone to the bottle. Though a good dad in his day – he'd nurtured Jaeger's boyhood love of the wild – after leaving the army he'd drifted into drink.

Whenever he'd been on the booze, he proved rude and abusive. At age sixteen, Jaeger had volunteered for Royal Marines selection as a 'crow' – a raw recruit. In a drunken fit, his father had told him he would fail the punishing selection course.

Jaeger had been determined to prove him wrong.

That was when he'd first met Raff. He'd been thrown into line alongside the big Maori, as they paraded in their underwear that first morning at Lympstone. They hailed from totally different backgrounds, but that meant sod all. Both were day-one crows and both were freezing their nuts off. They'd forged an unbreakable bond on the fearsome assault course and trekking over the Dartmoor fells.

Jaeger knew that his father had tried to curtail his drinking in recent years, but he didn't want either Luke or Simon exposed to that kind of crap.

As he had become more distant from his father, so Jaeger had grown closer to his grandfather, whose example had inspired him to try for SAS selection. But when Brigadier Edward 'Ted' Jaeger had been murdered by Kammler's people, he'd turned to Uncle Joe, the brigadier's younger brother and his former comrade in the Secret Hunters.

As the Galaxy took to the air once more, heading east out of Djibouti, Jaeger grabbed a ration pack from his bergen and wolfed down a cold, gloopy boil-in-the-bag meal. As in-flight food went, it wasn't great, but lying in a gently swinging hammock eating lukewarm rations was luxury compared with the physical deprivations to come.

Jaeger had few illusions: as soon as they crossed the border into China, they were going to be totally up against it, operating in some of the harshest, most unforgiving terrain the world had to offer.

Where they were going, they'd be glad of all the high-altitude and Alpine gear they'd stuffed into their bergens, plus the cross-country skis and other survival kit they had packed into the steel-framed para-tubes lying in the hold.

Then there was the risk of capture by the Chinese armed forces. Though they were heading into China for that nation's benefit – indeed, for the benefit of all humankind – the Chinese weren't to know that. As soon as they crossed the border, that threat would be very real.

A part of Jaeger wondered if Brooks couldn't have found a way to brief the Chinese, but he also understood the challenges involved. The CIA chief would have had to explain to his Chinese counterparts how his agency had supposedly verified that the world's most wanted man was dead, whereas in truth he was still very much alive.

Not only that, he would have to explain how Kammler had somehow wormed his way into China, with the help of a changed appearance and an assumed identity.

In short, raising all this with the Chinese had the potential to backfire spectacularly. It was a recipe for dark conspiracy theories, not to mention international mistrust. US–Chinese relations were always delicate, and on balance Jaeger could appreciate why Brooks – and Miles – had opted for the present course of action.

Still, he didn't fancy being captured by the People's Liberation Army, and having to talk his way out of this one.

46

With worrying thoughts of capture in mind, Jaeger decided to gen up on the mission. They had a 6,000-kilometre flight ahead of them before touchdown at the Takhli Air Force Base in central Thailand. They'd have precious little time thereafter for studying the target.

He tapped his iPad's screen, scrolling through Peter Miles's hastily prepared briefing notes. It seemed that Kammler and his forebears in the Reich had a certain history in the area that they were jetting into. As with so many things from the war years, what had first led the Nazis to this remote part of China beggared belief.

In May 1938, SS Hauptsturmführer Ernst Schafer, a German zoologist, had led an expedition into Tibet. Staffed entirely by SS officers, it was sponsored by the Deutsche Ahnenerbe – the SS Ancestral Heritage Society – a pseudo-scientific institution charged with proving that an Aryan master race had supposedly once ruled the earth.

Heinrich Himmler, chief of the SS, was one of the Deutsche Ahnenerbe's key backers, as was SS General Hans Kammler. They believed that centuries ago, a group of pure-blooded Aryans had emerged from Tibet, making it the cradle of Aryan civilisation. However crackpot that theory might seem, the SS Tibet expedition had set out to analyse the cranial dimensions and take plaster casts of the local people's heads, to somehow prove it.

Schafer had managed to persuade the British authorities to

allow him to access Tibet via India, which was then still a British colony. Travelling via Sikkim, a region of north-eastern India, the German team had made their way into the 'Land of Snows' – the mountainous Tibetan plateau. On 9 January 1939, they had reached Lhasa, Tibet's capital. There, Schafer had handed out Nazi swastikas, which ironically served to endear his team to the Tibetans.

In the swastika the Nazis had appropriated an ancient religious symbol popular in Roman times and revered in Buddhism and Hinduism. The Tibetan leaders had taken the expedition's swastikas to indicate a shared belief in the peaceful, tolerant tenets of Buddhism.

Of course, nothing could have been further from the truth.

Schafer and his people had headed to the famed Nyenchen Tanglha Mountains, overlooking Lake Namtso – the 'Heavenly Lake' – which lay sixty kilometres to the north of Lhasa. This area, they had concluded, was the epicentre of Aryan ancestry in Tibet – the long-forgotten Nazi homeland.

They carried back to Germany scores of ancient religious artefacts, together with the cranial measurements and casts, which they claimed proved their theory. Himmler was ecstatic: he greeted Schafer with gifts of a special SS dagger and a silver death's-head ring.

Hitler himself read Schafer's reports and was impressed. All the expedition team were promoted up the ranks of the SS, and the Nyenchen Tanglha Mountains went down in SS mythology as the legendary Aryan fatherland.

And now it seemed that Hank Kammler – son of the SS general who had done so much to further such ideas – had headed for this region. There was a dark symbolism in Kammler's hiding out in the Nyenchen Tanglha Mountains, of that Jaeger felt certain.

Kammler was nothing if not smart. A man of wealth, thanks to his father's post-war dealings, he'd sunk significant resources into projects in isolated parts of the world, including a remote private game reserve in Katavi, in East Africa – somewhere that had provided perfect cover for his germ warfare research.

It was there that Jaeger and his team had nailed him, or so they had thought.

Now, in the Nyenchen Tanglha Mountains, he had established a cover for his newest and darkest aspirations. According to the intelligence Jaeger was reading, if Kammler was breeding a clutch of INDs, he was very likely doing it from here. If Brooks and Miles were right, on the snowfields overlooking the Heavenly Lake, Kammler had set up a veritable devil's sanctuary.

A sanctuary from where he planned to unleash a new Armageddon.

47

'Truce?' Jaeger suggested, as he offered Narov a steaming brew.

She swung her legs off the seats. 'I did not know we were at war.'

Jaeger said nothing. Over the past seventy-two hours it had certainly felt that way.

He broke out his steel flask and mixed her a hot chocolate from some sachets in his rations. Raff and Alonzo would sleep until the cows came home, just as they always did. It was only Jaeger and Narov who were awake.

They were two hours out from Takhli, and once they touched down, they had to hit the ground running. They were poised to deploy on the most challenging mission they had ever faced, and they needed to gel as a team. Hence the mug of hot chocolate. Call it a peace offering.

Jaeger nodded at Narov's iPad. 'You've read the reports?'

'I have. Several times.'

'What d'you reckon?'

'From all the intel from St Georgen, we know that fissile material – uranium – has almost certainly been removed from those tunnels. Trouble is, no one knows how much was there in the first place. But we can make a good guess. There were how many in the gang who hit the film crew?'

'Six.'

'Six men can carry what, in terms of loads? Maybe thirty kilos each. So, presuming they made the one run, let's say they retrieved a hundred and eighty kilos from the tunnels. Plus they have a hundred kilos incoming from Moldova, or at least they think they have. And there are the previous flights . . . So what are they doing with all this material?'

'Multiple INDs.'

'Multiple INDs. Nothing else makes sense.' Narov paused, blowing on her hot chocolate pensively. 'Which potentially means multiple targets. And right now we have no idea where or what those targets are. Or their timescale.'

'What're you thinking?'

Narov glanced at him. 'If I were Kammler – a crazed mass murderer with a delusional ego – I'd have started building my INDs just as soon as the first raw materials were to hand. And I would have started to filter those INDs out to their targets as soon as they were ready.'

Narov was no Kammler. In truth, she was his arch-enemy. But Jaeger figured she was dead right. Kammler very likely had shipped out his first INDs.

Right now, though, as she perched on her seat sipping her drink, Jaeger was struck by another thought entirely. Even with her fine blonde hair pulled back in a scrunchie and no make-up to speak of, Narov remained stunningly beautiful. He let the image linger in his thoughts. Longer than he had ever allowed himself to do before.

'We have to presume Kammler has got his first INDs in position,' Narov repeated, seemingly oblivious to Jaeger's admiring gaze. 'Which means we've got to trace them. Stop them.' She paused. 'Where would Kammler make his targets, do you think?'

Jaeger took a sip of his own brew. Tea, laced with heaps of sugar. Raff had got him into it during their first week of commando selection. It was one bad habit that he'd never managed to shake. Ruth used to nag him about it incessantly. All that sugar would kill him. Jaeger knew many other things could kill him long before that.

'Follow Kammler's ego,' he ventured. 'Ego always has a

pattern.' He paused. 'What will he aim for? Urban conurbations? City centres? Places where an IND's lethality will cause maximum impact, but more importantly, mass panic and terror.' He paused again. 'Though if you think about it, he's not going to blow one device until he can blow them all.'

'Why not?'

''Cause if he blows one, the world is alerted. The search is on. Globally. City centres are shut down. All vehicles stopped; searched. The airspace cleared. You can't detonate an IND unless you can deliver it to target. He'll have to coordinate multiple strikes so that all go off at once. And that's got to lend us a little time.'

'Let's hope so.' Narov's ice-blue gaze met his. For once Jaeger figured he could detect a certain emotion in it, and it surprised him. Her eyes cried out fear; fear of what Kammler was capable of, especially if he was ahead of them in this dark game.

He felt an irresistible temptation to kiss her, to whisper words of reassurance. If he was honest with himself, he'd fallen hopelessly for this confounding woman. Yet at the same time, there was Ruth. Innocent until proven guilty.

He took a gulp of his tea.

He didn't know what the hell to feel or think any more.

48

Narov grabbed her iPad, and pulled up one of Brooks's documents. It was entitled: 'The inevitability of ISIS achieving a nuclear terror strike'.

'Did you see this? Background briefing.'

Jaeger shook his head. He'd trawled through the key documents – the mission-specific ones – but had then started to tire.

'You know how large your average IND is?' Narov continued. 'About the size of a small fridge. You know how much it weighs? As little as a hundred kilos. Basically, you could carry it in an SUV. So while it is not exactly Ryanair hand luggage, it's incredibly easy to hide. Carry across borders. Conceal. Deliver.'

She fixed Jaeger with a look, worry etched in her eyes. 'We have to presume that Kammler has developed multiple delivery systems. Plus the links he's forged with organised crime and drugs mean he's got covert trafficking networks he can utilise.'

'Yeah, but consider the upside,' Jaeger countered. 'It's us.'

He reached out to touch Narov's arm in a gesture of reassurance. Typically, she seemed to recoil – to freeze – at the prospect of any physical contact other than for the practical reasons of soldiering.

Jaeger shrugged it off. He glanced at his watch. 'We're one hour forty-five out from Takhli. When we touch down, there'll be an AN-32 waiting on the apron. It's two thousand klicks north to our target. That's five hours' flight time. We'll be on the ground tonight, and at the target by the early hours of tomorrow morning. Miles has confirmed that Bear 12 is airborne and flying a similar route to the one we've taken. It's got less range, so more fuelling stops, but it won't be far behind.

'I'd say seventy-two hours from now, the tungsten device gets delivered to Kammler's headquarters,' he continued. 'We'll be eyes on. We'll see it taken into his IND lab. Then we detonate. That's a very large part of the problem taken care of.'

'And then?' Narov challenged. 'How do we finish it?'

Jaeger shrugged. 'That I can't say. Not until we're visual. The plan of attack will shake out of whatever we find on the ground. But either way, this time we finish it. Finish Kammler. For good.'

Narov pulled up one of the satellite images on her iPad screen. 'There appear to be three separate facilities: what they think is the laboratory; the generator hall and plant; plus the accommodation block.'

'Yep. And they're well spaced out. The tungsten blast will take out the lab, that's for sure. But the rest of it: that's for us. We'll need some kind of diversion. And our usual calling cards: speed. Aggression. Surprise.'

'You've seen the thickness of the walls?' Narov queried. 'We'll need demolitions gear. Plus whatever kind of firepower Brooks can offer us, 'cause we're bound to be seriously outnumbered.'

'On that level at least we're sorted,' Jaeger confirmed. 'I've been told there's a real war-in-a-box waiting for us at Takhli. And I've made sure they included a Dragunov with your name on it.'

As Jaeger knew only too well, the Dragunov – the iconic Russian sniper rifle, with a ten-round magazine – was Narov's weapon of choice. He'd asked for a Dragunov SVD-S – the shortened lightweight version, with the folding stock – to be included in the weapons package that Brooks had prepared. As America's key ally in the region, the Thai military had proved extremely accommodating.

The ghost of a smile played across Narov's features. 'Thanks. You remembered. Uncharacteristically thoughtful.'

Was there just a hint of playfulness in her tone? It said a lot about their relationship, Jaeger reflected, when the only opportunity the two of them had for flirting was discussing the best means to kill.

'So, total weight?' Narov added. 'And how long do we need provisioning for?'

'Seven days. At that kind of altitude, we're constrained by how much we can carry. Assume twenty-five kilos per person, not including weapons. We'll have a pulk, with a further hundred-kilo capacity. So that's two hundred kilos between us. But with munitions, grenades, demolitions gear, batteries, comms kit, surveillance kit, and cold-weather and survival gear, we're left with precious little room for rations. We need to get this done quickly, or we'll be chewing on thin air.'

'What about the locals?' Narov probed. 'Brooks figures there are several dozen Chinese employed at the plant. Unsuspecting, of course, since the place has perfect cover.'

'We try to minimise local casualties. But it's going to be incredibly hard to ID friend from foe in the kind of fight that's coming. We'll do our best. Trust our instincts.' Jaeger paused. 'But Kammler and his people – no one gets out alive. The risks are too great.'

'No one? What about Falk?'

'Falk . . .' Jaeger shrugged. 'If he's onside and no risk to the mission, then he lives. But you better be damned certain . . .' He paused. 'For that matter, we all better be damn certain he's onside. Falk's phone calls . . . if they're designed to lure us into a trap, well, we're buggered. And so, my dear, is the entire fucking world.'

Narov nodded. 'We cannot afford to fail. But trust me: Falk

will not have betrayed us.' She fixed Jaeger with a look. 'As to your wife . . .'

Jaeger flinched. 'If she's in that place, the same rules apply. We have to be certain. But leave it to me. It's my call.'

49

As far as Jaeger was concerned, the Antonov AN-32 was the only aircraft with which to be attempting such a mission.

With its twin Ivchenko turboprop engines set high on the wings, it had an almost unrivalled high-altitude landing and take-off capability, a 2,500-kilometre range, plus a stall speed of under 100 kilometres an hour – which for tonight's operation was absolutely critical.

It was also ubiquitous across Asia, being flown by the Indian, Bangladeshi, Sri Lankan and several other armed forces, and scores of civilian operators, including any number of Chinese commercial airlines. A common workhorse of charities, it regularly flew missions of mercy into Asia's uncharted regions.

Hence the cover for tonight's ultra-secret flight.

The AN-32 was decked out in the markings of the International Committee of the Red Cross: the distinctive red and white livery, plus the iconic red-cross symbol splashed across the tailplane, wings and the underside of the fuselage.

Routed via northern Thailand, Myanmar, north-west India and Bhutan, the Antonov would be straying one hundred kilometres into Chinese airspace from the border crossover point. That an ICRC flight could have blundered that far off course was unlikely, unless the navigator was seriously incompetent. But it wasn't entirely impossible, especially amidst such wild and uncharted mountains, where detours due to bad weather would be common.

The one-hundred-kilometre insertion would take the

Antonov little more than ten minutes, and the aircraft wouldn't pause long to deliver the team to target. It was unlikely to be detected on such a short run, especially as it would be weaving a path between towering peaks.

The route back would take the same amount of time, and it was just possible that the Antonov might get intercepted or forced down. Should that happen, the pilot would claim to be a bona fide aid flight that had somehow strayed into Chinese airspace.

The idea of using ICRC cover wasn't without precedent. In 1997, the SAS had been tasked to snatch two prominent Serbian war criminals, Milan Kovacevic and Simo Drljaca, from Bosnia. Kovacevic was hiding out in a hospital. The five-man SAS team sent in to get him posed as Red Cross officials, gaining entry to the hospital with their 9mm pistols tucked beneath their clothing.

Code-named Operation Tango, the SAS mission was a resounding success. Kovacevic was spirited away to a waiting 'Red Cross' helicopter, whisked out of the country and subsequently tried for war crimes. His partner, Drljaca, tried to put up a fight. He didn't get to stand trial: he died in the firefight with the SAS.

Jaeger hadn't been on Op Tango; it was before his time. But he'd certainly heard about it. It had gone down in SAS legend, and it had inspired tonight's little subterfuge.

On one level, using the ICRC livery as cover wasn't entirely morally justifiable. The Red Cross relied upon its reputation for strict neutrality and humanitarianism to gain access to war zones. But during his years in the SAS, Jaeger had learnt that sometimes, whoever broke the rules won.

Who dares. And always for the greater good.

Going up against Kammler and his ilk, he'd also learnt some of the darker arts of the enemy. As a consequence, he had few qualms about the nature of tonight's deception.

He, Narov, Raff and Alonzo were dressed in unmarked white Alpine warfare gear – state-of-the-art Goretex jackets and trousers. Under that, each sported a Helly Hansen thermal top, plus layers of silk, and they had thermal gloves and white Goretex overmitts to protect their hands from the intense cold.

In the centre of the Antonov were piled their bergens, each sheeted over with a white Alpine camouflage covering, along with two steel cargo para-tubes. An expedition-spec pulk – a six-foot flat-bottomed fibreglass sled, which came complete with tow harness – completed the kit for tonight's drop.

The pulk was man-portable: you loaded it up, strapped yourself into the harness and hauled it across the snow. Once they were on the ground, the team would unload the para-tubes, load up the sled and be on their way. Their packs were stripped down to survival gear only, so they could exit the aircraft with the lightest possible loads.

All the heavy kit was packed in the para-tubes.

During the flight, Jaeger had been too wired to sleep. The groaning of the metal fuselage and the deafening howl of the Ivchenko engines made talk all but impossible. The AN-32 had been designed in the mid seventies, and Jaeger didn't doubt that this one was several decades old. At every twist and turn he felt as if it was about to shake itself to pieces.

But he knew the reputation of the aircraft. Like most Russian airframes, it was ruggedly built and engineered to last. He didn't doubt it would get them to their target, Chinese vigilance permitting.

He'd plugged himself into the aircraft's intercom, so he could listen in on the chat from the cockpit. Mostly it had been navigational, as the pilot, co-pilot and navigator talked each other through what they could see of the terrain below, to keep a check on their route. They were heading across the easternmost extent of the Himalayas, circumventing the massive 7,500-metre peak of Kula Kangri, which straddled the border with China.

Jaeger glanced out the nearest of the AN-32's portholes. He could see jagged-edged snowfields rearing up to their right like the white fangs of some impossible sky god, the heights washed in a silvery-blue moonlight. Kula Kangri had long been disputed by both Bhutan and China. So remote was this region that neither country had been able to substantiate its territorial claim.

'Border crossing in five,' the pilot calmly announced.

This was it: no turning back now.

50

Jaeger had had just a brief introduction to the Antonov's aircrew, and that had been first names only. The pilot, Bill, was very clearly American. He spoke with a tough East Coast – New Jersey – accent. Jaeger didn't doubt that he was ex-military. Dressed in the smart, iron-creased blacks, whites and reds of an ICRC pilot's uniform, he sure looked the part.

'Border crossing in five,' he repeated. 'Prepare for things to get a little interesting back there. We'll be going in lower than a snake's belly.'

Jaeger flashed a finger-down at Narov, Raff and Alonzo: universal symbol for *prepare to lose altitude*.

The Antonov's intercom was one-way only. Any comms with the cockpit had to go via the loadie, Pete, another American. He was perched on one of the fold-down canvas seats where the bulkhead separated cockpit from cargo hold.

The Antonov began to plummet towards the moon-washed snowfields. Jaeger felt his stomach contents lurch into his throat, and fought back the gag reflex as the pilot kept losing altitude.

When it seemed as if they were about to plough into the snow and rock at some 300-plus kilometres an hour, he heard the twin turboprops emit a piercing howl. The pilot piled on the thrust, and the AN-32 pulled up, blasting the tops of the highest drifts, then sped onwards, thundering into the night.

They were down so low that the aircraft's moon shadow was almost indistinguishable from her fuselage. As he craned his neck to get a view out the rear, Jaeger spotted thick flurries of snow kicked up by the Antonov's four-bladed propellers, swirling madly in the slipstream.

Deep gullies opened up ahead, and the pilot slipped the Antonov into their icy embrace, throwing it from side to side to edge past dome-like outcrops blasted bare by the freezing wind. At the approach of a vast series of ridges, which rose like a snow-blasted giant's staircase, Jaeger felt the aircraft going into a series of switchbacks, as if they were riding some runaway escalator.

Whoever the pilot was, and whichever unit he'd trained with, Jaeger figured it was time to settle back and enjoy the ride.

'Crossing border,' the pilot's voice confirmed. 'Going dark.'

Before now, theirs had been a non-covert flight, and they'd been flying through non-hostile airspace. Accordingly, the Antonov had been showing the normal lights that civilian aircraft used. Now, all had been extinguished, including any internal lighting.

Jaeger glanced around the hold. It was washed in a faint ghostly glow: moonlight reflected back from the snow rushing past just a few dozen feet below.

'Hook-shaped frozen lake at ten o'clock,' the co-pilot announced.

'Check,' the navigator confirmed. Jaeger could just imagine the guy crouched over his charts. 'That's Lake Le-Wen-Pu. You follow its course and it leads into the Le-Wen-Pu valley. The valley extends twenty kilometres north, with a gentle curve east.'

'Roger,' the pilot confirmed.

'Oh yeah, and watch out for yaks, yurts and prayer flags tugging at the undercarriage,' the navigator added.

Jaeger allowed himself a smile. He risked a peek out of the Antonov's window. The navigator was right.

Any lower, and they'd be kissing the snowfields.

51

Jaeger braced himself at the Antonov's open ramp.

Normally when preparing to jump from such an aircraft, you had the reassuring form of a bulky parachute strapped to your shoulders as the slipstream tore at your clothing and howled around your ears.

Not tonight.

All Jaeger had strapped to his back was his light-order bergen: even their weapons were packed into the para-tubes. The Antonov's airspeed was incredibly slow – seventy knots, Jaeger figured – so it felt little worse than driving down a motorway with the window down.

He reckoned the snowfield flashing past below was no more than forty feet away.

It felt close enough almost to touch.

The Nyenchen Tanglha Mountains were so remote that there was no official agreement as to how far the range extended. But what the maps could agree on was the highest peak – Mount Nyenchen Tanglha itself, at 7,162 metres. Plus there were some 7,080 glaciers, covering 10,700 square kilometres of terrain.

In short, a lot of snow and ice.

Snow and ice: there was a big difference between the two as far as this insertion was concerned. Tonight they needed to seek out just the right kind of snow.

Jaeger had picked the spot off a satellite photo, with the help of some of Brooks's finest meteorological experts. As he crouched at the open ramp, waiting for the loadie to give them the go-go-go, he prayed that he'd got it right.

The risks in what they were about to attempt were legion. Only Raff and Jaeger had ever made such a drop before, and then only during a series of highly experimental SAS arctic warfare exercises.

The loadie flicked two fingers in front of each of their faces. Two minutes to go. He was fastened to the Antonov's side with a thick canvas strap, just in case anyone lost it at the last moment and tried to drag him with them.

'One minute!' he yelled.

Jaeger bunched closer to the pulk and the steel drop containers, which were perched on the open ramp. He shook out the tension in his arms and shoulders, stamped his feet and beat his hands together. He needed maximum flexibility in his limbs for what was coming.

'Thirty seconds!' yelled the loadie.

Jaeger's eyes were glued to the jump light, which was set to one side of the ramp. Moments later it changed from red to green. This was it: show time.

He dropped his shoulder and drove the pulk off the end of the ramp and into the open void, as to either side of him Alonzo and Raff shoved out the steel containers.

For the briefest of instants he was aware of the objects silhouetted against the gleam of the snow, and then he followed in their wake, leaping off the ramp. As he tumbled into thin air, a part of his brain was yelling at him to pull his chute, even though he knew he didn't have one.

He felt himself buffeted by the slipstream as he fought to maintain a crouched position, legs pulled up beneath him and locked there with his arms. It was the kind of poise you'd adopt to bomb your mates in a swimming pool. By trial and error it had also proved to be the best kind of body stance for what was coming.

Jaeger had just the briefest of instants to wonder what madness had possessed him to jump when his feet hit the snowdrift.

The impact was surprisingly soft and silent, and moments later sixty-five kilos of Will Jaeger had ploughed deep into the spongy white mass, disappearing completely from view.

He lay on his back in a foetal position and gazed at the heavens above him. It felt like something out of a Tom and Jerry cartoon: he could see the shape his falling body had cut through the snow's surface, etched against the stars and the moon.

Jumping into snowdrifts: only the Brits could have dreamt up such an insane means to deploy into hostile territory. Yet tonight, for Jaeger at least, it seemed to have worked just fine. He'd made a near perfect landing in soft snow and was unhurt.

The boffins had assured him that on this flat, open, windswept plateau on the northern scarp of the mountains, the drifts would likely be a good eighteen feet thick.

Jaeger figured he'd sunk ten feet into this one.

The challenge now was to get out again.

52

Jaeger took a few seconds to calm his heartbeat, his breath pooling in the human-shaped snow hole like some ghostly mist. It was so cold he could feel his breath freezing in his nostrils.

Above the echoing silence, he could hear the droning of the Antonov as it did an about-turn. Moments later, its ghostly form flashed past overhead. Had Jaeger imagined it, or had the pilot given them a momentary wing wobble to salute their insertion? No doubt about it, the crew of the Antonov had been a class act.

Now to extricate himself from this snowy embrace. No time to delay, he reminded himself: the fate of the world was hanging in the balance here. Failure wasn't an option, the price of screwing up an unthinkable one. They needed to get moving.

He tore off his overmitts, placing his bergen beneath him to form a solid platform, and clambered to his feet. He pulled a length of paracord from his pocket and tied one end onto the pack's top strap. Then he tied the other end around his waist and groped for the sky. He was just tall enough for his fingertips to emerge above the surface.

He used his mitts to pat down the snow. He kept doing so until he figured he'd built up a firm enough platform. Then, using his hands to pull himself upwards and his boots to kick holes into the wall of snow, he wormed his way up and out, emerging like a caterpillar on his belly. That done, he turned and dragged his bergen out by its leash.

He took a moment to survey the scene.

Utterly breathtaking.

The snowfields rolled away on all sides like some gently undulating frozen sea. There wasn't so much as the blink of a light or any other sign of human habitation. Jaeger felt alone on the roof of the world.

On one side the range of peaks reared into the heavens, icebound and severe. He was thankful they didn't have to cross those. The Antonov had flown around them, saving the team the trouble. From their landing spot, it should be all downhill to the target.

Just then he heard a sudden sharp, pinging crack, which echoed across the snow. A glacier was on the move, ancient ice breaking under impossible pressure.

He glanced around, searching for the others.

No sign of them anywhere.

Likewise, the pulk and the drop containers had disappeared from view. On balance, he figured his team had a greater chance of extricating themselves from the snow's clutches than did the sled or the heavy para-tubes. There was no telling how deep those had penetrated, though finding them should be fairly straightforward. He figured he'd jumped around three seconds after they'd been shoved out. At the speed the Antonov had been flying, they should be no more than fifty feet away.

He retraced the aircraft's path, moving due south. It was easy enough to do so: by turning to face the Nyenchen Tanglha Mountains, which rose before him like a giant frozen wall, he was by default heading south.

The first hole he found was made by the pulk. Lighter than the containers, it had drifted further, being thrown forward by the Antonov's momentum. It had dropped rear first, upending itself in the snow. After a few seconds' tugging back and forth, Jaeger freed and righted it. Now to find the drop containers and load up the heavier cargo.

As he searched, he heard a figure struggling through the snow.

215

It was Raff. The big Maori was a good twenty kilos heavier than Jaeger, and as a result with each footstep he sank further into the soft drifts.

Raff had been less than enamoured with Jaeger's proposed insertion technique. He'd grown up on New Zealand's North Island, which had a warmer climate than its southern neighbour. With its pristine white beaches, parts of it were semi-tropical. As a result, Raff hated snow, ice and everything associated with the cold.

'How you doing?' Jaeger asked.

'I'm alive,' Raff growled. 'Nothing broken.' He glanced around at the frozen moonscape. 'Still freezing my bollocks off, though.'

Jaeger had just found the first para-tube. Laden with ninety kilos of kit, it had sunk deep. He nodded at the hole. 'This'll warm you up, mate. Get digging!'

Raff grunted and set his massive shoulders to the task. Soon he and Jaeger had dragged the first of the tubes out of the snow-drift's icy embrace.

To one side, Narov and Alonzo were likewise getting busy freeing the other tube. All four of them seemed to have made the jump pretty much in one piece.

Four: it was the magic number of UKSF patrols, the smallest unit you would regularly deploy in. In SAS parlance, four was a fire team. Four fire teams made up a troop of sixteen. Four troops made up a squadron of sixty-odd SAS blades – 'blades' being the term for the fighting men of the Regiment.

As four-person teams went, this was about as good as it got, Jaeger reflected. The fire team to die for. And right now, they had the fate of the world resting on their shoulders.

They started emptying the para-tubes, making five piles of kit: one, the largest, to be loaded onto the pulk and four of equal size to be packed into their bergens. Once the pulk was loaded, they zipped closed the waterproof cover and unfastened the tow straps.

Raff eyed the heavy sled, which was now piled with some hundred kilos of kit. 'I'm good to go. I'll set the pace. At least it'll get me bloody warm.'

The para-tubes had held four sets of skis. Raff took one, un-clipped the toe binding and slid the front of his boot in, hearing the reassuring snap as it clicked home. They were langlauf – cross-country – skis, and only the toe would be held firm. That left you free to lift your heel as you thrust forward, powering ahead.

Skis on, Raff grabbed the pulk's harness – like a rucksack's shoulder strap and hip belt, but without the pack attached – and strapped himself in. He fastened the D-ring clips to the harness, then grabbed his ski poles, slipping the straps around his wrists.

He glanced at Jaeger and nodded.

Jaeger fought to suppress a smile. Where Raff's braids were poking out from under his thermal ski hat, he could see they were icing up, like the frozen tentacles of some bizarre ice beast. Surely the world's coolest hairstyle, he reflected, but not right here and now!

'Okay, thirty minutes' march, then rest,' he announced. 'Pulk changeover time.' He checked his watch. 'We've got six hours' skiing ahead of us, and it's eight until first light. We're at serious altitude, unacclimatised and with much less O_2 than we're used to. Take it easy. No rush. Conserve yourselves for what's ahead.'

Grunts of acknowledgement all round.

'I'll take point,' he continued, 'then Narov, followed by Raff with the pulk, with Alonzo bringing up the rear. All good?'

Silent nods.

'Right, let's go.'

53

They say the weather is the single greatest danger you are ever likely to encounter in the Tibetan mountains. Sure enough, this storm had blown up out of nowhere, and with zero warning.

One moment Jaeger had been leading the march, skis sliding across a hard-packed field of snow, the heavens bright and star-lit. The next, a keen, biting wind had blown up out of the west and the sky had darkened ominously.

Tibet being twice the size of France but as barren and sparsely populated as anywhere on earth, it had proved difficult to get accurate weather forecasts. Generally, during the drier spring and summer months, you were more likely to encounter dust storms than any significant precipitation.

Yet by the feeling of the wind as it bit into Jaeger's face, a blast of wet and cold weather was coming.

Almost fifty per cent of the world's population relied on fresh water originating from Tibet's glaciers. Jaeger had read as much in Miles's briefings. Meltwater from the Tibetan plateau fed the rivers that watered much of China and India. When a storm hit at the kind of altitude Jaeger and his team were traversing – some 5,000 metres – it fell as snow.

Just as it was starting to do now.

The wind stiffened. Soon it was driving hard needles of ice into Jaeger's exposed features. He halted, peeled off his over-mitts, and rolled his ski hat down, transforming it into a white balaclava, the better to shield his face from the knife-edge blasts. The others gathered close, doing likewise.

With each passing second, visibility was worsening, gusts howling down from the northern scarp of the mountains. Jaeger reached into his smock pocket and pulled out a pair of snow goggles. He slid them on, shielding his eyes.

Raff pressed his balaclava-clad face close. 'Last thing we need – a fucking storm!' he yelled. He glanced at the mountain range. It was barely visible any more.

'Got to press on,' Jaeger yelled back. 'We stop too long in this shit, we're dead. Got to get lower . . .'

His last words were torn away by the wind.

Pulling his compass out of his pocket, he took a bearing, then signalled them all to move out.

They ploughed on, cutting into the teeth of the storm. To Jaeger's rear, the driving snow obliterated his tracks in seconds.

The weather closed around them. Soon he could barely see the hand in front of his face. It was horribly disorientating. Keeping track of time was as hard as maintaining direction. Forty-mile-an-hour gusts tore into him, threatening to blast him off his feet. He dreaded to think how Alonzo, who had just taken over pulk duty, was faring.

They were skiing through a near whiteout. The four of them closed ranks as the wind howled and screamed. The temperature had dropped to ten below, and the storm felt all-consuming. They were trapped within the belly of a raging beast.

Jaeger didn't doubt any more what danger they were in. This had morphed from a seek-and-destroy mission into a survival epic. They needed to find shelter. Urgently. Without it, they would perish, swallowed up by the savagery of the storm and ending up as deep-frozen corpses.

He thought back over a vital lesson he'd been given by his mountain and arctic warfare cadre instructor. You didn't fight the mountains – not if you wanted to survive. You had to learn to bend and flex to the vagaries of the wild.

He tried to scan the terrain before him, but in every direction it looked the same. He struggled to see through the churning mass of white. The air was dark with angry, violent snowflakes. It felt as if he were marooned in a world formed of snow and ice.

And already he felt frozen to the core.

The colder he got, the slower his body and mind seemed to work. In these kinds of conditions, hypothermia killed you by stealth. The more sluggish his brain became, the less likelihood there was of ever finding a way to safety.

He tried to get a grip. He'd been steeling himself to deploy and fight a human enemy – Kammler and his people – not a natural one. But he needed to get his head around this life-or-death challenge and focus.

As he pushed onwards, fighting against the savage whip of the ice-laden blasts, he noticed a bank of snow rising to their left.

As Jaeger knew well, snow was actually one of the best insulators. In the Arctic, the Inuit lived in igloos, which were basically domes made of blocks of snow.

He stopped. The others pulled to a halt beside him, their faces encrusted with a layer of wind-blasted snow and their breath condensing as thick icicles crusted to the exterior of their balaclavas.

He jabbed a hand towards the bank of snow.

'Time to get the hell out of this wind!' he yelled. 'We dig, or we die.'

54

Jaeger dropped his bergen, sank to his hands and knees and began to burrow into the snow bank. The others joined him, and gradually the space before them took shape. In a matter of minutes, they had excavated a basic snow cave large enough for all four of them.

They crawled in, dragging their bergens after them, and began to ready the cave to last out the storm. First they closed off the exit, so that only a hole large enough for a human torso to wriggle through remained.

Snow is a great insulator, as long as human body warmth doesn't melt it. Then, it becomes a sodden, freezing mess . . . and a killer. The trick is to lay down a waterproof membrane, ideally with a thermal mat on top – just as they were doing now.

That done, each of the four rolled out their goose-down sleeping bags, ready to crawl in and thaw their freezing limbs. But as Jaeger was about to do so, he remembered the pulk. There was no telling how long the storm might last, or what thickness of snow might fall.

In short, the pulk could be swallowed by the tempest.

Taking Raff with him, he ventured back outside. If anything, the blizzard was worse. The wind buffeted him one way and then the other as he groped in the thick darkness for the sled. Even as his gloved hand found it, a blast of incredible force plucked him off his feet and hurled him into the darkness.

He struggled to his knees, but the storm threw him down

again. He had to reach the pulk and secure it. Without it, they were dead.

He groped for it again, practically worming his way across the snow on his belly. His hands made contact, and he started fitting together the first of the marker poles, made of sections of a tough but lightweight aluminium.

Blanking the pain, he slotted together the second pole and handed it to Raff, who drove both poles into the snow, knotting the pulk's tow straps securely around them. Some five feet of tubing emerged above the ground to mark the pulk's position. No matter what depth of snow might fall, the two marker poles should remain visible. Plus they would anchor the sled to prevent it blowing away.

The two men crawled back exhaustedly into the cave, where Alonzo and Narov were already trussed up tight in their sleeping bags.

Outside, the storm howled and screamed. Inside, the four figures were ensconced in a cocoon of comparative warmth and safety.

Jaeger flicked on his head torch and eyed the others. It was a testament to their utter professionalism that the building of the snow cave had been accomplished almost without a word needing to be said. Their training, and their subsequent operational experience, spoke volumes.

'Right,' he announced, 'we sit tight until the storm blows out.'

By way of response, Raff held up his Nalgene water bottle, which was almost empty. 'Got me a pee bottle.' He slipped it inside his sleeping bag. 'You know what temperature urine comes out at? Ninety-six degrees Fahrenheit. Keep your pee bottle close – doubles as a hot-water bottle.'

Jaeger grimaced. 'Too much detail.'

Narov shifted restlessly in her sleeping bag. 'By staying here, we risk the shipment getting there before us. The tungsten.'

'We do,' Jaeger replied. 'But one, we're no good to anyone dead, and that storm will kill us. Two, no aircraft is landing anywhere near here in these conditions. Trust me, if the storm's stopped us, it'll stop any plane.'

'Tell me,' Alonzo ventured, 'just how goddam cold is it?'

'Breathe in,' said Jaeger, by way of answer. 'Feel your nose hairs freezing like needles? That's what happens when you're below minus ten. And right now I'd say it's way colder.'

Alonzo glanced around their shelter. 'Thank Christ for the snow cave. No need to keep watch, I guess?'

'No one but a dead man is moving out there. Get some sleep. Everyone.'

Pausing only to remove his boots, Jaeger crawled into his own bag. He checked his watch: 0400 hours. He'd been so focused on getting them to their target – *on stopping Kammler* – that he'd lost all track of time.

Much longer and that focus would have killed them. Seeking shelter had been the only call to make, and Jaeger knew it.

But he also knew that time was not on their side.

55

There was nothing overly flashy or brash about Nordhavn trawler yachts. With their smooth, clean lines, they were built for serious ocean-going journeys, and for those who liked to travel the world in no-nonsense, businesslike style. They were low-key, functional and practically unsinkable, which was the main reason why Kammler had chosen to use them.

Steve Jones didn't much give a damn. No sailor, all he cared about was whether this floating bomb platform would do the job they needed it to. The Nordhavn had a fridge full of beer and a gym, so he could handle it for a few days. But he'd be out of here just as soon as the present task was done.

He leant his massive, muscled, tattooed bulk on the rail and pressed a button on the bottom left panel of the hand-held console. On a flat stretch of deck aft, the four blades of a quadcopter drone began to rotate, spinning into a blur as they spooled up to speed.

He glanced at the figure on the bridge. 'All clear? Nothing on the radar?'

'*Niet*. Nothing. All clear.'

The Russian captain was a typically dour soul who kept himself to himself. There was one upside. He was pickled in vodka most evenings, which meant that he kept his hands off Jones's stash of chilled beers.

Jones swept his eyes around the stretch of ocean. Calm aquamarine water stretched as far as the eye could see, empty of any other shipping. That was just as he wanted it. This far out in the

Pacific, if there wasn't another ship in range, they were as safe as houses.

He rested his thumb on the left joystick and pushed vertically forwards. The whine of the quadcopter's engines rose to a screaming fever pitch, and seemingly effortlessly it rose into the air. Jones kept his thumb pressed forwards as the drone climbed, bringing it up to a good hundred feet above the surface of the waves.

Its cargo was visible now. Beneath the SUV-sized craft and gripped by four powerful calipers sat a black box not a great deal smaller than the drone itself. It was a life-size replica of the devices these airborne-delivery systems would be dropping over their targets, if today's little experiment went to plan.

The black box was crammed full of bricks – enough to replicate the weight of one of the devices Professor Kangjon was building. Jones didn't like the Korean. In fact, he didn't like anyone foreign. Or rather, anyone who wasn't a pure-blooded Aryan, which was how he viewed himself – a prime and perfect example of the breed.

He scrolled his thumb across the right joystick, pushing it towards the right, and sure enough the drone banked in that direction. Once he had it on the desired bearing, he flew it straight and level a good 500 feet, at which point he put it into a steep climb.

By the time it was some 800 feet away, it had clawed to over 1,000 feet in altitude – not a great deal lower than the kind of height at which the Fat Man bomb had been detonated over Nagasaki.

If Kammler's plan was to work, they needed to deliver a clutch of INDs to their targets simultaneously, for maximum destructive effect. And they couldn't just sail right up to the shoreline. For one, they'd be spotted by the plant's security. And second, as Professor Kangjon had indicated, only by detonating the IND as an airburst right above the nuclear power plant could they achieve meltdown. So what better way to do so than by drone?

Jones allowed the joysticks to return to their central position and the drone went into a steady hover. Perfect.

He scanned the horizon one more time: still blissfully empty. As he turned his gaze back to the drone, he could just imagine it hovering above a power station, poised to strike. With his thumb raised over the button on the bottom of the console, he pictured the cataclysmic detonation. The resulting devastation. The human cost. The terror. He couldn't wait, especially as it was Jaeger who would suffer the most.

Poetic justice, as Kammler had called it.

He punched his finger onto the button. There was a micro-second's delay as the message flashed across the air, and then the sharp crack of an explosion at altitude. In a puff of brown smoke the drone and its cargo disintegrated, shattered brick and aircraft parts cascading down into the sea.

Jones smiled. They were good to go.

He pulled out a satphone from his pocket and punched speed dial.

'The eagle has landed,' he announced, without bothering to introduce himself.

'And what the hell does that mean?' the speaker on the other end snapped.

The Eagle Has Landed was one of Jones's all-time favourite films. In it, a crack team of German operators were sent into Britain at the height of World War II to kidnap or assassinate Winston Churchill. Pity they hadn't succeeded, Jones reflected. It would have saved him and Kammler a whole world of trouble.

'All done and dusted,' he explained. 'It went like fucking clockwork.'

Kammler laughed exultantly. 'Excellent. I knew I could count on you.' He paused. 'Now, your next task is one I think you will relish. Professor Kangjon: I think he may be in need of your powers of . . . persuasion.'

Jones smiled. 'My fucking pleasure.'

'Make your way back as quickly as you can.'

Jones confirmed that he would. He went below and headed for the Nordhavn's gym. It was a bit cramped for a man of his size, but better than nothing, and at least it had a full-size punchbag slung from the ceiling.

As he began his workout, fists, knees, elbows and feet smashing away in a blur, he could see in his mind's eye the pudgy features of the North Korean professor being beaten to a pulp. The image morphed into the chief figure of hate in Jones's life: Will Jaeger. In his mind, he was kicking Jaeger into a cowed and bloodied heap . . .

The last time they had met, Jaeger had left him for dead, ensnared within a wild tangle of sharks. Well, as Jaeger should have learnt on SAS selection, Steve Jones didn't give up that easily.

Or die that easily, for that matter.

56

J aeger leant back from the SwiftScope's eyepiece. Set on a tripod and screened by vegetation, the scope's lens was camouflaged by a piece of 'scrim' – perforated khaki material – to prevent glare. Its 50x magnification lens gave a perfect view of all that was happening down below.

Jaeger's backside felt like a block of ice. His legs were on fire, his muscles on the verge of cramping up. He needed to shift about a bit in this freezing hole of an OP – little more than a shell scrape on the bare mountainside – or he was at risk of getting frostbite. But any sudden movement had to be avoided.

It was forty-eight hours since the blizzard had blown itself out. For four days they'd been trapped in that snow cave, riding out its blind rage. Four agonising days that had confirmed what Jaeger had felt on every mission he had ever been involved in: it was the waiting that was the hardest part.

It was six days since they'd leapt from the Antonov's open ramp and landed on Chinese soil. Or snow. Time was running out, and still there was no sign of the tungsten shipment.

They'd dug themselves out of the snow cave only to discover that their surroundings had been transformed. Ghostly snow sculptures rose before them, as if a horde of primordial monsters had stormed down from the mountains, becoming frozen in time. In between those bizarre forms, pans of ice were windblasted and scoured clear.

The landscape had had a certain dreamlike quality to it.

Everything was snow. Even the poles marking the pulk's position had been transformed. Raff had had to knock the snow off them before they could credit that the pulk was actually there – just buried.

Thankfully, the weather had turned. In fact, it had reverted to what were more normal conditions for this time of year – spring on the high Tibetan plateau. Under a shockingly clear night sky – washed free of the storm – they'd harnessed up the sled and set forth.

A few uneventful hours later, they'd reached their end destination and established the OP. Roofed over with branches and chicken wire – into which they'd woven twigs and vegetation, piling on some earth and snow for extra authenticity – it was indistinguishable from the surrounding terrain.

You would have to stand right on top of it and gaze into the six inches or so separating the roof from the frontal slope of rocks and boulders to get any sense of what it was. And as the interior was bathed in permanent shadow, the watchers were all but invisible.

A few dozen paces back from the OP, at the crest of the ridge, the snow proper began. There they'd built a second, slightly larger snow cave, the entrance to which was concealed by Alpine camouflage netting. This was the rest and admin area.

They'd put in place a perfectly concealed position to spy on their target.

Now to nail him.

But they were running short on food. As was invariably the case when calculating rations, Jaeger had underestimated just how many calories the human body needed to stave off starvation and as fuel to keep warm. Or rather, in the trade-off between extra food and extra weaponry, it was weaponry that had won.

As Raff had noted sourly, shame you couldn't eat bullets.

Jaeger could feel hunger gnawing at his guts. But one glance at the facility below them – the target – and he figured prioritising raw firepower over raw food was undoubtedly a good thing.

That facility was a well-secured natural fortress, and it would require a distinctly suicidal four-person squad to take it out.

They'd set the OP on the very fringes of the snowline, where the frozen whiteness petered out, to be replaced by bare rock and scrub. Below, a steep-sided gorge cut through the foothills of the Nyenchen Tanglha Mountains, and at the far end lay the vast expanse of the Namtso – 'Beautiful' – Lake.

Through the depths of the gorge ran the Boqi river, a twisting sliver of violent aquamarine blue, the striking colour caused by the salts carried by glacial meltwaters. And clinging to the side of the gorge, on a platform blasted out of the rock, lay the fortress that Jaeger and his team were keeping watch on.

It was the water that had drawn Kammler here, which had also been the means via which the Chinese government had allowed him in. Much of Tibet's water sat in lakes like the Namtso, which, being brackish, carried a high degree of salt. Salt water was no good for human consumption, and offered little scope for irrigation either, since the salt quickly poisoned the land.

Knowing this, and recognising the growing demand for water amongst a one-billion-strong population, the Chinese had opened up to foreign investment in using water for energy and for its purification. In due course Kammler had offered them a double whammy of a promise, here on the banks of the Boqi.

First, by piping the water from the smaller, glacial lakes above, his plant could turn it into electricity – hence the giant turbine hall set into the mountainside. Three massive water pipelines – 'penstocks' to those in the trade – brought the water from the highland lakes down the nearside of the gorge to drive the turbines situated inside the building.

The electricity so generated – massive amounts of the stuff

– went to serve the plant's main purpose: desalination. Removing salt from brackish water to make it drinkable was hideously expensive. Normally. But here, the electricity came dirt cheap, and Kammler had promised groundbreaking technologies to render the water potable.

For the Chinese, this was the holy grail of such research. No wonder they had welcomed Kammler – plus his money and technology – with open arms.

China had recently overtaken America as the foremost country attracting foreign investors. Kammler had been just one amongst many thousands of such businessmen.

All of this Jaeger had learnt from Miles's briefings. Now, as he gazed down into the Boqi river gorge, he was seeing it at first hand. The slab-sided desalination plant lay adjacent to the turbine house, and a short distance away was the accommodation block. It looked as if it must house a good two hundred people – workers and guards.

Tucked well to one side and clinging to the cover of the gorge's knife-cut wall was their main target – the laboratory. The entire complex was encircled by a double layer of high-tensile fencing, crowned by rolls of razor wire. A guard force patrolled the perimeter. They were armed with pistols, as was a civilian establishment's wont, but Jaeger didn't doubt that there was a well-stocked armoury close at hand.

It was a heavy security presence for a civilian facility, but no more than many others that Jaeger had visited. Commercial research was expensive and sensitive, and espionage always a danger. Kammler would have argued that he had to safeguard his investment, which would supposedly chiefly benefit China after all.

He had every reason to seek to import sophisticated technology for his desalination plant and laboratory. A dirt track snaked east along the riverside, giving access to the outside world: it was via this route that Kammler would be awaiting his newest, Moldovan delivery.

Somewhere in the laboratory was a sealed-off high-security area, with very restricted access. There, pretty much hiding in plain sight, he was amassing his highly enriched uranium.

And, as they feared, building his clutch of deadly INDs.

57

Of course, a place as beautiful as Namtso Lake attracted a smattering of tourists. Snowy peaks plunged abruptly into the turquoise waters, wind-sculpted ice crusting the very shore-line. And along the northern fringes, herds of sheep grazed upon the seasonal grasses that thrived amidst the yellows, ochres and greys of the lakeside.

But the lake's sheer remoteness kept the number of visitors down to a trickle, and few ever ventured to the far western fringes – into the Boqi gorge. Even if they did, all they would see would be a bona fide hydropower station, with all the usual associated facilities, security included.

Miles and Brooks had hit the nail on the head: this place was perfect for Kammler's purposes. In fact, the entire set-up was so smart and accomplished that it made Jaeger marvel at the sheer waste of such intellect. So much creative intelligence and cunning channelled into death and mass destruction.

What would a man like Kammler have been capable of, had he not been seduced by his father's twisted dreams of Nazi world domination? Of the rise of a Fourth Reich?

It troubled Jaeger beyond reason that Ruth might be down there. It was such a horrific thought that he blanked it from his mind. If he dwelt upon it, it would torture and destroy him.

He leant back from the SwiftScope and wriggled around, trying to work some life back into frozen limbs. Without a word being said, Raff took up position at the scope. What they were waiting on now was the arrival of the tungsten shipment – their Trojan horse.

Jaeger eyed the big Maori for a second. With approaching six days' growth of beard, and trussed up in layer upon layer of cold-weather gear, the guy looked like some kind of a cave troll. It never ceased to amaze Jaeger how much punishment Raff seemed able to take without complaining. The exception was the cold.

Raff truly hated the cold. It made him grumpy; bad company, just like he was now.

'Got an idea,' Jaeger ventured quietly. 'Want to hear it?'

'Just as long as it doesn't involve jumping into bloody snow-drifts,' Raff muttered, without removing his eye from the scope.

'Remember the heavy-water raid? 1942? We studied it in commando training. Started with Operation Musketoon, twelve commandos dropped by submarine off Norway's coast. They trekked across the mountains to sabotage a hydropower plant – Glomfjord. Pretty similar to this one.'

'Yeah,' Raff grunted. 'Commando legend. Sunk Hitler's nu-clear programme. And?'

'They were a small force,' Jaeger continued. 'Lightly armed. Nowhere near strong enough to take down the two hundred German troops defending the place. So you know what they did? They harnessed the power of mother nature to smash it to smithereens.'

'Don't drag it out. I got brain freeze.'

'They realised the pipelines were pointed directly at the power plant, like the barrels of a massive shotgun. You blow the pipes, the water spews out and slams into the target, carrying with it trees, rocks, boulders – the works.'

Raff took his eye away from the scope. Jaeger could tell that he had the big Maori's attention now.

'Think about it,' he enthused. 'We blow the pipelines, high above the plant, security fencing gets swept away, walls get breached; it's chaos. Gives us an edge, a way in.'

The hint of a smile crept across Raff's frozen features. 'Does this mean I get to go home early and get warm?'

Jaeger grinned. 'Pretty much. But you're the demolitions guy. How do we do it? Do we have enough explosives?'

'Damn right we do,' Raff growled. 'Wrap a collar of shaped PE4 around each of the pipelines, preferably at a point of natural weakness. Job sorted.'

'So,' Jaeger mused, 'we blow the tungsten bomb, lab gets obliterated. We blow the pipeline charges, perimeter fence and a lot else gets smashed to pieces. That's our way in – we go in hard on the tail end of that.'

Raff's smile glinted in the half-light of the OP. 'What's not to like?'

Quite a bit actually, thought Jaeger, though he wasn't about to vocalise it. As far as the rest were concerned, they were risking their lives. But in Jaeger's case there was also the possibility that his wife was down there. And when they blew the pipelines, would anyone in that plant survive the coming storm?

What was Jaeger then supposed to tell his son? *I killed your mother, but I had my reasons. The survival of the world was at stake.*

He blanked the very thought from his head. No son would ever understand.

But what other option was there?

58

R aff and Alonzo had volunteered to set the pipeline charges. Demolitions: it was their kind of thing.

They waited until nightfall before flitting due west, moving along the snowline until they reached the point just below where the pipelines exited the feeder lake. They crouched beside the massive steel tubes, each as high as a man's shoulders, the roar of the water loud in their ears.

The sheer power of the through-flow and resulting friction was such that it heated up the steel sides of the pipelines, which were utterly free of snow and ice. The bare pipes plunged away like giant serpents glistening in the moonlight.

Raff and Alonzo descended a short distance, tracing the route of the pipes to where they tilted over the lip of the gorge, dropping at a seventy-degree angle towards the plant. There they unslung their rucksacks and settled to their task. At this juncture the pipes, when blown asunder, would be pointing directly at the power station some five hundred feet below, like three giant gun barrels.

From their packs they removed the shaped daisy-chain charges. Each consisted of a string of chunks of NATO Plastic Explosive No. 4 – 'PE4' for short – the saboteur's tool of choice. Clay-coloured, and with a distinctive oily smell, it had a consistency like dough.

It could be sliced up, moulded, jumped on and even shot at, and it wouldn't so much as go *phut*. But if you triggered a small charge embedded within it – the detonator – it would truly go *kaboom*.

Raff threaded the first charge around the nearest pipe. He could feel the thrumming pressure as water thundered through at incredible speed. He did a repeat performance with the other two pipes, linking the three charges to one common fuse.

That fuse was set to sixty seconds, leaving just enough time for whoever triggered it to take cover. With an explosive velocity of some 7,500 metres per second, a charge of PE4 would scythe down anything in its path. Once they triggered the detonator, the pipelines would be history.

Charges set, Raff rejoined Alonzo on watch. The night was clear and still and not another living thing appeared to be moving, either on the snowfields above or below in the gorge.

'Anything?' Raff whispered.

'Nada,' Alonzo replied through a mouthful of gum.

In his arms the big American cradled a Colt C7 Diemaco assault rifle, with an under-slung 40mm grenade launcher. In terms of lightness, sheer accuracy and raw firepower, the assault rifle/grenade launcher combo was the only choice for such a mission. All had opted for it bar Narov.

Typically, she had insisted on deploying with her trusty Dragunov sniper rifle.

'I could murder a beer,' Alonzo muttered.

Raff blew into his gloved hands. 'Beer? Too fucking cold, mate. Give me a Big Mac and hot chocolate any time.'

He took a moment to check over his handiwork. As he ran his eye across the linked charges, he could just imagine the tidal wave of destruction that would tear down the mountainside once the pipelines were ruptured.

He hoped to hell Jaeger's wife wasn't down there. In truth, he doubted she was. As far as Raff was concerned, Ruth had very likely taken herself off to some wacky retreat. A few weeks away and a chance to sort her head. That was far more likely than her running here, to Kammler.

But still, he didn't envy his friend's dilemma one bit.

Sure, there had been no sign of Ruth during their observations.

They'd considered attempting a close-target recce to check. But on balance, the risk of compromise was too high, and no way could they afford to mess up. Not for anyone.

Raff and Alonzo turned to their final task: camouflaging the charges. Stunted trees and shrubs clung to the side of the gorge. They scattered some fallen branches over their handiwork until it was well hidden, then set off back to the OP.

It had just turned midnight on their third day above Kammler's lair. They expected the tungsten bomb – their Trojan horse – to be delivered shortly. Brooks was keeping a close check on it via the tracking device, and it was scheduled to be here in the next twenty-four hours.

Raff and Alonzo were back at the OP by 0300, Chinese time. It would be 1900 hours back in Germany – at Falkenhagen – and Miles had assured the team that he was on call 24/7. Time for the update that they were all were keen to hear.

Raff relieved Narov at the OP. She moved back to the rest area to try and get some sleep, Alonzo joining her. For the past forty-eight hours they'd been on half rations, and the hunger and cold were gnawing at their guts.

Raff glanced at Jaeger, who was hunched over the scope. 'Anything, mate?'

Jaeger held up a hand for silence. His focus was one hundred per cent on whatever he could see through the lens. Raff strained his ears. He figured he could make out the distant throb of a diesel engine in the valley below.

The SwiftScope they were using was a High Performance Nighthawk, equipped with an 82mm objective lens, providing increased light transmission. Basically, it delivered incredible night vision in anything close to decent moonlight.

Artificially boosted night-vision binoculars – NVGs – which utilised infrared light spectrums to see in the dark, were all well and good, but they tended to create their own distinctive glow. Not good when holed up in an OP overlooking a hostile target.

'Got something,' Jaeger muttered. 'Twelve X-rays, all armed:

assault rifles. Boarding two SUVs. Loading in bags of gear. Looks like Kammler's people are taking a little expedition somewhere.'

'Tesco,' Raff grunted. 'Running short on cornflakes.'

Jaeger smiled. 'Nah, mate. Chinese takeaway.'

Humour: the bedrock of British elite forces operations.

If that died, you might as well pack up and head home.

59

'First vehicle leading off,' Jaeger continued his commentary. 'Heading east down the dirt track. Two up, travelling in convoy.' He kept his eye glued to the scope as he swung it gently right, tracing the vehicles' passage. 'Showing full lights, not driving tactically, skis strapped to the roof: looks like a regular kind of a road move.

'Gone from view,' he added. He removed his eye from the scope. 'What d'you reckon, mate?'

Raff shrugged. 'Gone to RV with the incoming shipment. What they figure is a crateload of HEU.'

Jaeger nodded. 'My thoughts exactly.' He flicked his wrist and glanced at his watch. 'Time to check in with Falkenhagen.'

He disconnected the Thuraya satphone from its portable solar charger, punched out a short message, encoded it and sent it in data burst: *Sitrep: in position. Update?*

The two men stared at the Thuraya's screen, waiting for a response. Generally Miles got back pretty much instantly. A few minutes later, there was the ping of an incoming message.

It wasn't from Miles. Instead, the caller ID showed it was from Brooks.

Jaeger opened it: *Falkenhagen compromised. Condor missing. Your position believed blown. Take soonest direct action to sabotage Kammler. Urgent: make contact voice comms earliest possible.*

Jaeger had to read the message twice before he could even begin to grasp its import. Surely it couldn't be true? Condor was Peter Miles's code name. If Brooks's message meant what it appeared to, the Falkenhagen bunker had been penetrated and Miles was gone. Plus their mission had been blown to Kammler and his people.

Shit. Jaeger turned to Raff. 'Mate, what the fuck?'

'Only one thing to do: call Brooks.'

Jaeger punched speed dial for the CIA director's secure line – the one on which he'd assured Jaeger he would always be available.

'Jaeger?' a voice answered. 'No easy way to say this, but the shit's hit the fan. A force of gunmen hit Falkenhagen. The place is a mess. No guessing who's responsible. Miles is missing. MIA, KIA – we don't know. We have every reason to believe your mission is compromised, your position known. You're going to have to speed things up down there.'

Jaeger cursed. It was worse even than he'd imagined. He felt as if he'd had the rug whipped out from under his feet while going five rounds with Mike Tyson.

'How did they even find Falkenhagen? Penetrate the security?'

'No idea. They must have had someone on the inside.'

Jaeger's mind was reeling. 'So we've no idea who we can trust? Kammler's people could be anywhere – *anyone* – amongst us?'

There was a momentary pause. Then: 'Jaeger, I figure I can trust you. And I figure I can trust your team. And rest assured, buddy, you sure as hell can trust me.'

It was Jaeger's turn to pause. Brooks could be the one who had betrayed them. Sold out Falkenhagen; sold out Miles. But that didn't make any sense. Brooks turned? From all Jaeger knew of the man, it didn't add up.

A look of steel came into his eyes. 'Okay, so what do we do?'

'In essence, nothing's changed. You're there. You have your team. Kammler's very likely onto you. But he's got to get to you. And before he does, we – *you* – have to stop him. Finish it. Finish it before he finishes you.'

'So we're a hundred per cent on our own, right?'

'You always were. You're in China: apart from intel, I can't give you jack in terms of backup. You know what you gotta do. Finish Kammler. Nail that goddam sonofabitch once and for all.'

'Got it. Out.'

Jaeger killed the call. *Expect the unexpected*: it was his mantra. But he'd never for one moment imagined anything like this.

He eyed Raff. 'How much of that did you get?'

'Most of it.' A beat. 'But here's the thing: those two dozen guys Kammler just sent out? They ain't gone to RV with the shipment. Mate, they're coming after us.'

'Like how?'

'Kammler knows we're watching. If he sends his guys out on foot to comb the valley, we see them coming. This way, they drive east until they're out of sight, pull over, climb to the valley rim and come at us from the rear.'

'Across the snowfield?'

'Yeah. From where we least expect it. From where we're not watching.'

'So they'll be moving on skis?'

'Probably, yeah.'

'Right. We go out and meet them head on. Fire with fire.'

'Hit them where they'll least expect us.'

'Not *us*.' Jaeger eyed the scope. 'I need you here on watch. The priority has to be to get the tungsten bomb in. Eliminate the main threat. Do everything possible to avoid Kammler's people. Last thing we need is for it to go noisy before we hit the kill button.'

Raff's face hardened. 'I'd rather go out fighting.'

'No, mate, I need you here. Safe pair of hands to backstop the team. That tungsten bomb arrives, someone's got to call it. Trigger the blast. That's you. Got it?'

'Got it.'

60

Bent double, Jaeger scuttled through the brush and scrub above the OP, flitting from shadow to shadow. It was vital that he moved fast whilst also ensuring that he didn't give their position away. He ducked under the camouflage netting giving access to the snow cave.

'Heads up. Falkenhagen's been hit,' he hissed. 'Miles is missing. We're very likely compromised.' His eyes flitted around the cave, searching for something. 'Irina, I'm going to need you to lend me your sniper rifle. I'm going out to secure our rear. Take this.'

He handed her his Diemaco. He could tell that she and Alonzo were still in shock as they tried to grasp the enormity of what had happened. As he continued speaking, he grabbed his skis and slotted his boots into them.

'Look lively, guys. Depending which route they've taken, Kammler's people could be here any moment. Narov, join Raff on watch. Alonzo, set up a position looking east over the snowfields. We figure Kammler's sent out a party to take us from the rear. I'm going out to hit them first. And make no mistake: getting the tungsten bomb in remains our absolute priority.'

Narov tried to protest, but Jaeger silenced her with a gesture. 'No buts: I'm a stronger skier. No time to argue. Let's get moving.'

Dragunov strapped to his back, Jaeger set out east, skiing hard and fast across the moonlit snow. Thankfully, he'd only recently waxed his skis. He'd done so in order to help kill the boredom, but it was good that he had. They whispered across the snow.

The night sky was crystal clear. The moon was almost full, throwing the surroundings into eerie light and shadow. The illumination would be both a help and a hindrance. Jaeger would try to use it and the natural environment to his advantage. Old lessons that never died.

His mind raced. The two SUVs packed with gunmen had been lost from sight around the far end of the valley at around 0330 hours local time. He figured it would take them a good ninety minutes to scale the lower end of the gorge, especially with all the kit they would be carrying. It was 0430 now, so they could be cresting the ridge at any time.

They'd then have to ski west-south-west for a kilometre or so to bring them into the OP position from its rear. Jaeger figured he had twenty minutes maximum to execute the kind of deception he had in mind. He upped his pace. He could feel the sweat dripping down his back and soaking his silk inner layer as he pushed on.

Part of him felt physically drained. The lack of food, no doubt. But another part of him was fired up on adrenalin, and he felt as if he could ski like the wind. He'd have to if his plan was going to work.

The snowfield rose ahead of him gently, cresting out at a distant ridge. He was at his best going uphill. Few skiers could beat him in a climb. He just needed to make that ridge alive, and he should be good to execute stage two of his plan.

He halted when he figured he was some 500 metres short of the high ground. There was little point in taking cover, not for what he now intended. He turned and faced the way he had come, back towards the valley. He drew his pistol – a Sig Sauer P228 – and chambered a round.

He was a white figure standing amongst white snow on a moonlit night. They were unlikely simply to see him, and he couldn't think of any other way to draw their attention. He'd fire a shot into the air. As if it was intended to alert the rest of his team, positioned higher up the slope, to the appearance of the enemy.

Alert, hyped up, muscles coiled tense as a spring, Jaeger waited.

He checked his watch. *Any time now.*

Sure enough, the first figures hove into view.

Kammler's team were moving in single file, the lead skier beating a track through the snow for the others to follow; disciplined professionals, mercenaries no doubt, searching the terrain to either side of them as they went.

They clearly knew that Jaeger and his team had set their OP on the high ground, but they didn't know exactly where. Or at least that was Jaeger's gamble.

They kept moving towards him.

Like fish in a barrel.

Jaeger's heart was thumping. He knew the time had come. Time to go overt.

He raised his pistol and fired.

61

The shot rent the air above Jaeger's head, the hollow thud of the subsonic round echoing across the snow.

The line of figures came to an abrupt halt.

As they did, Jaeger turned and recommenced his line of march, making for the high ground. He was banking on several factors now. One, he was the better skier. Two, none of the enemy would have brought a long-range weapon with them. You wouldn't tend to, not when you planned to ambush a small force in a hidden OP.

From behind him he heard the harsh crackle of gunfire. Rounds snarled past to either side, kicking up angry plumes in the snow. He pushed ahead, knowing that his very life, plus those of his team, depended upon it.

He began to zigzag across the snow to confuse the gunmen's aim. The very worst thing would be one of them scoring a lucky hit and disabling him.

Eventually the fire from behind petered out.

He risked a glance over his shoulder.

The dozen figures had slung their weapons and turned in line to follow him. In a sense, Jaeger didn't blame them. Where else could a lone figure like him be heading, other than to join the rest of his team at their OP? Nothing else would make sense. Track Jaeger and the gunmen would bag the lot of them – or so they had to be thinking.

The way ahead was a mass of unmarked snow. Jaeger mapped out a route through the contours, one designed to maximise speed. All he had to do was reach the ridgeline ahead of his pursuers.

He drove himself onwards until his thigh and calf muscles were burning, his lungs heaving.

At last he crested the high point. For a few seconds he skied onwards, as if continuing his flight. Once he was out of view of his pursuers, he dropped down, clipped off his skis and crawled back to the ridge. Unslinging the Dragunov, he brought it to his shoulder and eased himself over the lip of rock and ice. The slope below came into view close up, via the Dragunov's PSO-1 4x magnification telescopic sight.

At first glance, the scope's reticule – its eyepiece sighting system – looked complicated. The horizontal crosshair was joined at the middle by a series of vertical arrowheads or chevrons, each spaced a millimetre or so apart. On the bottom right of the scope were two fine lines in the shape of a funnel laid on its side. Five marks were inscribed along it, like the lines on a ruler, numbered 2, 4, 6, 8, 10.

Like most former communist bloc kit, however, the scope was actually simplicity itself. And fortunately, the Regiment had taught Jaeger how to use just about every weapon known to man.

You placed the funnel marker over the target until it snugly head to toe. At that point you read off the number, as Jaeger did now: 8. The lead enemy gunman was thus 800 yards away. He raised the rifle slightly, getting the topmost chevron lined up with the target's chest. Each chevron represented 200 metres extra distance.

Like that, he adjusted for the bullet drop over 800 metres. He calmed his breathing, closed his eyes, and settled. Just for a beat. Then he opened his eyes again, took one long, slow breath, and held it for an instant, confirming his aim.

Sniper training. Never hold your breath for too long or your body would begin to shake ever so slightly. One of the key principles that had been ingrained in him. Instinctive by now.

He squeezed the trigger.

There was the sharp report of the weapon firing, and the lead figure crumpled into the snow. Instantly Jaeger went about acquiring his next target. The column of men had hit the deck, dropping to one knee and unslinging their weapons. There were a few sustained bursts of fire, but they fell well short of the mark.

At this range Jaeger had them pinned down in the open and they knew it.

He had to keep each move calm and deliberate, although he knew how thin the line between life and death was. The only thing keeping him alive was the distance.

Via his scope, he had recognised the weapons Kammler's men were carrying. Each was equipped with a Chinese-made Type 79 folding-stock sub-machine gun. A good weapon and perfect for close-quarter combat, but accurate up to no more than two hundred yards.

Jaeger fired again. A second figure keeled over. Knowing they had no option but to move, the ten surviving gunmen rose to their feet and started to fan out, trying to rush his position. All twelve had to die. He couldn't afford for even one of them to get away and raise the alarm with Kammler.

But even as he steeled himself, Jaeger was struck by an utterly chilling thought. He'd been lying here repeating the mantra 'one bullet, one kill'. But he'd missed something. Something vital.

The Dragunov carried a ten-round magazine . . . and there were twelve gunmen coming after him. And in his haste, he'd only grabbed the one magazine.

For a fleeting second, he wondered why he'd volunteered to do this. It had been vital to draw Kammler's gunmen away from the OP. But he could have sent Raff. Or Narov. Or Alonzo.

He knew the answer. Sure, he was the best skier, but it was more that he'd never ask one of his team to do something that he wasn't willing to do himself.

If they were going to survive this, it would take a gamble.

And so he was here, with ten gunmen to kill and with only eight bullets to do it.

At best, there was only one way this was going to end: sooner or later, he would have two of Kammler's men on his tail, each armed with a Type 79 machine gun, and he'd be all out of rounds on the Dragunov.

And Jaeger knew that no pistol was a match for that kind of weaponry.

62

Thirty minutes into the race of his life, Jaeger saw one of his pursuers break away.

He'd taken out eight of them with the Dragunov, two rounds having missed their target. Kammler's four remaining men had dispersed across the snowfield in an effort to outflank him. One had now fallen away, but the remaining three were slick operators and none seemed about to give up the chase.

Jaeger reminded himself that they would be well fed, whereas he was half starved. The pursuers kept pace with him, matching ski thrust with ski thrust as he blazed a trail through the moon-washed whiteness. Up ridgelines, down valleys and across snowfields the race continued.

Inch by painful inch he felt the hunters gaining. He realised his greatest problem now: he was beating a path through the snow for his pursuers to follow, which had to make it easier on them. He was drenched with sweat, his lungs heaving fit to burst.

Still he powered onwards. He pulled ahead a small distance on the steeper climbs, only to have his pursuers close the gap again on the descents. Knowing it made sense to seek the higher ground, he veered south, his back to the lake, and began to climb into the mountains.

He reached a vast expanse of fresh snowfall, reminding himself of the avalanche risk. For a split second, he was back in the Alps, guiding some soldiers along the Kuffner Ridge on the Mont Blanc massif, assessing the danger as he moved.

He dragged his mind back to the harsh reality of here and now. An avalanche was the least of his worries. He was running out of options fast. He couldn't keep skiing forever, and with no more Dragunov rounds, the odds were not good.

And then he was struck by a flash of inspiration: maybe there *was* a way to finish this.

As he reached the top of the slope, he crouched low and removed a grenade from one of the pouches he wore slung around his belt. He turned and checked behind him.

The slope was the perfect angle and the snow pack fresh and deep.

Below, the three figures were surging up the diagonal path that Jaeger had cut across the snowfield, four hundred feet below and closing fast.

He waited until they were directly beneath him before pulling the pin and letting the retainer clip fly, then hurling the grenade in a high arc. It landed hard a good forty feet downslope, a puff of snow marking where it had disappeared into the soft whiteness.

Jaeger turned and dug deep with his ski poles, pushing into a powerful traverse. From behind him there was the dull thud of the grenade's detonation, the thick snow muffling the blast. He felt the shock wave of the explosion beneath his feet, and pushed on, skiing for all he was worth.

For a second or so nothing happened, and then the slope behind him started to move.

There was a dull crack as the surface broke, a chasm opening where the entire expanse at the epicentre of the blast began to surge downhill. As the snowfield collapsed across an ever-widening front, it pulled more of the mass above into churning chaos.

The noise of the cataclysm grew to a thunderous roar. Jaeger figured he'd put enough distance between himself and his handiwork to stop, and he turned to see a boiling wave of jumbled snow and blocks of ice tearing downhill like some kind of frozen tsunami, with a force that would carry everything before it.

Or not quite everything.

Of the three figures that had been in pursuit, one had somehow made it across the front of the avalanche before it could claim him. It was some feat of skiing. The others were swept away, arms and legs flailing helplessly as they were buried under hundreds of tons of snow.

Snow that would settle into bullet-hard ice as soon as the avalanche stopped.

But one of his pursuers remained alive.

Jaeger felt their eyes meet across the ravaged hillside. Whoever this lone figure might be, he didn't unsling his weapon or unleash any rounds. He was clearly too disciplined, knowing the range was too great. Smart – conserving ammo. Knowing Jaeger was all out of rounds on the Dragunov.

It was one-on-one now. A manhunt.

Jaeger knew that he was close to dead beat. He had to find a way to finish this. Almost as one, he and his pursuer turned back to the hillside and recommenced the deadly race.

After twenty minutes, Kammler's man was gaining on Jaeger, even on the uphill stretches; closing for the kill. Sooner or later, he'd have his target within range of his sub-machine gun.

The words of Jaeger's SAS instructors blazed through his mind: *Fight from the time and place of your own choosing.*

He knew what he was looking for; knew what he had to do.

63

Jaeger topped a small rise, and the scene that opened before him looked as good as he could have hoped for. A flattish plain stretched ahead, wind-scoured so that his tracks would show no trace. It was wide open, and dotted here and there with exposed rocky outcrops.

He skied ahead and chose a small, snow-sculpted heap of boulders that protruded from the whiteness, dropping behind it and kicking off his skis. He drew his P228, chambered a round, and settled the barrel on the topmost surface of the rock. Like this, prone on his belly and mostly in cover, he would be practically invisible to his pursuer as he topped the rise.

Maybe one hundred feet would then separate the two of them. It was doable.

As he calmed his breathing in preparation for what was coming, he reminded himself of the P228's accuracy. No other pistol came close.

Sure, the stopping power of the 9mm round was less than the heavier .45-calibre pistols. But Jaeger's P228 was loaded with hollow-point ammo, which was available in certain SF and es-pionage circles. A hollow-point round did pretty much what it said on the tin. The tip of the bullet was hollowed out, so that when it hit, it tore itself apart, causing maximum lethality.

At twenty-five yards – so about the same kind of distance he now had to engage at – he'd reliably achieve a grouping of less than three inches on the ranges.

But this was a different situation altogether. The negative impact of acute stress, physical exhaustion and raw fear would play havoc on anyone's aim. All he could do was try to calm his breathing, settle his nerves and relax into the shot.

A head appeared above the ridgeline. Jaeger waited for the torso to follow. He needed as large a mass as possible to aim for. The eyes of his pursuer scanned the way ahead. He must have noticed that it was devoid of his prey.

Moments later, he had dropped flat on the snow.

Jaeger cursed.

This guy was good.

He figured he'd recognised the gait, too, if not the features. He could have sworn it was Vladimir Ustanov, a man with whom he had crossed swords more than once. Narov had told him about the sighting in Dubai, and now here was Ustanov, hunting him across the Tibetan snowfields.

During their previous showdown, in the Amazon, Ustanov had proved to be an utterly single-minded operator and a cold-blooded murderer. He'd captured one of Jaeger's expedition members – Leticia Santos, a Brazilian and one of Jaeger's favourites – and tortured her horrifically.

When Jaeger had gone in to rescue her, it had brought him face to face with Ustanov. And now here they were again, second time around.

Jaeger kept his aim firm. He just needed Ustanov to make one mistake; to show himself. The distant figure kicked off his skis. He must know that Jaeger had gone to ground, which meant it was Type 79 sub-machine gun versus P228 pistol.

Jaeger reckoned he had one advantage. He was certain that Ustanov had hit the deck without unslinging his weapon. When he moved to do so, Jaeger could take his chance.

He steeled himself to take the shot, knowing he'd probably only get the one opportunity, for once he fired, his position would be revealed.

He waited.

An eerie silence settled over the freezing mountainside that had already claimed several lives.

The cold seeped into Jaeger's underside, but he knew that the slightest movement could spell death. He kept his hands firm on his pistol, his aim on where his adversary had gone to ground unwavering. As he kept scanning the terrain, he could just make out what he figured was the shadow of the man's torso.

At last he saw Ustanov make his move. He rolled slowly in the snow, sliding the machine gun around on its sling until he was lying on his back with the weapon resting on his stomach. He rolled over once more, back onto his front, and now he had the Type 79 held firmly in his hands.

Slick. The guy sure was a smooth operator.

Jaeger waited for his chance. It came in the two seconds it took for Ustanov to raise himself onto his elbows to swing the Type 79 into the aim. Before he could squeeze off any rounds, Jaeger fired.

The 3.9 inch barrel of the P228 was scored with six rifling grooves, forming a spiral that spun the bullet as it left the weapon, the action lending it accuracy. The pistol barely gave a kick as Jaeger let rip.

He kept his eyes glued to his sights. The hollow-point bullet ripped into the metal of Ustanov's machine gun, throwing off shards of shrapnel, the power of the impact tearing the weapon out of his hands.

Jaeger heard the man scream and instantly broke cover. He would have a matter of seconds at most.

Surprise. Aggression. Speed.

Jaeger sprinted forward, urging his tired legs to power across the hard snow. He could see Ustanov scrabbling about to get his hands on his weapon. He found it and brought it to his shoulder, and for an instant Jaeger could see the bloodied mess of his adversary's face.

But he couldn't close the distance in time.

As Ustanov steadied his aim, Jaeger could taste bile in his mouth.

He knew that he was about to die.

64

U stanov pulled the trigger to unleash the killer burst. All he got from the sub-machine gun was a dead man's click. Either his weapon had misfired, or it wasn't functioning properly; more likely the latter, after being hit by Jaeger's round.

For a few seconds he fought to get his weapon operational, before throwing it to one side and reaching behind him, groping for the pistol that he would have holstered in the small of his back.

But Jaeger was closing the range fast. He thundered on, and from somewhere in the pit of his stomach came a scream of primeval range as he bore down on his adversary.

This was the man who'd thrown several of Jaeger's friends from a helicopter's open doorway, during their Amazon expedition, in an effort to get him to surrender. The man who had bound, beaten and abused Leticia Santos and tortured Jaeger with images of her suffering.

As Ustanov whipped his pistol around to his front, Jaeger dropped to one knee with the P228 in the aim. From thirty feet he opened fire, pumping seven rounds into the target in under three seconds.

Ustanov slumped forward and lay still, the pistol still gripped in his hands.

Jaeger closed the final yards, keeping the figure covered. He came to a halt. From close range it was clear that it was indeed Ustanov, but also that he was very, very dead. The man was a mess. No one could have survived the kind of barrage that Jaeger had unleashed.

He reached down and prised the pistol from his grip. It was a Chinese QSZ-92 – the 'Type 92 Handgun' used by the People's Liberation Army. Fitted with a dual-stack magazine, it carried fifteen standard 9mm rounds, or twenty of the smaller armour-piercing variant. In short, it was a good weapon that packed more bullets than Jaeger's Sig, with its thirteen rounds.

Jaeger was glad this hadn't turned into a prolonged pistol duel.

He felt an outburst of raw emotion. It washed over him, taking him by surprise. An explosion of power and energy surged through him: hatred, relief, adrenalin and, strangely, pleasure.

Soldiers did experience such emotions in combat. Jaeger had seen it enough times to know it was simply a part of human instinct. A sudden release of endorphins that flooded through the system, resulting in a feeling of euphoria that was clearly at odds with the brutality of killing.

But he'd also witnessed the ensuing guilt that soldiers some-times experienced. Killing wasn't meant to feel good. Soldiering was a job, and this was just the sharp end of what could be a very brutal profession.

Jaeger didn't try and fight the emotions. Up here, in the midst of this wilderness, alone, alive, he let it pour out of him. 'Screw you, Ustanov and screw you, Kammler,' he yelled. 'I'm coming for you. I am coming for you all.'

His body was shaking with adrenalin. He tried to compose himself and focus. Deep breaths. In and out. He closed his eyes. *Slow it down, buddy. Slow it down.*

With Kammler's hunter force eliminated, he needed to focus on the task in hand – getting back to the OP and finishing the job they'd come here for.

He checked the magazine of the QSZ-92. It was full. He tucked it into the rear of his waistband. Always good to have a backup backup weapon. He ran a practised eye over the dead man's machine gun. The mechanism was ruined, bent and buckled where Jaeger's shot had ploughed into it.

Then he turned back to the bloodied corpse and began to search it.

Tucked into an inner breast pocket, he discovered an Iridium satphone. It was a top-of-the-range Extreme 9575 – a compact, reliable and durable piece of kit. The only country that couldn't get an Iridium signal was North Korea, due to US trade sanctions. Across China there was blanket coverage.

On the spur of the moment, Jaeger powered it up. After a few seconds, a message icon popped onto the screen. There was no ping, so Ustanov must have it set to silent mode.

Jaeger opened the message: *SITREP please. And it better be positive. K.*

He paused for a moment, his mind and heart whirring.

K.

Hank Kammler.

65

Jaeger sensed the advantage swinging his way.

He took a deep breath, then typed a reply: *Two eliminated. Closing in on others. We have casualties. Will return to base when mission complete.*

He read it over a few times, checking it had the right ring to it, before pressing send. As he waited for some kind of response, he rifled the dead man's daysack. He discarded everything but the spare magazines of ammo for the pistol, and the twenty-four-hour ration pack.

That he ripped open so he could feast on the dead man's food.

As he wolfed down slabs of chocolate and energy bars, he kept one eye on the Iridium's screen. A message icon appeared.

Leave wounded. First priority to eliminate enemy.

He typed a one-word confirmation, and was about to power down the satphone when he thought of something else. He checked his watch and then typed out a short message for Raff.

Kammler hunter force eliminated. One turned back, presumably heading your way. Intercept him. My ETA your position 0800. Three pink elephants. Out.

That last line was a part of the team's agreed comms-under-duress procedure. It was devised in the form of a question and answer. If any of their number were feared captured and forced to make contact, they would be asked the prearranged question 'Who did you meet at Piccadilly Circus?'

The prearranged answer was 'Three pink elephants.' When

he saw that phrase in the message, Raff would know that it was genuine and from Jaeger, despite it having come from an unrecognised satphone.

Message sent, Jaeger moved a distance from the dead man. Despite the food he'd eaten, he could feel the fatigue washing over him, as the adrenalin drained out of his system. He slumped against a nearby rock, feeling an overwhelming urge to rest; to sleep. He fought it. *Get a grip, Jaeger. When in doubt, have a brew.*

He broke out the tiny stove that the ration pack contained and lit the solid fuel block, then gathered up some snow and melted it over the flame. Throwing in several sachets of sugar and two tea bags, he left it to come to the boil. Milk added, he settled back on the freezing ground and blew on the mug to cool it. As he drank, the warm fluid provided a jolt of relief and much-needed energy.

Once he was done, he stuffed what remained of the ration pack into the dead man's daysack, slung it on his shoulders, clipped on his skis, fetched the Dragunov and turned back the way he'd come.

To the east, the sky was brightening, bringing with it a little warmth. It was 0630, and Jaeger had a long ski ahead of him.

He gave a wide berth to the avalanche slope, which in turn led him down towards what he assumed was a frozen lake. He'd avoided it on the way in, with his focus on getting to high ground fast. Now he needed the quickest route back to his team. He decided to chance the lake.

At these kinds of temperatures, the ice should be metres thick and more than capable of holding a man's weight. Still, he took precautions. He paused at the edge, unstrapping the daysack so that it was slung over one shoulder only. That way, if the ice did give way, he could ditch the pack and not be dragged under by its weight.

He inched onto the ice, reminding himself of the drills if he did go through. He'd practised them repeatedly on exercises in

Norway and the Arctic. They'd used chainsaws to cut holes in the ice, purely for the purposes of learning how to survive such a fall.

The drill was to ski in with all your gear on. You then had to remove your skis and bergen and clamber out, all before the freezing water sapped your energy and pulled you under. The technique involved driving your ski poles into the ice beside the hole, and using them as an anchor to haul yourself free.

Counter-intuitively, the first thing you then had to do was find some fresh snow to roll in, which would soak up the excess water. Priority number two was to start a fire to warm yourself and dry out. Without a fire, you'd freeze to death in no time.

Thankfully, Jaeger had to do none of that while crossing the frozen lake. Apart from the odd eerie groan from below, it held firm.

The journey was made easier now in that he was able to follow the hard-packed ski tracks of several figures – those who had until recently been his hunters. At one stage he paused to read an incoming message from Raff confirming that Kammler's lone surviving gunman had been dealt with.

Jaeger smiled. Raff: bulletproof reliable.

Hopefully Kammler would be none the wiser now there was no one left alive from his hunter force to warn him they had failed. Plus Jaeger's message suggesting otherwise should have bought them some time, or so he hoped.

He paused at the corpses of those he had shot dead, scavenging food for the others. With that crammed into his daysack, he figured they had enough provisions for whatever lay ahead.

But with a man like Kammler, it was never over until he could gaze upon the dead man's features.

66

Professor Pak Won Kangjon wandered into the strongroom where they stored the weapons-grade uranium.

He eyed the wooden crate lying before him on the room's bare concrete floor. It was fresh in from Moldova, a former Soviet state gone to rack and ruin, or so he'd heard. At least the uranium, being former Soviet stock, should be near one hundred per cent pure.

He felt a thrill of excitement at the thought of dealing with such a potent source of raw power. He signalled to his assistants – fellow North Koreans who were also here on false papers, and likewise at Kammler's mercy – to break open the crate.

They worked quickly and in silence, levering apart the planking.

Once it was removed, the professor set them to dismantling the lead shield. It was a simple enough affair: six slabs of metal, each covering one face of the HEU cube, joined at the edges by pressure bolts.

When they were done, he picked up a Geiger counter. He approached the small pile of dull silver metal – atrociously expensive; impossibly heavy – and ran the device over it.

Not a sniff of a reading.

Which didn't mean much. Contrary to popular belief, HEU could be famously un-radioactive, at least before it went fissile. He didn't understand why they made such a fuss about lead shields. It was only a few curies of radiation, and it was never going to kill. In North Korea they'd been far more relaxed about the whole thing.

He ran his gaze over the pile of bars. They were strapped down with tough plastic straps designed to hold them firmly in place inside the lead sarcophagus. As he eyed the cube of metal ingots, something struck him as being a little odd.

This was supposed to be 100 kilos of HEU – enough for two power-plant-busting INDs, with a few ingots to spare. But it didn't look like 100 kilos' worth to his practised eye. It looked to be around twice that amount.

He'd read a report recently stating that hundreds of tonnes of Soviet-era weapons-grade uranium was unaccounted for. Maybe they'd got lucky. Maybe the Moldovans had messed up. But surely they weren't so stupid as to have miscalculated the weight?

Either way, this was a chance to ingratiate himself with Kammler. If he could verify his discovery – that the shipment was twice what they'd paid for – maybe he could redeem himself in his boss's eyes. Perhaps even earn himself a bonus.

He ordered his assistants to lift the cube of HEU onto a nearby workbench. Before he made any announcement, he would need to be one hundred per cent certain. He couldn't afford another screw-up.

He feared his next mistake might very well prove a life-ending one.

He took a seat at the bench and examined the block. One of the ingots had shifted about a little in transit, leaving a square hole large enough for him to poke one of his pudgy fingers through. The metal felt cold to the touch; cold and incredibly dense. He could almost sense its raw power.

He pulled a Maglite from his pocket and shone the flashlight through the hole, focusing the beam so that it illuminated the interior. He expected to see HEU all the way through, confirming that there was more here than they had been anticipating.

Suddenly Professor Pak Won Kangjon stopped and stared.

His torch beam had caught upon something yellowish-brown in colour lying at the centre of the cube. It looked to him like a lump of . . . plasticine. But what was a lump of plasticine doing crammed into the centre of a cube of weapons-grade uranium?

Moments later, he felt his blood run cold. As he moved the beam around, it glinted upon a wire. He dropped the torch and backed away from the bench. Surely to God it couldn't be . . .?

Somehow he found his voice. He barked an order, then turned and stumbled from the room. As he hurried ashen-faced down the corridor, his assistants swung closed the heavy steel door that secured the strongroom, and locked and barred it.

The last thing the professor wanted was to be the bearer of bad news, and this surely would be the worst kind imaginable. Kammler, he knew, was not beyond shooting the messenger. But if he didn't raise the alarm, he feared he was dead in any case.

He stopped at his desk, and dialled his boss's number. A voice barked an answer.

'Mr Kraft, I have been inspecting the new shipment,' Professor Kangjon stuttered. 'I am afraid there is something not quite right with it. You see, inside the uranium someone seems to have placed what looks like an explosive charge.'

There was an outburst of expletives on the other end of the line.

The professor visibly cringed. 'Yes, Mr Kraft. Please come see. Right away.'

As he replaced the receiver, his hand was shaking.

How on God's earth could this be happening?

67

As he neared the rear of the OP position, Jaeger pressed the toggle of his SELEX Personal Role Radio and spoke into the mouthpiece. With a three-mile coverage, he was well within range.

'Jaeger, coming into rear of the OP.'

'Got it,' Alonzo confirmed.

The American operative was keeping a sharp watch as Jaeger skied in. He jerked a thumb over his shoulder darkly. 'Narov's forward with Raff. There's been a . . . development. Best you go see.'

Jaeger clipped himself out of his skis. 'What kind of development?'

'Buddy, you need to speak to those two. In fact, maybe I'd better join you.'

Together Jaeger and Alonzo crept through the bush, bringing some of the scavenged rations with them, and slipped inside the OP. The four of them were jammed tight in the darkness. The confined space was fetid and stinking – the result of several days' occupation by unwashed humans who had been forced to urinate and defecate where they lay.

They were on 'hard routine' – a practice pioneered by the SAS, in which all signs of human occupation were kept to an absolute minimum. It required peeing into bottles and wrapping your own faeces in a combination of cling film and plastic bags, a bit like a dog walker would do with their animal's mess.

Hard routine could prove critical to a mission. If you left

human waste lying round your OP, and especially if the bad guys had search dogs, it was a dead giveaway. Plus it would inevitably attract wildlife, another telltale sign. In fact, you might as well run a Union Jack up the flagpole.

But Jaeger could sense something else overlying the rank stench. There was a dark tension to the air; a deafening silence. You could slice the atmosphere with the proverbial knife.

Clearly something had gone wrong; something that seemed to have set his teammates against each other.

He eyed Raff and Narov. 'Tell me.'

For a long beat, no one spoke. It was Raff who finally broke the silence. 'The tungsten bomb was delivered to the laboratory maybe an hour ago.'

Jaeger gave a start. 'Then why haven't you blown it? What're you waiting for?'

Raff's features darkened. 'Peter Miles is down there. Kammler made a show of bringing a figure out of the accommodation block and marching him across to the lab. It was Miles.'

'Fuck.'

'If I had had my way, we would have blown it anyway,' Narov hissed. 'We risk the lives of so many for one man, when we have every reason to believe he would want us to press the button. His life to save the world – Miles would not hesitate.'

Raff ignored the comment. 'He had a black bag over his head,' he explained to Jaeger. 'Kammler removed it in full view, so we could get a good look. Miles has been beaten half to death. Trust me, Kammler knows we're watching.'

'We figure they scarfed him up at Falkenhagen,' Alonzo added, 'then shipped him here. We think he arrived in the SUV that brought the tungsten device.'

Jaeger grabbed the SwiftScope and swung it around until the lab was in full view. 'Any sense where they're holding him exactly? Any chance we can bust him free?'

Raff was about to answer, but Jaeger silenced him with a gesture. He kept his eyes glued to the scope for a few long seconds before sinking back, a look of utter shock and horror on his features.

'It's her,' he whispered hoarsely. 'She's down there. With Kammler.'

No one needed him to explain who he meant. Ruth Jaeger had just made an appearance at the plant.

One by one they took a turn at the scope as Jaeger slumped against the back wall of the OP in a dark and brooding silence. Kammler was standing out the front of the plant, the distinctive figure of Ruth kneeling before him, bound and gagged.

It was Narov's voice that broke the quiet. 'I still say we blow the charge. Two lives sacrificed to save the world . . . It is what Miles would want. As for her, she'd be better off dead. She doesn't deserve—'

'And what the fuck do you know?' Raff cut in accusingly. 'She's tied up, or hadn't you noticed?' He turned to Jaeger. 'Trust me, he's holding them both as captives. He's using them as human shields to safeguard his lab.'

'*Fuck.*' Jaeger felt as if his mind was about to explode. '*Fuuuuuk.* So what the hell do we do?'

Three sets of eyes stared back at him blankly.

68

'You know what Miles would say?' Narov reiterated. 'Even though he is being held hostage, he would still tell us to detonate. He would sacrifice his own life to save countless millions. I do not understand what we are waiting for.'

'You wouldn't,' Jaeger fired back at her. 'It's called compassion. Empathy. And basically you're devoid of it.'

'Yeah,' Raff cut in. 'You'd sell out your own grandmother.'

Narov turned on them. For a moment it looked as if she was about to lash out, but somehow she managed to hold herself back.

'Let me tell you something about my grandmother,' she hissed. 'The man who raped her . . .' She paused. 'That man was SS General Hans Kammler.' She jabbed a finger in the direction of the plant below. 'That bastard's father. Which makes *him* my half-uncle. So rather than selling out my grandmother, I'm here to make sure she's avenged!'

Jaeger shook his head in disbelief. 'Kammler? Your uncle? But you've never breathed a word.'

Narov glared. 'And I should tell you because? When did you ever give a damn about anyone other than your turncoat of a wife? She came here against all our wishes and against everything we stand for. She should die along with the rest of them.'

Jaeger's eyes flashed anger. 'What, because she's the hostage of a madman?'

'Okay, guys, knock it off,' Raff cut in. 'Time's running out. What the fuck are we supposed to do?'

Silence. Brooding and toxic.

No one had any suggestions.

Jaeger felt the Iridium vibrate. He pulled it out expecting another of Kammler's messages seeking an update from the recently deceased Ustanov. But he saw instead that he had an incoming call, the ID showing it to be 'K'.

Hans Kammler himself.

He was torn. Should he or shouldn't he answer?

If he didn't, that would sow the seeds of doubt in Kammler's mind that all was well with Ustanov. And while Kammler would know Ustanov's voice, surely he wouldn't know those of all his team? It could be any one of them speaking on behalf of their boss.

He let the call go to voicemail. No message was left. Instead, the Iridium began to vibrate again.

Jaeger grabbed his khaki scrim and wrapped it around his face, flicking the Iridium to 'speaker'. The combination of the scarf and the broadcast-mode should muddy his voice enough, or so he hoped.

He pressed answer.

'Good morning, William Jaeger,' a voice rang out.

Kammler's.

'Plus the delightful Irina Narov. And the redoubtable Raff and Alonzo. Do I have you all present and correct, and hanging on my every word?'

Jaeger glanced at the others: how in God's name did Kammler know they had Ustanov's phone? And how on earth was he supposed to respond? He didn't feel as if he had any alternative but to answer.

'We're here,' he confirmed through gritted teeth.

'Welcome,' Kammler continued, 'although I understand you've actually been here for some time. You should have popped down earlier to say hello. Oh, if you're wondering how I know you're here? The Iridium: great technology. Sometimes the Americans do get it just right. It has a camera front and back and a remote interrogate function. Look at you all. Crouched in your stinking, shitty little dark hole.'

He guffawed. 'Say hello, everyone. Give Hank and his buddies a wave.'

69

Jaeger could have kicked himself. Why hadn't he thought to disable the Iridium's camera? It was so easy to do: a strip of gaffer tape slapped over the aperture, for those who didn't have the brains or the nous to master the software.

As it was, Narov reached for the satphone, pressed a few buttons and disabled the video function. At least now Kammler couldn't spy on them.

'Such a pity – you've gone,' Kammler continued, 'And you know how much I love a little theatre. Talking of which, if you look out of your hovel, you'll see me outside my laboratory with two of those who are so very dear to you.'

Jaeger crawled across to the OP's opening. Kammler was surrounded by a phalanx of gunmen now. Bodyguards. Jaeger recognised one of them instantly: it was the massive, muscle-bound hulk of Steve Jones. He'd never believed he could feel so much hatred. He felt an irresistible urge to dash down the hillside, all guns blazing.

'All sitting comfortably?' Kammler's voice queried. 'Then I'll begin.'

Jaeger saw him give a signal, and the bound forms of Ruth and Peter Miles were forced to their knees in front of him. Jones strode up behind them and drew a pistol. At a gesture from Kammler, he smashed the butt into Peter Miles's head. The elderly man keeled over, but Jones grabbed him by his hair and dragged him up again.

'So I think you probably get the picture,' Kammler purred.

'We have a newly arrived shipment of uranium in the lab. A shipment that you clever people seem to have rigged with some kind of explosive device. But as you see, I am infinitely smarter and, for what it is worth, far more ruthless.'

With that, he raised one leg and kicked Ruth between the shoulder blades. Even from a distance, Jaeger heard the scream of pain as she keeled forward. Steve Jones reached down one massive beefy arm, grabbed a twist of her hair and dragged her viciously back into the kneeling position.

Jaeger felt as if he could howl with rage. He was burning up with it. His fingers clenched into an iron fist, the nails drawing blood from his palm. 'Fuck you, Kammler,' he snarled.

Kammler laughed. 'Oh, I don't think so . . . Now, this is what we're going to do. You will explain the detonating mechanism and how we disable it. You see, we are a little concerned it may be pressure-activated: we remove a bar of uranium, it goes bang.' He paused. 'You are going to show yourselves, drop your weapons and come down to join us. Together we will defuse your bomb.'

Jaeger didn't answer.

'I am asking nicely, but in truth it isn't a request,' Kammler continued. 'Do what I say, or Peter Miles dies. And shortly after that, your beloved wife. But I think ever so slowly . . .'

Jaeger covered the Iridium. He eyed Raff and Alonzo, a sudden clarity burning in his eyes. 'He's a bloody madman. But we know more about his plans than he suspects, and he knows less about ours than he believes. Which means we can play him.'

He looked at each of them in turn. 'Here's what we do: we act as if agreeing to his demands. But you two – you go blow the pipelines. They go bang, it's utter chaos down there. On the back of that, we fight our way in. You two take the desalination plant, we take the accom block. Once we're clear, we combine forces to hit the lab.'

'What about Miles and Ruth?' Raff queried.

Jaeger gritted his teeth. 'They'll have to take their chances. In all the confusion, we have to hope they break free. What other option is there? Blowing the pipeline – it's the one thing he'll never expect.'

One by one the others nodded their silent assent.

Jaeger spoke into the handset. 'I hear you, Kammler. We'll come down and defuse it, but once we've done so, we walk out of there with my wife and Miles. Do we have a deal?'

'Agreed. Come on down to join us.'

'We're coming. Front entrance,' Jaeger confirmed.

He killed the call and glanced at Raff and Alonzo. 'Mission's on. Head for the pipelines. Pronto. And good luck.'

Alonzo and Raff grabbed their weapons and their daysacks.

'See you in paradise,' Alonzo muttered as he crawled out of the OP.

Jaeger smiled. 'Have me a beer ready when you get there.'

With that, they were gone.

Jaeger stuffed extra grenades and magazines into his own daysack, turfing out anything he didn't need. He paused at the Thuraya, undecided whether to take it or not.

It gave them comms with Brooks, which was important. It also gave them the means to detonate the tungsten device, though he wasn't about to do that any time soon. If he did, he'd kill two of the people closest to his heart.

On balance, he decided to take it. He didn't want anyone else – Narov, for instance – on that trigger.

He heard Raff's voice crackling in his SELEX earpiece: 'One-minute countdown, boss.'

'One,' he confirmed back.

They were sixty seconds and counting.

70

Jaeger and Narov emerged from the bunker into the full glare of the mid-morning light. By their reckoning they were fifty seconds short of the detonation. They walked forward until they were silhouetted on the ridgeline where Kammler could see them.

As they began to move downslope, Jaeger felt the Iridium vibrate. He answered.

'Nice to see you, Mr Jaeger,' Kammler announced. 'And you, Ms Narov. I have heard so much about *you*, of course. Now, if you would leave your weapons there and keep your hands where we can see them . . . But you are four. Where are your two friends?'

'Just getting their shit together. They'll be—'

Jaeger's words were cut short as a massive concussion rang out along the ridgeline, seeming to shake the entire hillside. He turned to see debris hurled high into the air, as a pall of grey smoke fisted skywards above the pipelines. An ear-splitting roar swept down the valley like a gigantic express train thundering through a long and ghostly tunnel.

The noise seemed to bore into Jaeger's head, even as the torrent of water foamed down the mountainside like a tidal wave on steroids. The leading edge of the flood plummeted with such force that it tore boulders from the hillside, hurling them high into the air, so that they landed in a shower of sparks. Second by second, the churning head of the tsunami thrust a boiling mass of rocks, trees and mud ever closer to the plant.

Jaeger and Narov started to run, slipping and sliding downslope. Below them, the unstoppable surge hammered into the plant's defensive perimeter. The high-tensile fencing buckled and broke, as if it was straw caught in a monster hailstorm. Coils of razor wire crashed down. Massive boulders slammed into the concrete fence posts, which broke with a series of deafening cracks.

The first of the buildings to be hit was the generator hall, which lay directly below the ruptured pipelines' triple barrels. Within seconds, water-driven rocks and debris hammered into its rear like a volley of cannon fire. As the cascade carved an ever deeper path, so the flow grew in power, ripping doors from hinges and punching in windows.

Boiling water thick with debris surged inside the generator hall, bringing with it a thick sludge of mud, gravel and shredded tree branches. The flood engulfed the first of the massive turbines, short-circuiting the electrics in a cloud of roiling steam shot through with angry sparks.

The tsunami thundered onwards, the roar from the ruptured pipelines reverberating across the valley. It swamped the accommodation block and hydrolysis plant. Scores of local workers turned and fled. They had one aim only: to save themselves.

The only building that escaped the devastation was the laboratory, tucked into cover and set a little higher up the valley. But as the surge engulfed the last of the generators, the lights flickered out. All of the machinery – including Professor Kangjon's 3D printers, which had been diligently constructing the components for the final clutch of INDs – ground to a halt.

In the high-security end of the lab, Professor Kangjon crawled out from under a table where he'd taken shelter. He groped for a light switch. His fingers found it and flicked it several times, but nothing happened.

The lab had few windows and it was frighteningly dark. The professor had always been afraid of the dark, ever since he was nine years old and the North Korean security police had come for his father in the middle of the night, hustling him away, never to be seen again.

He switched on his Maglite and tried to find his way to the exit. He had only one thought now: to get the hell out of the building and save his own skin.

On the heels of the floodwater came the assaulters.

Jaeger thundered downslope, trying to keep one desperate eye on his wife and Peter Miles. But as he flashed through the scrub and vaulted over boulders, they were lost from view. He broke through a patch of dense cover, and spied the shattered perimeter fence lying barely a few dozen feet before him. He raced for it, Narov hot on his heels. His eyes darted right again, and he realised that Kammler and his hostages had disappeared.

Maybe Ruth and Miles had seized their chance to escape.

Or had they been dragged away by their captors?

Jaeger just didn't know.

Right now he had to concentrate on the job in hand, which was eliminating Kammler's gunmen. He forced himself to blank all other thoughts from his mind.

Speed, aggression, surprise.

Speed, aggression, surprise . . .

71

As Jaeger and Narov charged through the gap in the wrecked perimeter fence, they were up to their knees in swirling water. It slowed them, making them easier targets. The roaring from the ruptured pipelines masked the sound of the gunshots, but Jaeger saw the kick and spurt where the first of the rounds tore into the floodwaters.

Narov dropped to one knee in the cover of a boulder, bringing the Dragunov to the aim. 'Engaging! Push for the accom block! Will cover you!'

Jaeger knew how utterly critical it was that they seized the initiative. Hit by total surprise by the avalanche of floodwater, the enemy would be shocked and in disarray. Before they had time to regroup, Jaeger and his team had to finish this.

He powered onwards, wild bursts of gunfire chasing his heels. Via his SELEX headpiece Narov provided a quiet, steely commentary as she went about her work with the Dragunov.

'Enemy down, laboratory, ground-floor window far left . . . Enemy down, laboratory . . .'

Sprinting like a man possessed, Jaeger gained the cover of the accommodation building, his momentum making him shoulder-barge into the prefabricated wall. He felt a jolt of pain from the impact, but blanked it completely.

'In place, accom block, eastern wall,' he panted into his SELEX.

'Copy,' a voice breathed back at him. It was Raff. 'Turbine hall clear. Going into desalination plant . . . now.'

'Copy,' Jaeger confirmed.

'Coming in to join you,' Narov radioed Jaeger.

'Move on my fire!' he confirmed.

In his present position, he was pressed against the eastern wall of the accommodation block. Like this, he was sheltered from the fire coming from the direction of the laboratory, set some four hundred feet up the valley.

Four hundred feet was approaching the limit of the Diemaco's effective range, but not so Jaeger's grenade-launcher. As he'd learnt on ops in Afghanistan, the 40mm fragmentation grenade was a perfect anti-personnel weapon in such terrain. Basically, the hard valley floor would do little to soak up the blast, shrapnel scything out and ricocheting in all directions.

The grenade had a lethal radius of over thirty feet: anything caught within that distance was dead. It had a danger radius of over four times that: if you were within 120 feet of the blast, you could suffer serious injury. As a result, you didn't need pin-point accuracy; you just needed to lob a round in the general direction of the bad guys.

With practised hands, Jaeger flicked a lever to open the M203's breech, slotted in the snub-nosed grenade and slid back the launch tube. He flicked up the M203's sight, which sat atop the weapon like a tiny ladder and allowed grenades to be fired accurately over anything up to 500 feet.

He was good to go.

He braced himself, eased one foot and his shoulder around the wall of the accommodation block and took aim. As he did so, a burst of incoming fire kicked up the dirt just a little low and to his front. Kammler's gunmen must have seen where he'd gone to ground and were waiting for him to show.

As Jaeger sighted on their muzzle flashes – his weapon held at a twenty-degree angle to lob the grenade – the enemy gunmen walked their rounds ever closer to his position, using their bullet strikes to adjust and raise their aim.

Just as they seemed poised to nail him, the incoming fire

ceased abruptly. Narov's voice crackled through the SELEX: 'Enemy down, laboratory, central window . . .'

That's my girl, Jaeger told himself.

He squeezed the M203's trigger, feeling the reassuring kickback of the weapon firing. The half-kilo snub-nosed projectile left the muzzle at 250 feet per second. He counted out two seconds in his head, knowing that Narov would have treated the crump of his opening fire as her signal to move.

The grenade struck, the dirty-white plume of its explosion spreading out low to the ground, then punching a fist of smoke into the air. Jaeger ducked back into cover, slotted in another round, reached around the corner and fired again.

Within ten seconds, he'd peppered the eastern flank of Kammler's laboratory with a scything wave of shrapnel. But even as he unleashed the fourth of his twelve 40mm rounds, he feared that his wife was very likely somewhere in that building.

Jaeger forced such fears from his mind, otherwise they'd push him to the edge, which was just what Kammler wanted. He had to reason Kammler would try to keep her out of the line of fire. She was his main bargaining chip, and it would do him little good to get her killed.

Narov dashed into the cover of the wall beside him. They paused for a few seconds to catch their breath. To gain entry into the accommodation block, they'd have to move around the southern wall where the deluge had hit, and go in through a broken doorway.

And that was going to expose them to the full brunt of the enemy's fire.

72

There was a burst of fire from barely fifty yards away: the distinctive *crack-crack-crack* of an assault rifle unleashing an aimed burst. Moments later, Jaeger heard Raff's voice come up over the SELEX.

'Desalination plant clear. Five enemy accounted for. Covering your move forward.'

'Roger. Out.'

Jaeger rested against the wall as he ratcheted a fresh 40mm grenade into the launcher's breech. Beside him, Narov threw the Dragunov onto her back with its sling, and drew her pistol. Like Jaeger's it was a Sig Sauer P228, only Narov had lucked out: she'd managed to get one with an extended twenty-round magazine.

Somewhere on her person she'd have her diminutive Beretta 92FS tucked away. Narov always carried a backup to her backup weapon. Which reminded Jaeger: he still had Vladimir Ustanov's QSZ-92 stuffed in the rear of his waistband.

Narov's P228 was as good a weapon as any for clearing the accommodation block, and she certainly wouldn't be using her sniper rifle. It was far too long and unwieldy for the rapid-fire close-quarter-battle environment they were about to step into.

Jaeger had a sneaking suspicion that Kammler had pulled most of his gunmen back to defend the laboratory. He'd counted two dozen earlier, during Kammler's piece of theatre with the kneeling hostages. That number, added to the dozen skiers that Jaeger and his team had eliminated earlier, made thirty-six in all.

He doubted whether Kammler's original guard force would have numbered a great deal more. But presumption was the mother of all fuck-ups; they needed to clear every building to be absolutely certain, and quickly. Even now, desperate and under attack, Kammler could be about to trigger those bombs that had been delivered to target.

He eyed Narov. 'On my signal, join me at the doorway. We go in as one.'

Narov nodded her silent assent. She stuffed the P228 barrel-first down the front of her combats and slid the Dragunov into her shoulder again. Then she leant out from behind the wall, sweeping the terrain around the laboratory for targets.

As she unleashed her first round, Jaeger broke cover.

'Moving now!' he yelled into his SELEX.

He sensed rather than heard the bursts of grenade fire, as Alonzo and Raff unleashed 40mm rounds from the cover of the desalination plant. He sprinted for all he was worth, knowing he was exposed to every gunman positioned at the laboratory. Sure enough, and despite the suppressing fire, rounds slammed into the masonry either side of him.

Change of plan, Jaeger told himself as a caved-in window opened on his right shoulder. He dived through it, landing on his front in a pool of filthy water and rolling once to break his fall. Moments later, he was on his feet in a crouch, soaking wet, his Diemaco levelled and doing a rapid sweep of the room.

It was empty.

He had intended to wait for Narov at the building's shattered doorway. It was standard operating procedure to clear a building in pairs, so you could watch each other's back. But the fire had been too intense, and he needed to warn her.

'Gone through first window on right,' he radioed.

'Seen.'

As he crouched at the window to give covering fire for Narov, Jaeger noted that his assault rifle was spattered with grime from where he'd landed in the water and dirt. He'd need to clean it, for sand and grit could seize up a weapon's working parts. But no time for that now.

Seconds later, Narov dived through the shattered window. Jaeger turned away, and they both flicked on the flashlights attached to their weapons. It would only get darker the further into the building they went.

Wordlessly they moved across to the doorway leading out of the room, gravel and debris crunching underfoot, water sloshing around their ankles. Everywhere there was sodden furniture turned on its side, or rammed against the walls by the sheer force of the flood.

Jaeger clambered over a soaking mattress jammed up against the doorway. The door itself had been forced open and was lying drunkenly, half ripped from its hinges. He stepped around it into the corridor, pivoting left, his P228 swinging into the aim. At the same instant Narov took up a mirror position behind him, so they were back to back, covering either direction.

They began to move down the eerie, echoing space, checking the rooms on either side. Doors had been ripped open by the floodwater, leaving the place littered with wreckage and seemingly deserted.

They reached the far end of the corridor, where a flight of metal steps led up to a second floor. Jaeger paused, moving to one side of the final door before the stairs. This one was covered with steel sheeting, and despite the floodwaters, it remained intact. Narov flattened herself against the doorway's other side.

Reaching around, Jaeger tried the handle. Once. Twice. It didn't budge. Firmly locked. There was no point trying to kick it in. This wasn't the movies. He was more likely to break a leg or injure himself than bust through a steel door.

'Blowing the lock,' he mouthed at Narov.

73

Standing to one side, in case whoever was behind the door tried to open fire, Jaeger shrugged off his pack and readied a charge of PE4. Contrary to popular myth, trying to shoot open a lock was not a smart idea, especially when using a handgun or an assault rifle.

As soon as you opened fire, those on the other side of the doorway would know you were coming. Nothing like advertising your intentions. And even if you did manage to shoot up the lock, more often than not you'd jam the working parts, fragments of shattered bullet lodging in the lock's innards. Plus rounds hitting a steel lock at close quarters would spit out chunks of shrapnel, threatening to injure the shooter.

Jaeger had learnt that much on day one of SAS room-clearance drills. A metal-reinforced door such as this would require a special 'thread-cutter' shotgun, which fired a solid twelve-bore slug. And right now, they didn't have any such weapon to hand.

It was just as easy to blow it using a shaped charge of PE4.

Jaeger moulded the explosives to where the door's hinges met the frame. The detonation would cut them in two, as well as blast the wood apart. The combined effect should tear the door outwards, its very weight ripping it free.

Charges set, he triggered the thirty-second fuse, and he and Narov took cover in an adjacent room. There was a sharp explosion, followed by a thick cloud of smoke and debris billowing along the corridor. They emerged from cover to find the door hanging at a crazy angle, the lock struggling in vain to keep it in position.

Even as they approached, weapons in the aim, the lock gave way and the door tumbled outwards with an almighty crash. Jaeger was the first through, Diemaco levelled and flashlight piercing the smoke-filled interior.

The first thing that struck him was the faces: row upon row, eyes wide with terror. Desperate voices were crying out frantically in what Jaeger figured had to be Chinese. His flashlight flitted over the crouched figures, hands raised and panic etched across their features.

It was instantly clear that this sad mass of humanity were workers, not soldiers.

They were dressed in ragged, stained boiler suits, and looked underfed and in terrible condition. Jaeger was suddenly aware of the stench in the room. It reeked of unwashed bodies. Sickness. Fear. There were dirty mattresses lying against one wall, plus a battered toilet bucket.

What the hell had Kammler been running here? Some kind of slave camp?

'Any of you speak English?' he barked. 'English?'

'Me,' a nervous figure volunteered from the darkness.

Jaeger's eyes came to rest upon the man who had spoken. 'Why are you here?'

'Chinese workers. Locked up. To stop escape.' The speaker gestured at the others. 'We all try escape. Boss catch us and lock us here. He make us work or we die. Underground. Many people die.'

'What were you doing underground?'

'Making chamber. Tunnel. On far side of laboratory.'

Jaeger's mind flashed back to the St Georgen tunnel complex. Hundreds of thousands had died constructing the Nazi-era labyrinth that honeycombed the Austrian mountains. It looked as if Kammler had been doing something similar here.

The question was, why?

Jaeger sank to his haunches, getting eye to eye with the speaker. The haunted look in the man's eyes spoke volumes.

'Why a chamber? What sort of tunnel?' he pressed.

'Is shelter. This place attacked, boss stays underground; boss stays safe. Is shelter. And – how you say? Headquarter.' The speaker pointed to himself. 'Hing made foreman. All shot if try to escape. Boss is a madman. Hing and his team prisoners. Those the rules.'

Jaeger straightened up. 'Well they're not the rules any more. You're free now. All of you. Go out to the right and down towards the river. Wait there until we're done, okay.'

Jaeger explained that once he and his team had cleared the entire plant, they'd come back and furnish whatever help they could. For now, though, the workers had to lie low at the riverside.

He paused. 'But not you, Hing. You're coming with us.'

74

So far Jaeger and his team had been clearing lightly defended buildings; ones that Kammler could afford to let fall. But at the laboratory complex they would be assaulting a well-defended target. And there, Jaeger didn't doubt that Kammler's gunmen would have been ordered to make a last stand.

He sank back into the cover provided by the thick stone walls of the turbine hall. He, Narov and Hing – the Chinese worker-slave – had joined Raff and Alonzo in preparation for the final assault, though who exactly it would prove final for, he dreaded to think.

The accommodation block had been deserted apart from that roomful of workers. Anyone else with any sense had long fled. Jaeger and Narov had learnt from Hing several key things. One, that he had fired a weapon when he had served in the PLA, the Chinese People's Liberation Army. And two, that he hated Kammler almost as much as they did.

Having been compelled by Jaeger to join them, Hing argued that because he hated Kammler so much and could operate a rifle, it made him useful. More to the point, he knew his way around the plant intimately. It made sense to Jaeger, and so Hing had been included as the fifth member of their team.

Raff and Alonzo had scored six definite kills, plus however many of the enemy their grenade fire might have accounted for. But no one was kidding themselves that this was going to be easy. Time and experience had taught Jaeger the savagery of a cornered dog.

Ahead of them lay an uphill dash across 250 feet of largely open terrain. All around the laboratory the vegetation and natural cover had been bulldozed clear. Any way you tried to approach it, you were an easy target.

The plan was to keep it simple-stupid. One pair would rush the target, as the others lobbed 40mm grenades into it, in an effort to keep the enemy's heads down. That pair would in turn provide cover for the others to follow, with Hing bringing up the rear.

But they were running short of grenades, and Jaeger could sense the initiative turning in the enemy's favour. If he'd been Kammler, he'd have done exactly as he had done: drawing his main force back to the lab and waiting for the enemy to come.

To all sides it was a kill zone.

He eyed the others. 'You ready?'

By way of answer, there was the double *clatch-clatch* of Raff and Alonzo ratcheting grenades into their launchers. The steely look in their eyes spoke volumes. If Jaeger had to attempt such a suicide run, there was no one better to watch his back. And Narov's.

He turned to her. 'Toss for who goes first?'

Narov flashed a thin smile. 'I am the lady. You should allow me the honour.'

Jaeger grinned. Narov: always at her very best in the midst of a shitfight. He had to admit, it was what he loved about her.

They spent a moment scanning the ground ahead, mapping out the route that would provide the best cover. There were precious few options.

Jaeger was tensing himself for the go when he felt a vibrating in his pocket. No doubt Kammler calling with another sick ultimatum. Well it was too late for that. It was time to end this, one way or the other.

The slight *brrrrr* of the Iridium was audible to all. Narov glanced at him. 'You are not going to answer?'

'Why? Let's do this.'

Narov remained inscrutable. 'Check. You never know.'

Jaeger pulled it out. The caller ID displayed an unrecognised number. Not Kammler. He pressed answer, flicking the satphone onto speaker mode.

'This is Falk,' a scared-sounding voice hissed. 'I know you have no reason, but you have to trust me. My father has your wife and Peter Miles here in his bunker. Underground. He's kept me locked away ever since I made the calls to you, Irina.' He paused for breath, then continued. 'Irina, you *can* hear me?'

'Falk, I'm here. Keep talking.'

'It's good to hear a friendly voice . . . This place is like a total fortress. To find a way in you have—'

The voice was cut off by a distant scream of rage and a wild burst of gunfire. The call remained live for a few seconds. In the background, Jaeger could hear Kammler raging.

'My only son! The heir to the Reich! And you are trying to betray me? Who were you calling? Tell me?'

'Who would I be calling at a time like this?' Falk remonstrated. 'I was searching the internet, trying to work out how to treat the old man's injuries!'

'Let the shrivelled bastard die!' Kammler snarled. 'Let them both die! And next time, son or no son, those won't be warning shots. They will be aimed to kill.'

The call died.

75

For a second, the four of them eyed each other in stunned silence. Right now, right at this pivotal moment, that was the last thing they had been expecting.

It was Jaeger who spoke first. 'You believe him?' he demanded of Narov. 'You believe what he said?'

'You think that was another bit of theatre? That fear: no one fakes that.'

'Then he's in the underground shelter. The one the workers built. That's where Kammler's taken them. Got to be.'

Jaeger took a few seconds to explain to Raff and Alonzo what Hing had told them. 'Doesn't change shit,' Raff growled. 'We still have to take down Kammler's laboratory.'

'He's right,' Alonzo added. 'Only one way to do this.'

Jaeger held up a hand for silence. 'Just one second.' An idea was crystallising in his mind, one as crazed as it was beautiful. 'Kammler's taken himself, my wife and Miles into his bunker. That means that any reason we had not to blow the tungsten bomb has just evaporated. He's not disabled the device – I'd bet my life on it. Trust me, guys, it's still there and it's still live.'

He scanned the faces for a second. Raff and Alonzo looked stunned by his suggestion; Narov transfixed by it.

She reached out and grabbed his arm with a grip like iron. 'Then what are you waiting for? Blow it. Finish it.'

Jaeger reached into his daysack and pulled out his Thuraya. He glanced at Alonzo and Raff. 'Guys, I'm making the call. You good?' They were a team of equals, and he wanted this to be unanimous.

'I got no way to call it,' Alonzo objected. 'I never met this Falk guy. I'll go with what you say.'

Raff eyed Jaeger, doubt creasing his brow. 'You know Falk. You know if you can trust him. Plus it's your wife that may be in that lab, if he's full of shit.'

Jaeger could sense Raff's reluctance. He desperately needed his support. Raff was his best friend, godfather to Luke, and he and Ruth had been close. 'Raff, I'm taking the shot.'

'Fuck it.' Raff shrugged. 'We try to rush that open ground, we're dead anyway. Blow it.'

Jaeger bent over the Thuraya and typed in a single word in caps: GUNNERSIDE.

In 1942, a team of British and Norwegian commandos had been sent in to occupied Norway on a mission to sabotage Hitler's nuclear programme. Against impossible odds, they had succeeded. That operation had been code-named Gunnerside.

During his teens, Jaeger had read every book he could get his hands on about those World War II commando missions. It had been the catalyst that had spurred him to undertake Royal Marines selection. He'd never forgotten the Gunnerside story, and it had seemed like the perfect code word to trigger the tungsten device.

As he prepared to press the send button to get the message winging its way to Daniel Brooks, he hoped to hell it wouldn't spell the death of those he loved. He paused for a second, his thumb hovering over the button.

Fail to prepare, prepare to fail.

He turned to Narov. 'As soon as the charge blows, we need to hit Kammler's bunker. Hing is our guide.'

He grabbed Hing's hand and clamped it onto Narov's shoulder. 'Show her the shelter. Understand?'

Hing nodded. 'I show. I show.'

That decided, Jaeger pressed send.

76

That one word – GUNNERSIDE – winged its way across the ether, bouncing from satellite to satellite, en route to Daniel Brooks. Wherever he might be, he'd assured Jaeger that upon receipt of the code word, the tungsten device would be detonated within ninety seconds, and probably sooner.

It was time to get into some good cover.

Jaeger led his team in a dash for the eastern side of the turbine hall, and they took up position in the shadow of its massive wall. They now had that building plus the desalination plant between them and the coming blast.

They crouched and waited.

There was one other crucial piece of intel that Hing had revealed: though the entrance to Kammler's headquarters and nerve centre was heavily defended, there was another way in. Concealed in a mass of dense scrub was a 'window set in ground', as Hing had described it.

In other words, a skylight, one that opened directly into Kammler's bunker.

The plan they'd settled upon required Alonzo to advance to the front entrance. From cover he would lob in a few 40mm grenades, in the full knowledge that they would have very little effect on the bunker's heavy steel door. He would then unleash continued bursts, using as many remaining magazines as they could muster.

That should give the impression that the team were preparing to fight their way in via a full-frontal assault. Kammler's gunmen should gather at the entrance, waiting for the attackers to show themselves and to pick them off, one by one.

Which should leave Raff, Jaeger and Narov free to make for the skylight, with Hing acting as their guide.

Assuming they could locate it – and Jaeger hated assuming anything – they'd drop through and take Kammler by surprise. From there they would fan out and clear the rest of the complex from the inside, from where it would be as vulnerable as any regular building.

There was one other refinement that Raff had suggested. The subterranean complex had its own backup electricity supply, provided by a generator positioned in a separate building. Before going in, they'd disable that, plunging the bunker into confusion and darkness.

It was a decent enough plan under the circumstances. It had flaws, but at this stage, with such limited resources and time, it was the best they could muster.

Of course, somewhere within the scheme of things were Ruth and Peter Miles – if they were still alive. But they'd cross that bridge when they came to it.

Jaeger's Thuraya buzzed. He glanced at the screen. One word: LURGAN.

When the Operation Gunnerside commandos had gone in to sabotage Hitler's nuclear programme, the cipher they had adopted for the target was Lurgan. That was the agreed code word now, signalling thirty seconds to detonation.

Jaeger yelled out a warning to his team. The roaring from the ruptured pipelines high above had lessened, as the feeder lake was mostly drained of its water, but it was still loud in their ears.

He turned to Hing, showing him how to keep his mouth open to ensure the coming blast didn't damage his eardrums.

In his head Jaeger was counting down the seconds now: ten, nine eight . . . He mouthed a quick prayer: *Please, God, make that device still operational.*

Four, three, two . . .

77

In the dark and deserted strongroom inside Kammler's laboratory, a tiny radio receiver secreted at the heart of the tungsten pile bleeped once, almost inaudibly.

The message had been received and understood.

An instant later, a charge of detonation cord was ignited, which triggered the fifty-kilo block of RDX to blast apart at a velocity of 8,750 metres per second.

As the RDX exploded, it fragmented the one hundred tungsten bars that were packed around it into a million shards of twisted, razor-sharp shrapnel. The metal's immense density and hardness enabled it to absorb the full force and energy of the explosion, transforming it into raw destructive power.

The blast tore outwards, the strongroom vaporising as a storm of jagged metal pulverised its bare concrete walls. The deadly tungsten vortex expanded with irresistible force, scything down all that stood in its path. Walls, doors and windows buckled and disintegrated.

The 3D printers – Kammler's IND factory – were vaporised.

The wave of devastation thundered outwards, those of Kammler's gunmen left to defend the laboratory dying in a hail of shredded metal. As the blast exited the building, it tore off the roof and ripped away the outer walls. Red-hot shards of tungsten sliced through the SUVs that were parked nearby. The fuel tanks were lacerated, the vehicles exploding in a sea of flame.

Set to the rear of the laboratory was a 20,000-litre oil tank, for heating the lab through the harsh winters. It was torn apart, fire blooming orange and angry from where the ruptured tank spurted oil. A massive cloud of dark smoke billowed above the shattered remains of the laboratory, as the tsunami of blasted shrapnel thundered onwards across the valley, spending the last of its awesome power on the gorge's walls.

As the roar of the explosion died away, Jaeger emerged from cover to a scene of utter devastation. Where the laboratory had once stood, there was now a mass of torn wreckage, wreathed in oily smoke and hungry licks of flame. Finally, they'd done it: Kammler's IND factory was no more.

He ran his eye across the wider complex. It only remained now to take the bunker. According to Hing, that lay at the far southern end of the boundary fence, beyond the shattered lab and hard against the wall of the gorge.

Jaeger led his force on what he hoped was the final assault now. But in the back of his mind was a nagging worry: what evil might Kammler have been brewing, as he hunkered in his lair?

In the strange way that time seems to slow to an agonising pace when in the midst of life-or-death combat, he felt as if he'd been here, fighting, for a lifetime. In truth, it was only forty-five minutes since Raff and Alonzo had triggered the pipeline charges, but that was more than enough time for Kammler to wreak havoc.

'Time to split,' Alonzo announced, as he prepared to move towards the front of the shelter.

Jaeger nodded. 'Let's do it. When you go noisy, we'll give it a minute, then go in. Stay in your position and cover the entrance, in case any of the fuckers try getting out that way. If it's anyone but us or the hostages, nail 'em.'

'Got it,' Alonzo confirmed.

With that, the two parties dashed their separate ways.

78

The Nordhavn 64 trawler yacht didn't look at all out of place on its berth at wharf number 47, in New York's Chelsea Piers Marina.

Just three years old, and with its bright white superstructure gleaming from a fresh steam-clean, it spoke of understated wealth, plus a very businesslike and functional ocean-going luxury.

No gin palace this.

Owners of Nordhavn 64s were serious players in the yachting world – global-traveller types. Places to go, new horizons to see: that was what the Nordhavn was all about. With its 59-foot waterline hull length and a 3,000-mile cruise range at a steady nine knots, the vessel was all about eating up the sea miles.

It was 10.30 p.m. New York time – so 10.30 a.m. China time – when the two figures – a man and a woman in their late thirties – emerged from the bridge and closed up the vessel as if they were going out for a night's partying. The Chelsea Piers Marina was a great location from which to do so: the Chelsea Market, the UCB Theatre, and many of New York's finest bars, cafés and clubs were just a few blocks away.

The Sokolovs left the Nordhavn knowing that they were never going to return. A fisherman by profession, but one who had drifted into more nefarious business due to the vagaries of fate, Mr Sokolov had thrilled to the few weeks that he had skippered the vessel. He would never be able to afford such a fine boat himself, even though he had been very handsomely rewarded.

In return for undertaking a long ocean-going journey and following some simple instructions, enough money had been wired into his offshore account to start a new life wherever he and his wife might choose. Or they might simply buy a seaside dacha – a penthouse retreat – and retire to their native Russia.

For the Sokolovs, it was a dream come true.

Deep in the Nordhavn's bilges lay an inspection pit for checking the state of the fibreglass fuel tanks. It had provided ample space to conceal the wooden crate with the simple console bolted onto it. Mr Sokolov guessed the package contained drugs. What else could it be? He presumed that now he had activated the console, as instructed, it would signal the drug gang's pickup point, and they'd home in to wharf 47, to collect their cargo.

He'd heard about such things before: drugs runners even left bales of narcotics at sea, with a homing beacon attached. That way, trafficker and recipient never had to meet. Far safer. Far fewer risks. He didn't doubt the switch he had flicked would trigger that kind of a pickup.

Even so, the call that he had received from Mr Kraft to trigger the console had come as something of a surprise: he'd not been expecting it for some days.

But his was not to reason why: he had executed the final stage of his contract.

Now to disappear.

79

Some 3,500 miles away, the Petrovs exited the Nordhavn 52 that had been their home for the last few weeks. Fitted with a 1,670-gallon fuel tank and a 1,514-litre fresh-water tank, the yacht lying at berth in London's St Katharine Docks Marina was built for ocean-lapping journeys. Displacing 40.82 metric tonnes, she had proved remarkably stable during the long voyage.

A former fisherman, Mr Petrov had been recruited by the same Russian criminal cartel as his friend, Mr Sokolov. When both had been made the same offer by the mysterious Mr Kraft, it had seemed too good to be true.

Well, if it looked that way, it generally was.

In recent days, Mr Petrov had started to worry about just what their vessel was carrying.

He'd not raised it with his wife. He didn't want to worry her. It was more than enough stress sailing between continents and trusting to luck that their mystery cargo wouldn't be discovered.

Most people they had met along the way seemed to think it perfectly natural for a Russian couple in their mid thirties to own a two-million-dollar yacht. In their minds, every Russian was an oligarch and should boast at least one such vessel. Well, the reality was far different. And Mr Petrov for one was very glad to be getting off this ship and away from whatever might be coming.

Mr Kraft's surprise call had woken him in the depths of the night, but Mr Petrov didn't care: it couldn't come soon enough.

He'd flicked the switch on the console and shut up the yacht, then he and his wife had hurried along the quayside to meet their 3.30 a.m. Uber.

Mr Petrov wanted out of London.

He had a bad feeling about what was about to happen and he couldn't seem to shake it.

When taking the contract, he'd agreed with his good friend, Mr Sokolov that it was most likely drugs they'd be carrying. It wasn't the first time they had run such cargoes. If rich Westerners wished to ruin their lives by jacking up on heroin, more fool them. But as he'd approached Britain's coastline, he'd been gripped by this unshakeable worry.

Upon taking Mr Kraft's call, he'd tried to book flights leaving from London's City Airport, just a short drive away. But at such notice there had been no availability. Instead, they would need to travel right across London to Heathrow Airport. From there, he'd booked British Airways direct to Moscow, leaving that evening.

As he stood on the quayside, Mr Petrov checked his watch. The taxi was late. No doubt still trying to find its way onto the marina. He searched for any sign of the car: most likely a black Mercedes or Audi.

A few blocks west, the floodlit towers of London's City banking district rose like a monument to the power of the financial markets. A stone's throw away lay the historic Tower of London, where Britain's royal rulers had once locked the treasonous, to await their execution at nearby Tower Hill.

Mr Petrov wanted out of this city, before he and his wife ended up imprisoned in the Tower themselves.

80

Five thousand miles from St Katharine Docks, Hank Kammler settled back in his executive chair in his subterranean command bunker, smiling grimly. Three calls made: three devices primed to blow. He could hear the clock ticking in his head: the countdown had begun.

Whatever Jaeger and his people might try now, of one thing he was certain: they weren't about to stop the carnage that was coming.

The fuse had been lit.

He was no expert, but he knew enough to envisage what was about to happen. When the Little Boy and Fat Man bombs had been dropped over Hiroshima and Nagasaki, they had been detonated several hundred feet above the cities. That had maximised the immediate destructive power of the blasts.

By contrast, the first of Kammler's INDs would be detonated at ground level. The blast effect would be lessened, but conversely the radioactive contamination would be increased, because the radiation wouldn't disperse in the air. Those parts of the cities that weren't flattened would be rendered uninhabitable for decades.

Hundreds of thousands – maybe millions – would die: either an instant death from the blast, or a lingering one from radiation poisoning. That alone was some achievement.

It had taken seven decades to get to this point.

The humiliation of the Third Reich was about to be avenged.

And once Kammler's gunmen had finished off Jaeger and his

team, he would slip away to another place of hiding. He had many.

It was all coming together, despite the damage inflicted here by a few desperate individuals.

Such was war, Kammler reflected.

Plans evolved as necessity dictated.

And revenge truly was a dish best served cold.

81

There was a squawk of static in Jaeger's earpiece. Message incoming.

'Going dark,' Raff confirmed.

Seconds later, the dull, rhythmic thud of the generator ceased. Raff had considered a few options for stopping it: blowing it up, cutting the wires, slicing through the fuel pipe. But in the circumstances – and once he'd picked the lock on the generator shed – it was just as easy to press the STOP button.

Sure, Kammler might send out his gunmen to get it restarted, but to do so they'd have to leave the bunker's entrance, which any second now was going to get hosed down by Alonzo. And the big African American wasn't exactly short of ammo: Jaeger and Raff had handed over all their remaining 40mm grenade rounds.

Screw it, Raff told himself. He ripped off the generator's fuel hose and stuffed it in his pocket. Now it definitely wouldn't start.

Raff's radio message had been the signal. As Alonzo opened fire, the noise of the blasts echoed through the stunted tree cover. Jaeger figured Kammler had set his command bunker here, in the densest thicket of bush, so as to hide it from the air.

Well, thanks to Hing, they'd found it anyway.

Jaeger glanced over his shoulder and saw Hing give a reassuring thumbs-up. He added a tug of the earlobe, which in this part of the world signified that all was well.

Hing struck Jaeger as being remarkably cool under such

303

circumstances. But then you didn't exactly get wrapped in cotton wool in the People's Liberation Army. Having found himself working for Kammler and enduring whatever horrors that had entailed, the man would have a core of inner toughness.

Raff rejoined them, and they crept closer to their intended point of entry. The skylight proved to be perfectly disguised amongst the vegetation. Without Hing, they would never have found it.

It allowed natural light to enter the bunker complex, and there was also a thin metal ladder running from the skylight down to the floor inside. Clearly it was designed to act as an emergency exit in case of fire or attack.

In his left hand, Jaeger cradled a grenade. He counted down the seconds. When he figured they were long enough into Alonzo's assault, he crept forward, pulled the pin and rolled the grenade across the skylight.

By the time he heard it come to a stop, he was dashing for cover. The standard NATO fragmentation grenade had a four-second fuse, and a lethal rage of five metres. The delay gave Jaeger just enough time to go to ground. Moments later, there was a deafening crack, and the howl of shrapnel cut through the air.

The team were instantly on their feet, sprinting for the breach. Jaeger reached it first, dropping some seven feet through the shattered opening, aiming for a clear patch of floor in the smoke-filled interior.

He hadn't even bothered with the ladder. He needed speed and surprise. He landed in a crouch, his P228's flashlight sweeping the room as he steadied himself. He blanked all else from his mind, scanning for human figures.

He panned right with his weapon, the torchlight dancing in the ghostly swirls of smoke. The light caught on a form slumped over a desk.

Kammler.

82

Behind him Jaeger heard a second pair of boots thump down. He knew instinctively that it was Raff, and that he would be sweeping the room on the opposite side. A third figure vaulted in beside them: Hing. Narov had to be bringing up the rear.

'Kammler at my eleven o'clock,' Jaeger intoned into his SELEX. The bastard looked injured, or at the very least stunned by the blast. 'We need him alive. I repeat: alive.'

It was vital they captured Kammler living, breathing and sentient. He was the key to stopping all of this. His knowledge. His say-so. His authority. His orders to call back those sent to wreak devastation and vengeance. Or if not, his leads so they could hunt the bombers down.

Jaeger spotted a target. To the far right of Kammler a figure was reeling about, senses dulled by the blast, as he struggled to bring his weapon – a Type 79 sub-machine gun – into the aim. Jaeger nailed him with his torch beam: *phzzzt, phzzzt, phzzzt.*

Two shots to the body and one to the head, just to make sure he was finished.

'Enemy down,' he breathed into his SELEX.

Inside his head a voice said, 'Three.' He'd fired three rounds from the P228's thirteen-round magazine, so ten remaining.

A fourth figure dropped in beside him. Narov, weapon at the ready. They swept the room, seeking further targets. As they did so, Jaeger marvelled at what they had stumbled into here. Banks of computer terminals and stacks of complex communications gear lined the walls.

The place resembled an ops room for a small but very tech-savvy army.

Jaeger noticed Kammler trying to move. 'Taking Kammler,' he barked.

As he broke from his stance and began to steal across the room, a figure darted out of cover, weapon raised at the shoulder.

Raff nailed him before he could squeeze off a shot.

'Enemy down,' he breathed calmly.

The big Maori was in his element. He was never more at home than when he was fighting in the darkness and closing with the bad guys at close quarters.

Jaeger moved in on Kammler warily. But as he stole ahead, keeping light on his feet, a figure flashed past on his right-hand side. In a blur of speed, Hing launched himself at Kammler – his former boss, jailer and tormentor – hands reaching like claws to rip the man's eyes out.

Kammler moved surprisingly fast for someone of his advanced years. He whipped up the compact form of a Type 92 handgun and let rip. Two 9mm slugs hammered into Hing, stopping the man dead in his tracks. He went down hard.

As Kammler went to pivot around with his weapon, Jaeger fired, blasting the gun out of his grasp. Moments later, he smacked him around the head with the butt of his P228, Kammler reeling and collapsing against the wall.

Jaeger grabbed him by the hair, jerking his head backwards. There was a cut across his cheekbone, but otherwise he seemed merely stunned. He kicked the man's legs out from beneath him, Kammler dropping like a sack of shit.

'Room clear,' Raff's voice intoned over the radio.

'Room clear,' Narov echoed.

'Secure the entrance,' Jaeger ordered. 'Plus Hing's down. Check Hing.'

He spent a brief moment frisking Kammler, making sure that he wasn't armed, then knelt until they were eye to eye.

'Hello, Mr Kammler. You invited us to drop in. Well, here we are.'

He brought the barrel of his P228 into Kammler's face, until the muzzle was jammed hard against the man's bleeding cheekbone.

'Got a few questions.' He ground the muzzle closer, blood starting to seep round the hard edges of the weapon. 'I'm going to ask this only once . . . where are Ruth Jaeger and Peter Miles?'

Kammler's face twisted into a cruel smile. 'You're too late. To save them. To stop any of this. Heil Hitler, and long live the Thousand Year Reich.'

Jaeger took a step back and kicked Kammler square in the chest. He reeled backwards.

Jaeger glanced at Narov. 'He's all yours.'

Jaeger eyed Raff, who was bent over the fallen form of Hing. The big Maori shook his head. Fearless to the last, Hing had died doing what he'd vowed to do – going after Kammler.

Jaeger moved towards the doorway. 'Right: let's clear this place.'

He and Raff eased themselves through the command bunker's doorway and out into the pitch-dark corridor beyond.

83

Narov settled down in a seat facing Kammler, getting comfortable.

This was a moment she was not going to rush.

She'd waited a very long time.

He was fastened to his chair in a similar way to that in which she had secured Isselhorst in his house in the Heidelberg woods. If anything, Kammler was even more comprehensively constrained. Not only was his body taped to the steel frame, but she'd also wrapped his entire face and head with gaffer tape, leaving only a thin strip for his eyes – the windows onto the soul.

She needed the eyes free so she could better gauge how high the terror needle was pointing.

She'd cut a small hole in the tape around Kammler's nose area, just large enough for him to breathe. Otherwise, he was enshrouded completely.

Just as she wanted him.

'So, you know who I am,' she began in that calm, eerie monotone that was so universally unnerving; utterly devoid of feeling. Mercy, compassion, empathy – her voice lacked it all, and it was doubly unsettling for it.

'You can nod to agree with what I say,' she continued. 'Oh, you cannot nod? Well then, you can blink with your eyes. One blink means you agree. Two blinks mean you do not. Blink once, now, to show me you understand.'

Kammler didn't so much as twitch an eyelid.

Without warning, Narov lashed out with stunning power, swinging her pistol around in a 'ridge-hand strike', a martial arts technique that brought the topside of the weapon crashing into the side of Kammler's head.

The force of the blow was such that it sent the man and chair toppling over. Of course, there was no scream from Kammler, for his mouth was firmly taped shut. Narov reached down and dragged him up into a sitting position, then settled before him again. As she did so, a series of muffled shots echoed through the darkened corridor: no doubt Jaeger and Raff, going about their clearance work.

There was little sign of injury to the side of Kammler's head, but that was mainly because it was a mass of gaffer tape. There could be any amount of damage below.

'So, we try again.' Narov intoned, her voice still chillingly flat and unemotional. 'Blink once to indicate that you understand.'

Kammler blinked.

'Good. Now, I have only one question for you. You will answer it truthfully, or you will experience suffering of a level you would never imagine possible.' She paused for effect. 'Do you understand?'

Kammler blinked once.

'Apart from those we have just destroyed in your laboratory, do you have any other INDs in existence?'

Narov wasn't particularly worried about radiation leaking from the lab. Uranium was not nearly as radioactive as people seemed to believe. Only when a nuclear device was properly detonated did it produce a cloud of lethal fallout.

By way of answer, Kammler blinked twice.

'There are no more INDs? Are you certain? Please think very, very carefully. You see, we are only really just getting started . . .'

Kammler blinked once.

'To be clear, Mr Kammler, there are no INDs anywhere in the world that you control? They were all here?'

Kammler blinked once.

At that moment, a voice rang out from the far end of the corridor. 'Falk Konig! Falk Konig coming through!'

Narov spun in her seat as a pathetic figure stumbled through the doorway. Kammler's son was a pale shadow of the man that Narov had grown close to barely a few months ago. Back then, the German-educated conservationist had been running Kammler's private game reserve at Katavi, in East Africa.

Falk had been something of a hero figure to Narov, despite the blood that ran through his veins. Disregarding that fact – no one gets to choose their parents – his tireless efforts to safe-guard Africa's big game had won her undying respect. The two of them had bonded over their mutual love of animals – the elephants and rhino first and foremost – even amidst the dark secrets of the Katavi reserve.

Kammler's son had rebelled against the family's legacy. His taking a different surname was all part of an effort to cut the ties to their Nazi past. But when Hank Kammler disappeared, Falk Konig had been branded an accessory to his father's crime, and he too had become a global fugitive.

A hunted man.

Only Narov – and Jaeger to a certain extent – had chosen to believe in him; to keep the faith.

When she and Falk had first met, he had been a dashing six-foot-two wildlife warrior, who flew daring sorties across the African bush tracking the poaching gangs. His shock of wild blonde hair and straggly beard had lent him a somewhat hippy-ish air – an exotic if dishevelled eco-warrior look.

Or so Narov had thought. The figure that stood before her now was a pale shadow of that. His hair was matted with dried blood, his eye sockets were sunken and dark-ringed, and he hobbled on an injured leg.

Narov felt a surge of sympathy for him, quickly followed by a stab of unease.

Jaeger must have sent him here for a reason.

No doubt the son knew something of his father's dark secrets.

84

Narov got to her feet. 'Take my chair. You look like you need it.'

Konig sank into the proffered seat. For a moment he stared at the mummified figure opposite – his biological father – in horror.

Then he shook his head. 'You brought this on yourself, Father. You would not listen to anyone, myself included, and now you're finished. It is all finished.'

A flash of defiance burnt through Kammler's eyes, mixed with something that Narov hadn't expected: a fleeting look of triumph. *Of victory.*

It was a look he couldn't hide.

But what did Kammler have to feel triumphant about? Unless . . .

'Tell me,' Narov urged Konig. 'Is there anything he could have done to ensure we cannot stop him?'

Konig shrugged. 'I don't know. He brought me here almost as a hostage. I was being hunted; he offered me some kind of sanctuary. I was innocent of any crime, but damned because he is my father. So I came with him. What choice did I have? He said he would share with me his new dream if I could be loyal. I acted that part. For a while. But once I realised what he actually intended, I tried to call you.'

He cast a glance at his father. 'He grew increasingly suspicious. Paranoid. He cut me off from his inner circle and pretty much locked me away. But this much I do know. He was building eight devices, eight being the sacred number of the SS. And some have already been dispersed to their targets.'

Narov glanced at Kammler. His eyes bulged with impotent rage. From that very look, she knew that he had lied to her, and that his son was telling the truth.

'So, we have one or more INDs already at or near their targets?' she queried. 'Presumably he was waiting for all eight to be in place before a synchronised detonation?'

Konig nodded. 'Nothing else makes sense.'

'Do we know the targets?'

Konig shook his head. 'He never said. But one thing he did boast about: he said that if you took a forty-kilo bomb and detonated it over a nuclear power station, you would achieve meltdown, so increasing the destructive power exponentially.'

As Konig spoke, his father had been making agonised noises from behind his gaffer-tape gag. Narov didn't doubt that he was trying to stop his son selling the Kammler family's secrets. Thank God Konig was a far better man than his father.

'How has he delivered them?' she probed. 'To their targets?'

'I can't say. But nearly all nuclear power stations sit on the coast, as they need water for cooling purposes. Even a forty-kilo device is relatively small in size. You could sail a pleasure yacht to the location, anchor offshore and wait for the signal to detonate. It's weird, but most of those nuclear stations don't even have an exclusion zone. They're sitting targets.'

Narov turned to Kammler. 'You lied to me,' she began, in a gentle whisper. 'I warned you that if you lied, it would get much worse. Now I need you to tell me where your INDs have been sent, and how we stop them.'

She pulled her chair closer. 'I am going to enjoy this next bit. And trust me, you will answer.'

85

Kammler stared back at Narov through the gaffer-tape mask, his eyes burning with hatred.

She delved into her daysack, pulling out a small medical pack. She removed two syringes – the same ones with which she had recently threatened Isselhorst – and held them up where he could see them.

'Two syringes,' she announced. 'One full of suxamethonium chloride, a paralytic. The other contains naloxone hydrochloride, an anti-opioid. I will spare you the complex science. The first is a respiratory depressant: it stops you breathing. Completely. The second reverses the effect.'

She stared into Kammler's eyes. 'Too long under the first, and you suffocate to death. Not enough of the second soon enough, and the effect is irreversible. But you know the best part of it? You are fully conscious the entire time, and you get to experience in clarity what it feels like to suffocate and die.'

She pulled her commando knife from her sheath, bent to Kammler's forearm and began to slice away enough tape to attach a tourniquet, searching for a usable vein.

'I insert a two-way valve so I can pump in both the chemical and the antidote. That way, I can make you experience what it is like to die over and over and over again.'

She reached up with the knife and cut an opening where Kammler's mouth had to be. She smiled. 'If you don't want me to go ahead, now is the time to talk.'

She had partially freed Kammler's lips. They were surrounded by a ragged rosette of torn and sliced tape. His expression was a mixture of fear and rage, as he turned his bile on his son.

'You always were a filthy little commie shit! A traitor of the worst sort!' he spat, the words mixed with gobbets of blood. 'You bring shame—'

Narov's pistol hand whipped around in another blow, the vehemence behind it throwing Kammler to the floor once more. In an almost involuntary action, Konig reached to help his father, but Narov stopped him.

She dragged Kammler up by his hair.

'Is that the answer to the question I asked? No.' Her voice rose an octave, the trace of a killer rage burning in her eyes. The effect was utterly terrifying. 'Your son has more honour and integrity than you could ever wish for. So, answer very carefully, or keep your mouth shut.'

She turned to Falk. 'You don't need to see this.'

Falk shook his head. 'I should have done more to stop him. I *could* have done more to stop him.' He paused. 'I am staying, at least until we have the information we need.'

Wordlessly, Narov turned back to Kammler. 'So, I insert the first shot. This will stop you from breathing. During that time you can think about how you want to answer. The question is: where are your INDs dispersed and how do we stop them? After one minute without oxygen, your brain cells start to die. After three, you will suffer serious brain damage. Better have your answers ready.'

She held up the first syringe and carefully flicked any air bubbles to the top. The last thing she needed was to inject air into Kammler's veins and kill him. She pushed the syringe until the first drops of liquid spurted out of the end.

That done, she reached out and inserted it into the valve hanging out of Kammler's vein.

She plunged the syringe home. For a second there was no visible reaction, and then it was as if the top half of Kammler's body just seemed to cease functioning. The regular rise and fall of his chest cavity, the intake and outflow of breath, even the movement of his eyes – all had stopped.

But his eyes remained open. Frozen wide with terror.

She checked his pulse. It was there, beating away. He had simply stopped breathing, and was utterly helpless to do anything about it.

Kammler was alive and conscious, yet experiencing what it was like to die.

86

Jaeger eased his head around the concrete support beam, his flashlight probing the darkness.

Kammler's bunker appeared to be designed in a T shape. At the lower terminus of the T lay his command cell; at the right-hand end was the entranceway. It was when he'd cleared the left-hand arm that Jaeger had discovered Falk Konig, locked in a side room.

It had made sense for Raff to take the right arm, moving towards the entrance. As for Jaeger, he felt driven by a burning need to find his wife – and Peter Miles. He figured they would be in a room positioned somewhere off this dark corridor, as far from the entrance as possible.

But more haste, less speed: he couldn't rescue them if he got himself killed.

He stole along inch by inch, balanced on the balls of his feet.

Up ahead he spotted movement. A hint of a dark patch of shadow braced against a doorway. He swung his weapon around just as the figure showed himself. Or rather, *herself*. Suddenly Jaeger was face to face with his wife.

She stepped forward, further into the light. No denying it – she was still beautiful. His finger hovered bone-white over the trigger, but his brain felt utterly paralysed.

'You wouldn't,' she whispered. 'Kill the mother of your own child? After all we've been through . . . You and I, Will Jaeger, we're a team.'

Silence. Jaeger was utterly lost for words. He kept his gun in the aim, though he knew in his heart that no matter what she might say, or do, he didn't have it in him to pull the trigger.

She gestured at a pistol she had gripped in her hand. 'I was waiting. For you. In good cover, just like you always taught us. I could have taken the shot. I didn't. I wanted to talk.'

Jaeger found his voice at last. 'Then talk. Like for a start, what the hell are you doing here?'

'It's obvious, isn't it? Kammler – he's our coming saviour.' A glazed expression came into Ruth's eyes. It was one that Jaeger recognised from having come face to face with extremists the world over. Call it brainwashing. Blind fanaticism. Whatever. It always had the same look.

'We humans, plague-like, are eating up this precious earth,' Ruth continued. 'Devastating it. Destroying it. Kammler plans to put a stop to all that. He's an eco-saviour for our times; for the new age.'

She glanced at Jaeger imploringly. 'I tried talking to you back in London. Tried to share this. But you wouldn't listen. No time. Never any time. Nature needs protecting – *from us*. Wipe out half of humanity to save it: it has a simple and beautiful logic to it, don't you see?'

Jaeger felt punch-drunk. Narov had been right, all along. Kammler and his wife – there always had been that bond between them. They shared one, overarching belief: wildlife and environmental protection. She had run here, to him, to join forces in some kind of unholy alliance. Some kind of save-the-world-via-Armageddon death cult.

'Nothing to say?' she probed, a hint of emotion choking her up now. 'Can't you see, this is the right – the only – thing to do. Can't you see that?'

'I can't,' Jaeger countered. 'All I can see is someone who is desperately lost.' He paused. 'One thing you are right about. I should have been there when you needed me. I wasn't. Which makes this my fault.'

'Don't.' She reached a hand towards him tearfully. 'I don't

317

regret this. This awakening. It's what I wanted, always. I'm only sorry—'

'I'm the one who's sorry,' Jaeger cut in.

'No, no,' she countered, shaking her head vigorously. 'There's no time. Not for apologies. Regrets. The clock's ticking. No time for anything but to *join us*. No time—'

Her words were choked off as a huge, hulking figure burst out of the shadows and without a word of warning slammed a massive fist against the side of her head. She catapulted into the darkness, hitting the wall with a horrific thud, slumping down in a heap at its base.

'That shut the bitch up,' her assailant snarled.

Jaeger had recognised him even before he spoke. Steve Jones, his nemesis. Now to finish this. As Jones tried to duck back into cover, Jaeger pulled his trigger.

Click.

He tried again. *Click.*

His P228 had misfired.

He dived for cover even as Jones opened fire. Rounds hammered into the concrete pillar, and for an instant Jaeger felt a jabbing stab of pain in his left thigh.

Shit, he'd been hit. It felt like a flesh wound, but even so, he could sense warm liquid oozing down his leg.

Hugging the pillar, he checked the topside of his pistol. There was nothing stuck in the ejector port, so maybe the magazine was jammed. The P228 was normally bulletproof reliable, but their weapons had taken a hammering as they'd charged through the dirty floodwaters.

Jones stepped more fully into the corridor now, weapon levelled in Jaeger's direction. 'Dead man's click or fucking stoppage,' he grated, 'doesn't make a fat lot of difference when faced with this.' He brandished his weapon, a Type 79 machine gun. 'Long time no see, Jaeger. And by the way, welcome to hell.'

Jaeger didn't answer. Injured, with his gun jammed and no spare mags remaining, he was in a whole world of trouble right now.

'Come here seeking your little wifey, did you?' Jones sneered. 'Let you in on a secret: we ruined her.'

He fired again. Rounds tore chunks of masonry off the wall, ripping into the pillar. Hands working feverishly, Jaeger slipped the magazine off the pistol, but it still wouldn't unjam.

'Well, you've seen her,' Jones sneered. 'Your loyal wife? Somehow I don't think so.'

He reached to the floor and dragged Ruth forward. She looked a mess. Barely conscious. Jaeger's heart skipped a beat as Jones yanked on her hair, bringing her upright.

Was Jaeger imagining it, or did he see her lips move, mouthing: *I'm sorry.*

'Let her go,' he rasped. 'I'll fight you any which way you choose, but let her go.'

'I'll do better than that,' Jones snarled, letting Ruth's head drop with a sickening thump. 'I'll offer you a chance. More than you ever did for me on selection. I put down my Type 79; you put down your spud gun. We fight. No shooters. We end it. Here.'

Jaeger figured he had no option: he'd have to kill Jones first, before he could go to his wife's aid. He slid his pistol out into the corridor, the metal making a rasping noise on the rough concrete floor.

'Kick it away,' Jones barked, as he menaced Jaeger with his weapon.

Jaeger did as he was told.

'Good boy.'

Jones paused. He gripped his weapon and brought it around, slamming the butt into Ruth's head, before spinning it back, barrel pointed directly at Jaeger once more.

'*Now* we're ready. Ready to see what you're made of, Jaeger, you fucking pussy.'

'You're dead,' Jaeger whispered under his breath. 'This very day, you die.'

319

87

J ones lowered his machine gun to the floor and booted it into
the shadows.

Jaeger stepped further into the open. As he did so, he felt an
excruciating pain shoot through his leg. He was wounded and
facing an uninjured Jones: not the best place to be. But his burning hatred of the man, plus the rage that was surging through
him, had to give him an edge.

The two figures approached each other warily. Jones was
a good six foot four, and with all the performance-enhancing
drugs he used, he was as muscle-bound as Jaeger remembered.
He almost didn't look human.

Jaeger had always been faster, but with an injured leg, there
was no telling. He went into a combat stance, his feet shoulder-
width apart, toes slightly turned inwards, knees slightly bent,
arms up and out in front of his face, ready to lash blows.

It was then that Jones did something utterly unexpected.
Reaching down to his thigh, he drew out a blade. What had
once been Narov's commando knife – all seven inches of tapered, razor-sharp steel – was now gripped in his hand.

'Recognise this?' He smiled evilly. 'I said no shooters. I didn't
mention blades. I call it the Shark Killer. Though it's just as good
for disembowelling humans. Take a look at what I did to Old
Man Miles.'

Jaeger didn't reply. His entire focus was on the coming fight.

They circled each other like big cats, ready to pounce. From
his martial arts training, Jaeger knew that so often the key to

such a fight was to strike first and strike hard. The man who hesitated was dead.

He made his move – and it was fast, very fast.

He drove the outside edge of his right boot low and hard into the side of Jones's knee.

Jones tried to whip his leg back to avoid the blow. But it was a case of simple cause and effect; the attacker will always have a speed advantage. Jaeger's kick made partial contact. It wasn't the devastating strike that he'd hoped for; no crippling crunch of bone. But it was a start.

Jones backed away, regaining his balance, just as Jaeger swung the side of his right hand hard into his bull-like neck. Again, it was a glancing blow, but it opened the door for the next move. A split second later, he drove his left fist straight out like a batter-ing ram, smashing into Jones's windpipe with devastating force.

Jones's shaven head whipped backwards violently, then re-bounded forward from the impact of the killer strike.

The fight had lasted barely seconds. But as Jaeger watched Jones's massive form crumple to the floor, he felt a stab of sheer agony shooting through his good leg, which gave way beneath him. Even as he had collapsed, Steve Jones had struck Jaeger a savage blow with the knife.

Jaeger found himself sprawled in a heap, his knifed leg a mass of spurting blood. He started to crawl, trying to drag his body to a safe place.

Behind him, Jones was starting to come round. Jaeger heard a voice spitting out the words. 'Was I too quick? Didn't see the blade? Oh yeah! I'm going to enjoy every last minute of this.'

Jones sheathed his bloodied knife and staggered to his feet, towering over Jaeger's prone form. 'I have wanted this for so long,' he sneered. 'I am going to kick your head until what little brains you have are smeared across the walls.'

He moved to give himself room for the run-up. 'I'm gonna beat you to the very brink of death. But you ain't gonna die. Not yet. Not today. Oh no. This is far too personal . . . I'm gonna keep you alive. You know why? So you can watch your family fry.'

Jaeger was hunched against the wall, bloodied and helpless before the towering figure of his assailant.

'You think that by hitting this place you can stop us?' Jones scoffed. 'We're *unstoppable*. And we're coming for the Jaeger clan like you'd never imagined possible!'

As Jones braced himself to attack, Jaeger felt something digging into the small of his back. Suddenly he remembered: the Chinese QSZ-92 – the pistol that he'd taken from Ustanov.

His backup backup weapon.

As Jones began to charge, Jaeger whipped out the hidden handgun. There was a momentary look of disbelief in the big man's eyes, before his kick to Jaeger's head became a desperate attempt to boot the pistol from his hands.

Jaeger fired. The first round struck Jones high in the leg, two further shots following. By the time Jones's body joined Jaeger's on the cold concrete floor, he was splattered in blood and gore.

As for Jaeger, he was drifting into a dark unconsciousness.

88

Suxamethonium chloride – known as 'sux' for short by medical practitioners – is widely used in hospital procedures. It is also the perfect poison for those intent on murder.

It had taken three doses for Narov to break Kammler; three near-death experiences administered by her hand, before he had crumbled.

As he had begun to talk, the scenario that had unfolded had made Narov's blood run cold: three INDs moored at three world capitals, set to detonate in thirty-eight minutes and counting.

Right now she was hunched over the Thuraya satphone speaking to Brooks, her voice tight with tension and fear.

'Boat one is the *Adler*, a Nordhavn 64 yacht moored at New York's Chelsea Piers Marina. Boat two is the *Werwolf*, a Nordhavn 52 moored at London's St Katharine Docks. Boat number three is the *Fireland*, another Nordhavn 52, docked at the Tel Aviv Marina.'

Brooks repeated the details back to her. 'Okay, I'm on it.' He ordered Narov to stick by the Thuraya and not to move a muscle.

In addition to the three devices parked in those city marinas, Kammler had confessed to five other planned attacks, designed to hit nuclear power plants; five other Nordhavn yachts complete with their forty-kilo INDs, eight being the sacred number of the SS. Thanks to the sux, Narov had extracted the full details.

Target one was the Qinshan nuclear power plant, set on the East China Sea, on the very outskirts of Shanghai, a city of twenty-four million souls. Target two was America's Calvert Cliffs plant, on the Chesapeake Bay, just to the south of Washington, a city of eight million. Target three was France's Flamanville nuclear plant, west of Paris. There had also been a Canadian target and a second plant in China. Thankfully, due to the destruction of Kammler's lab, none of those devices had been dispatched. Which made the priority dealing with the nukes that were in place and primed to blow.

Narov didn't relish Brook's position right now. He had to coordinate three seek-and-destroy missions, on three different continents, and with precious little time. There would be no chance to attempt to defuse the devices; the only option would be to blow the yachts out of the water.

Weapons-grade uranium wasn't particularly radioactive, not unless you could smash together two heavy lumps with immense force. It was the collision of two such masses that led to fission, the self-sustaining chain reaction that would engender a nuclear explosion, which in turn would produce massive amounts of radioactivity.

If the devices were torn to pieces in the yacht's holds and sent to the bottom, they would be rendered relatively harmless. It was all up to Brooks now.

Narov turned to Falk. 'Go find Jaeger and Raff. Plus Alonzo. We need to regroup, in case there's anything Brooks needs from this end.'

'What about Peter Miles and Jaeger's wife?' Falk queried.

'Search for them too. But I don't hold out any great hope.'

Falk hobbled off to do as he'd been bidden. Narov knew him to be a brave and courageous individual, and she wasn't surprised that he had done the right thing. But right at this very moment, she needed him out of the way for an entirely different reason.

Once he had gone, she reached for a freshly charged syringe of sux, which she inserted into the tube hanging out of Kammler's forearm.

She brought her face close to his, so she was speaking barely above a whisper. 'I guess you thought it was all over? I am afraid not.' She paused. 'You see, Mr Kammler, this is *personal*.

'I am going to tell you a story,' she continued. 'It is 1943. Sonia Olchanevsky is a Russian Jewess of great beauty. For three years she has fought with the French Resistance. But she is captured and sent to the Natzweiler concentration camp. There, amongst other horrors, she is raped. One man basically makes her his slave and his mistress.'

She paused. 'I am curious: have you ever heard this story?'

'No,' Kammler rasped. 'Never. I swear.'

The repeated administrations of the drugs seemed to have broken him. Perhaps, having peered into the face of death, his dark soul had finally been revealed to him.

'The man who raped Sonia Olchanevsky was SS General Hans Kammler,' Narov continued. 'Your father. And Sonia was my grandmother. Your father raped my grandmother, which makes us . . . almost family.'

She moved closer, until her mouth was next to Kammler's ear. 'That makes Falk my half-cousin and you . . . my half-uncle. Now, as I understand it, the term for killing your uncle is avunculicide. It is a bit of a mouthful, but it will do for now.'

With that, she drove the final shot of suxamethonium chloride into Kammler's bloodstream.

'Goodbye, dear uncle. Today is judgement day. For you, it is long overdue.'

Kammler's gaze fixed itself on Narov for the briefest of instants, his lip curled in arrogance and hatred.

'Tell Jaeger,' he hissed, 'now I am become death—' His head slumped forward, cutting off the last words.

Narov leant over and checked his pulse. There was none.

Hank Kammler was dead. But what a weird way to phrase his final words: he hadn't *become death*. He *was dead*.

Weird. And chilling, in an odd, intangible way.

Why in his dying breath had he sounded so exultant?

And why the personal message for Jaeger?

89

The Super Lynx powered up the Thames, swooping over the river, pushing towards its 200 mph maximum speed. By the pilot's calculations, they were one minute out.

'Delta One, Stinger Three, sixty seconds out,' he intoned, speaking into his helmet microphone. 'Go live with LTD.'

'Roger that,' came the reply from Pete Iron, the SAS Counter-Terrorism troop sergeant, who was positioned with one of his corporals, Fred Gibson, at the London City marina.

Ever since 9/11, the SAS had maintained a counter-terrorism team based at the SAS's ultra-secret London headquarters, just a stone's throw from Whitehall. Ready and waiting for just such an alert as they had received today.

The call to action had come barely twenty minutes earlier. They were to destroy a Nordhavn yacht moored in St Katharine Docks, no matter what the risk of civilian casualties or collateral damage. The cut-off point was 0359 hours.

If they failed, the team had been warned, the proverbial sky would fall.

Iron and Gibson were crouched barely a hundred metres from the target. From their kneeling position adjacent to the dock's Zizzi restaurant, they could see the vessel's name clearly.

Werwolf was stencilled on her stern.

'Stinger Three, Delta One, lasing target now,' Iron radioed the pilot.

'Delta One, Stinger Three, copied.'

The SAS sergeant fired his tripod-mounted Thales laser target designator – LTD for short – at the *Werwolf*, knowing that the hot point of the laser – where it bounced off the hull – would act as a guide for the coming strike.

The pilot put the Lynx into a howling right-hand turn, bringing its nose around to face the marker – the smoke grenade that Gibson had lobbed onto the target. The helo swept in low across the river just to the east of the century-old Tower Bridge.

Some eighteen minutes earlier, just as the Lynx was being scrambled, Special Branch had got busy dragging some seriously confused yachties from their beds. They'd had only a few minutes to evacuate the dock, getting any public the hell out of there.

For a brief moment Sergeant Iron wondered how those yachties would react when they saw their beloved boats getting peppered with chunks of shrapnel. In truth, he didn't much care.

To receive an order such as this – an air strike on a civilian vessel in the heart of London – it had to be a crisis of gargantuan proportions. He wondered who could have dug up the intelligence to back such a ballsy move.

Above him the Lynx slowed, creeping closer to a firm firing position, its nose rotating around towards the target.

'I see your laser,' the pilot intoned. A lengthy pause. 'I have lock-on.' Another pause. 'Engaging now.'

There was a second's delay, and then a burst of violent fire bloomed on the Lynx's snub-nosed rocket pods, slung to either side of the aircraft, and a pair of CRV7 precision-guided 70mm rockets streaked towards the marina.

The 4.5-kilo explosive-point-detonating warhead was capable of penetrating a T-72 main battle tank's armour. Unsurprisingly, the steel hull of the Nordhavn 52 was torn open as if it had been attacked with a giant tin-opener.

The twin warheads penetrated the deck, detonating deep in the bowels of the vessel. It struck Sergeant Iron as being a tad overkill, as the two-million-dollar yacht was ripped asunder from the inside, vomiting chunks of molten aluminium in a boiling sea of flame.

As the smoke cleared, he could see what remained of the burning hulk of the Nordhavn sinking fast, the water hissing and gurgling as it sucked the twisted red-hot wreckage downwards. To either side, other boats had suffered fairly extensive damage.

He winced. Some very wealthy individuals were going to need some serious repair jobs on their oh-so-shiny vessels.

And the rebel within him loved it.

He looked at his watch: 0358.

'Bang on schedule,' he noted to the figure crouched beside him.

Corporal Gibson nodded. 'Job done. Let's get out of here.'

90

Narov punched answer, clamping the Thuraya to her head. 'Yes.'

'It's Brooks. Crisis over. Tel Aviv was first. The Israelis don't mess around. Scrambled an F-15 Strike Eagle and put a Harpoon anti-ship missile through the yacht. *Fireland* vaporised. New York was second. A Black Hawk headed up the Hudson and put a Hellfire through the *Adler*'s bridge. London was last. Typical of the Brits to push it to the wire. Slammed a couple of CRV7 rockets through the *Werwolf*'s deck at 0358 precisely.'

'Two minutes to spare,' Narov noted. 'More than enough.'

Brooks smiled. She was one cool customer. He was glad she was on the side of the angels. 'You managed to extract the other information we needed?' he asked.

'Eventually,' Narov confirmed.

She passed the details of the other ships and their targets to Brooks. Thankfully none of the five vessels had yet to set sail, or so Kammler had claimed. Those five, plus the three already destroyed: she allowed herself a rare moment of self-congratulation. Soon now, they'd get them all; all eight of the killer devices.

'I'll get teams scrambled to take them down,' Brooks confirmed. 'Any chance the crews might have got word from Kammler to scarper?'

'Unlikely.' She glanced at the corpse slumped it its chair. At last he looked almost at peace. 'He certainly won't be warning anyone now.'

'Maybe you can connect me to our . . . friend. I'd like to let him know in person that he failed.'

'That might be a little difficult,' Narov replied flatly. 'The questioning: it was most robust. His heart failed.'

'His heart? He's dead?' Brooks cursed. 'I was looking forward to putting that bastard on trial.'

'Were you? Why? He didn't deserve a jail cell; to be made a rallying point for the Nazi cause. He deserved what he got.'

Brooks didn't argue. Kammler was dead and the world was undoubtedly a safer place for it, no matter what the means of his removal. The CIA man knew Narov as a straight talker, which was rare in this business. He appreciated it.

'What about you guys? Any casualties?'

'Peter Miles has been beaten to within an inch of his life. He needs urgent medical attention. Jaeger has suffered serious blood loss due to an arterial wound. He's in and out of consciousness, but we've stabilised him.'

'You?'

'Unwounded.' She paused. 'But some of Kammler's men are unaccounted for. Among them his deputy, Steve Jones. He's injured, but he got away.'

'How?'

'There were some vehicles parked in a subterranean hangar, in a hidden cave in the cliff. Jones managed to get to one of those. We tried to stop him, but he got away in a hail of bullets.'

'Jaeger's wife?' Brooks prompted.

Narov's face darkened. 'Same as Jones. We understand she's injured, but no sign of her either. We figure she and Jones made a joint getaway.'

'Right, how long has that vehicle been mobile?'

'Twenty minutes. Thirty at the outside.'

'We'll find it. Don't worry, we'll find it.'

'And then? Bear in mind what it might be carrying. It's unlikely, but it might just be loaded with—'

'Understood. Don't worry, it's history. Even over China, we have ways and means.'

'Good. But don't go starting a third world war. We were so close to Armageddon this time . . .'

'Leave it with me. Time to come clean with the Chinese, but since Kammler planned to hit two of their foremost nuclear plants, I think they'll cut me some slack.

'And Jaeger?' Narov probed. 'Do we come clean with him too? About his wife? That vehicle?'

There was silence for a beat, before Brooks answered. 'I think not. Better for all if he doesn't know. At least not yet; not before it's all over.'

Narov allowed herself a fleeting smile. 'Understood.'

'Keep this line open. It's a fast-moving situation.'

Narov told him she would, and killed the call.

91

Narov left the command cell, making her way towards the kitchen area, where the injured were being treated. Raff had got the generator working, so at least they had power and light.

As she stepped through the mess left by Jones and Jaeger – the blood and detritus from their savage close-quarters battle – her eye caught the glint of a half-obscured blade. Her heart missed a beat.

It was instantly recognisable.

She bent and retrieved it. This dagger meant the world to her.

It had once belonged to Brigadier Edward 'Ted' Jaeger, SAS war hero and founder of the Secret Hunters, the man who had helped rescue Narov's grandmother from the World War II concentration camp.

Ted Jaeger had been a man of true compassion: when he'd learnt that Sonia Olchanevsky was pregnant as a result of rape, he had offered to be the unborn child's godparent. He had been Narov's mother's godfather, and he had treated Narov herself as if she were his own niece.

It was from Ted Jaeger that she had first heard of her family's dark history, and had first been drawn into the work of the Secret Hunters. When she had met Will Jaeger, she'd wondered whether he could ever be worthy of his grandfather's legacy.

Now, as she moved towards the kitchen, she knew in her heart that he most certainly was.

After their battles here in Kammler's lair, she had to admit it: Jaeger had the Secret Hunter spirit in spades. She also knew that without him they would never have got Kammler.

The plan in the Amazon to switch the aircraft's cargo: that had been Jaeger's brainchild. The tungsten bomb – their Trojan horse – his inspiration again. Plus blowing the pipelines, a touch of true Jaeger genius.

She looked the bloodstained dagger over. It would need a good clean, she thought. But it was home. At last.

She stepped through into the kitchen, seeking out Raff and Alonzo. They were crouched over Jaeger's barely conscious form. She could see where they had cut the combat trousers off him and slapped a tourniquet on his right leg.

'How is he?' she asked tightly.

Raff shrugged. 'You know how he is. Soft as shit. He'll pull through.'

The humour: it had to mean that the worst was over.

'And the others?'

'Miles is unconscious but stable,' Raff explained. 'With some proper medical attention he should be okay. And Falk will be fine.' He paused. 'We lost Hing, but assuming you got Brooks to rustle up the medevac, the rest should be good.'

'He promised. I'll chase him.'

Narov turned and left the room. She could only get satphone reception from the command cell. As she made her way down the corridor, her mind wandered. Hunting Kammler had been her life's mission. But now *his* life had been snuffed out, that dark evil extinguished, and the debt she owed to her grandmother had been repaid.

So what was to be her life's work now?

What mission was there that could draw her close to Jaeger, as their work in the Secret Hunters had done? She didn't know, but she lived in hope. As the brigadier had often told her: life rewards the persistent. It was a dream that she would nurture.

She dialled Brooks's number, and he reassured her that a medevac team had been scrambled. It should be no more than twenty minutes away. 'And the vehicle?' she queried. 'The geta-way car? Jones and his . . . sidekick?'

'Found,' Brooks confirmed.

Narov felt her pulse quicken. 'And? How are you tracking it? What are you intending? Whose take-down is it – ours or the Chinese?'

'I can't say,' Brooks demurred. 'That's beyond highly classi-fied. But what I can tell you is this: I'm eyes on a video feed of that vehicle, even as we speak.' Brooks paused. 'I can patch you in, if you have a screen handy and a broadband connection running.'

As it happened, Narov had. With Falk's help she'd managed to log onto the base's wireless connection. She passed Brooks the details and a grainy image flashed up on a nearby screen. It showed a Great Wall Haval H6, a Chinese manufactured 4x4 that was hugely popular in the country, speeding along a frozen track that snaked through a grey-walled gorge.

'Thermal imaging reveals four individuals aboard,' Brooks re-marked. 'So along with Ruth Jaeger and Steve Jones, we have two other escapees. Don't suppose you have any idea who they might be?'

'None.'

As the powerful 4x4 took a series of sharp bends, it slewed alarmingly, spraying snow and dirt from its wheels.

'Notice the less-than-impressive handling,' Brooks added. 'No fault of the vehicle. See how low it sits on its springs. We figure it's armoured, and whoever's at the wheel isn't used to how the extra weight affects the cornering.' Brooks paused. 'But armour or no armour, it won't help those aboard much with what's coming.'

'Which is?'

'Put it this way: they could be riding in an Abrams main battle tank, and they'd still not stand a hope in hell of surviving.'

At last, Narov told herself.

'As it happens, the . . . termination is due about any time

now,' Brooks added. 'Keep your eyes on the prize . . .'

The seconds ticked by as Narov studied the screen closely. She could barely stand the wait. It was like watching some kind of computer game – not that Narov was in the habit of doing so much. With those who truly deserved it she preferred hunting – and killing – for real. Just like now.

Suddenly, there was a blinding flash of light, which whited-out whatever observation platform Brooks was using to track the vehicle. As the image adjusted, and pulled back into focus, Narov could see shattered chunks of smoking debris scattered across a wide swathe of the gorge.

She didn't have a clue what asset – what weapon – Brooks had deployed in the strike, but whatever it was, the 4x4 had been totally obliterated. Shredded into blasted, fiery ruin. And whoever had been riding in it had been vaporised along with the vehicle.

Narov smiled. At last: Steve Jones and Ruth Jaeger – good riddance to the both of them.

92

Jaeger stumped down from the Range Rover. His right leg was still painful, but he hated using the walking stick. While it was healing, he wasn't too proud to lean on Narov's arm.

She'd offered to drive, for which Jaeger had been grateful. He wasn't supposed to get behind the wheel, not with the powerful painkillers that he was taking.

What mattered most right now was that he was alive, he was out of hospital and he was about to see his boys again. Plus the world was safe – for now, at least. Until another madman like Kammler tried to wreak havoc and destruction.

Luke and Simon strode across from the far side of the playing field: muddy, soaked and steaming, but proud in their new school colours.

They'd lost the match, yet they'd played like demons, which was all that really mattered in a game of rugby. Or indeed in life, Jaeger told himself. As they approached, he marvelled how a few months at a school such as this could have turned his sons from boys into young men.

They had matured so much. They weren't just bigger, taller and with voices noticeably gruffer; they walked with a new sense of purpose.

They stopped a few yards short of him. Eyes smiling, but a little unsure whether to go for a hug in front of all their rugby mates, and with this stranger of a woman standing by their father's side.

Jaeger eyed the thick mud plastered over them. 'Glad I

cleaned the Pinkie for you guys – caked in all that crap!'

Pinkie: it was their in-joke. During World War II, the SAS had learnt that a light pink colour was the best camouflage for their vehicles while on desert operations. Not brown or khaki or yellow or ochre, but pink. SAS Land Rovers were still painted that hue for desert ops, hence the nickname for the Range Rover.

Despite the mud, they piled into the vehicle.

'So, does every SAS soldier get a gorgeous blonde to ride shotgun?' asked Simon, Jaeger's adopted son, tilting his head in Narov's direction.

Jaeger choked back a chuckle. 'Sadly not. But just to be clear, she's driving; I'm crook; and I'm *former* SAS. Plus you need to wind your neck in.'

'Hey, I'm winding it.'

They laughed.

Narov got the vehicle under way and they pulled out of the school grounds, heading for the motorway.

'So, guys, this is Irina,' Jaeger announced, realising he'd failed to do the introductions. 'She offered to help me get you home, so be real nice to her.' He paused. 'She can be very scary when she wants to be.'

The boys looked at each other.

'Like we're ever not nice.'

'Yeah, as if.'

'You know why we lost the match?' Luke volunteered. He lived, ate and breathed rugby, and like his dad he was one bad loser. 'We got greedy in the second half. We thought we'd won. We took stupid risks and paid the price.'

'Just like your father tends to,' Narov volunteered flatly.

Jaeger rolled his eyes.

Luke glanced at his dad, his face all serious for a second. 'I miss Mum.'

'I know. We all miss her.' In a way, Jaeger did.

After Brooks had contacted the Chinese authorities, they had descended on Kammler's lair in force. They'd flown the wounded out to the nearest hospital, which had been equipped with the most advanced medical facilities. That had been critical to Jaeger and Miles's recoveries.

It was in hospital that Jaeger had learnt all that had been discovered about his errant wife. The remains of Ruth's laptop had been retrieved from the scorched wreckage of Kammler's lair. That, plus her emails, had revealed the full extent to which she had been seduced by Kammler's crazed schemes.

In his own gentle way Miles had explained to Jaeger that Ruth's warped allegiances had been more anchored in trauma than in any coherent beliefs or philosophy. She'd demonstrated all the classic symptoms of Stockholm syndrome.

Stockholm syndrome was something studied during the kidnap and ransom phase of SAS counter-terrorism training. Jaeger remembered it well. It was named after a Stockholm bank heist in which the hostages had ended up siding with the robbers. It referred to the propensity of a hostage to bond with his or her captor, especially if they shared similar values and views.

Jaeger had forced himself to contemplate this with regard to his wife. It would explain an awful lot of her behaviour over the past few months, though forgiving her would still take time. Serious amounts of time. As for the love, it was there, but warped forever by grief and anger.

Several bodies had been discovered in the getaway vehicle, one of which was that of a woman. The Chinese authorities had promised DNA samples to confirm that Ruth Jaeger and Steve Jones were amongst the dead, but they were taking their time.

It was hardly surprising. Brooks and the CIA had hardly rushed to alert them when Kammler was plotting world devastation from Chinese soil. Why would they hurry now to share their findings?

Even so, Jaeger had few doubts that his wife had perished in that vehicle. Still, until he had absolute confirmation, he wasn't going to say anything to the boys. They had more than enough to deal with.

'Any news?' Luke pressed. 'Anything?'

Jaeger shook his head. 'Nothing concrete. But let's not lose hope. Let's not give up.'

He felt like a Judas saying it, even though he was just trying to shield them from the worst. He glanced at Narov. She looked just like she had when he'd first met her. Cold. Detached. Unemotional.

Only of course deep down she wasn't. Jaeger knew that. In a way, that was what he loved about her. Her impenetrable calm. Her blunt honesty. Her straight-talking no-bullshit ways.

Her quiet, unassailable strength.

He figured it was time to lighten the mood a little. He'd try some corny jokes. Another long-lived Jaeger family tradition: on long drives, Dad cracks the worst ever jokes.

He turned to the boys. 'So . . . why don't they play poker in the jungle?'

Luke rolled his eyes and groaned. 'Don't tell us – too many cheetahs.'

Jaeger grinned. 'Very good. How about this. What's a Hindu?'

Luke groaned again. 'Lay eggs. Ha ha. Very funny.' He nudged Simon in the ribs. 'I guess everything's gotta be okay if Dad's started on the crappy jokes.'

Simon grinned. 'Talking of Hindus, we're learning all about it at school. It's kinda cool.' He put on a deep, gruff, God-like voice. 'Now I am become death, destroyer of worlds! Lord Krishna, the blue-faced dude.'

The colour drained from Narov's face and she snapped her head around. '*What* did you say? Now I have become *what*?'

Simon shrugged. 'Death, destroyer of worlds. That's how the quote goes. Like I said, Lord Krishna.'

'Yeah, but some guy called Oppenheimer also used it,' Luke added. 'When the Americans detonated the first atom bomb.

We learnt about it in history. Kind of summed up the moment pretty well, too.'

Narov flicked her eyes across to Jaeger. There was a hint of panic in them that he was at a total loss to comprehend. 'There's a services just ahead. I'm pulling over.'

She turned in and brought the Range Rover to a halt. As she did so, Jaeger could sense the fear that had crept into the vehicle.

'What's going on?' he queried.

Narov eyed him nervously. Worriedly. It was hugely unsettling. If *she* was so perturbed, then whatever was happening had to be some seriously heavy shit.

'I . . . terminated Kammler. That much you must have realised.' She was trying to choose her words carefully, mindful of the boys sitting in the rear. 'But you know what the weirdest thing was? He died almost *triumphantly.*'

She locked eyes with Jaeger. 'His last words were choked off mid sentence. But you know what they were: *Now I am become death* . . . I didn't get the significance of it at the time.' A beat. 'I do now.'

Jaeger felt his blood run cold. The pieces were falling together in his mind, and it was utterly chilling. 'Are you saying what I think you're saying?' he ventured.

'We've been fooled.' Narov answered, as if confirming his worst thoughts. 'Kammler tricked us all, even those supposedly closest to him.' She shook her head, horrified. 'There weren't just eight devices. There's another out there somewhere.'

'Jesus,' Jaeger muttered. 'Nine. And the last one presumably primed to blow.'

Narov nodded darkly. 'Plus there's this: Kammler's final message, it was personal. He said: *Tell Jaeger.*'

93

Jaeger's eyes widened. He was gripped by an unshakeable fear. A phrase had come unbidden into his head, from the time of his bloody fight with Steve Jones in Kammler's lair. It had slipped from his mind during the long hours of unconsciousness that had followed. But it was back now with a vengeance, triggered by Narov's recollections.

He turned to the boys, doing his best to hide his consternation. He thrust his debit card in their direction. 'Here, you know the code. You guys must be starving. We'll see you in McDonald's in five.'

The only answer was a pair of doors slamming and the boys were gone.

Jaeger turned back to Narov. 'Before I shot him, Steve Jones said something. Something like: *I'm gonna keep you alive so you can watch your family fry.* It's only just come back to me.'

Narov's gaze hardened. 'So it *is* personal. For both of them. Against you and your loved ones. If there is a device still out there, it is being targeted at you and them.'

'But how? And where?'

Narov pointed towards the pair of golden arches that rose above the service area. 'The boys. Has to be. Kammler tortured you with Ruth and Luke before, remember. This time, Ruth ran to Kammler. To his side. That leaves only the boys.'

Jaeger glanced towards the darkening horizon, in the direction of the coast. The school rugby match had ended late. It was dusk. Darkness descending. In the distance, a pair of floodlit towers rose above the clifftop, surrounded by a weird, ghostly halo of alien blue light.

It hit him suddenly, in a blinding flash of realisation. 'The reactor at Hinkley Point,' he whispered. 'Has to be.'

A forty-kilo IND detonated at Hinkley – it would cause meltdown at the plant. Cataclysmic devastation. It would fit Kammler's bill perfectly . . . and the boys' school just nearby would be one of the first places to be hit. Might even be close enough to be flattened by the blast.

He turned to Narov. 'Hinkley's smack-bang beside their school. Plus it's coastal, so perfect for his fleet of yachts. The prevailing wind spreading radioactive fallout all across the country. Bristol, Reading, Oxford, London . . . all those cities in its path. And from there on into western Europe, like so many Chernobyls . . .'

His mind was awakening to the full ramifications; the full horror. 'We've been outsmarted. Completely. It was always *nine*. How could we have been so dumb? How could we have missed it?'

Narov shrugged. 'Shit happens. And we're not perfect.'

'The ninth device – it's his last laugh on us all. His gift to a devastated world.'

'Not if we can stop him.' Narov's voice was tight with tension. 'Hinkley's what, twenty minutes' drive away?'

'Less. Fifteen.'

She slammed a fist into the Range Rover's wheel. 'Then what are we waiting for? But what about the boys?'

Jaeger glanced towards the twin towers. 'We do not take them any closer to the threat. They sit tight here. I'll call someone who can fetch them.'

He checked the time and date on his watch. *Jennie*. Raff's girlfriend normally worked nights, but she had the long weekend off. Raff was planning to take her away on a surprise break. He grabbed his mobile. He'd give her a call.

He went to throw open the Range Rover's door, but paused

for an instant. The date. Utterly chilling. He didn't believe in coincidences.

'You know what date it is? The thirtieth of April. Anniversary of Hitler's death. It's pre-planned. Got to be.'

'Only one way to find out.' Narov fixed him with a look. 'We have to get moving. Go tell the boys.'

'Weaponry? Whoever's crewing that boat, what the fuck do we have to fight them with? Our bare hands?'

Narov reached behind her back and withdrew a compact pistol. Her Beretta 92FS. Jaeger didn't know how she'd managed to keep hold of it, but he wasn't entirely surprised.

'Never go anywhere without it,' she breathed. 'Go warn the boys.'

'Make some calls and get a chopper scrambled from Valhalla,' Jaeger called over his shoulder as he darted from the vehicle. 'They should be able to get here pronto.'

Valhalla: their slang for Hereford, the SAS's base, lying just north of the Bristol Channel. It made sense to call for as much backup as possible.

'We will be there sooner,' Narov yelled after him.

94

It was the noise that had alerted them. The weird, ghostly roar of a machine of some sort rising fast into the night sky. Only no aircraft that Jaeger and Narov had ever heard of took off directly from the sea, and especially not under such conditions.

Whatever the mystery machine might be, it remained utterly shrouded in darkness, almost invisible to the naked eye. The only exception was the rear underside, from where Jaeger could make out a faint, pulsing red glow.

That blinking devil's eye was the only sign that the hidden aircraft was powering into the heavens.

Jaeger turned his head ninety degrees, so that he was facing east towards the shadowed outline of the Somerset coastline. Not a mile away, the ghostly structure of the nuclear power plant was lit up like some kind of giant spacecraft marooned on the low cliffs.

The proximity of the two – the power station and the approaching aircraft – was terrifying.

Narov crouched in the stern of the boat, edging it forward, trying to match their desire for speed with the need to make a covert approach. In the circumstances, stealing the rigid inflatable boat had been their only option. There had been several craft moored in Bridgwater Bay, but the RIB had been the one to go for.

Fast, stable, relatively silent and riding low in the water, it was the preferred assault craft for seaborne special forces the world over. It had made double the sense to take the RIB, for there was a stiff wind blowing and a big swell on the sea. The RIB was just about unsinkable and able to master far worse conditions than these.

Once they had got under way, powering out to sea, Narov hadn't even tried to argue when Jaeger had demanded her pistol. Whoever was on the vessel that had to be out there somewhere on the dark waters, Jaeger was determined to be the one to take them down.

As Narov nursed the RIB closer to where the launch platform had to lie, a form began to emerge from the dark line where the night sky met the sea. Jaeger could just make out the vessel, silhouetted as it was by the moonlight that bled through the clouds.

It had the classic lines of a Nordhavn yacht, Kammler's chosen delivery vessel for the untold mass murder and mayhem that he had planned to visit on the world.

As the ship materialised from the darkness, Narov powered the RIB right down so they could creep up on their prey silent and unseen. The RIB inched closer, Jaeger holding his breath and praying that the roar of the mystery aircraft would mask the noise of their engine.

Whoever was crewing the yacht was bound to be far better armed than Jaeger and Narov, who boasted the one Beretta between them. If the crew got wise to the RIB's presence, they'd be able to lean over the ship's rail and shoot them up in the water. They'd pick off Jaeger and Narov at a distance, well before the Nordhavn came within the pistol's range.

Much as Jaeger hated it, they had to creep in stealthily, even as the aircraft streaked towards its target, the devil's eye blinking ever closer to the cliffs.

Jaeger didn't doubt that the airborne platform was somehow fitted with the last of Kammler's INDs. The ninth device – the one they had all missed, believing that Kammler, in his hubris and megalomania, would have stuck rigidly to the Nazis' sacred number.

He figured the mystery platform had to be a drone of sorts. Right now, it was just minutes away from drawing level with the power station and stealing into its airspace. That was what the flashing red light had to be for – it provided a reference point, so the drone's operator could steer it through the dark skies to the exact point of detonation, one calculated to cause maximum devastation and the catastrophic meltdown of the power plant.

The RIB nudged ever closer to the Nordhavn. Moments later, the silhouette of the yacht was looming above them, a dark, slab-sided form etched against the moonlit sky. Jaeger reached out one arm to fend off the vessel. The last thing they needed was to collide with its hull, alerting whoever was aboard.

That done, he began to drag them hand-over-hand towards the ladder lashed to the Nordhavn's side, guiding the prow of the RIB through the choppy water. His eyes scanned the deck above, checking for any movement or a sign they had been discovered.

Nothing.

Momentarily he clocked the vessel's name bolted to the hull: *Grey Wolf*. Kammler's chosen code name. Like the man had said with his dying breath, this one was personal. A gift from Kammler to Will Jaeger – the deaths of his nearest and dearest. Or so Kammler had intended.

Well it's personal for the both of us, Jaeger told himself grimly.

With his left hand he made a grab for the ladder, and without a word to Narov swung himself onto the rungs. Hand over hand he powered upwards, light on his feet despite his recent injuries and blanking out any residual pain.

With infinite care he inched his head above the level of the hull, his eyes sweeping the Nordhavn's deck. A massive figure was standing erect in the dimly lit wheelhouse. Or rather, his bulk seemed to be propped against one side of it, as if he needed the support to remain upright.

Steve Jones, it had to be. Somehow he'd escaped from the getaway vehicle, that's if he'd still been riding in it when Brooks had taken it out. And by the looks of things, he was still nursing the injuries Jaeger had inflicted upon him during their brutal fight in Kammler's lair.

But if Jones was here, did that also mean . . .?

95

Away to their east, the pulsing red light of the drone was fast approaching the airspace above the nuclear plant. No matter who might be crewing this ship of death, they had to be stopped. No time to lose.

Jaeger didn't hesitate. He vaulted onto the deck, soundless as a cat, and flitted towards the wheelhouse, moving stealthily and sticking to the darkest shadows. The door had been left ajar, and within moments, he'd slipped inside.

He found himself on the lower deck of the bridge, with Jones on the floor above. He located the stairway leading upwards, keeping his feet to the outer edges as he climbed, where there was less chance of any of the steps creaking under his weight.

He reached the top seemingly undetected. From there, he eyed the figure hunched at the wheel. The massive shoulders, the bulging muscles, the shaven head: it was Jones all right. His gaze seemed glued to the prow of the yacht, and beyond it the drone as it powered towards the target.

Jaeger scanned the bridge from end to end. Jones seemed to be alone, but propped in one corner was the distinctive form of a Type 79 folding-stock sub-machine gun – the same as Kammler's men had used.

He would have to be doubly careful.

He stole across towards his nemesis, the Beretta levelled at the big man's head. Still Jones didn't seem to have heard or seen anything. Suddenly Jaeger froze, as a deafening burst of static hissed out of the Nordhavn's speaker, set into the yacht's bridge.

A voice came over the radio. 'What was the detonation code again?'

Jones cursed. 'How many bloody times . . . HK300445. It couldn't be more bastard obvious.'

'I asked for the code, not a barrage of abuse,' the voice replied coldly, before repeating it back at Jones. 'HK300445.'

'You got it. Bravo, Einstein.'

'Concentrate on keeping a steady course, if you think you can manage that.'

The radio link died and Jones cursed some more.

Jaeger felt his blood run cold. The code *was* obvious. HK for Hank Kammler, plus the numbers 300445, Hitler's date of death. But it wasn't that that had so poleaxed him. Distorted though it was over the radio link, he could have sworn that he recognised the drone operator's voice.

It had sounded distinctly female. Horribly familiar. But most shockingly, it had sounded as if she was in control of this last-minute apocalyptic mission.

Jaeger felt a surge of rage burning through him now. What had Kammler and Jones done to her? Moving as silently as a striking snake, he stole forward, aiming the muzzle of the Beretta at the point where Jones's bullneck met his shaven head, so keeping him covered.

When he figured he was close enough, he raised his hand and brought the butt of the pistol down in a savage ridge-hand strike, driving it into Jones's skull. Steel met bone, the power of the blow whipping Jones's head forwards, and the big man's lights went out. He dropped like a stone, his forehead cracking against the Nordhavn's wheel.

Jaeger knelt over him, using the fingers of his right hand to force Jones's jaws open. Then he jammed the muzzle of the Beretta as deep inside the fallen man's mouth as he could, and pulled the trigger. He'd angled the barrel upwards, ensuring the round would tear up through Jones's brain.

Blood and mangled grey matter splattered across the

Nordhavn's floor. Jones's mouth cavity and his skull had served as a makeshift silencer, deadening the shot, just as Jaeger had intended. He bent over the body, making sure to be totally certain. There was no doubt about it: Steve Jones's gaze was empty, blank and stone-cold dead. *Finally*.

Feeling a kick of elation, Jaeger straightened up, running his eyes across the Nordhavn's prow. A shadowy figure was crouched there, hunched over some kind of device. The drone operator – it had to be.

Jaeger darted out of the wheelhouse, moving forwards stealthily. Sure enough, the operator was bent over a console that had to be controlling the airborne delivery system, one loaded with an IND and primed to blow any second now.

As he crept closer, Jaeger realised with a massive punch to the guts that that silhouette was known to him: the cascade of long hair; the poise; the lithe form. Somehow, both Ruth and Steve Jones had survived the strike on the getaway vehicle. Maybe they'd bailed out en route, sending it and its remaining occupants onwards as a decoy? Smart. But not smart enough. Jaeger and Narov had been one step ahead of them. Now to end it, once and for all.

Jaeger levelled the Beretta, letting out a strangled yell. 'Ruth! The boys are out there. Luke and Simon. It's over! Call back the drone! It's over!'

At the sound of his voice, Ruth Jaeger all but dropped the console. She turned towards him disbelievingly, shock written across her features. Jaeger saw her hands hover over the terminal, as if frozen with indecision, the drone coming to a halt maybe 150 feet short of the nuclear plant.

There was a look bordering on madness in Ruth's tortured, harrowed eyes. Her lips moved but the words were inaudible. What the hell was she trying to say? Eventually Jaeger realised what it was: *Sorry. Sorry. Sorry.*

'The boys!' he screamed. 'They're out there! Call back the drone!'

Ruth's eyes flashed wide now, the look in them one of utter hellish insanity. Somewhere in there was a burning hatred too, though a hatred of what, Jaeger just couldn't fathom. The next moment she'd turned away from him again and set the drone powering towards its target.

Jaeger's hands began to shake. A voice screamed inside his head: *Kill her! Kill her! Kill her!* Despite the night chill, sweat poured into his eyes. He tried to steady himself to take the shot, but his brain was unable to make his hands function any more.

The drone crossed into the airspace above the nuclear plant. Any second now and it would detonate. *He had to take the shot.*

Suddenly a figure darted out of the shadows. Lithe, powerful, untainted by emotion or mercy or love. Commando knife clasped in hand.

In one smooth movement, Irina Narov leapt at Ruth, driving the blade in deep. There was a chilling, bloodcurdling scream. Jaeger tore his gaze away from the sickening scene: two women – one that he had loved; the other that he had grown to love – fighting to the death.

The drone wobbled above the nuclear plant, hanging there like some impossible apparition. Jaeger swung the Beretta back to cover the two figures, but they were locked in mortal combat and he couldn't risk a shot, even if he could bring himself to open fire.

As Narov fought, she drove the blade in further with one hand and wrestled the console out of her adversary's grip. That done, she pirouetted, bringing her leg up in a savage karate kick, which drove Ruth Jaeger, stumbling, back into the shadows.

An instant later she collided with the ship's rail, fell backwards and tumbled into the darkness.

'How do I fly this fucking thing!' Narov screamed. She gestured at the console. 'I know how to fight, not to fly!'

Jaeger forced himself to move. He sprinted across the deck, whipping the console out of Narov's grasp. As he did, the drone began to bank east, slipping into a crazed descent towards the nearest of the nuclear plant's twin cooling towers.

He swept his eyes across the bank of joysticks, lights and dials. In his latter days in the SAS, they'd used drones extensively, mainly for remote area surveillance work in the Afghan badlands. For sure he should know how to fly this thing.

He flicked one thumb onto the left joystick, piling on the power, and with his right thumb levelled off the craft. As he did so, he realised with a kick of revulsion that the console was slick with blood.

His wife's blood.

He blanked such thoughts from his mind. All that mattered now was to fly the damn thing. Pilot the drone west, away from the coast, and ditch it at sea.

That way, the experts could lift it in due course and fully disable the mechanisms. Retrieve any HEU and fully neutralise the threat.

Jaeger stabilised the drone, then banked it around, bringing it away from the coastline. When he judged it was far enough from land, he put it into a dive, and it plummeted towards the surface of the sea. There was a flash of white in the darkness, and it ploughed beneath the waves.

Moments later, the noise of the drone's engines died as it was sucked into the sea's hungry depths.

The Hunt was over.

Jaeger dropped the console and rushed to the ship's rail. His eyes scanned the dark water desperately, though he knew that it was hopeless.

Irina Narov had done her work well. There wasn't the slightest sign of Ruth Jaeger anywhere.

Her bloody form had been dragged into the icy depths, just as Kammler's final nuclear device had been.